Storm-E

'Do you love me, I

'Yes, I do.'

'I don't love you, though.'

'You love no-one, least of all yourself. What you're doing here is to commit a mindless act of spite against yourself. Come back with me, Celia, marry me, have my children. I will teach you about love. It begins, it always begins, with an act of surrender.'

James Sorel-Cameron was born in Shropshire. He was educated at Newton Park College, Bath, and at Malcolm Bradbury's Creative Writing Course at the University of East Anglia. Married, and with five children, he now lives in West Cumbria where he is a full-time teacher of English. *Mag*, his first novel, was published in 1990, and his second novel, *A Generation of the Dark Heart*, was published in 1991.

Storm-Blind

James Sorel-Cameron

Mandarin

for Bridget

A Mandarin Paperback
STORM-BLIND

First published in Great Britain 1993
by Sinclair-Stevenson
This edition published 1994
by Mandarin Paperbacks
an imprint of Reed Consumer Books Ltd
Michelin House, 81 Fulham Road, London SW3 6RB
and Auckland, Melbourne, Singapore and Toronto

Copyright © 1993 by James Sorel-Cameron

The right of James Sorel-Cameron to be identified as the author
of this work has been asserted by him in accordance
with the Copyright, Designs and Patents Act 1988.

A CIP catalogue record for this title
is available from the British Library
ISBN 0 7493 1588 1

Printed and bound in Great Britain
by Cox & Wyman Ltd, Reading, Berks

Contents

                    Fair encounter
Of two most rare affections! Heavens rain grace
On that which breeds between 'em!

                    SHAKESPEARE, *The Tempest*

        O what authority gives
        Existence its surprise?

                    W. H. AUDEN
                    The Sea and the Mirror

Book One
DUTIES

One . . .

In the first years of this century, in the north of England, a girl named Anna Brand went alone into a small wood and was caught there by a sudden storm.

She had always been afraid of this wood; sometimes her brother had made her come here, but she had never before come here alone. Although not directly intending to become lost, she had deliberately turned off the paths into bracken and brambles, had sought the isolation of the dark tree trunks where the light flittered about an abiding darkness and, even in the calmest weather, there was a restlessness of growth and hidden movement. She was young enough to be afraid of what she could not see, what she could not clearly imagine; and she was old enough to court that fear, allow it to dance in her blood.

She had made her way far enough into the wood to be out of reach of the path, to be fully immersed, to allow the chill of the shadow to settle her hot flesh. She was poised and intent, listening to every rustle and scamper about her, standing very still, the sound of the wood held in tight focus, small patterns that she followed until they disappeared or blended into other sounds. The light was leaden and still. The earth reeked of green dampness, brown dampness, the sour stink of growth and decomposition. The longer she stayed, the more entranced she became, the fear coming in a clear pulse that made her feel alive, that opened a wildness within her.

She did not mark the first blusters of the storm, registering them merely as a tightening of her awareness, as if her concentration was magnifying the creak of the boughs, the shiver of the leaves. The first patter of the rain she heard as the sudden ticking of hidden clocks. The first rumble of the thunder seemed to come from below her, a growl of the benevolent earth.

The lightning brought her out into the open again, the sudden blink of the world, with the thunder rolling in behind, the rain

3

slashing in through the gaps in the canopy above her. The sky went dark, concentrating suddenly before the lightning tore it open again.

Her fear, which had been lulled, now leapt in her. She turned and stumbled, gave a little cry, lost her directions, suddenly pathetic below the forces that gathered about her. She ran to a tree and hid her face against it, trembled and wept.

Be sensible, she told herself. None of this has anything to do with you. She turned and leant her back against the tree and bided out the storm, the billowing cold wind that made the wood retract under it, the squalls of rain that diffused amongst the tree tops, gathered and then poured in vile streams about her. She huddled in her cloak, stamped her feet and endured it, looking through the trees for a lightening in the sky, looking for her way back to the path, imagining the warmth of the house that waited for her; content with herself so far.

Several thousand miles away, although in a land under the same flag, her brother Harry was blind drunk. In a low building with thick walls and an earth floor, he stumbled about, grasping at things he could not properly see, to fight them or to throw himself against them to be held and comforted, to be allowed, one way or another, to spill his supercharged emotions. From the edges of the room native eyes watched him, curious, furtive, predatory, afraid; watched also the other Englishman who was not drunk, or not drunk enough. He too watched Harry Brand, but watched him from a distance, from the space with which he always surrounded himself. His name was Lionel Drewer.

When Harry, reeling forward towards the walls, lurching back, finally fell over his own feet and pounded the earth with the dead weight of himself, Lionel stepped forward, stooped and took his comrade under the shoulders, lifting him up like a sack.

'Where's that damn black bitch?' Harry said.

'Enough now, Brand.'

'Drewer?'

'Yes.'

'Get me out of here.'

'Yes.'

Outside the night was a thick purple pall, unbroken by any star, the air velvety, moist. Lionel pulled Harry clear of the building, out into the dark. It was three miles to the barracks, three miles of

4

malignant black dust, stones, the scuttle of nocturnal insects. With a grim smile, Lionel steadied Harry, shook him until he buckled and began to vomit, sustaining him whilst he did so, then shuffling him upright and propelling him home, the precision of his own direction and the strength of his determination beginning to be picked up in his comrade's tottering limbs.

Soon the night had enveloped them entirely. A faint vibration in the darkness kept the track immediately before them perceptible. They did not speak. Harry was mostly asleep, walking blindly, but walking, the young strength of him instinctively firing him on. Lionel guided him, proud of his youth, proud of his comradeship, proud of his drunkenness, for he felt that when he drank, he poured fuel on his strength, made it flame. They were spending their youths here with the blind courage of men, of soldiers whose lives were provisional and which must therefore be lived in their entirety. There was no tomorrow. They belonged to no-one but themselves. Life was a storm that they raised and rode within them.

. . . *two* . . .

She was sitting on a sofa in the deep shadow of her mother. From the moment Lionel Drewer entered the room, he was aware of her strangeness, although he did not at first identify it with her, not registering her distinctly, assuming it to be a turn of his customary claustrophobia in the social situation rising with new intensity as he moved amongst the furniture of formality.

Harry, his comrade and host, steered him with ironic appreciation of his awkwardness.

'Mother, may I introduce Captain Drewer? Lionel, my mother.'

He knocked together his heels and hinged his body at the waist to take her offered hand. It was the languid smile that made him angry, the affluence that could afford to be amused at his angularity, the hidden web of social balances that constricted him to the point where everything he did or said seemed coarse and brutal and was consequently amusing. He loved Harry, but he did not want to be with him here in this world of mirrors and masks.

'We have heard so much about you, Captain Drewer.'

What had they heard? How had Harry translated their intimacy into a currency that could be exchanged here? He shuddered at it.

'May I introduce my daughter, Captain Drewer? Anna?'

He moved his neck stiffly in the ring of his collar and found her eyes upon him, looking from under the darkness of her forehead. He drew up, took a breath, thought she was about to jump out at him.

'Miss Brand.'

'Captain Drewer. I am very pleased to meet you.'

It was given in the style of the mother, but the formality was not, in the daughter, a mask: she did not smile as she said it, for the smile would be the sign of calculation, the self-satisfaction of the move well-played. The girl did not smile; her pleasure was a serious pleasure, the expression of it innocent and direct. It took him at once; it was he who smiled.

'I am very pleased to be here, Miss Brand.'

At which his smile was returned, a glow below the shadow which seemed a secret offered to him, slipped inside his tunic and pressed warmly against this breast.

Harry then moved him on to meet others whom he greeted automatically, the uncle, the cousins, a neighbour. He was brusque, wanted this over, wanted to ask Harry about his sister; but when at last they could move together to the edge of the room, out of the social concourse, he did not ask, did not know what he would be betraying.

They stood by the window and Harry was telling him who was who and what was what, spicing the information with mild local scandal that meant nothing to him, as they meant nothing to him. His mind could take in nothing but the girl on the sofa whom he watched intently, stared at, hoping that she would not turn and catch him thus, for he wanted to digest her there completely, and he did not want her compliance in this, could not have borne it.

She did not turn, kept her small body tilting forward on the sofa, her head slightly to one side as if listening to something, trying to catch the tone of something, frowning, alert. She was not in any conventional sense beautiful: small, solid-fleshed and solid-featured; but there was something alive in her at which he marvelled: a strangeness, a difference that filled him with an urgency of which he had no clear understanding, that perplexed him and brought a fine perspiration onto his flesh.

It was not her womanliness; that he could have understood. She was not, indeed, a woman in that sense at all. Women were predictable, in either their attainability or their unattainability; in the latter class of which were all the women who might ever have come into this room. This girl, this Anna Brand, came upon him as a potential, as someone not yet become woman; in whose becoming, in a bolt of terrifying imagination, he realised that he might be a participant.

And then, at the perfect moment, she did turn into the heat of his watching; and he felt between them a fall across which he yearned to leap, knowing that it would be a dreadful leap, but knowing also, from the way she considered him with her eyes narrowed and her mouth just open, that were he to make that leap, she would rise at once and reach out for him.

. . . *three* . . .

She was dancing at the summer ball with Captain Lionel Drewer, her brother's comrade and friend, and their guest. She had danced with him for most of the evening. She did not know whether his repeated invitations were for want of another partner, or for form's sake, or for her brother's; and she did not know why she was prepared repeatedly to accept.

He did not dance well. Drilled in the mechanics of the dance, he was unable to do more than step out the pattern in frantic concentration upon the rhythm of the little country band; with certainly more concentration than they were applying to it. He was, however, incapable of allowing the music to move in him; or, if it moved in him, he seemed afraid of it, unable to release himself into its flowing and dipping and turning.

She loved to dance, to reel about the shiny floor in the arms of some bright boy, laughing and turning, flirting her body within the quick discipline of the dance-steps. She could forget herself as she danced, could become anonymous as her partner was anonymous.

She cared for none of them, nor for herself, as she danced. Her sense of herself as a body and a mind faded. But she could not dance with Captain Drewer like this. She urged herself upon him but his monumentality was beyond her. He would not let her forget herself, nor him; on the contrary, dancing with him intensified his presence, and her sense of herself before him.

Imagining him against her brother, she had expected beauty; or, at the least a rugged grace. He was not beautiful in any feature, and his ruggedness, if such it was, was sallow and creased beyond his years. He was very tall; pressing her head against him, his chin would have had substantial clearance above her. As she danced with him, she was aware that his height supported a bulk of bone and flesh that seemed out of the range of her imagination. She did not know how to regard him at all. The elements of his face – eyes, nose, mouth, chin – were proportionately substantial; none exaggerated into grotesqueness, but each determined by heavy lines and angles. His hair was oiled flat, and like his moustache, was severely black. 'What d'you think of my captain then, Nan,' Harry had asked her. 'He's quite remarkable,' she had said, and every observation confirmed this; about every physical aspect there was something to remark.

The music ended and, in the hiatus, she stepped back and looked at him, felt herself in the narrow range of his concentration again, as she had felt every moment they had been in the same room since his arrival. She lowered her head meekly and stood before him, at his pleasure for a while, before lifting her face. laughing, taking his arm and directing him towards the cold collation. It is time, she told herself, to find out about him.

'My brother tells me you are a dangerous man, Captain Drewer.'

'I hope I am dangerous, Miss Brand, to the enemy.'

'Ah. The enemy. But there are no enemies here.'

'Certainly not.'

'So you would not be a danger here.'

'How could I be a danger here?'

'I don't know. I don't quite know what Harry meant when he said you were dangerous, but I don't think he was talking about the enemy.'

'I expect he meant that I am not to be trusted not to knock things over in drawing rooms, not to spill my food at dinner, and not to offer pleasantries from the barracks that would not be pleasant in the ballroom.'

'I don't think that's what he meant either.'

'What, then?'

'I really don't know, but I think I would like to know.'

'What do you expect of me, Miss Brand?'

'Something . . . I expect something that I do not expect.'

'You alarm me. I have no idea how I might fulfil your expectation. You place an obligation upon me.'

'I don't mean to, really I don't. Oh, please, Captain, please, I don't mean you to give some performance for my curiosity. That would be horrid. I know so little about . . . things. We are all so protected, don't you think?'

'Don't you think it proper for young ladies to be protected, Miss Brand?'

'No, I don't think it . . . proper. We are protected even from ourselves, or it seems so to me. I want to know everything. I want to understand. You men make the world and hide it from us. I want to know why you are dangerous, Captain. Please don't condescend to me. I shall not think well of you if you do.'

'It is hard to explain such things in terms that you might understand, Miss Brand.'

'If I do not understand, then I shall say so, Captain Drewer.'

'I think that your brother understands that I am not entirely domesticated. I live, you see, too much in army camps, in strange countries. And I must confess that I prefer such places to . . . to society. They seem more real to me.'

'Why?'

'Perhaps it's because such places seem to me closer to the extremities of life. I will confess to a serious pleasure in danger. That, I think, is what your brother means. Danger makes me feel alive, and sometimes, perhaps, I assume too readily that my companions feel as I do.'

'What dangerous things do you do?'

'We ride fast horses over uncertain terrain. We climb precipices. We hunt animals that might destroy us before we have destroyed them. We fill our idleness with excitements and recklessness.'

'And fighting?'

'When there is fighting to be done, yes, we fight.'

'And . . . and vices?'

'Vices, Miss Brand? What are you asking me?'

'You know well enough what I am asking you, Captain.'

'Every pleasure is a vice if it is pursued too profoundly. Yes, we are in that sense, I suppose, vicious. Or I am, at least. I sometimes find life too small for me.'

'Particularly in society?'

'Particularly in society, yes.'

'Particularly amongst women?'

'Society belongs to women, Miss Brand, surely.'

'It most certainly does not. It is the cage into which women are put . . . some women. I also find life too small for me, sometimes.'

'With respect, Miss Brand, I think you know little about life. There is much more to it than you yet realise, even in society.'

'You are like my mother who prefaces every answer to every awkward question with, "When you are married, child . . ." I shall not be married. Marriage is a great delusion. For a moment the cage opens and you are free to fly, only to find you are in another cage, a tighter cage, a cage that you have unwittingly stepped into with your own free will and which, therefore, you have not the remotest hope of ever escaping.'

'What will you do with your life then, Miss Brand?'

'When I have come to an understanding of what it is that my life really amounts to, then, Captain Drewer, I shall be able to answer your question.'

. . . *four* . . .

Alone in her bedroom, now that she could in solitude and darkness be herself, she found that she was very angry with him. A muscular pulse beat at her temples and she allowed the complexities of emotion that had been constricted within her throughout the evening to unravel themselves in a livid, writhing heap.

Firstly, she thought, how dare he do this to her? How dare he? He was an ugly man, clearly, an unpleasant man. He had taken her brother from her. He was a corrupt man, she knew he was corrupt;

and he would corrupt Harry too, had probably already done so. She hated it. It filled her with contempt and loathing.

She wondered what form such corruption took: riding horses and climbing mountains, however, were not a part of it. It would involve something more profound, intimate, something physical; something that tapped the animality of their natures. She thought then of animals, thought of their chomping mouths, their blind predations, their soulless instincts. Captain Lionel Drewer liked to play at the extremities of life, did he? Society dulled him. He was disgusting. She lay awake and a card-house of denunciations against him rose in her mind.

Then came the remembrance of his watching and she grew afraid. What did he see when he watched her like that? What imaginations did he make upon her? She grew cold, for she knew that she had flirted with him. She had not meant to; she had meant to question him seriously; but serious questioning, amongst the sweetnesses of a cold collation, could only sound like flirtation. She had turned to him in her innocence and he had used it against her. He had begun to corrupt her too, to play her in a game, to use her according to rules that were hidden from her.

She lay awake and listened to the noises of the sleeping house, expecting to hear amongst them his footfall, his moving through the darkness to where she lay. She dreamed of a scream rushing through her unable to break the silent smother of his devouring.

And as she was struggling through the folds of her dreams, he sat up in his room at a small table; before him, a blank sheet of paper upon which he was impelled to write, although what he would write, and to whom, he did not know. He felt merely the need to lay out sentences, to give form to what he felt, to have it out with himself. For the moment the pen hung above the paper, the ink drying in its nib.

That he was in love with her was a truth beyond the faintest stain of scepticism. What followed was the formal opening of his love; the purpose, to acquire her as his wife. He was a practical man and an honourable man, and there was no other admissible direction. That this proceeding was uncertain, that she or her family would be most unlikely to entertain his proposal, was a possibility he accepted clearly, not permitting it to deflect him for a moment. It would be as it would be. As the committal to military engagement always held the possibility of death, so here he risked terminal social humiliation. Such a risk was inevitable. He did not consider his chances of success, did not question his suitability, did not begin to imagine his offer from her point of view. This was not to his purpose. He could only know his own course and he set himself to do it with a single-minded stoicism.

What did catch him, and sent his thoughts twisting away from their line, was the contemplation of his own life. Love and marriage had been social things which he had implicitly renounced by the way he lived. He was, by the standards of the family he sought admittance to, a pauper. He had no possessions that he would not have thrown away without a thought. He was ready at a moment to go anywhere, do anything that his duty required of him, had ambitions only to be urgent and useful. He belonged to no-one but his regiment and himself. For society, he had intense companionships with men who he felt were his equals, images of, or complements to, aspects of himself. Such a life he accepted as the dark liberty of his profession. He had indeed a residual contempt for those of his comrades who took wives, adulterating their calling with domesticity. He had not known himself remotely capable of the emotions which now gripped him by the heart, and he did not know what would become of him as a result of them. Perhaps he secretly hoped for rejection, for the hurt that would enable him to draw a cloak of misanthropy about him tightly.

He thought also of women, for he was not without appetites and not without the knowledge and exercise of those appetites. He had visited the native paramours, dark and silky as the night. Their breasts expanses of loose, spicy flesh, the pelted openings of their sex like ripe fruit, they were of a different order of beings. It was not so much their race that made them different, but the silent understanding they had of the operations of desire. If they were, as the accepted wisdom was, of a lower order to the women of his own race and class, then their lowness put them in touch with the truth of sensuality, a human reality that was explicitly denied by his society, but which existed nevertheless, was potent and profound. He admired them deeply, and was grateful for what they were able to give him so freely and fully.

The complexity of his present situation was that what he felt for Miss Anna Brand was compounded with the rising of these appetites within him. He had not thought it imaginable to feel as he felt for the native women towards any respectable woman; but he did feel it, more strongly than he had ever felt it before. The native women were never, finally, individuals; they were a whole sub-world into which he sank when he needed it. Anna Brand, however, was emphatically an individual, now, in his thoughts of her, the most precisely experienced individual that he had ever known, full of a complexity that involved him completely; and the engine that hummed behind this involvement was desire. It frightened him, what he sought to bring to this girl, but it was inevitable. He no longer had control of himself.

. . . *five* . . .

Her mother sat at her writing-desk in the shadow between two tall windows through which fell the strong glare of the afternoon.

'Sit, child,' she said, turning her chair round to face her.

She sat on the sofa. The seriousness of the summons to this meeting, and the seriousness of the presence of her mother, set up a giggle that troubled the pit of her stomach. She drew herself in and breathed deeply, felt she had been called in here to be subjected to some dreary admonition, some weight of maturity that was about to be laid upon her.

'Do you know what I have to say to you?'

'No, Mama.'

'Well, then.' She looked at something on her desk, a distraction, a prevarication. 'Since your father's loss,' she began, 'you have perhaps been too much on your own. There are things that he might have given you that I cannot give you. I feel his loss most deeply at moments like this.'

The evocation of her father's memory made her sad; but then she felt that it was contrived to make her sad, and she resented it. She drew herself up.

'What is it, Mama?'

Her prompting brought out her mother's irritation, brought her smartly to the point.

'Captain Drewer has been to see me, Anna. He asks my permission to approach you with an offer of marriage.'

Of course. She had known it would be this, not consciously perhaps, but now that it was said it was almost a disappointment; only this, after all.

'Well? Anna? Have you nothing to say to me?'

'I . . . I don't know what to say.' And being forced to say even this brought the tears to her eyes, all of a sudden, tears of bewilderment streaking down her face. She felt as if she had been pushed out into an empty space in which it was hard to breathe.

She heard her mother's steep inhalation.

'Please . . . please don't be distressed. I will inform Captain Drewer that his offer is not . . . not welcome.'

'No, Mama. Please. I will see him. Please.'

'Anna, if you agree to see him, he will take it as encouragement.'

'Nevertheless . . .'

'Do you mean to encourage him, then?'

'I don't know . . . I don't know . . . please, Mama.'

'Very well, very well.' She summoned herself, re-railed herself on the practicalities. 'Let me then tell you how things stand. Listen closely to me. Whatever you decide, you must not do it in ignorance. D'you hear what I say, now, Anna?'

'Yes, Mama.'

'Captain Drewer is a professional soldier, a man of some considerable reputation and prospects within the service; but the wife of a professional soldier leads a strange, peripatetic life, and although the respectability of such a life is beyond question, it is a life that will not allow you the settled society, the belonging, to which you are accustomed. You will meet and mix with people who have not been brought up with the protection and privilege that you have. Now, Captain Drewer is not a rich man. You have some money of your own, but your circumstances as his wife would not be the circumstances you are used to. These things may not, at your age, seem to matter; but they will matter to you, and you must consider them. Will you promise me that you will consider them, Anna? Will you?'

'Yes, Mama.'

There was more to be said; the awkward bits.

'Tell me, child. Do you like him?'

'I . . . I don't know.'

'You do not dislike him, though?'

'I do not . . . dislike him, no.' Did she dislike him? She had thought that she did, but now she had to say it out loud, she did not want to say it, did not want to be pinned in this opinion.

There was a pause. Her mother wanted it settled one way or the other, was uncomfortable at her daughter's lack of immediate decision. Her refusal to make an immediate decision was only partially to irritate her mother, however; for rising within her was a turmoil that blocked her thinking. She wanted to leave, to be by herself to come to some understanding of this immensity; but if she left now, there was so much that would never be answered. She needed answers. She needed to know all the things that were left unsaid about such matters. She had always wanted to know, but now she had to know; not that she seriously thought she would receive any such knowledge from her mother.

'Mama?'

'Yes?'

'Will you tell me . . . ?'

'What, child? What is it?'

'Will you tell me the duties of a wife?'

'The duties of a wife? They are . . . to love your husband; to honour and obey him . . . to be faithful to him in all things . . . to . . . to make him a home . . .'

'To bear his children?'

'Yes, to bear his children.'

'And will you tell me how that happens?'

'Do you really not know?'

'How might I know such a thing, Mama?'

Her mother sighed, set her teeth. Anna thought that she had offended her, but it was done now, the offence, and she would not, could not, having got this far, go back.

'Please, Mama. Please.'

She sat again, turned away, put her hand to her head, then looked at her daughter, and spoke with a quiet clarity.

'He . . . your husband . . . he will come to you at night, child. He will touch you in the way of love. He will touch you intimately. That is all you need to know, except . . . except that it is an act of love to which you must, in your duty, submit. And in your submission, you must not be afraid and you must not be distressed. If you really love your husband as you should, as you must, you will accept his touching. And if you can accept it, freely and clearly, then it will not be a burden to you. Anna, there are some women for whom it is a burden, this touching, this intimacy. If you cannot, in your heart, accept such intimacy from this man, then you must wait. You must not marry him until you can accept it, not marry him at all until you can accept it, not marry any man until you have this clear in your heart. D'you understand what I tell you, Anna? Do you?'

She had submitted to this advice with a bowed head, her face ablaze. When it was done, in the waiting pause that followed it, she lifted her face and saw in her mother's watching a tenderness that she had not remotely expected. It was a tenderness of sympathy and pleasure. She rose at once and came to her mother, knelt at her feet, buried her tears in her mother's lap and felt the heavy, ringed hands come upon her head in benediction.

She felt that she had been told exactly everything that she had wanted to know; and, knowing it, at that moment, she knew that she might accept Captain Drewer as her husband.

. . . six . . .

He paced the lawn until he was afraid of marking it with his impatience. He withdrew and sat on a garden seat on a rise below some trees, to wait and to watch. The house before him caught the afternoon light, its stones glowing as if molten, its many windows reflecting the light in slivers of intensity. Its sheer beauty diminished and excluded him.

He sat in shadows which lengthened over the lawn towards the house. He was overcome by physical discomforts, as if his bowels and lungs were lumped and recalcitrant, his bones twisting at their joints, his nerves sparking against one another. He was outside the mechanism of his life at this moment, and he hated to be so. Within the house, women were passing judgement upon him, and his inadequacies were too many for him. He wished there was some physical test that he might be put to, some action that might determine his merit. But he was condemned to be still and to wait, and he was without hope in such a situation. He wanted only for it to be over so that he could pack and leave and never come back here.

If the shadows reach the house before she has come to me, he told himself, then she will not have me. This magic allowed him to concentrate, to watch the long stains of the dark spread across the grass and the borders, up the terrace, towards the door through which, for no logical reason, he knew that she would come; she or her mother, or her brother.

He could not bear to think of Young Harry at this moment, for he felt that he had betrayed him, had come here as his honourable friend and had used that honour basely. He dreaded the regiment when Harry returned, questioning, joking, telling the others that poor Drewer had gone moon-struck over his little sister and made an ass of himself. He would ask for a transfer, find a grim little frontier in some wind-raddled pass where he would grow dry as the dust. The shadows touched the walls of the house and he felt the hot pulse of tears in his throat.

A glint as the light changed in a window, in the door, and she was there on the terrace, turning, looking for him. He looked behind him and considered a flight into the woods, into the moors beyond. Turning, he saw that she had seen him. She raised her hand to him, began to move down the terrace steps.

He did not mark the change within him, but he was moving towards her, almost running, stumbling. Whatever pains he had endured in his waiting, he had left them; they did not belong to him any more.

They met in a clear space of lawn with the eyes of the house upon them, of which, as they met, he became aware, restrained by his awareness.

She lowered her face under his proximity.

'Captain Drewer,' she said simply.

'Miss Brand.'

'My mother has . . .'

'Yes.'

'She has told me that you wished to speak to me.'

'I wish . . . yes, to speak to you, to ask you . . .' He had not the words for this. He turned from her. He was unable to do this. He would go away.

'Let us walk a little, Captain,' she said. 'Will you . . . will you take my arm?'

17

He did so, and they walked in silence, with slow steps, through a gate into a walled garden where the flowers rose high and the last bees buzzed drowsily in the evening air.

'Miss Brand,' he began at last. 'I do not have the words for what I want to say to you. I want only to prove to you what I feel for you.'

'There is so much that I too do not understand and cannot express; but I think we must try to say the words, Captain Drewer. Please don't be afraid. We are quite alone here and what passes between us, whatever its outcome, will be between us alone. You have my word on this.'

He struggled with it, closing his eyes, trying not to be aware of her too closely, trying to recover only the dream of her to which he could speak, to which he had spoken often in the hours that had led up to this moment.

'Miss Brand,' he said rapidly. 'I am in love with you and I wish to make you my wife. Can you . . . will you marry me?'

She did not respond at once and, having felt certain of her acceptance from the moment of seeing her, in her silence he began to feel that he had been deluded, that she was going, quietly and kindly, to turn him away. He was appalled.

'Miss Brand?' he said desperately.

'I need . . .' she began. 'I need to understand this, Captain. I need to know what you mean.'

They had been walking, their voices paced to their footsteps. Now she stopped and turned to him, took a pace away from him, looked at him.

'I do not understand love, you see,' she said. 'I know what it is meant to be, but I am very young. I have spent so much of my life in solitudes. I have read many books and have, perhaps, lived my life through them. We have known each other for such a short time. Will you . . . will you promise to be honest with me?'

'That is an easy promise, Miss Brand.'

'Is it? I'm not sure that it is. Honest even with things that may hurt me, things that may hurt you. Could you be honest enough to say, "You should not be my wife", if that were honestly what you felt?'

'I don't know.'

She smiled. 'Good, then. Forgive me if what I ask offends or pains you, but there are some things that I must have clear.'

She paused and he waited, eager for her questions, eager to satisfy her in whatever way he might.

'Tell me, Captain, have you ever loved another woman?'

'No. Never.'

'Have you ever asked another woman to be your wife?'

'Never.'

'Have you ever . . . touched another woman in the way of love?'

He gasped at this question, but could not avoid her eyes.

'I . . . I have.'

But when he had admitted it, he was overcome with gratitude for her having pressed him to this honesty. He felt humbled. He wanted her to know him in everything.

'How could you touch a woman in that way and not love her?'

'For . . . for pleasure, and . . . and in exchange for money.'

This perplexed her. She really did not know of a world where such a thing might be possible. She released his hands, stood before him with her hands clasped before her.

'Is that not shameful?'

'Yes. Now, it is shameful. Telling you about it is shameful.'

'But at the time it was not shameful.'

'At the time it was . . . Miss Brand, please. Must I tell you of this? The follies and shames of my life are many. I have no pretence of being a good man, nor even perhaps a decent man; except in this; in my love for you and my desire to have you the guide and reference of my honour from this moment to the end of my life.'

He reached out his hands, palms open, and she placed her hands in his.

'What would it be like to be your wife?' she asked simply.

'It would be . . . a rough-and-ready life, perhaps. You know my profession, and the obligations that it places upon me. Perhaps soldiers like me should not have wives. I have thought this in my ignorance. I can only say this. You have made me aware that there is a great part of myself that is as yet unused, empty. I do not know what I can offer you apart from that, and that is as uncertain as life itself.'

She pondered, put her head down.

'Have you nothing to ask me?'

'Only the one question, Miss Brand.'

'But you don't know who I am. There must be something that you want to know.'

'There is really nothing. I want to come to know you in ways that I cannot explain to you now. I want you as a part of my life. What you are now, what you have been at other times, I don't care about any of that.'

'I will not marry a man who takes casual risks with his own life, Captain Drewer.'

'No more. Never again. Miss Brand, I am now taking the greatest risk that I have ever taken. The rest is triviality, games played by men who have no loyalty but to themselves.'

'I had not thought to marry. I do not know whether what I want out of life can be contained within marriage. I know people who have been diminished by the claims marriage makes upon them. I dread waking one morning, in perhaps a year's time, and thinking my life is over now. I think I am too young, too young to marry.'

He noticed that she had begun to cry. She did not turn away, did not put her hands to her face. He watched the opening of her emotion with an impossible tenderness. He stepped forward and put his arms about her, drew her to him. She submitted passively to his embrace. She lifted a great sigh and he felt her breasts rising against him, causing a physical lurch within him that shocked him. He lifted his arms from her, but her hands came around him, pulled him to her with a sudden jolt. He looked down and her face lifted, eyes closed. He bent his head and kissed her mouth, lifted his hands to hold her face to his. A torrent of joy opened within him.

. . . *seven* . . .

She was to be married to Captain Lionel Drewer. The moment of her acceptance propelled her into a complex social mechanism in which she had little active part. Arrangements and objects were brought to her, not so much for her approval as for her acknowledgement: she was asked formally to approve them but had neither the knowledge nor the power to disapprove. It was hardly real to her, any of it; and yet she was grateful for it, enjoyed it as a wonderful pampering she had never before experienced, and because within it all there was a still space in which she was allowed to settle herself privately to the enormity of what she was about, to the simple fact of her marriage which all this busyness seemed designed to obscure with frills and formalities, with dates and menus and schedules, with lengths of fine cloth and lists of guests.

She began to imagine her parents' marriage, to recover, in the active silence of her mother's solicitude, her lost father; not as an individual, but as a presence, as a force who had completed her mother, who had made her what she was. She imagined their love, their intimacy out of which she and her brother had been born. That her mother had been capable of this was a revelation which made her weak with its beauty, with the sheerness of its loss which now and forever had determined her mother. She grew nervous of her own capability to deliver such commitment, nervous of exposing herself to the extremity of it. And thus she came to think of Captain Drewer and her heart grew thick within her.

I don't know him. I don't love him. I don't want to be his wife. These cries came to her tongue and she clamped her hands over her mouth to keep them in. At times she was terrified, saw him as a devouring force who would secure her and subject her to nightmares of degradation. At times she was afraid of herself, afraid that when she was alone with him, she would shrivel into a whimpering child. At times she imagined what she had always dreaded, waking three months from now to a tedium that would stifle her to death over long, sickly years. The day of her marriage, meanwhile, tumbled towards her.

The night before, her lover was to be found in the lounge of a small country hotel. His body was limp, dulled by brandy, inert amidst the hissing of flames in dusty mantles, the crackle of an over-heaped fire and the shivering cross-currents of draughts. He felt as if something had been turned off within him, as if he lay at a still point in the world from which it would require an unimaginable effort to lift himself.

Harry Brand sat with him, watching him with a sobriety that made him uneasy. A clock chimed.

'Two o'clock,' Lionel said.

'Are you going to sit it out all night, Drewer?'

'What am I doing here, Brand?'

'I thought the general idea was that you were to be married to my sister.'

'Brand?'

'What?'

'Do I have your blessing?'

'Do you need my blessing?'

He did not know what he needed; some sort of confirmation, some sort of belief in himself.

'Will it be all right?' he asked.

'Why should it not be all right?' Harry said with a cheeriness that had the edge of cynicism cancelling it.

'Have I betrayed you, Brand?' he asked.

Harry laughed.

'My dear fellow, of course you haven't betrayed me. It's the most wonderful joke in the world: you and my sister, neither of you remotely domesticated, getting married. I can't believe in it at all.'

Lionel had no more to say, wanted to be on his own, was on his own, yes, for the first time, out in the open. He closed his eyes again and tried to think of her, tried to bring her features into his mind, could not, could only incarnate within him a warmth, a fleshliness, a possibility that was terrifying, rushing at him as he sat in a blank space and trembled.

She rose at dawn, rising from a shallow sleep to stare out over the greyness of the sky and the darkness of the woods and hills of her home for the last time.

She lay long in her bath, her flesh soft and malleable, considering the comfort and security of it, the comforts and securities of her childhood and her home for the last time. She was not sad, not at this moment afraid. A consciousness of herself here, now, in these closing moments, absorbed her with a quiet curiosity. When she rose from the water and presented her nakedness for her maid to wrap in her big towel, she smiled and raised her hands out, lifted herself up. She saw her maid blush deeply.

Weighted down with white satin, stitched in with ribbon, braided up with flowers, all like some baroque parcel, she was taken to the church by Uncle Spencer. She had to stop herself from looking about her continuously, from wanting to see them all, to note what they wore and how they looked, to spread smiles amongst them. She felt light-headed and wonderful, wanted to skip down the church, to rise on tiptoes, to throw back her head and hoot. Harry was there and he would have understood.

Captain Drewer was there, sworded and medalled with a foolish cap under his arm. From the glittering surface upon which she skimmed, she wondered what he was doing there, who had invited this indigestible lump of a man, why she had to stand next to him. Then, when the cheerful hymn-singing stopped and the rector began to apply the clauses of the contract upon her, she felt herself begin to close up. The swirling merriment was stilled. She had felt light and breezy; now a solid heat grew in her. She seemed to gather and grow, to throb as if she were about to become a great bruise. Tears came to her eyes; not the easy tears of her bright emotions, but tears squeezed out of the press of her.

Questions were put to her and her drilled affirmations came out in little gasps. Her hand was lifted and she looked up into the watching eyes of Captain Drewer. She was afraid. She wanted to throw herself upon him, to cry out for his help. He caressed her finger with his ring, stooped and put his face to hers, an instant of contact, a sudden fierce stillness.

. . . *eight* . . .

Lionel Drewer stood in a small dressing room that was next door to the bedroom. He needed a new and complex courage now, and applied to a brandy flask for it, then cursed himself and went to the basin to rinse his mouth. He looked at himself in the glass above the basin and was disgusted. He was blotchy and greasy. So much mattered now that had never mattered in his life before. Before it had always been his empirical qualities, his training and obedience and integrity, that had been put to the test. Now, he himself was to be tested and it was hopeless.

A few seconds from where he stood in this tangle of procrastination lay his bride. His duty was to step in to her, to lie down beside her and to consummate his marriage to her, perhaps to conceive a child upon her. Out there in the night, how many thousands,

23

millions, of men were at this instant going to their women with an eager facility that he half-envied, half-abominated?

He rehearsed the nightmares that were now about to be realised: her screaming at his touch; her leaping at him with lascivious greed; his own desires overwhelming him with their cruelty; his own simple physical ineptitude. His previous experience he now regretted sharply; it had given him a knowledge of, and a taste for, the pleasure of love in the intoxication of depravity; it had not equipped him for this; for the application of his pleasure to a virgin bride for whom he felt such tenderness and care that to hurt her would be the worst thing he could ever do.

Perhaps she would be asleep. How much, anyway, did she know? He suspected her of knowing enough to expect something vital from the experience that the ungainly penetration and discharge of his member could not fail to disillusion. How much longer could he delay? Did he want her to be asleep? Was it necessary tonight to fulfil this rite?

And this was the worst of it: that however hard he writhed with apprehension, however much self-disgust he banked up within him, he wanted with an urgency that hurt him to go in to her, to uncover the nakedness that he had struggled so hard not to imagine, to press himself upon that nakedness and bring himself to fulfilment within her. He could not stand it. He knew what he was and he loathed himself for it.

He put out the light in the dressing room and stood in the darkness, wrapped it round him as if it would disguise him. He stepped out onto the landing in which low nightlights flickered. Like a thief he took the paces to the door, then halted. What was the protocol here? To knock, surely. And if there were to be no answer? He groaned at his indecision. He knocked lightly; too lightly; she could not have heard. Was he expected to knock like some policeman? He turned the handle of the door and slipped quickly into the room, closing the door and turning the key in the lock.

A lamp was alight on a table by the bed, and in its glow he could see her lying on her back, the covers up to her chin, the weight of the bedclothes covering her body completely. Her head was to one side, towards him, the eyes closed. Her hair was loosed and sprayed about her face; he noticed for the first time the length and glossy darkness of it. Released from its braiding and combs, it looked wild, exotic. The roundness of her features looked softer than he had recalled. He

24

had not thought her beautiful when he had seen her first, in spite of
the complexities she had at once presented him: she seemed now so
tender, so soft, that he could not bear it.

Quickly, he went to the lamp and extinguished it, slipped his
gown from his shoulders and slithered under the bedclothes,
keeping as far from her as he might, cramming himself to the edge of
the bed. The sheets were cold and, although a warmth spread from
where she lay, he drew back from it as from a furnace. He shivered
heavily. He could not hope to sleep in this position.

But he did sleep, or begin to, for he was shot awake again by her
moving, a heavy rustle that he could not interpret.

'Lionel?'

'I woke you. I'm sorry.'

'I wasn't sleeping . . . where are you?'

Her arm came out and he took hold of her hand before she could
find him. He pressed her hand to his lips. She wore a nightgown,
stout material that was buttoned at the cuffs. He was naked and had
assumed that she would be naked too. He was appalled at himself
and at once began to wriggle to leave the bed and to find something
to wear, a shirt, some drawers; but she had her hand locked round
his.

'What is it?' she said, and he heard the concern in her voice.
He was obliged to stay and, at the very least, to give her rest and
reassurance.

He shuffled closer to her, keeping hold of her hand. He leant
across and kissed her forehead, touched her eyelids, her mouth. Her
free hand came across and met his, ran down his arm to his shoulder,
then quickly, glancingly, touched down his body, registering his
nakedness then as quickly withdrawing. Quickly he covered her
mouth with his mouth and kissed her, feeling as he did so, as she
shaped her mouth to his, the trembling that spread down from his
kiss to fill her body, to make it active below him.

He could not resist it then, had laid his hand upon her breast
before he had decided to, could not remove it, could not believe the
soft, full slackness of it, could not possibly have imagined the resilience of the nipple that pressed against the nightgown. He lifted his
mouth from hers to breathe and heard her gasp, heard the breath
catch in her throat. He fell back from her at once, released the hand
he had clutched and lay on his back, clasping in rage the stupid
arrogance of his member.

A while later she took his hand and pressed it. They lay on their backs, side by side, clasping hands, trembling in the darkness.

'Whatever must be done, my love,' she said slowly, 'you must not be afraid to do it.'

'There will be time enough,' he said. 'Time enough. Sleep now.'

'No,' she said. 'You must do it. I want it to be . . . to be complete.'

'Do you know . . . ?'

'Tell me. Tell me what I must do.'

'Hush, then.' He would try, he would at least have to try.

He turned on his side and placed his hand upon her belly which quivered with quick weeping. He fell back from her again. It was impossible.

'How can I . . . ? I cannot touch you as you weep, Anna. I cannot cause you fear and pain like this. How can I?'

'I am afraid, yes, I won't pretend. I won't put on a brave face. I need your comfort. I need your faith in me. I want to be your wife. I don't want to be a child under your protection.'

He waited, steeled himself. He would have liked to have relit the lamp so that he might face her, but that would have been a further complication for her. He had, anyway, a vivid, inescapable image of her, and his mental discipline was to bring this awareness of her into alignment with the blindness of his desire; to translate, in other words, his love into his desire and his desire into his love. It required, not the physical submission that he had thought it would, but a clarity of action, control, precision.

He kissed and touched her face, lowered his head down to rest upon her breasts, felt down her belly, felt the shape of her thighs, discovered the extent of her carefully. She was not weeping now; she breathed deeply, lifting herself with each breath. She had her hands at her sides, the palms down, pressing onto the bed. He drew up her nightgown, lifted it clear of her. He put his mouth upon her mouth and, holding her head, he slipped his tongue into her, touching her tongue quickly then withdrawing as she arched her back and gasped. He wanted to laugh then, with delight at her, with the pleasure of her reaction; he was bringing her to a physical immediacy which fascinated him. He knew that he had only begun, that what was to come might yet shock her into panic, into disengagement; but his own desire was now so secondary that he was ready at her first cry to leave her. He laid his open hand over her vagina.

26

The small cluster of her pubic hair surprised him. He had assumed only native women were so endowed, the last vestiges of animal pelt. It brought her into a different perspective. He had imagined her nakedness pale and submissive, a featureless expanse of rounded whiteness, but there was a complexity here, something that might catch onto him somehow. He was intrigued. He kissed her again quickly.

'Is it . . . as it should be?' she asked.

'It's . . . a miracle,' he said.

Suddenly she brought her hands together, covering his hand which covered her vagina, pressed his hand briefly then slid them quickly back to their stations beside her. Then, at once, her vagina opened and his fingertips slipped into the moist complexity. She gave a little cry of alarm and he took away his hand.

'Is it done?'

'If you want it to be done, it is done.'

'Is it done?'

'No.'

'Then . . . then, do it.'

He knelt over her and a rush of cold air filled the space between their bodies. He brushed the hair from her face and held her cheeks, kissed her. He stepped his knees, one by one, between hers. A rank sexual smell rose up and he breathed it in. She was taking deep breaths and holding them in.

'This,' he said. 'My love, my love.'

He touched her with the tip of his penis, moistened it at her. He held her face to his, lowered himself upon her. It occurred to him to discharge himself at once; he could have done it at will; but he felt that this would have been a deception. With infinite caution he pressed into her, touched a resistance and drew back. The pleasure was beginning to master him: his penis was numb, but in his thighs, at his anus, at the base of his spine, on his chest where her breasts were flattened beneath him. She seemed to grow beneath him, to spread herself receiving, her breathing now quick, now strong. He was having to twist and writhe himself to contain and control his pleasure and, as he did so, he had slipped forward.

She shook free her face and cried out, jerked up her body against his. She beat her hands on the bed, then, as if to still them, she whipped them round his middle, twisted and turned, as if to throw him off, as if to hold him down, he did not know. He felt himself

27

vanish upon her, a dead weight of useless flesh, a catalyst now used and neutralised. His hands lay at his sides, his face was buried in the pillow at her shoulder. His penis lay deep inside her and, as he remembered it there, in a motion of surrender, the semen flowed from it in quick beats.

They lay thus for a while, then he felt her begin to relax, to shift herself under him. Quickly he slipped from her, dropped back into his space of the bed which was now chill and wretched. He knew of animals that, once they had delivered their seed, had nothing more to do but die. He understood the biology of this. He was not touching her now. She was shifting and twisting in her own darkness as if her own part in the act was not over, as if there was a whole secret part of it that belonged to women alone, and from which he was excluded. Of course there was. He imagined her accommodating his seed within her, drawing it up somehow into her womb. She seemed in this very powerful, and he could not have reached for her then with anything adequate.

He wondered if he should leave her, sneak away to the daybed in the dressing room; but exactly as he thought this, she said:

'Don't leave me, Lionel. Where are you? Where are you?'

'I'm here.'

And he rolled himself towards her and she rolled herself to him, and they bound themselves in one another's arms and turned and writhed together; and she covered him in tears, struggling to get closer and closer to him, feeding on the touch of his mouth upon her face.

'My love, my love, Anna, my love,' he said.

When at last she began to still, her breathing eased and deepened into sleep, he remembered his nightmares, of his desires and of her desires, of his failure and of her panic; and they had all come true, all of them in their way; but they had not mattered. No, not at all. He did not know whether it had been good or bad, he knew only that it had been achieved openly and fully, and without shame; and the immensity of that achievement made him weak with relief.

. . . *nine* . . .

She awoke to a slit of pale light that parted the heavy curtains. She lay on her back beside her husband, in the dawn of the first day of their life. They had, in the night, separated. He lay sleeping heavily beside her. His face was towards her, but she could not see him clearly. He was shadowy and strange, entirely strange to her now. She was not sure what she felt towards him. She took an inventory of herself. Her head throbbed with a large pulse that did not ache but which, she felt, would ache when she lifted herself. Her limbs seemed enervated, her bowels watery. Her thighs hurt. She put her hand down and she felt sticky and sore there.

She remembered what had happened clearly, understood it mostly, but had no reaction to it. He had hurt her; she remembered that, had felt herself tearing inside; but when it was over, she had not somehow wanted it to be over; when he had laid upon her, she had not disliked his weight, had struggled up against it, but it had been a strong struggle; when he had touched her she had been glad to be touched, had shed tears of embarrassment, but they were warm tears and they came to her again now as she remembered.

It had certainly been far more physical than she had imagined it would be; or rather, she had known that it would be physical, but she had not imagined seriously what that meant. There had been a practicality to it that she had not expected. She wondered if it had pleased him, hoped that it had; for she found that she wanted to please him, that above all she wanted to prove herself his, to be proud of herself in this. She was ashamed then of her tears and fright, afraid that she had spoiled it for him. She did not know. She felt her tears begin to deepen and, before they broke, she slid from the bed into the cold morning.

She watched him carefully lest he should wake, slipped on her robe and made her way to the bathroom. She was concerned at the blood she had shed. She examined herself carefully, but could find no further cause for alarm. She stripped and washed herself. She

29

stretched and tensed her muscles. She ached, but did not hurt. She felt, below a blurred surface, resilient and clear. She wondered what the time was, wondered if she might summon a maid yet. She would have to go and collect a clean nightgown from the bedroom wardrobe and then she would have to return here to put it on. It all seemed complicated and she felt tired, felt that she wanted to be back in her bed, to lie in through a long morning. She tiptoed back along the corridor.

He was standing by the window in his dressing gown. He had opened the curtains and was set against a fall of grey light. As she appeared, alarmed by him there, he turned to her, stepped forward.

'Good morning, my love,' he said.

'Hello.' She was embarrassed by the soiled linen under her arm, went to the wardrobe.

He came to her. She saw him in the glass of the wardrobe, saw him watching her, trying to read her mood. She dropped her head and stood still and he put his hand on her shoulder.

'I need to . . . a nightgown. . . .'

'There was blood? It is . . . usual.'

'Is it?' She turned to him.

'Yes, the first time.' He put his hands on her shoulders, peered into her face. 'I . . . I thought you would know.' He drew her to him, held her submissive, squeezing out her tears onto his breast. 'Were you hurt?' he asked.

'A little.'

'Was it shameful?'

'No, not shameful.'

'Are you sad, now?'

'Why should I be sad?'

Then, after a silence, 'It's early. Go back to bed.'

'Yes.'

'I will leave you to rest.'

'No. I don't want to be left.'

'Come, then.'

'I must change my nightgown.'

'Anna?'

'Yes?'

'May I look at you?'

She did not understand this, looked up at him. He moved her away from him, held her shoulders with straight arms. He smiled at her and she pressed him a smile in return that, once she had committed herself to it, became warm, a smile of complicity, of greeting, their true good-morning.

'May I?' he asked.

'What?'

'Look at you?'

'Of course you may, Lionel.'

'No . . .'

'What? What is it? What do you want?'

'I want you . . . to take off your gown.'

'I have no nightgown on.'

'I know.'

'Oh . . .' She felt the blush flooding her face and neck and breasts.

He stepped away from her, closed his eyes.

'Forgive me,' he said. He turned and went out of the room.

When she had recovered her breath, she began to giggle. She shed her gown and ran quickly for the bed, slipping into the sheets which were cold and tangled, in which she had to twist and struggle to create a nest of warmth. She curled up and waited, suddenly excited, her tiredness gone.

He was a long time out of the room. She wondered what complexities there were in masculine ablutions that should keep him. She was cross with herself for her stupidity in failing to understand him. There would come a time when they would understand each other completely. She would do for him whatever he asked of her. She trusted him. It was an adventure.

When he returned he came in like a disgraced boy, avoiding her eyes. When he shed his gown, she saw that he wore a shirt and a pair of drawers that came down to his knees. She had to put her face in the pillow to stifle her laughter. He entered the bed formally as if sitting down for some function.

'Anna, my love,' he began. 'You must know that to shame you in anything is the last thing that I desire. I have many corruptions that, in my weakness, I may seek to exercise upon you. You must never give in to them, and you must never be afraid to bring me to task for them. Please . . . please don't weep . . . Anna?'

'I'm not weeping. I'm sorry, my darling. Here. Here I am.'

Lifting the covers and letting the cold air into her nest staunched her laughter at once, as did the shock that made him blink and gape. He looked and then turned away.

'No,' he said. 'You mustn't . . .'

'You are my husband, and I want you to look at me and to touch me. I don't want to live with you in my own little secrecy. It is not dishonourable. Is it? Lionel? Are you ashamed that I should lie here like this?'

'But when I asked you. . . .'

'I blushed because it took me so long to understand, because I am naïve and clumsy, and before I had a chance to right myself you had run away to put on those . . . those stupid drawers. Do you usually sleep in those?'

'No, I . . . I had not thought to bring nightwear.'

'You had thought we would sleep naked?'

'Forgive me.'

'Stop it!' She flung back the covers and lay there, blank and bare, waiting for him, beginning to laugh. He removed his garments, flung them to the floor, then took her to him.

She had forgotten the implications of this, felt them at once as he shifted himself to allow his swelling penis to lie against her leg. All her fine bravado was blown away. She closed her eyes, then opened them to look at him, to register his face upon hers, his seriousness and his concern. At once she wanted to retreat, to say that it was only a game, that she had not known what she was saying, that she needed more time. She moved herself away from him, felt the space where his penis had lain as a blush on her leg. She touched the space to find a smear of moisture there.

He kissed her, opened his mouth over hers and she felt the cutting edges of his teeth, tasted the metallic sting of his saliva. The intimacy of the kiss eased her, softened her, allowed her breathing to deepen. She thought of his penis there in the darkness below and wanted to see it. It frightened her a little; she thought of it as some internal organ, livid and bloated, slimy with visceral fluids. He caressed her face and neck, touched her breasts which glowed with the blushing she had now learnt to take pleasure in. She smoothed her hand down his side, noting its knotty unevenness, the hard, coarse texture of his musculature. It was intriguing to her in its difference to the soft padding of her own body which he now touched and smoothed. They were on voyages of exploration, discovering each other and themselves, coming through thickets of puzzlement to moments of clarity and understanding, flushed with pleasures of breathtaking simplicity. In this escalating intimacy, it was natural for her, at last, to take his penis into her hand, to dismiss her fears of it in her knowledge of its hard runnels, its smooth, moist tip, its sheath of loose skin. It was a part of the knottiness of his whole body. She understood it. And as she touched him there, he began to stroke her vagina, to open it into a palpable, moving space, swelling, liquid with an anticipation that made her turn and lift her body. And when he rose and laid himself down upon her, it was so natural that it made her laugh; when, after a moment's imprecision, he slid into her, deep through a twist of hurt, it was right, it was the great liberty of the flesh; the caressing within her was the reality for which all other caresses had prepared her; not only his caresses, but the caresses of her mother, the movement of water and wind upon her flesh, the gentle operations of her own organs within her. She lifted herself to caress him as he caressed her, drew back as he drew back, rose again as he strove into her, strove to dissolve the hardness of his penis with her softness, but growing hard somewhere against his hardness, gripping him with her thighs and arms.

My husband, she said to herself.

. . . *ten* . . .

They were to live in a bungalow in an avenue of bungalows in the grounds of the barracks at which his regiment was stationed. The bungalows were built on sandy soil amongst old pine trees; each surrounded by neat, white paling which enclosed, at the front, a small flower garden, and at the rear a larger, less presentable space of rough lawn and washing lines.

He showed her the bungalow embarrassed at its meanness, its darkness, the raw newness of its plaster and planking already touched by damp and grubbiness. She, however, noticed none of this, paced her way through the small rooms proudly, happy with their containment, happy that there would be little room here for any distance between them. The bungalow seemed to her designed for the first years of a new marriage, minimal and spartan. Apart from which, it was theirs, their home, within which they could bring forth their children.

There were three bedrooms: their large bedroom and two smaller bedrooms, one of which would be his dressing room; the other was to house her servant. He too had a servant, a soldier who lived in barracks but who was to come at dawn and leave at dusk.

'Mayn't we do without servants?' she asked.

'No. I don't think we may,' he said, touching her shoulder. 'Wilkie will be here shortly. He's been with me for a while.'

Wilkie was a stout young man, red-faced and busy. She offered him her hand to shake and he was surprised at the gesture. Lionel left him with her to move her trunks into the bedroom, to unpack such household things as she possessed, to put up her pictures, to tell her the form regarding provisions. She tried to imagine him as a man with a private life, with desires and pleasures, but it was difficult to imagine him as anything other than he was now.

'Captain Drewer prefers the Blue tea, m'm,' he said at one point. 'Captain Drewer has his bath at six, m'm; cold water, m'm. I've filled the Captain's decanters, m'm, but his usual blend is out of stock, so I've taken the liberty of substituting for it a new blend that I hope he'll not mind too much.'

As she heard these instructions, as she watched Wilkie tidy her things neatly away, she felt that she was being offered a pattern of life to which she would be expected to adhere, a tight pattern which this little man kept in trim; and to which, she half-suspected, her presence was seen as an interference. She sensed about her a world of functional masculinity, coded and hard-edged. She disliked it, and disliked Wilkie, or tried to; but he was as impossible to dislike as he was to like. It was not dislike, she told herself, but discomfort, and she set herself to explore this discomfort, to know its edges and constrictions.

When Wilkie had gone, she articulated her worst possible case, namely that she was here as an item of soft furnishing, or as a domestic pet. There seemed little for her to do but to wait for Lionel to return from his duties. In waiting for him, she grew warm and active again and her fears were softened.

He was not gone long and, when he came in, she was pleased to settle him down in an armchair and to make tea for him. The kitchen range which Wilkie had tended before he left intimidated her, but

34

she managed to bring the kettle to the boil without disaster. She had looked into the larder and noted the meat and vegetables that Wilkie had laid in; the prospect of having to make a meal for him hung darkly over her. I will learn, she told herself. I will become competent, will peel potatoes and make gravy. She racked her memory for childhood hours spent in the kitchens, for the games they had allowed her to play there in the fiction of helping them. She was determined, but out on a giddy ledge here. That which ordinary women, real women, performed as part of their nature was quite beyond her upbringing.

'What will you do with your days, my love?' he asked her over the tea.

'I will cook and sew, of course. What do you think women do, Lionel? They have their duties too, you know.'

'Then Brady will be redundant.'

'And who is Brady?'

Brady was to be her maid. There was, before the tea was done, a quiet tapping at the back door. Lionel went and brought her through, a dumpy, sleepy-eyed girl in a new uniform that did not quite fit her. She bobbed and blushed and took the tea things, although they were not strictly finished with, through to the kitchen to make herself busy.

Anna had not seen her face properly, for she had not lifted it once. She listened now and heard the clatterings of the kitchen and wondered how this girl would change the landscape here, whether they would become friends, whether there would be problems that she would have to make judgements upon, take the responsibility of. She was nervous and looked to Lionel for support, or at least for some basic priming, but he, smiling, said he'd leave her for an hour to settle Brady in.

'Where are you going?' she asked.

'To the mess.'

'Mayn't I come with you?'

'No, my love. You will have your own society here, such as it is.'

She sulked a little after he had gone. She understood that he had his duties to attend to, but the idea of his spending his social time in masculine enclaves seemed an outrage. She did not want her own society; she wanted his.

After a while, however, sitting alone in the gathering evening, she heard a quiet humming coming from the kitchen, and she remembered Brady there. She would go and ask Brady to light the lamps, but she did not go at once. The humming made her feel strange, awkward; she did not know whether she approved of it or not. She could not make out a tune as such, but the tone was sweet and lilting, personal in a way that she had not expected. Its proximity worried her. This girl was to be living very close to them; there was not much that they would be able to conceal from her. The reality of sharing her home, her marriage, with this stranger came to her. She rose and went to the kitchen door.

Brady, peeling potatoes, stopped humming when Anna appeared, turned and made an awkward bob in her direction, without taking her hands from the potato water.

'May I sit and watch you work, Brady?' she said.

'If you please, m'm,' the girl said.

It was not an entirely consistent response, and Anna knew that she had surprised the girl with her request. She had thought to make an offer to help the girl, but did not know how to; so she sat at the kitchen table and began assiduously to question her.

She was one of a family of eight, her father a soldier, her mother dead. She was fifteen. This was her first position in service, although she had helped at home. Corporal Wilkie was a comrade of her eldest brother and had told her all the things that would be expected of her here, had trained her up properly.

Anna wondered if Corporal Wilkie had further interests in Brady. She was glad, though, to have a girl without experience, without previous mistresses with which to compare her. Many of her fears were allayed. She would at least be able to direct this girl, to assume a superiority without its tenuity being exposed too soon.

'And when you're not at work, Brady,' she asked, 'what do you like to do?'

'I don't know at all, m'm.'

'D'you like to sing?'

The girl blushed, presumably remembering her humming.

Anna stretched out and placed her hand upon the girl's red wrist.

'I am glad to have you working here, Brady. I hope you will be happy.'

Brady's cooking erred on the side of the overdone, but when Lionel made a wry face at his cutlet, Anna became proprietorial and told him that he would have to be patient and tolerant, that Brady would do them very well, and that he was to keep an eye on Corporal

Wilkie in that direction. Lionel was visibly impressed by her tone, nodded appreciatively.

. . . *eleven* . . .

It was strange, that first day, to walk away from the bungalow and to approach his old world, the other side of such monumental differences. He did not know how he would manage it. In the event, he re-entered the life of the regiment with scarcely a ripple of the surface. He took up his duties, reconnected himself with the trivia of the mess as if there had been no change. It was bizarre, for he was entirely different and, although he found that he could, with a conscious straightening, present himself amongst the forms and motions of his old life in the image of his former self, that self was now a shell within which swelled livid, visceral excitements that would catch at him continually with extraordinary bouts of remembrance. He held himself more tightly and formally amongst them than ever before. They congratulated him, meanwhile, shook his hand and bought him drinks in celebration, but it was a formality and, when it was done, they did not refer to it again, had done all that was necessary and proceeded from there as before; but he no longer belonged here as he had belonged, that was obvious.

He sought a moment's privacy with Harry, had assumed that this would happen in the course of things, but he found that it was hard to achieve. Harry greeted him, but always seemed to be going somewhere else, looking off past him.

At last, after a week or so, he took a bottle of whisky up to Harry's room, having ascertained first that he was there and that he was alone. He rapped on the door and, hardly hearing the response, entered.

Harry was sitting on his bed, laying out a hand of patience. He looked up and watched Lionel, wary, caught out. Lionel collected a couple of glasses and splashed the spirit into them. He handed one to Harry, who took it; then he pulled up a chair and sat, raised his glass. After a moment, carefully, Harry returned the gesture. They drank together and that made it easier.

'Well? When are you going to come and pay your respects to your sister, Brand?' Lionel began.

'Not my sister any more, old man.'

Lionel considered the tone of this: casual, but a fraction too studied. He drank off his glass, refilled it, reached over and put a splash more in Harry's glass. Harry sighed, brushed his game of patience onto the floor and sat up on the bed, elbows on his knees, face down.

'What the devil's got into you, Brand?' Lionel asked.

'You're a married man now, Drewer, that's all.'

'A married man, yes. To your sister. We are brothers now, surely.'

Harry looked at him through narrowed eyes, his head to one side.

'I . . . I was in a bit of trouble the week before you got back here,' he said softly.

'I heard something. You broke a brother officer's nose.'

'Trussel.'

'Trussel? My dear Harry, where, on God's earth, did Trussel find the meat to rouse you?'

'That's it, d'you see? he said . . . he said that you'd married my sister because you couldn't marry me.'

There was a moment's whiteness, then Lionel felt the blood come into his eyes, the bolus of rage in his throat. He turned away to contain it, to drive it down to safety, and when he turned back, Harry was watching him at last, peering up at him.

'You did well to break his nose, Brand. I'd've broken his damned neck.'

'You see? You see?'

'What?'

'I don't want to get drunk with you, Drewer. I don't want to come climbing or hunting any more. None of that's any good now.'

There was something in this that Lionel did not understand, some intonation that he could not quite read. He puzzled at it for a while, trying to find the right words to open it; but then he stopped, felt the spirit go cold in his belly, and did not want to know any more. He took out his cigarette case, offered it to Harry who took a cigarette and reached for a match. In the glow of the match, Lionel caught the wastage in Harry's face, the lines of excess at his eyes, the rictal quiver of his mouth.

'Tell me, Harry, why did you never say you had a sister?'

'Didn't I?'

'You told me about your parents, your home, but I never knew you had a sister.'

'I don't know why. It never occurred to me. She was . . . a child, I suppose. I didn't think she mattered much to anything. She was just . . . just Anna. We were children together. We . . . all that didn't matter any more when I was . . . when we were . . . when I heard you were to be married, I was drunk for three days. I couldn't understand it. I couldn't understand you. I couldn't understand why I had to get drunk. Everything seemed stupid.' Then he shook himself to clear the morbidity of this, looked up, said, 'Well? Is she a good wife to you, Drewer?'

Lionel smiled but did not answer, did not know what answer would have eased the boy. He drained his glass, screwed out his cigarette.

'Come to dinner tomorrow night,' he said as he stood to leave.

'No, I can't . . . I've an engagement. . . .'

'Nonsense. We shall expect you at eight.'

'Please, Drewer. Not yet.'

Lionel stood and looked down at him.

'So be it, Harry. So be it.'

He left the bottle there.

. . . twelve . . .

In the morning of her first working day as the wife of Captain Drewer, she received a visit from the Colonel's wife. Mrs Radstock sat in the bungalow's little drawing room with a rigidity that made Anna imagine her backbone as a long, knotted block, bone and cartilage fused by decades of formality. She wore white gloves, a black hat, was so covered with swathes of heavy cloth that Anna came to see her face too as part of her clothing.

Anna was welcomed to the regiment, offered felicitations upon her marriage. Mrs Radstock hoped that she was settling in, asked if she had everything she needed, asked if she was satisfied, so far, with her servants. She inquired a little way into her background, far enough, Anna felt, so that she might be placed socially.

'You and your husband must come to dine at the Black House soon, Mrs Drewer,' the Colonel's wife said as she departed.

'I shall look forward to that keenly, Mrs Radstock.'

No precise invitation was forthcoming.

It was so clinically formal, this visit, that Anna felt exhausted by it. She felt as if she had been fitted with a tight new garment, a uniform. Mrs Radstock had behaved as a doctor or solicitor might have behaved, rigorous and professional, impeccably detached. She had wondered, in the frequent empty spaces of the interview, what opinion was being formed of her here, what report would be made upon her; but that had not been the point. The point had been merely to check her through, to make sure that Captain Drewer had not encumbered the regiment with anyone socially or temperamentally unsuitable. She imagined the woman with a great ledger of all the regimental wives: against Anna's name would be placed the smug tick.

On the second day, she was visited by a group of the other wives, the women who were situationally her equals; and so she became enrolled in the female society of the regiment, offered the diversions and small usefulnesses that were established to fill in the hours when active domestic ministry was not required of them. There were visits into town, to the dressmakers and haberdashers, to the cake shop and tea room, the library and stationers. Anna watched them exercising their little choices, making fussy little purchases out of fussy little purses. She noted with surprise their avariciousness, and listened to them complain of the meanness of their little town, comparing it unfavourably with the grand London shops which they all claimed to have visited and at which they pretended to have spent sums that they spoke of in hushed voices. They took tea together, behaving in one another's drawing rooms with expert manners that made Anna feel positively coarse; and then, on their way from their hostess's door, they worked up an embroidery of comments about her and her home that made Anna blush with their cruel vulgarity. They simply did not seem to know any better. They had books and music, but they read and played as if they were arranging ornaments. Their aesthetic reactions were divided into a vile flaring of the nostrils for disapproval; otherwise, a soft simpering. They played games of cards, at which they were at their very worst, displaying a pettiness and lack of charity, a lack of the simple pleasure of the games, that was beyond Anna's comprehension. They bewildered and dispirited her, day after day. She had come into another world.

Their children seemed uniformly unhealthy and unhappy, some bloated and sickly, others wasted and sad. They looked around the drawing rooms into which they were brought with restless, vacant eyes. To bear Lionel a child seemed the purpose of her life at this time; she willed it to happen with an excitement that, in her solitude, was everything. Here amongst these pale, pointless infants, she began to grow uneasy. Was this formaldehyde world a place into which to bring children?

'Lionel?' she began one evening when Brady had cleared the dinner. 'Why are they all so . . . so senseless?'

'Who, my love?'

'The women. The other wives. My . . . my friends.'

'Are they?'

'Yes.'

'Senseless.' He lifted the word clear to expose it.

'Insensitive, unaware . . . yes, senseless.'

'You have found no-one . . . sympathetic?' he asked.

'No. No-one. You are surprised? Do you know any of them?'

'No. How might I know any of them? Garland's wife's a pretty and amiable sort of woman, isn't she?'

'Lionel, she's a doll. Oh, she's less vicious than the others perhaps, but that is only because she is less intelligent.'

He paused, took out his cigarette case and offered it to her. She took her cigarette carefully, with a customary smile of complicity. Cigarettes were an indulgence she had acquired since her marriage. She only smoked in the evening with Lionel, did not entirely enjoy it, but relished the sharing of the narcotic with him against the dictates of convention. As they smoked, a sensual ease came between them.

'I am sorry you have no friends here, my love,' he said.

'It's not important.'

'I want you to be contented.'

'I am.'

'To be purposeful too.'

'I shall write a book.'

He laughed.

'You are not to mock me, Lionel.'

'I am not mocking you, Anna. I am delighted. You are right. They are a dreary, senseless lot. You have your independence and I would be wretched if any of them claimed that from you. I don't want you to have friends, if you must know.'

She was quickly glad of this, felt liberated by it, rose the next morning and went visiting with the sprightly step of one who has nothing to prove but to herself, who has no obligations but those encamped in the citadel of her heart.

. . . *thirteen* . . .

Her initiation into the life of the regiment was consummated at the Klejinski Ball. On the plains of the Klejinski, seventy years before, the regiment had suffered a glorious decimation. A scrofulous collection of illiterate social misfits, dressed in blazing uniforms, braid and buckles, gasping with sunstroke, raging with lice, gutted with dysentery and syphilis, officered by schoolboys hard-cocked with blind, bloody ignorance, had one long afternoon become myth; had been locked four-square against scything sweeps of cavalry and grape-shot, and pulverised into a knot of mutilated defiance. Five hours they had held the field and, as the sun set, the survivors had straggled out over the ramparts of the dead, extricated themselves from their disembowelled, dismembered comrades; and, bestial with fatigue and cruelty, they had mustered in the great, dusty emptiness and marched home. Thereafter, on the anniversary, the regiment crowned itself with celebration. The brigades paraded and the names of the dead were called, a pause after each one as if he might somehow rise up and answer; and in the pause a swell of sympathetic emotion touched the breasts of men who, whilst on parade, hardly knew themselves from the men next to them. For the men then followed beer and fiddlers and as much fornication as could be smuggled into the adjacent shrubbery. For the officers, and their ladies, and for the local gentry, there was the Klejinski Ball.

Anna and Lionel danced tirelessly through the first hours of the ball with an assurance and pleasure that drew a certain, cautious admiration. They were not ostentatious – marriage to Anna had effected no great miracle upon Lionel's footwork – but they were inexhaustible, and so brightly concentrated upon one another, taking sustained pleasure in the dancing, rising to the band with competitive smiles, honouring one another at the end of each set with a steady, judging look.

The regiment approved. It seemed that marriage had civilised Drewer. And his wife, the rumours about whom were that she was rather young, rather stand-offish, was here revealed as a positive asset, an ornament to the social life of the regiment that was sadly lacking in such ornaments these latter days. She was not exactly beautiful, but then that was always a distraction, a temptation for the mooning boys to fall in miserable love with. She was small and well-fleshed, but delicate and lively in her movements; there was something daughterly, sisterly, about her to which the calloused old imaginations of the regiment warmed palpably.

Later Lionel danced with Mrs Radstock, and with the widow of an old brigadier who had been good to him when he had first joined the regiment; but he could not do more than step through the dances, his awareness of Anna intensified in his separation from her. He watched her dance with his superiors. She was incredible. If men must go and fight and die, if their world meant anything beyond the blind butcheries they inflicted upon one another, then what Anna was tonight, what she was always with him, was the motivation; for she was life itself, with no other purpose than to take a clear and free pleasure in itself, and to bring that pleasure to those whom she touched in any way. If soldiering was, as he believed, manliness at its most rigorous and perfected, then she was the other half, the womanliness without which men were sterile in everything they assayed. The personal intensity of his love for her was that evening expanded into a love for them all, and for all they represented and defended; not only the nation and its sheltering millions, but the truths and honours which he felt were embodied in the nation at its best. The two halves of his life came together here and he was seamlessly happy.

The tinge of the dawn was coming amongst the pine trees and the blocks of the barracks buildings when the last dance ended. Captain and Mrs Drewer were amongst the first of those who had stayed the full course (and only advanced decrepitude excused one from the full course) to make their farewells to their hosts.

They walked the half-mile to their bungalow across the turf, their steps springy, the dew beginning to rise about them. They did not speak, but when the first bird of the morning began to sing, they stopped simultaneously and stood in the fall of its song and looked up into the bowl of the sky.

Brady and Wilkie were waiting for them to return, a little sleepy-eyed, a little shamefaced, but ready to be about their duties of unty-ing and unbuttoning, tidying away the discarded fineries. They asked the master and mistress independently about the ball but received brief, distracted answers. Yes, it had been splendid, splendid.

They met briefly, Brady and Wilkie, for a quick cuddle before Wilkie trotted off into the morning and Brady bundled herself off into bed. She was tired beyond sleep; lay on her back and listened to the noises of the adjacent bedroom; she tried not to, but could not stop herself. The purposeful, wordless, rhythmic restlessness was there tonight as it was every night, and it cluttered her dreams.

She had had an important evening. Wilkie had brought a bottle of sweet wine and they had chatted and become merry. He had grab-bed her as she passed and had plumped her down on his knee, at first in an avuncular manner, but she was not as naïve as he had thought her to be: she had five older brothers, after all. It had been cosy to be cuddled by Jack Wilkie, but she had been clear-headed enough not to believe his endearments, not to be ignorant of what he was about. His kisses had been alarmingly deep, and they had made her head fizz. His caresses had proceeded from reassurance to exploration, but she had resolutely kept him out of her skirts. At last she had conceded him her breasts which he had kissed and sucked greedily. This was going too far, and she had jumped up from him; turned and had been ready for him when he came in pursuit; had submitted to his embraces there whilst deftly unbuttoning him and, to his alarm, had brought him to a rapid ejaculation; after which he had subsided into a comfortable lassitude. They had cuddled and dozed, rousing to make themselves presentable for the return of the master and mistress.

44

In the aftermath of this intimacy, Brady found herself pleased with her evening, pleased with the attentions of Jack Wilkie, which had made her feel desirable and wholesome; and in her handling of the situation which made her feel strong. Surely she did not love him, had anyway no intention of marrying a soldier; but it was good now to know a little of that, to know how it all worked within her, the mechanism of arousal, something of the mystery that was in progress through the wall, which frightened and allured her.

Captain Drewer terrified her. She thought him monstrously ugly and was appalled that her mistress should submit the soft nakedness which she never sought to conceal from her maid to that man. Brady imagined him marked by some hidden deformity and although, theoretically, she could imagine herself surrendering to a man like Jack Wilkie, she could not settle herself to the hideousness of a man like Captain Drewer. It made her shudder to think of it, to think of it happening a few feet from her solitary bed. It must be love, she told herself, that must make the difference. She could not understand that, could not imagine it, could not comprehend how love, in which she did not fully believe, could make the difference. She had begun to nurture an amassing affection for her mistress, a loyalty to her that would admit to no intimation of criticism from her family and friends, and certainly not from Jack Wilkie who had been teasingly impudent at her expense, and had been firmly put down. In the darkness of the night, Brady was afraid for Anna Drewer, longed to be called in to her, to have her come weeping for comfort. In the tangle of these jealous fantasies she at last fell asleep.

Anna and Lionel took the pleasure of their marriage bed that night, as every night, but that night, crowning the triumph of the ball, with a new register of delight. They were tired now and proceeded slowly, calmly, roused silently by the memories of the dancing and the others, all the others who had clustered close, but who were not admitted to this sealing act of the evening, towards which every rising pleasure led, as surely as the whole ritual of the regiment led to moments like the glory of the Klejinski plain.

When the pleasure had triumphed and faded, they unpeeled their weary flesh and lay apart. He would have to rise in an hour to be on parade, to bolt on his professionalism; it did not seem possible that he would manage it, drained and limp and, at this moment, without the remotest motivation to do anything; but he would manage it, and manage it well, as he always did. She wondered, as she often wondered, what Brady could hear. She closed her legs tightly to keep it all within her. They fell together into a small sleep and dreamt of light, warm light running in horizontals through the trees at the dawn or dusk of some majestic day. They lay like gods, golden and eternal in the moment of their love.

. . . *fourteen* . . .

It took a while, perhaps for her to settle, perhaps for her mind to be ready, perhaps for her body, but at last, in the ineffable secrecy of her body, it happened. She noted the signs but did not dare to trust them too early; the small queasiness, the failure of her menstrual blood. She waited whilst the certainty grew within her, afraid of self-delusion, afraid that, even if it had begun, she might by her wanting and willing it cause it to falter and fail.

She dared not mention it to Lionel yet, but she could not keep it from Brady. Lionel was dining in the mess and Anna ate alone, went early to bed. Anna sat in her nightgown before the glass watching Brady pull the brush through her hair which was growing thick and awkward, causing Brady to have to pull the brush, to jerk at the roots of her hair, causing her continually to apologise as Anna winced. Anna did not resent the pain; it was superficial and bracing. Brady hated causing it though, and Anna could see the girl's eyes begin to brim with the frustration of it.

'That'll do,' she said.

'I've not done, m'm. I'm sorry.'

'No. That'll do for now, my dear.'

The affection of this made the maid's eyes flood, but Anna caught her hand as she turned away, pulled her down beside her and took her head against her belly.

'Hush now, dearest,' Anna said. 'Look up at me.'

Brady lifted her face and Anna kissed her forehead, took her hand and placed it there, where her face had been.

'You know it, don't you?' she said.

'You're with child, m'm, aren't you?'

'Yes. Hush. I've not told the Captain yet. Oh Brady, you know all our secrets, don't you? No, no, you mustn't be ashamed. I am going to need you more than ever now. You will look after me, won't you? Won't you?'

'Yes, m'm. Oh yes.'

And Brady hurried off to her bed, trembling with the fear of her knowledge, desperate to be asleep before the Captain returned, but longing, without really thinking about it, for Jack Wilkie to come knocking at her window, longing to let him in.

Lionel returned earlier than usual, warmed but not blurred by the brandy he had drunk. He had hoped to find Anna still awake, was a little irked at the silence of the sleeping bungalow. He undressed carelessly – let Wilkie sort it out tomorrow morning – and slipped in cold and naked beside his wife.

She lay on her back, breathing lightly. He did not think at first that she was asleep, but when he whispered out her name she did not answer. He moved close to her warmth, wary not to let his chill disturb it. He breathed in her sweetness and grew hard, shuffled away to try and settle himself to sleep.

Anna, who was not remotely asleep, felt his restlessness beside her with a teasing, detached pleasure. She did not respond to his arousal as she would have done, even yesterday. Poor Lionel. What would he do now that its purpose was answered? A shadow came over her satisfaction at this thought, but did not obscure it. All that was irrelevant now, and she trusted him to sustain her in this new adventure as he had sustained her before. In a few moments, she would turn to him and tell him, but for the moment she lay in the darkness and stored up the pleasure of her revelation, swelling with the simple joy of it, and of him, and of herself, the simple, natural completion of everything.

The news filled him with delight. He wanted to stand out in the night and bellow his triumph. In the morning, the houses seemed filled with a new brightness, a purposeful quiet. Leaving it to go about his duties was at first an irritation, but later, as she grew, as she progressed into maternity, he began to hate his work. He wanted only to be with her.

His world proceeded with blunt oblivion: inspecting, drilling, trudging out across cold, bleak countryside to practise the instincts of a war he knew would never be fought, or at least never again in the way they interminably practised it. His men were fat and slovenly, fractious, and fostering a sense of themselves that was out of place in their calling. They needed the desperation of battle. They were becoming domesticated, bourgeois, nesting themselves into the life of the barracks.

He knew that these dissatisfactions were as much a reflection upon his own state as upon theirs, that he too was a long way removed from the simple purity of his calling. The consciousness of this hypocrisy within him did not make it easier to bear. His anger with them at times seemed to swell his anger at himself, the frustration of his futile soldiering when there was so much of such importance waiting to be engaged with at home.

She did not have an easy time of it. She sunk into watery lethargies and migraines which locked her head in contraptions of pain. He spent hours with her lying against him, weeping with sheer exhaustion. He massaged her numb, aching flesh and came to know her body in another dimension, to understand its fragility and mortality as it gathered itself about its purpose. He learned a new respect for her, and for womankind; for he knew that this was a physical testing that would have shrivelled him. Masculine courage was external, deliberate, indulgent: this courage was a struggle with the mechanics of being, with the nature of flesh itself. He strove always to come closer and closer to her, as if he might in some way be a part of her struggle, share her anguish. He was proud of her need of him, of the way she turned when he entered and broke her emotions over him. She was mysterious and bewildered and, day by day, the drama of her pregnancy involved him completely. Had they summoned him away at this time, he would have refused them, thrown his commission down and fought them back from her.

As the time drew nearer, he began to be vividly afraid of what she would have to endure in her approaching encounter with life as it rent itself clear of her, as she was opened and vulnerable to the slip of death. He yearned sympathetically to put himself at risk again; caught himself once spinning a bullet round in the chambers of his revolver, pulling himself back from this insanity and going quickly in to where she slept, heavy-bellied and breasted, restless and sweating, kneeling down beside her to ask in the silence of his shame for her forgiveness and her understanding.

. . . *fifteen* . . .

He came back one evening from a route-march through bitter autumn rain, wet and tired and angry. One of his men had fallen into a waterlogged gulley and had broken something; not a bone, something internal, a rupture. The man lay on his stretcher white-faced and whimpering. When they had uncovered his back, a vast blue swelling disfigured the pallor of his flesh. Lionel felt personally compromised by this accident and was fighting angry, looking for someone to exorcise that anger upon: the man's comrades who had not been taking care, the imbeciles who had initiated this stupid day's drudgery; upon the man himself who looked up at Lionel with a clearer response to his anger than to his own hurt.

'I'm sorry, sir,' he said.

'Shut up, Hicker, you bloody, damn fool.'

The man began to cry and Lionel had to walk away to stop himself slapping the stupid face.

By the door of the infirmary where they had brought the man, he saw a woman. He assumed that it was the man's girl, or sister; he knew that he had no wife. He was furious that she should be here, that some meddling cretin had sent some message. He strode towards her, his fists clenched, the orderlies parting and going for cover either side of him. Then he recognised the woman.

'Brady?'

'She's . . . she began just after you left, sir.'

'Is it over, Brady? Is it?'

'No, sir, it's. . . .'

He did not want to hear any more, not from a servant. He was running across the sticky grass, the wet air clogging his face; he flailed his arms about as if to clear the obstructions. The unevenness of the ground stumbled him and he came to the bungalow at last in a damp sack of held panic that was, as he kicked the gate, abruptly rent by her scream.

The scream was terrible. It halted him with an image of her torn open, the pain terminal, leaping out of the terrible exposure of her torn organs. He could not bear it, actually turned to flee into the closing darkness. A second scream came, lower than the first, pushed down into the moan. He clenched himself to the sound. He turned and faced himself clearly, stepped into the fetid bungalow, through the rooms towards her.

At the door of her room he saw her on the bed, in an inflammation of lamplight, her back arched up under the great nakedness of the belly, her legs opened, between them a horrible leaking wound. Her head was rolling from side to side, swollen in sweat, the eyes clenched. She did not seem to be there at all; she was lost in the drowning of her mortality. He stepped forward, but they caught his arms; the doctor, a nurse or midwife, bundled him out. He tried to struggle but was suddenly weak.

He sat in an armchair, flaccid and trembling, and the doctor brought him whisky which he drank in one blind swallow.

'Now, now, Drewer,' he said. 'We can't have you bursting in like that. You're the last person she needs at the moment. She's doing very well, very well indeed.'

'The pain,' he said.

'There is always pain, dear boy, that is how these things are arranged. Come now. Be calm. She's more than a match for it.'

So he waited, the screams coming at progressively tight intervals, each like a blow on his head but, as to a succession of blows, he grew numbed to them in time. He could not understand why he was shut out from her. His impotence drugged him. He slept fitfully, in the filth of his fatigues. He imagined that she was dead. He had not known how much of himself was embedded with her. He felt as if some amputation had taken place within his head. He began to lose all memory of her, all sense of her and of himself. His awareness of the present was of a garish smearing upon an infinitely descending darkness.

The maid, Brady, knelt before him and unlaced his boots. He looked down at her and hated her fussy practicality, submitted to it stupidly. He told her to fetch him a cigarette. The tobacco made him cough but that roused him. His head ached and his mouth and throat were full of ashes.

'What's going on?' he asked.

'You were asleep, sir.'

The screaming had stopped. He lifted himself in his chair, turned his head to listen, shook his head as if he were deaf.

'Brady?'

'You were asleep, sir.'

'It's over?'

'Yes, sir.'

'Where's that damn doctor?'

'He left, sir. I wanted him to wake you, but he said you should sleep.'

'My wife?'

'She's asleep now, sir. And the child.'

'Child?'

'A son, sir.'

He felt firstly stupid, blushed like a schoolboy who has wet his bed. He tried to lift himself out of his chair, but could not seem to put the necessary tension into his limbs.

'Help me,' he said.

Brady came and took his arm. He grabbed at her shoulder and pulled himself up on her. He went to the door but could not open it. Brady opened it, guided him in.

The nurse was there, sitting on a chair at the side of the bed. She rose when he entered and put her finger to her lips, then curled it, beckoning him forward to the cot.

The child lay, perfectly pink and tiny, its head shocked with a tuft of black hair, breathing quickly and making a small sucking sound. It puzzled him. He had no reaction to it.

'A boy, then?' he said.

'Yes. Sssh.'

He turned at last to Anna. She lay on her side, beached in her exhaustion, open-mouthed, her hair in sodden tangles. He touched her cheek and it was burning. He wanted more than anything to strip off and to lie down beside her, to take her in his arms and to feed off her heat, to touch her rawness with his mouth. He looked at the nurse and at Brady.

'The instant she wakes you are to rouse me. D'you hear?'

'Yes, sir.'

'The instant.'

He returned to the drawing room, poured more whisky, sat with it, sprawled in the armchair. He lit another cigarette. The rain was splattering on the windows and the wind gusted against the faces of the house. He felt grey with tiredness but could not have settled to sleep. Brady appeared.

'Where's Wilkie?'

'Sir . . . it's four o'clock. The doctor said. . . .'

'Damn the doctor.'

'Can I fetch you anything, sir?'

'What?'

'Would you like something to eat? May I run you a bath, sir?'

He regarded the maid, Brady. He had always seen her as a frightened little thing, scurrying away behind Anna's skirts. Anna had an affection for her and he was glad of that, did not consider that it concerned him further. At this moment, however, he hardly recognised her, rosy and plump and smiling there. Her control of the situation, and of him, perplexed him.

'Was it . . . a difficult affair in there?' he asked.

'No, sir, not at the end. It took a time, sir, but it was not . . . not too hard on the mistress, not really. She was . . . was wonderful, sir.'

'And it's all . . . all as it should be?'

'Oh yes, sir. Oh yes.'

'It's a fearful business.'

She smiled at him quietly, as if he understood a secret at last. He watched her and she blushed. Under the trembling of his exhaustion, a thawing tenderness went through him. His eyes filled with tears. His belly and thighs quivered.

'Come here,' he said.

She came at once and he grabbed her hand. He did not look at her, did not want to allow his desire to fasten upon the nature of her specific womanliness. He needed only something to hold onto, a substitute, someone to absorb some part of the energy of his tenderness. Did she understand this? He could not believe that possible. Did he pull her to him? He did not consciously do so, yet she was there, kneeling on the floor between his legs, her well-fleshed body pressed against his, her breath even and deep as he held her, gripped her and shook with the outrush of his ungainly love which she absorbed in her warm, patient flesh, nestling into him, sustaining him.

. . . *sixteen* . . .

To Captain and Mrs Lionel Drewer, a son, Lewis Henry Carrow.

Harry Brand was surprised to be asked to godfather his nephew, and was more surprised by his own unthinking acceptance. He had visited his sister and her husband a couple of times as he was honour-bound eventually to do, but he did not like it there. There was something indecent about marriage, about this marriage at least. He felt that he was prying, hated their smiles and the little touching they bestowed upon one another; a trailing hand on a shoulder, nothing more, but suggesting a deep physical understanding that he could not stomach. He wanted to be no part of it, did not want to touch it even with his imagination.

With the child there, it became somehow easier. They had opened out, the child between them, upon whom their attentions could be focused rather than upon each other. He was a fine little fellow, Harry thought, sulky-faced and surprisingly stocky. Harry was encouraged to hold him and he liked to lift him up to the light, to feel him wriggle.

There had been many hurts revealed within Harry when they had married. He had felt betrayed in ways that he did not care to understand. His life up to then had, in childhood and manhood respectively, been lit by moments of emotional intimacy with his sister and with Lionel Drewer; they, independently, had had access to his most private times. He had felt they were combined against him. Little Lewis, then, was offered to him as a token of reconciliation, and he was glad to accept it.

He became thereafter a frequent visitor to the bungalow, dropping in at odd moments when he needed a little quiet, glad of the distractions from his own company, in which he had found himself too much recently. Although he could not imagine himself in such a situation, he began to feel a sentimentality towards this little domestic circle of which he was a tangent. He even drew it thus: a circle, quartered, with a tangent along which he wrote his name; and in the quarters, Anna, Lionel, Lewis, Brady; the latter perhaps as an afterthought, his schoolroom mathematics not up to dividing the circle into three; but when she was there, Brady came to belong there. She seemed indeed essential to the domesticity of the bungalow, moving quickly and freely between Anna and Lionel, never forward, but always there with a quick smile and a quiet confidence in the movements of her small, plump body.

He found himself thinking about Miss Brady more than he ought to. He thought it would be most delightful to roll that confident little body about in a big bed. Remembering this fantasy, the next time he visited the house, when Brady appeared with little Lewis cradled on her forearms, he blushed and had to turn away. They were alone in the room for some reason at this moment, and Brady gave a little laugh which mortified Harry; it was as if she could read him. When he left, he pressed a coin into her hand.

'And what's this for, sir?'

'For . . . for all you've done for my godson, Brady.'

'Then, thank you, sir.'

He had expected her to refuse it, had wanted perhaps to discomfort her with his money. Her acceptance of it made matters worse. It established a secret between them.

Jack Wilkie's designs upon the affections of the Drewers' maid were both more advanced and more realistic than those of Lieutenant Brand. Brady, he had decided, was the girl he would marry. He had plans to gather up a little capital, abandon his soldiering and settle down behind the counter of a small shop with a steady wife. Brady was perfect. He admired her growing confidence in the Drewer household, watched her blossoming in the duties of housekeeper, cook and nursemaid, and began to value her very highly.

One evening, with the Drewers out to dinner and little Lewis asleep, sitting together in the kitchen in the big chair, he decided that tonight was the night to make an issue of it. It was so warm, so soft, so easy here. He wanted only that she should feel as he did.

She sat athwart him, with her warm, damp hands about his face, giving him little petal kisses that made him laugh. He bounced her a little and tried to slip his hand up her skirt as if to steady her, but she was too quick for him.

'Come on, Brady,' he said. 'They're out. Let's make the most of the time, eh?'

'I'm not your little Nellie from the Clarence Hotel, Jack Wilkie. If that's what you want, you're in the wrong shop.'

Wilkie gaped, felt himself blush and heard her laugh in his ear.

'It's only because I care for you, Brady,' he said, feeling a rush of sincerity behind his words.

'Much you'd care for me if I let you away down there.'

'If . . . if anything was to go wrong, I'd marry you, sweetheart.'

'Ah, but would I marry you, Jack Wilkie?'

He was hurt by the tone of this. He had, unthinkingly, revealed his big plan and she appeared flatly unimpressed.

'Well, I know I'm not the Captain . . .' he began, not really knowing where this thought was going, nor indeed where it had come from.

She did not give him time to complete the thought.

'The Captain?' she said, jerking back from him. 'What are you saying?'

'I meant no offence.'

She leant back onto him, pressed him down. He was not sure whether this was tenderness or aggression.

'Tell me what you did mean, then, Jack?' she insisted.

'Oh, nothing, sweetheart. You know.'

'What?'

'How he looks at you sometimes.'

'How does he look at me sometimes?'

'There'd be nothing wrong with it.'

'With what?'

'Being kind to him, what with his wife in her confinement. He's a man with appetites, Brady, I know he is.'

She paused to have this clear.

'So you think he's taken his pleasure with me, do you?' she said.

'I don't know, do I?'

'But you like to think it, don't you?'

'It's no business of mine, is it?'

With deliberation, accuracy and considerable force, she punched his nose. A starburst opened the front of his face, and when it dimmed and the pain thumped in behind it, she was there with a cold cloth to catch the dribble of blood, tilting back his head in the chair.

'That,' she said decisively, 'was for thinking such a thing of such a man. You don't know anything, Jack Wilkie.'

He groaned.

Later she came and sat back on his lap, undid her blouse and took his hand into the fat of her breasts.

'And there's a little pleasure for you, Jack, to show that I don't hate you.'

Across the lawns and along the drives of the barracks, they could be seen taking the air, Captain and Mrs Drewer, with their maid wheeling the baby-carriage before them. They were regarded with a general sentimentality, a family whose life seemed to have none of the edges and frictions of normal families. The more malicious, perhaps, wanted them to be subjected to some tragedy, not so that they might be brought down, but so that they, the malicious ones in their envy, might sally out darkly and swaddle the weeping wife in sympathetic condolence.

For the Captain, a promotion: Major Drewer. A universal warming to this. A changed man; always a first-rate soldier, of course, but now acquiring the graces necessary to seniority. He might go far.

There was talk of the regiment achieving a colonial posting, an excitement, a chance to prove themselves, the pattern of militarism to be imposed upon some slack civilian administration caught between the superstition and dishonesty of the natives and the rapacity of the colonials.

In high summer, the regiment paraded in full ceremonial before the monarchy, embodied in a frail, delicate figure on the dais between the tall seniority in their gleaming boots, impeccable breeches, thick-chested tunics from which decorations glared in their clusters, with the plumes of their helmets quivering and the slant of their sword-sheaths subject to the small rattle of adjustment. Across the drill ground the divisions and companies were placed in four-square bristling stacks, dark-blue masses picked with red and silver and black. A haze of dust covered the ground with two inches of restless blur in which the blocks of men stood massive in their silence and uniformity. About the edges of the ground waited a profusion of the civilianry, pastel parasols and tumults of crinoline, suits of dark formalities and the badges of civic office, inhabiting a quiet chatter of smiles and compliments.

Then began the band with a bass-drum pulse, a clatter of snare-drums, the metal bellow of bugles, and a tune threaded through on the fifes. A gathering of emotion in every stomach, a lifting onto the toes, then a shout, an indecipherable, drawn-out yell, at which the blocks began, one by one, to move, paced to the beating of the band which had set into the massed pulse of the afternoon. Beneath the band came a fierce susurration of civilian applause, a distinguishing cheer, yet undistinguished in the force and purpose of the marching files, the precise snap of commands, left-turn, right-turn, the blocks coming in a long, straight sweep before the dais, heads snapped aside, sword-backs pressed into pink faces, eyes too fierce to blink turned upon the watery gaze of the monarchy; each face staring and registering, each individually printing the figure in the brain, an icon the more fragile the more precious, and deserving of the fierce combined loyalty. Give us the chance to prove ourselves, to test the pristine immaculacy of this machine you have come to honour in the furnace mouth of your enemies' devouring; give us this that our wives may be gentle and our merchants prosperous, that our children may be nurtured amongst the airy spaces of our learning; give us this that your watery watching of us may spill with tears for us, tears that we will wear as our medals, that will glitter in the rain on our memorials; give us this that the nation shall be one in the strength of our sacrifice. Just a nod would have done it, would have sent them streaming out to the horizon.

Anna Drewer watched them parade and her eyes filled with tears at their perfection; at Lionel's fierce features glimpsed for a second amongst the turning files; at the clutching of little Lewis at her skirts, eighteen months old and set down by Brady to totter over the grass to her, clinging on but quiet in the majesty and noise of the parade; and at the knowledge that her lover's seed had found her again, that the whole intense drama of birth was beginning again within her.

... *seventeen* ...

With a rapid percussion, Lionel's boots hit the steps of the central staircase of the regimental headquarters. His ascent was aggressive but he did not run. The high ceilings about him sounded with a battery of echoes. The whole building was charged with energy and he was late, was furious to connect himself with that energy.

Two sentinels clicked their heels and flung open the doors of the big room at the head of the staircase to admit him. The other officers looked up at his appearance, nodded, then stooped their heads over the maps that were spread over the great table around which they clustered. Lionel advanced and placed himself two paces behind Colonel Radstock, to attention. Radstock glanced back at him and nodded, which Lionel accepted as a sign of inclusion. He stepped up to the table and they made a space for him.

He couldn't believe the maps. They were not the empty plains of some colonial continent, but the heart of the civilised world, Europe, packed with villages and towns, roads and rivers and railway lines. An intelligence officer was speculating in broad lines across the map.

'Well, gentlemen,' Radstock said at last, drawing himself up, glancing beyond them all to the window which occupied a whole west wall of the room. 'We know our duty.'

'It's a game,' someone said. 'No-one wants this sort of war. It would be ludicrous.'

'That,' said Radstock, 'is not our concern. Our concern is to have the regiment equipped to embark, prepared to do battle against a fearsome adversary, within forty-eight hours.'

His words straightened the men about the table resolutely. There were a few moments of silence, then Radstock moved away towards the window as if there was something there that puzzled him. The men broke into clusters and began to talk with suppressed urgency.

Lionel moved away, dazed. He hardly comprehended the speed of it all. A host of problems filled his mind, things he would have to attend to at once, things that would have now to be neglected in the pressure of the moment. The complexities of his life suddenly had become inflamed, vital.

He came out of what seemed like a trance to find the room as it had been before, the clusters of men talking and smoking, serious-faced, some leaning on the map-table, a couple beside Radstock, who seemed not to be aware of them even as they talked, proposed things, offered; whilst the Colonel stood with his hands clasped in the small of his back, his head raised to the view from the window.

Lionel watched Radstock and wondered what he felt at this moment. He knew what he felt, knew as soon as he thought about it. He was possessed by a dark joy, a finality, a certainty. He walked over to the map-table, acknowledged a greeting, exchanged a tight commonplace, then stared down, put his hands onto the maps. Here it was, then. He had wanted it and he welcomed it now, felt no quiver of doubt, was proud that, now the time had come, his imaginings were substantiated by the lift of his emotions. He was filled with urgency, with the logic of his training, oiled and firing. He glanced up at the men about him and wondered if they felt as he did. He saw them through the haze of his excitement. He wanted to find one to embrace. He wanted to shout out: This is our purpose. This is why we exist, why we have honour and status. Without this, we are a sham.

He thought then about the nation, the country, the quiet boroughs and dark counties that burgeoned out there under their gentle weathers. He looked across at Radstock, still by the window, still looking out into the quiet summer landscape, and he knew what was calling to the Colonel. He himself did not belong out there. He was a stranger, an indigestible human fragment in a quiet world. It was not given to such as him to be rooted and environed. He was made for the task of war, and if it maimed or killed him, if after it he was shuffled away from the purposes of peace, having become a stranger again, then that was right, that was the nature of the world.

Radstock turned to them eventually and the room fell quickly silent.

'Gentlemen, we will reconvene at fourteen hundred hours, by which time our specific orders will have arrived. In the meantime, confide in your junior officers but not yet in the men. Those of you who have families, I would suggest that your duties there should be attended to as expeditiously as possible. Good morning to you.'

At which point Lionel, for the first time since he had entered the room, thought of Anna.

'What is it about?' she asked eventually.

'A large and powerful nation has compromised the neutrality of a small, defenceless nation. We are pledged to defend that small nation. But it is also about a threat to the integrity of our own nation, to the way of life we cherish and must therefore defend.'

'A just war, then.'

'Yes. I believe so. It is not for us to question the decisions and motives of those who govern us. We are their instruments, and our obedience is their strength.'

'Sit down, Lionel. I can't abide you standing there, lecturing me like that.'

He sat, reached over and collected her hand.

'Do you trust me, Anna?'

'Yes.'

'Will you be proud of me?'

'Oh yes, always proud of you. But afraid for you . . . am I allowed to be afraid for you?'

'Yes. But Anna, be clear of this. Men will die in this war. I must be prepared to die, cannot send any one of my men to face death without being prepared myself to stand beside him. That is what I am. You know this. You understand it. I cannot face you if I read in your face a wish that I were not going.'

She was silent and a hurt grew between them.

'I will bring something of myself home to you, in some way. I promise.'

'How can you promise that, Lionel? How?'

'I promise,' he said quietly in the silence that followed.

'You'd better leave,' she said, after a while, 'unless you want to watch me cry.'

He stood and lifted her, held her against him as she wept.

'Give me your blessing,' he said.

'Yes. Always. Always. Yes.'

. . . *eighteen* . . .

There were, in fact, to be ten days before the regiment left for the
embarkation point and, although Lionel returned at night, he was
drawn and preoccupied. He came to her bed charged with a sexual
energy, a need of her, that was fierce and blind, and she brought
about its release quickly, feeling that it was little now to do with her
pleasure. This hurt her, but more than that it frightened her. She
never quite came to the point of admitting that these encounters
were distasteful to her; if it was necessary for her to sustain and
minister to him thus, then she was ultimately glad to be able to do
so; but the calm, mutual solicitation that had marked their sexual
contact during her first pregnancy was entirely missing. When he
was released, in the brief minutes before he slept, he came close to
weeping, clinging on to her as his futile semen dried to powder on
their flesh. He slept and she lay awake and watched him. She
touched him and kissed him, covered him in her minute attention,
laid her head over his heartbeat, breathed in the dark scents of him,
taking infinite remembrance of him.

When she was certain that he was deeply asleep, she went from
the bed and sat up in a chair, kept vigil over him. She would sleep
during the day when he was out amongst his men. Lewis slept with
Brady. Before her lay the blackness of his absence; now she needed
to watch and to consume, moment by moment, his presence. She
did not speculate on his fate, could not have brought her mind to
that; nor did she rehearse her memories of him. He was here, the
living weight of him, and with a blank intensity she sat before him
and took him into her with a concentration that brought her to
strange starts. She saw him once as a great animal, a beast, lean, sour
flesh over knotty bones and claws. At another moment it seemed that
she had entered him completely, that she breathed with his breath,
beat with his pulse, dreamed his dreams which were of shouting and
gunfire, livid skies slashed with explosives. Later, she was able to
reduce him, to soften him into something small-limbed and helpless,

a child, a baby, an embryo which she could draw up into the safety of herself and feed with her blood. In these vivid involuntary metaphors, she took her possession of him, claimed him and digested him, spread herself through the mysteries of his body.

Before dawn, she slipped back in beside him, grew warm and then covered his body with hers as he began to come out of his sleep, and for a moment they were soft and warm together, before he pulled himself up, kissed her and padded off to his dressing room. She slept almost at once, woke long into the morning but lay in bed, wracked with enervation and headache, her stomach churning with bile, careless of anything but the moment of his return, drunk with the promise of another night of him.

She knew that Brady was concerned about her.

'Just three more days,' she said, 'then there'll be time for everything.'

'You mustn't be ill, m'm,' Brady said. 'You have the baby.'

'Time enough for the baby, my love, time enough.'

But, two days before they were due to leave, a new ferocity of pain woke her abruptly from her morning's sleep. When the pain had, if not subsided, at least been accommodated, shifting her limbs, she became aware of a visceral stickiness between her legs. She stopped breathing. Then the life jerked in her and she cried out.

Brady was with her within seconds. From the kitchen she could hear Lewis beginning to cry.

'Oh, Brady, Brady. . . .'

She lifted the sheet but could not bear to look herself. Brady looked, gave a little whimper, then clambered at once onto the bed and took her in her arms whilst she shrieked and shrieked, whilst the pain and shame and wretchedness possessed her.

Later it was Lionel who held her whilst the long weeping drained out of her.

'The first casualty of the war,' she said, her first lucid thought, and it shivered through her like iron.

. . . *nineteen* . . .

Major Drewer was summoned from his duties to be beside his wife in her bereavement. Brady found much to be busy with, not least Lewis, who seemed to have caught something of the tragedy and whom none of the usual treats and pleasures could ease. Brady paced up and down the kitchen with him in her arms, trying to calm him, using his wretchedness as a foil to her own, deeply afraid that he too was in danger. The whole world was in danger, rushing over a precipice. Brady was terrified.

She felt her mistress's loss intensely, had had no idea that love could turn so cruel, could cut back at those who shared it with such brutality; but in the subsequent necessities, she had to hold in the pain which lay like a cobblestone between her breasts. She knew that this was her trial, to keep everything going, to keep a patina of normality over the house lest everything fell into chaos.

The worst was having to answer the door, to receive the little notes of condolence from the wives who gathered and who were piqued and rude at Brady's insistence that Mrs Drewer could receive no-one, absolutely no-one, that she was under strict orders from the doctor and the Major. One of them actually barged her way in, plumped herself down in an armchair and snuffled loftily whilst the wretched Brady, who had left Lewis on the point of hysterics, was commanded to bring tea. Brady did not bring tea, went to the bedroom and summoned the Major, who had the old crow out of the front door in fifteen seconds.

In the kitchen, Brady found another visitor, Jack Wilkie. He had come, unknowing, to try to milk a little extra in the way of affection from Brady on the eve of his embarkation. He found himself dandling a squalling Lewis on his knee. Brady almost found a smile at the sight of his woeful alarm.

'Give him me, then, Jack Wilkie. A fine brave soldier you'll be.'

The Major appeared.

'What are you doing here, Wilkie?'

'I just came to . . . to do a bit of your packing, sir. Sir, I've just heard the . . . the terrible news, sir. . . .'

'Yes, yes. Can you manage to look after my son for two minutes without making an ass of yourself?'

Brady returned Lewis, his mouth temporarily stopped by a rusk, onto her sweetheart's lap; then she followed the Major through to the drawing room.

'Mrs Drewer's sleeping now, at last, thank God,' he said. 'Brady, you're a miracle. No, don't cry. Spare me that. I'm sorry. Look . . . I'll mind the boy for an hour. Get yourself out of the house. Get some fresh air. Take Wilkie with you, if you like. Or, if you'd rather, I'll keep him busy here.' He came and embraced her, briefly and strongly; then he released her and sat her down on the sofa. 'Brady, this is a nightmare. I'm going to send Mrs Drewer north, to her mother's house. I want you to go with her. You write to me if anything goes wrong, if she needs anything that they cannot give her there. D'you understand?'

'Yes, sir.'

'You'll go?'

'Please, sir, please.'

'Good girl. Bless you, Brady.'

She walked resolutely away from the bungalow, into the belt of woodland that separated the barracks from the heath where the soldiers went manoeuvering. She did not choose the direction, merely wanted to be away from the others, merely wanted to find somewhere to hide herself and cry. Jack Wilkie was beside her, but she took no notice of him, determining vaguely to send him away when she found somewhere to be alone.

At last, breathless and unsure of what was supposed to be going on, Wilkie ran ahead, turned and stopped her.

'Wait a minute, wait a minute, sweetheart. Where're you going?'

'Go back, Jack. Go back.'

'No.'

'I don't want you to watch me.'

'Watch you do what?' He looked nervously about him. 'Brady? What're you up to?'

She turned and headed into the tress, ready to turn and strike him if he followed her. He did not seem to be following her. She found a patch of yellowing bracken, waist-high, and she waded into it. In the middle of it, she sank to her knees, bowed herself over, squeezing at the lump behind her breasts, trying to break it open, trying to cry and wail. It would not come. She heaved at it, struck at her breast-bone, gasped. It would not come.

All at once she felt foolish; as if you could empty your emotions like your bowels. She struggled to her feet, dusted down her dress, looked about her. He was about a hundred yards off, walking cautiously, peering about him. She did not call him, waited for him to see her, which took him a long time. He did not advance at once and, when he began to, he came cautiously, watching for her to run from or call or come to him.

At last he came to the edge of the bracken, some ten yards from her, where he waited.

'You all right, sweetheart?'

She did not answer him.

'You need a hankie?'

A little laugh broke out of her nose. He began to wade through the bracken.

When he came to her she knew at once, as if a clear shaft of logic had fallen onto her, what was going to happen now.

'Oh, Jack,' she said. 'Give us a cuddle.'

He took her firmly but stiffly, hugged her like a sack, his face aside. This was no good. With a deft sweep of her foot, she kicked away his balance and they went tumbling down together. He groaned but she clung on, rolled on top of him and nuzzled her face into his neck.

'Brady?' he said, writhing below her.

She stopped, knelt up, looked down at him. 'What?'

'What're you up to?'

She smiled, leaned over and kissed him. 'You're going away to the wars, Jack. There's no more time, is there?'

'No more time for what?'

'For . . . for waiting till you're ready and I'm ready and all the world's sweet and tidy. It'll have to be now.' She began to cry then, a little. 'Oh, Jack, you go and get killed and then where would I be, wishing and wishing for the rest of my life that I'd been better to you.'

He understood then, gave a breathy whistle, patted her on the back.

'What about. . . ?'

'You let me worry about that. You'll be long gone.'

'No. No, what I meant was . . . what about the mistress?'

This pushed the tears out of Brady again, with more force.

'She wouldn't mind it.'

'I'll bet she would. You'd lose your place as soon as. . . .'

'You be quiet, now. She wouldn't mind. You don't know. You just don't know.'

She cried a little more, laying on him. He held her still for a while, then, carefully, rolled her over onto her back.

To begin with, as he was removing his tunic, shaking it out and folding it, tucking it neatly under her head, she was nervous. Little rushes of panic rose and she wanted to change her mind. It was his functionality that disturbed her, the furtive peeks over the bracken, the way he pulled his braces and made them thwack against his chest before slipping them from his shoulders. When he came to touch her, however, burrowing under her skirts and stroking her calves, kissing her knees, she became certain again. Poor Jack Wilkie. She'd rather it was Lieutenant Harry, much rather it was the Major. She just wanted it. When he kissed her, at last, in the place she had always denied him, a shudder went through her and she braced her body against the hard ground. She closed her eyes and grappled out her hands for him, unable to find him until he lifted over her and settled down in the tight saddle of her thighs, bolting himself into her with a jerk that lifted her. Then she opened her eyes and watched the thin, high clouds across the depth of the sky, saw the wafer of a daylight moon. She thought of her mother then, of her mistress, glad now to come into this community with them, submitting to this hunched creature, this slow pumping within her. It was warm, then, and easy, an easy gift to give. She squeezed herself tight and he groaned, panted.

'I'd better . . . not . . . before. . . .'

'Go on, Jack, go on.'

And it was done, with a gurgle in the back of his throat and a quick looseness inside her.

When he rose from her and stumped off on his knees into the bracken to urinate, when she lay there exposed and messy, she began to cry again, a little at first, but she trembled with it; it seemed to come not from her throat, but from her chest and stomach, from her thighs and her womb. She rolled aside and curled herself up, pressed her face into the earth and the weeping stamped through her.

He came over to her and touched her shoulder, kissed her neck, but he was useless to her now. The whole tension of the day, of what had led to it and what was closing around it, sprang in her and she unloaded it shamelessly and loudly.

'Hush now, sweetheart,' he said. 'Hush now. I didn't mean to hurt you. I'll marry you, Brady. I'll come back from the war and make it right with you. I promise you, I promise you.'

She turned to him and flung herself around him, curled herself into his distant assurances.

'Don't go. Don't die, Jack. Don't go.' They were ritual words, placing her within him so that she could receive his comfort. She would have been appalled had he conceded to her.

The house was still when Brady entered. She bundled her underwear into the bottom of the laundry basket, needed time to wash and sort herself out, but she thought she'd better see what was what first.

Lieutenant Harry was in the drawing room cradling a glass of whisky in his lap. He pulled himself to his feet when Brady appeared, at which entirely unmerited social distinction she blushed.

'Oh please, sir. Don't let me disturb you.'

'Oh, I was just . . . just on my way.' He swallowed the whisky at a gulp.

'Excuse me, sir. I was . . . out for a few minutes. Is the Major. . . . ?'

'He's . . . he's with Mrs Drewer. She's awake. He's taken Lewis in to see her.'

'Then if you'll excuse me, sir, I expect they'll be wanting me.'

'Wait. Wait a moment, Brady.'

'Sir?'

She held her head down, ashamed of herself suddenly, ashamed to be here before him with the manifestations of Jack Wilkie still active between her legs.

He moved close to her, lifted his hands as if he wanted to touch her, but did not finally find the resolution to do so.

'Brady?' he said quietly. 'You'll be all right? You'll manage all right?'

'Yes, sir.'

'If . . . when all this is over, when we come back, I'll make it up to you.'

'Sir?' She looked up at him, found his face troubled, serious, confused. This was what Jack Wilkie had been saying to her, half an hour ago. What was this?

'You are more than a servant here, Brady. You know that. Lionel . . . Major Drewer . . . he may not show it at times, but he is . . . he has the highest regard for you, as do I. As do I, Brady.'

She smiled, understood. He wants it too, she thought. He wants to go off to war with what I've just given Jack Wilkie. If only there were a way in which she might have given it him. If only she hadn't been in such a hurry.

It was curious, though, this sexual sentimentality that seemed to possess them on the brink of war. It was as if they needed to remind themselves that they were men in other ways than soldiers, that they were men as opposed to women, not just soldiers as opposed to other soldiers. It was a warm, silly thing. She and the mistress would be better off without them. Let them go off and have their war. Let them go off and get killed. There were always more men than you wanted anyway. Men weren't important. What they did didn't matter for more than a moment, as far as they were concerned.

'Thank you, sir,' she said at last, and then, with an outrageous rush of boldness, she reached up and put a kiss on his cheek. 'There, sir. That's to bring you safe home again.'

. . . *twenty* . . .

Anna insisted on rising and dressing. There was to be a parade, a ceremonial marching-off to war, but she could not face that. It was enough that she should stand in her home, with her son at her side, and bid her husband farewell in private formality. The events of the preceding days had bleached her into a state where formality was the only alternative to collapse. She would collapse when he had gone, would shut herself away and give in. For the moment, she must straighten her back and give him the benediction of her love.

She sat in the drawing room with Lewis on the floor at her feet, building stacks of wooden bricks. She watched his absorption in his making, piling the bricks up and up until they tumbled in a rattling chaos about him; at which his eyes brightened and he gave a little cry of pleasure before beginning again. Watching him at this made her uneasy in a way that she could not define. Brady sat in a chair by the window, sewing and looking out for Lionel. The clock ticked and they waited.

'He's here, m'm,' Brady said at last, bundling up her work and preparing to leave. 'Would you like me to take Lewis?'

'No.' She wanted to ask Brady to stay, had not thought she would have to do this alone; but she would have to. The presence of Lewis would protect her. She stiffened herself.

Brady waited until the door latch rattled and then slipped away.

Lionel wore his smart travelling cloak over the dark uniform. He seemed wet.

'Is it raining?' she asked.

'A little. A light drizzle.'

He approached her and stood before her. She wanted to rise, but could not. Lewis mumbled one of his baby-words into the stuff of her skirt where he burrowed.

'Come now, Lewis,' she said. 'You must be a brave boy for your father.' She attempted to disentangle him, but he squirmed deeper against her.

Lionel moved forward and sat down beside her, at an angle, looking down at the boy.

'Leave him be,' he said at last.

'When . . . when can I expect to hear from you?'

'I'll write by the end of the week. As soon as we settle anywhere.'

There seemed nothing further to be said.

'How are you today, my love?' he asked.

'Me? Oh, I'm . . . much better, much better.'

'I cannot stay for more than a moment.'

'No.'

He took her hand, leant over and kissed her cheek. His lips were cold, clammy, and she shivered. She closed her eyes, put her hand across and laid it upon his breast where, distantly, she could feel the twitch of his heart.

'Be quick, my love,' she said. 'Be quick now.'

He rose from her. She heard him turn, felt him look at her, heard him turn again, heard the doors close and felt the silence fall like a curtain.

He strode from the house quickly. He was free now, clear of it, of her, of everything that had stood in his way, glad that she had been so minimal in her valedictions, that he had not had to engage himself there at all. He had dreaded that last moment and was now greatly relieved of it.

He paused under a tree and lit a cigarette; surveyed the dank landscape, the moving men, the baggage wagons. He could see the parade ground and could hear the sergeants calling the musters. He inhaled the smoke fiercely and felt its narcotic fizz in his blood. He looked up at the wet, grey sky and glowered at it consciously. He walked out, flicking the cigarette down, hoping that it would somehow catch fire to something.

As they marched through the town to the railhead, the women were gathered on the pavements, waving little flags and cheering, blowing kisses, jumping up to see over one another's heads. They did not seem, somehow, to be a crowd, more a long, bulging row of individuals. There were men there too, but they were different, restrained, jealous perhaps, perhaps inspired, but privately. The women were the reverse of private, seemed each to glow out at the men with a specific eroticism, as if, were the men to break ranks, they could have had any one of them for the asking, as if wanting them to do this. He did not look aside, but he sensed them as patches of heat, imagined them bodily, thick-thighed and stout-breasted, accessible to mindless, energetic copulations, the thoughts of which put a sharp bite into his heels.

Suddenly one of them, a girl not more than sixteen, her head a chaos of golden hair, ran right in front of him and clasped herself around the neck of a young soldier, kissing his ear and putting a ragged flower in his cap. The soldier stumbled and laughed and the girl dropped away, shrieking with delight as she dodged the marching feet of the following platoons.

Lionel watched the flower, limp and blue with a stain of yellow in its heart, bobbing in the man's cap; and this somehow brought his mind to his wife. It was the delicacy and fragility, the intimacy of this flower, and it filled him with a sudden sadness, a regret, a longing to turn and dodge back for one more touch of her, one more kiss, one more breath of her in him. The vigour of this emotion brought tears to his eyes that shamed him.

'Jenkins!' he yelled. 'Take that bloody flower out of your cap.'

The flower was flung down and passed between Lionel's legs as he marched. A dread touched him, the dread of moments like this catching him as he went into battle, blunting him, making him vulnerable.

She did not collapse. After he had gone she had played a little while with Lewis, sung him a little song and held him on her knee whilst he fingered the lace of her dress. Outside the band began to play, and she remembered the parade in the summer, a few weeks ago. All that was over now, and a clear space surrounded her. She heard the music become distant; finally only the distant rattle of the drums could be heard with the silence at last squeezing out even that. It was a dream and now it was over. She sighed.

Brady came and collected Lewis for his rest. When she returned, Anna asked for tea.

'And . . . something to eat, I think, Brady.'

Brady brought her some thin biscuits which she consumed greedily, rousing her hunger further.

'Is there any cold meat in the house?' she asked boldly.

She and Brady sat in the kitchen and tucked into cold beef, cold potatoes and pickles, shared a jug of beer between them.

'The doctor says I can travel in a week.'

'Yes, m'm.'

'We'll have to pack everything, you know. The Major's things are to go into store, with all the household stuff, of course. We will not belong here any more. Will you be sad to leave, Brady?'

'No, m'm. There's not much here I'd want to take with me.'

Anna was not completely easy at taking Brady away from her home, from her family and her childhood, in spite of her assurances.

'You'll like the north, Brady,' she said. 'We'll live quietly, the three of us. They say it won't last long, this war, but I think it might. I think we've got to be ready to wait and wait. We'll be all right, won't we?'

Brady had gone heavy, had lost interest in her food.

'What is it, sweetheart?' Anna said, reaching across for her arm. 'They'll be back. What is it? Is it Wilkie?'

'I've not been a good girl, m'm,' she said suddenly.

Anna was alarmed by this.

'Brady? What've you done?'

'What I shouldn't've done, m'm. With Jack Wilkie.'

It took a few moments for the implications of this to come clear. When they did come clear, Anna gasped. A strange tingling filled her head. She was shocked, certainly, but it was, she quickly realised, the shock of excitement.

'When?' she said.

'Just . . . just the other day. Oh, m'm, I'm sorry. I've let you down.'

'Where was it, Brady?'

'Where?'

'Here?'

'No . . . in the . . . woods.'

'Might you be . . . with child?'

'No, m'm.'

'Are you sure?'

'Quite sure. This morning.'

'I see.'

'Will I . . . will I have to go?'

'Go where?'

'Away.'

'Good heavens, no. Brady, no. You mustn't go.'

'You're not . . . not angry with me, m'm?'

'No. Angry? Ought I to be?'

'You won't tell the Major?'

'The Major? What's it got to do with him?'

She took her maid's hand and clasped it. Brady remained retracted, uneasy; there was something more to be revealed. Anna waited and watched, avid to hear, wondering what confidences she might offer Brady in exchange.

'M'm, I wanted to be with child.'

'Oh, Brady, I know, I know, so did I, so did I.'

'But it's different for you, m'm.'

'Of course . . . perhaps . . . under normal circumstances, perhaps. . . .' It was different, of course, socially different, the natural child of a servant girl beside the legitimate offspring of the gentleman and his lady, born with a name and a position; but it was also the same, the same impulse, the same warm thrill of the act, the same biological urgency, the miracle of making life; and at this time,

72

in the silent days that lay before them, that might last until the ends of their lives, the impulse took precedence over everything else. She understood. She gripped Brady's hands and was proud of her; it was a courageous thing to have done.

'Do you love him, Brady?'

Brady paused, then said, clearly, 'No, m'm, that's the problem. Oh, I like him but . . . but he's so . . . so stupid sometimes. You see . . . you see, it is shameful. I went with him. I made him do it, but it could've been anyone. Anyone.'

This at last set Anna back. The daring romanticism in which she had begun to shroud Brady's confession was blown away. A shudder passed through her. She knew that such encounters happened, but could not imagine them outside a range of brutality that she could not believe Brady capable of. Anyone. Just for the sake of it. Memories of her intimacy with Lionel filled her and she tried to imagine those moments not with him, with anyone, just for the sake of it. It appalled her with a vehemence that by its ferocity betrayed her knowledge of its possibility.

'Oh, Brady,' she said. 'That's terrible.'

Brady's face was down. Tears plopped onto the table before her.

'Brady?'

She waited until the face rose and presented her with the full force of its misery.

'What was it like?'

Brady did not seem to understand this.

'Brady? Tell me. What was it like?'

Anna, quite suddenly and without the first notion of where it came from, giggled. Brady's tears stopped at once, lost in her surprise.

'M'm?'

'Well?'

'I . . . I don't know, m'm. It was the first time.'

'Did he . . . did he do it properly?'

'I . . . I suppose so.'

'I mean, as far as you were concerned.'

There ensued an incredible conversation that Anna could not have imagined having with anyone, not ten minutes before it happened. She found herself explaining to her maid the operation of sexual pleasure, in glaring, personal detail, in a vocabulary that she never knew she possessed. Later it occurred to her that she had committed the most appalling act of disloyalty. How would she be able to face

Lionel again? How would Brady be able to look at him knowing so much about him? But when would these awful encounters take place? When?

Lying in her solitude, awake in the deadest hour of night, she felt the loneliness come for her at last, the pitiful, wretched, sordid emptiness of her bed, and the smallness of herself within it. She wanted to call Brady, to take her in her arms and cry with her; but even as she desired it she felt its falseness: it would be an escape into sentimentality, into weakness, and that would be the real betrayal of her husband whose loneliness she must match with the certainty of her own. She understood, for the first time, the task before her and she wept.

Lionel was also awake at that moment, a hundred miles away in his embarkation billet, a cloth-curtained cubicle in a hall surrounded by his comrades. He was unable to sleep for the noises of the multitude of men about him, the dreamers and the insomniacs, coughing and cursing, the excitements and terrors. They seemed to him not individuals now, but one large body, their variousness melded into a corporate being that was capable of anything, any height or depth of humanity that would be attained involuntarily, with a surge of corporate instinct. No-one would be to blame for anything; no-one would be any more or less responsible than any other. It was the logical conclusion of what they were, an army on its way to a glad war. It was too momentous to submit to sleep.

He tried deliberately recalling Anna, as if she might reclaim him, bring him to a sense of the proper limits of his personal humanity. He felt her at that time as immensely distant, fragile, standing alone in the night and looking into the darkness trying to find him. I will survive, he said to himself, I will return; but as he said it, and believed it, he knew with a certainty that what would survive, what would return with him, would not necessarily be a consolation to her.

. . . twenty-one . . .

They were in action almost before they knew where they were. A series of marches and takings-up of defensive positions was executed with what Lionel knew to be blind map-work across the dreary Flanders countryside, through small mining towns, under grey, leaking skies; then suddenly the troops moving across their line were not another regiment trying to find their way, were wrongly dressed, moving wrongly. A moment of puzzlement, of re-orientation, a shout, and then the guns began; then they were under a blistering canopy of red-hot needles, fumbling to lock into the machinery of their training. It worked. With a professional panache that filled Lionel with pleasure, his men dropped into positions of shelter and direction and were pouring back rapid fire with a mutilating energy, the ground glittering with a moving scree of spent cartridge cases.

Lionel was lying with his legs soaking up the dampness, peering through binoculars at a landscape filled with tiny stumbling figures, smeared with smoke; was slithering back, dodging behind walls the top of which exploded into a scatter of brick-dust; was snapping orders at stumbling parties of orderlies with ammunition boxes; was pulling a man masked in blood down from the firing position, getting the gap filled, bellowing for the stretcher party. He was cool and certain and intense. His breath was strong and his heart clear. Dusk fell and the action petered out, too soon, too soon.

Walking amongst his men that evening he felt the old contentment, the certainty of his profession. The men looked up from their tin plates, from the steam of their mugs of laced tea, and smiled at him, their eyes and teeth bright in the murk of their faces.

'Good,' he said to them. 'A good day. Well done. Well done.'

They had made a beginning, an opening move; today they had held the line, tomorrow they would take the action to the enemy. The world hummed about him like an engine, pushed its pistons through him. He went up to the line where fresh troops, virgin men, lay watching the darkness. He strode amongst them, exchanging salutes, watching them contract as a flare went up, as a shot rang out.

There was no attack the next morning. The orders came for retreat. The men were puzzled, but perhaps relieved. They pulled on their packs and trudged back the way they had come, singing songs that irritated Lionel with their jaunty insolence. He did not understand the retreat and, as he thought about it, began to understand the truth that this war was to be on a scale that he would never be able to understand, that he and his men were merely a fragment of gigantic plans involving complex deployments of whole armies, whole nations. There was never to be the decisive moment, the crucial place at the heat of battle when his behaviour and the behaviour of the men about him would be the fulcrum of decision. He felt cheated.

They retreated into still countryside, beside leafy rivers along murky roads. They billeted in barns and stables. The locals viewed them with suspicion and approached them with avarice; they had the shadows of war climbing over them and they were uneasy at these alien troops passing through and leaving them in their wake.

Then they were not retreating, but advancing, or flanking, the enemy expected over every rise, behind every mist. From the horizons came the stamping of artillery, great, slow billows of smoke. The news came that the enemy were behind them now, now were rushing in on the left and right, now fleeing before them, now massing for an overwhelming offensive with new weapons which would sweep them away like lice; none of it made sense. There was only the long dreariness of marching, the orders and counter-orders, the clattering of the field telephones, the poring over maps in lamp-lit barn-garrets, the grey, gritty sleeps on ragged camp-beds in draughty farm buildings, the irritations of lost supplies, the harsh draughts of whisky drunk amongst brother officers who were growing edgy with the incomprehensibility of the campaign, with the lack of action and the fear of it that when it came at last, which it surely would, tomorrow or the next day, it would come in a form that none of them was able clearly to anticipate.

Alone at night, he scribbled brief, cheerful letters to Anna, but they meant less and less. He wrote to her in clichés that did not match any reality, any memory, any truth. He seemed to be modelling her, in his letters, into a type: the waiting woman, fragile and brave on a lone and windy shore, doing her duty as he was doing his. He had a photograph of her in his writing case but, after a while, he stopped looking at it. He needed to have a smooth, trouble-free image of her, needed only to believe in her, in the abstraction of her. He wrote the letters dutifully, but was always relieved when he had finished them, when they were sealed and waiting for Wilkie to take the post-bag.

One night, Wilkie came in whilst he was writing, or rather when he had paused in the writing and had lost the thread of what he was saying in a cluster of more immediate concerns. Wilkie moved as always silently and efficiently about him, tidying his things, collecting his boots for polishing, setting out his razor for the morning.

'I'm just writing home, Wilkie,' he said.

'Yes, sir.'

'Have you a message I can send my wife for Brady?'

Wilkie stopped for a moment, and Lionel could see a calculation on his face.

'Well?' he said.

'Yes, sir. Thank you, sir. Please send Miss Brady my regards.'

'Your regards? Something a little more . . . affectionate?'

'Whatever you see fit, sir.'

'Wilkie? How far have you gone with that girl?'

'Sir?'

'Do you have . . . an understanding with her?'

'I think . . . I think she's a bit sweet on me, sir.'

The idea of the resilient Brady being 'a bit sweet' on anyone, let alone Jack Wilkie, did not convince Lionel.

'You haven't . . . taken advantage of her, I hope, Wilkie.'

'Certainly not, sir,' Wilkie said mechanically, straightening himself formally under this questioning, closing himself up.

'Be straight with me, Wilkie. We're going to be in battle soon, and I need to know how things stand at home. I need to have my mind at rest. Brady is very important to my wife, and to me. I need to know how important she is to you, and you to her. D'you understand me? Well?'

'Yes, sir.' Still the mechanical response.

'Then tell me honestly, Wilkie, and I will believe what you tell me. Have you been intimate with her?'

'Intimate, sir?'

'Have you fucked the girl, man?'

The obscenity made Wilkie start, blink, blush.

'Well?'

'Just the once, sir.'

'I see. Thank you.'

'It was her idea, sir.'

Lionel, suddenly, could believe this. He was not angry, as he thought he would be. He was intrigued, perhaps even envious. He suppressed a nervous movement. He dreaded, above all, Anna finding out.

'I'll look after her, sir. I promise,' Wilkie was saying.

'Yes. We'll all look after her. Let us hope to God that we are able to. Go on, now, Wilkie. I'm not about to give you a sermon. What shall I write? "Wilkie sends Brady his love"? Would you be happy with that?'

'Yes, sir. Thank you, sir.'

He returned to his letter with the impetus of finding a way of inserting this sentiment in it without revealing any more. Wilkie left him to it.

Later, he felt troubled by this exchange, did not know what had prompted him to it. He felt he had stirred up thoughts and emotions that he did not need to have stirred up at this time, that he dared not brood upon for fear of where they would lead him. He thought of Brady, though, with more strength than he could think about Anna. Her intimacy with Wilkie presented him with images that he could not avoid, that troubled him, roused him even.

For the first time since he had left home, his sexuality came to the surface; not the delicate sexual interchanges of his marriage, but the blunt arousal and release, the primitive mechanics of it that he had known before; and he knew, as he followed these thoughts through, that they were right, that they belonged to this world. Was there, after all, a basic discrepancy between his two lives; an opposition where he had imagined there to be balance and harmony? Where then did his loyalties lie, finally?

. . . *twenty-two* . . .

Within forty-eight hours of his exchange of confidences with Wilkie, they were moving into battle. The feints and retreats were over. A massive engagement was begun, was growing in length and depth and carnage, and they were to be fed into it. A quietness came over the men, a determination as they marched through a sullen, deserted landscape towards a monumental thundering of artillery, a horizon curtained in smoke, amongst greasy wagon-ruts and oily puddles which, the closer they came, began to tremble with the enormity of the barrage.

Beside the road, making way for them as they marched, were ambulance wagons, stretcher parties and the host of the walking wounded. They tried not to look, tried to concentrate on the fury before them, but could not avoid the wasted faces, the bundles of human mess that were littered about them. If they did, inadvertently, catch the eyes of one of the casualties, they had a glimpse into a darkness, a blankness, as if the humanity had been blown away however much of the body remained. And there were so many of them, so many, a dense, moving wreckage tumbling out of the battle, jammed on the roads, piling up.

They arrived in the line at dusk and rested in shallow trenches and behind walls, taking over from the remains of a shattered battalion who slipped away through them silently. They waited in the darkness, staring into the gulf before them across which they were to attack at dawn: a shattered terrain of rubble, lit by occasional flares, punctuated by stray shots, pocked with the soft shapes of bodies. It seemed at times that the darkness was permanent, that daylight had been driven out; but the dawn began to seep in upon them, and those who had despaired of its ever coming now grew cold and alone in its steady revelation.

As the hands of his watch congrued at the set moment, Lionel raised his arm and the companies rose together, moving silently, many-limbed, spiked and armed, a vast insect, undulating over the contours of the wreckage, moving out into the nakedness of the morning. They could see only shadows before them, thick with mist.

A first, nervous shot came, a bright spark in the gloom. Thinking of Brady, of the warm clasp of her thighs, of how proud she would be of him at that moment, Jack Wilkie felt the bullet pass through him like a sudden gust of air. It did not hurt. He stopped, puzzled, then when he tried to move again, he fell and caught his shoulder on something hard that jammed up through him. That hurt, fearsomely, rammed a charge of pain right through him. He tried to wriggle away from it, but his body seemed to quiver and float independent of anything he tried to do with it. He lay back then and watched the torrent of blood flooding out of his receding self. He didn't understand.

Then the machine-guns began with a low splattering, flashes in the mist, and the singing of the bullets, their soft, percussive thump as they buried themselves in flesh, the cries of the men who received them, of alarm, surprise, rarely of pain, not at first. The line faltered, fell and was jammed into the rubble and wreckage under a ceiling of the fire which was lowered then, throwing up water and dirt and fragments, as if the ground had come to life, was effervescing with the violence.

Lionel pushed himself into a corner of broken wall and for the first time looked across at his men, saw them squirming and cowering, little distinction between the fallen and the rest. It appalled him that they should have been so easily neutralised, so quickly put down. He peered ahead and saw thirty yards of broken ground. Behind him was a declivity, a collapsed cellar filled with rubble. He dropped down and signalled, yelled for them to move into this declivity, watched two, three, a dozen receive his signal and begin to worm their way towards him. One of them raised himself and was knocked sideways, thrown down onto his back, splayed open. Bloody damn fool, Lionel thought.

'Be *careful*, damn you!' he roared, then set his mind forward again to work out a way across that ground.

He did not feel the slightest edge of fear, any more than he felt pity for the men who had fallen. There would be time to assimilate such things. He wanted to light a cigarette, but felt, with the men clustering down below him, that it would be inappropriate. The problem was to cross that ground with as few casualties as he could manage, with enough force to take the fighting into the stronghold of the enemy, to be in a position to strike at him, to kill him. He wanted that, not with anger nor with lust, but because that was what he was there to do. He and his men were at an insupportable disadvantage, had suffered unrequited damage, were losing; and that was blankly unacceptable.

Along the line the men were beginning to rouse, to find firing positions and to begin to provide something of an answer to the machine-guns, to provide him with the cover he would need to sustain his advance. A lieutenant made his way up to him and he explained what he intended.

'I'll take the lead, sir,' the man said.

'No you bloody well won't, Hartforth. You get those idle buggers up behind me. I want to feel them panting up my arse. And no-one, but no-one, is to do anything until we're amongst them.'

He glanced down behind him at the draggle of men. They looked up at him with a grim fidelity that made him smile.

'We're going to drown the bastards in their own piss,' he said, and felt their laughter push him as he made his first move, rolling out from his shelter and elbowing his way down into a length of ditch, nipping along it until it fell open and he had again to go down on his belly to the next junction, which proved to be a dead cow, the stench of it reaching into his belly and gripping him, making him fight for breath, rolling over and over until he went down into a shell crater which was deeper than he had expected, tripped him face down in six inches of filth from which he rose spluttering to face the last run, ten yards to a blank space at the end of the German firing-line. He could see them there, the lids of their helmets like machine valves. He did not know whether they had seen him, whether they were firing at him. He was tensed every second for the blow that would drop him out of his fury. He did not know if the others were behind him, knew that he mustn't look back, must drive himself on that final quivering stretch, a mere insect against the flame.

He felt a tug at his tunic at which he turned, furious, ready to strike or shoot at the distraction. A grinning face looked up at him and a filthy hand offered him, as if it were a fruit, a chubby grenade. He looked and saw Hartforth and the others scuttling into the crater, beginning to clog it. He snatched the grenade angrily, felt almost cheated of that blind run, armed it and began to count. This he enjoyed, clutching the fat knot of death in his hand, knowing they were watching him, knowing that it was in his power to let it fall, let it take over, to wipe everything clean in an instant; but when it came to it, his arm worked automatically, went out straight, gathered its muscles and lobbed with a sporting precision. He crouched briefly but, the second he heard the rip of the explosion, he was up and running, wanting to be there, to be directing its fury personally.

Almost without a thought the last yards were gone and he was there. It was strange to be there so easily, to find only smoking bodies, a wreckage of equipment and an enfolding swirl of foul smoke. One of the bodies shifted and he fired his pistol into it. Something, someone, emerged on his right and he fired again. The others were now piling in behind him and there were decisions to be taken, four to hold off anything to the left, the rest with him to make their way right, Hartforth to try to signal back that they had broken in, to bring up support as they cleared the line.

They moved rapidly and caught a nest of them about a machine-gun, trying to wheel it round to bring it to bear upon them; but they had caught them off-guard, and Lionel stood back to reload whilst his men executed rapid fire into the thick confusion of bodies, jerking and wheeling and tumbling together. They surged forward. Lionel supervised cover whilst a couple of his more experienced men brought the machine-gun down, quickly fingered its neat intricacies, and then turned it along the lip of the defences. More seemed to be joining them, spreading out, driving the enemy back, prising open a window in the line. They had made their incursion and could now get to work.

Around them was a swirling roll of mist and running figures, the stench of cordite, the confusion of roaring and shouting and shooting. He watched a man disembowelling a shrieking sack with his bayonet, turning the guts over with a farmyard deftness. A blond head between two upraised arms emerged from behind a pile of sandbags and stared at Lionel with a pitiful virginity; he fired quickly and the features crushed into a bloody rag. He caught some-one running, hit him in the small of the back, watched him stop and put his hand to the wound, try to hold himself up before tumbling in a muddle of limbs. A sudden gust of scorching air pushed him sideways and seconds later his eardrums were swamped with the explosion. He pulled himself up, shook his head and dusted off his shoulders. Then someone ran at him and grabbed him, held his arms at his sides and struggled to throw him down. It was strange to

82

be grappled like this, weaponless, like a schoolyard tussle, almost laughable, out of context. He could not see the face, but felt the alien breath on his cheek. He struggled and managed, by stooping over, to lift his assailant off his feet, to slam him into an edge of the entrenchment, where he gasped and fell loose. Lionel shook himself and turned with his pistol raised to see a small, dark-haired German glowering up at him, trying to edge his feet forward to trip him. He stepped back and fired into the torso which jumped at the bullet. He watched the man's face cloud, as if this were not at all part of the game, as if Lionel had entirely misunderstood. Lionel shrugged apologetically and turned. One of his men was sitting idly with his back against a wall, smoking a cigarette, which annoyed Lionel. He stepped up to admonish the man but as he came to him, he saw that the lower halves of both his legs were smashed and bloody. He moved away, annoyed with himself. He saw two of the enemy with hands raised and he moved towards them on the instinct to finish them quickly, but found they were being covered by two of his men. He wondered then at his instincts, strode off, moving back quickly into the responsibilities of his rank, the consolidating of the position, the marshalling of his men, pulling them back into a body to see what else they might achieve.

A whole section of the German line had fallen to them. New companies were flooding in and taking up what they had attained. Enough, Lionel thought, for the moment, enough. He went to find Hartforth, traced him back to the edge of the defences where they had made their first incursion, where he lay dead with a great jagged tear across his throat, his face white, his eyes open. Lionel sat down beside him on the parapet and blankly lit the cigarette that he had been craving all morning, the tobacco smoke curling giddily within him, making him choke. The reek of death then filled him, of blood and the filth of spilled guts. He opened his hand which he found was locked, almost welded, into the butt of his pistol. The pistol dangled on its lanyard between his legs whilst he chafed his cramped hand, found blisters beneath the filth.

He had survived, then. His hand was bleeding and there was a rent in his breeches about which dried blood and filth were clotted. He did not remember receiving these hurts, which only now began to reach him. He had survived. He looked at the dead Hartforth, knew that Wilkie was out there somewhere, others too, he recalled, whom he would never see again. He recalled their faces, their names, what he knew about them, tried to recreate the complexity of them in his mind. It was a wearisome and futile task.

He wondered if there were any design to who lived and who died, and knew that there was not. It was entirely random, entirely meaningless at this level, who lived, who died, whom you killed, who killed you. He considered these things but did not feel anything. They said that if the wound was big enough, the pain did not come, something shut down the connections between the damage and the brain; the numbness in his mind was of the same order. He was neither relieved to have survived, nor distraught at the carnage about him. He wondered how many he had killed personally, began to try to count them, but that too was meaningless. He had been a part of something, a tiny part of something that had killed massively, beyond calculation, randomly, composed of both armies, two unstable chemicals that had come together and had reacted with the blindness of their structure. Later, he knew, he would feel differently, would see and remember things differently. At the moment, he was quite depersonalised. If he had any serious desire, it was to continue, to find more of them to kill because the job was not finished, there were still hours of daylight, still enough men, surely, to make a go of it.

. . . *twenty-three* . . .

Lifting and running in that first assault, Harry Brand had felt the wind carry him like a song, had felt the mist part before him; then, a moment later, there had been obliterating light which had seemed, for a slow second, like some revelation. He had fallen to his knees, thrown himself back to welcome the God in whom he hardly believed, and then billows of blackness had swallowed him.

The next thing he was aware of was a disparate cocktail of noise, muffled clatterings and groanings very close, almost within his ears. At a distance he could hear a sustained pulsing roar that might have been distant battle, or might have been the roar of his own metabolism. After a few seconds, he knew that he was still alive;

where he was, and how much longer he might remain alive, were uncertain.

He felt a hand on his arm, a woman's hand, cool, affirming. Around his head was something muffling, but the rest of him came alive at that touch. He knew that he had legs and a belly, could feel the pull of the air in his lungs; although, he told himself a moment later, he might be imagining these things, might be the dupe of lusty nerves reaching into amputated space. He felt no pain, but that was not a reassurance.

'Where am I?' he said, the words coming up like phlegm.

'Hush, Lieutenant. You're all right. There's someone here to see you, but you mustn't tire yourself. Don't talk if it hurts you.'

The woman's hand withdrew and he reached up to regain it. A man's hand connected with his, a knotted grip that made him feel weak with its strength.

'Harry?'

'Drewer? Where am I?'

'You're in hospital.'

'Is it . . . over?'

'What? Is what over?'

'The . . . the war.'

'No. Not the war.'

'Where am I?'

'A field hospital, Harry. But you're going home. It is over for you. You'll be all right now.'

'I was hit?'

'Yes.'

'Where?'

He felt a bolus of emotion in his throat, but it jammed there; and then he knew what had been done to him.

'My eyes. It's my eyes, isn't it?'

'Yes.'

'My eyes. What about . . . what about the rest of it?'

'You're all right, Harry.'

'My arms? Legs?'

'Yes.'

'I've still got my balls, have I?'

'Yes.'

He didn't know whether to believe this, didn't know whether to believe any of it. It might not have been Lionel. Lionel was dead. He did not know how he knew that, but he did know it.

'I'm not sure,' he said.

'What're you not sure about, Harry?'

'Put your hand on me, Drewer.'

'Where?'

'On my fucking balls.'

He felt the sheets lift, felt the hand slide over his thigh, felt his penis become active as the fingers reached it, moved around it and under it. The sensations made him angry, but he had not the strength to express that anger, had not the strength for anything.

'All right?' Drewer said.

'Yes.'

The touch was withdrawn.

'Lionel?'

'Yes?'

'Are you . . . dead?'

'No.'

'Will you be coming home with me?'

'No. Harry?' He heard the tone change, tighten.

'What?'

'Be good to them at home.'

'Who?'

'Anna. Lewis. And Brady. Her young man died out there today. A lot of them went today, and there'll be other days.'

Harry could not talk any more. He waited, suspended, until Lionel's hand slipped from his. For a long time he felt him there watching him, and then he realised that he had gone, that he was alone, that the noises were receding, swelling, receding again, a meaningless insanity of sound; and all that was left to him was the darkness, the swaddling about his head that would be there for ever, the prison of himself to which he was condemned.

Lionel went from the hospital out into the night. The sight of Harry reached him as nothing else had that day, nothing. Death was certain, unequivocal; but that, that swaddled head, the gurgling voice, the cold contact beneath the sheet with the clammy flesh of him, that appalled and disgusted him. The boy he had loved was gone, was replaced by a bundle of limbs and organs. He hated it, wanted to go back and cover the bundle of the head with a pillow, to snuffle out the grunting animal there.

That he had mentioned his wife, his son, to him, revolted him. That that creature would be going back, would take this horror home to them, was an outrage. He did not want them to know, did not want any part of this to touch them, not like that. The bereavements he knew they could find the proper ceremonies to contain; but that, that disgusting, mutilated living corpse, that he felt would destroy them. They had to be able to believe in its nobility and purpose. There had to be nobility and purpose in all this somewhere, for there was none here. They held the nobility, the waiting, grieving women, the widows and the orphans, those who gave their distant dignity to death, who held the secret flame of each life in their hearts.

The memories of the day then came back to him in a tumult, a chaos, a horror, for he had fallen into the terrible, the fatal error of knowing them as she would know them. His blistered hand remembered the pistol, the mass of it, the living twist of it that he contained in the muscles of his forearm as he fired, the snap of hammer and percussion, the jump and skew of the body before him, below him, caught by its final logic, the black pit below the veil of cordite, the well that filled with blood, the heart diverted in its purpose, pumping and pumping and pumping the blood that did not feed, that rushed to the vent and spilled into the filth of the world, the dead filth that covered the world, red pus that stank and corrupted the land, sacks of it, mounds of the sacks, too many to count, too many to bury, too many to understand. There was no understanding. There was no meaning. He had no meaning, no more than the dead amongst whom, by a meaningless fall of fate, he was not yet numbered; but by killing he had become one with them. As they were nothing, so he was nothing. He thought of Anna and he thought of what he had done that day and he did not want to see her any more, could not face her again, wanted to die. She made life and was life in her making: he was dead.

A week later, during the counter-attack, he vanished physically as he had vanished spiritually, was lost in the roar and confusion of battle, flung back against a dirt wall firing his pistol until it jammed in his hand, accepting the advancing obliteration with a sigh of relief, pushing out his chest as his enemies swarmed over him, teeth and blades and bullets, as the darkness and violence swallowed him.

. . . *twenty-four* . . .

Anna and Brady and little Lewis found their peace quickly in the north. The house was cold and largely shut-down. Many of the men had rushed to join the army, the war apparently generating massive national emotions which Anna could not comprehend or respond to in any way. She was glad to be here, as far away from it as she could be, in the quietude of her waiting.

She wandered through the rooms of her childhood, felt her former self as a shadow to which, at times, she could fancifully give substance, but it made her feel foolish to do so, childish, sentimental. She walked the woods where she had made her dreams, but the mists and frosts of winter made it an alien place; she felt cold and displaced here; but she was not dispirited, for she felt that it was right to feel this, that the cold and the emptiness were the proper setting for her time of waiting.

She spent much time with her mother, sitting in the drawing room and eating alone at the long table with her. They did not speak much. Anna felt her mother's attention upon her, testing her, asking in the silence if things had turned out as they ought to have. She set herself to a serious implicit affirmation, in everything she said and did, of her married life; it was not a difficult task, and she took pride in it.

She was pleased, also, to watch how Brady fitted in amongst the other servants. She had been apprehensive lest their northern insularities might have turned sour upon this healthy, open southern girl. Brady, however, had the gifts of deference and hard work, and their suspicion of her soon softened. Brady would confide in Anna and together they would giggle over the rituals and hierarchical ignorances of the other servants. They never spoke of the men they had lost, although they spent a great amount of time in one another's company.

Lewis provided the most sustained focus of their attention in those first months. He was a strange child, would accept affections from none but Anna and Brady, and these he needed, at times, with an insatiable vehemence. When she was with him, taking him out walking, reading to him, he regarded her with a fierce attention, seemed to take little interest in what she showed him or read to him, but watched her, absorbed her attention of him entirely, throwing open his arms often for her limitless embraces.

It had been strange to be a mother. She had been nervous of Lewis as a baby, had hardly known how to treat him. She had grown envious of Brady's confidence in handling him, wondered what she should be doing, watched this little stranger grow into himself independently of her. Now, however, she found that somehow he had located her, had learnt what she had to give him, and she gave it entirely, delighted in his laughter, enfolded his crying to her breast. He might, she told herself, be all that is left me in the end.

She spoke to him, and to him alone, of Lionel, speculated on what Daddy was doing, what Daddy might say to this or to that, created Lionel for his son in a shameless sentimentality that, when Lionel returned, she wondered how he would ever be able to embody.

She thought of Lionel continuously in her solitude, lapsed into her memories of him, her concerns for him, which grew in her like a bruise; and in the night she longed for him sexually with a pitiful desperation that made her feel weak and small. That he might never again touch her, that no-one else ever again should touch her like that, as no-one ever could, made her shrivel and cower into jagged, claustrophobic dreams from which she rose, dark-eyed and heavy, the weight of her solitude too much for her.

Some weeks after their arrival a new curate arrived in their parish and came to the house to pay his respects. His name was Michael Fairfield and, after a nominal attendance in the drawing room, her mother retired and left Anna to entertain him.

Young, he certainly was, hardly older than she, fresh from university and bright with the new challenge of his calling. He was fair-haired and slender, with an expression that was clear without being cheerful, immaculately dressed and mannered; quite unlike the rector whose somnolence and flatulence had been a local joke for as long as Anna could remember. After finding him rather too much of a good thing, too bright and too keen, on subsequent visits, Anna began to take to him.

He became a regular visitor, brought news of the world beyond their domain, of the ignorance and hardship of the people that made Anna feel that she ought to venture out about duties in the parish, although the prospect of this made her cringe with inadequacy. He was good for her, certainly, gave her something to do, if only to settle herself to the common tasks of politeness and sociability when he called.

Fairfield joined Anna and Brady as the select group who could handle Lewis; he took the boy up sturdily, bounced him on his knee, at which Lewis was surprisingly silent; and when Fairfield put him down, he showed such reluctance that Fairfield laughed and took him up again. Anna was impressed, although on later reflection, she knew that the implication of this was that the boy was beginning to need a father.

One early evening, sitting on opposite chairs close to the drawing-room fire, Fairfield opened a new intimacy with her.

'May I ask you a personal question, Mrs Drewer?' he said.

'A personal question?'

'Personal to myself, I mean. Forgive me.'

'Please.' She drew back a little, but found that she could trust him not to embarrass her.

'Do you think I should join up?'

'The army, Mr Fairfield? Good heavens, no. Do you feel the . . . the call to join up?'

'So many of my friends have gone, some have already fallen. I open my newspaper with apprehension every morning now, and with, not shame, but with a sense that perhaps I am hiding here, hiding behind the cloth.'

'I do not think, forgive me, that you would make a good soldier, Mr Fairfield.'

'Not in peace time, certainly not. But this war is different. Somehow this war has grown to challenge the heart of our nation, of everything we hold dear. Every young man must feel the call, especially those like myself who have enjoyed the privileges that our society affords.'

'I think . . . I think that you are fulfilling the duties of your privilege here, amongst your parishioners, to the fullest extent. I do not understand what this war is about. No, please. I don't want to understand. If that sounds insensitive, it is because I have faith in what we are doing, faith in what my husband is and does. I think I can understand also why so many young men are rushing to this war, and I think their motives are noble and true. But you, Mr Fairfield . . . no, not you. You have . . . finer talents that are needed here. You are not hiding here, but hard at work to bring the better world that, whatever it is about, surely this war seeks to bring, or else what is its purpose?'

'What indeed?' he said, then was silent for a while; then said simply, 'Thank you, Mrs Drewer.'

Later, in the new range this intimacy had given her, she imagined talking to Fairfield about Lionel, and about the army, about the certainties and nobility of the world it inhabited; but she could never quite bring herself to this. She did want, however, to share confidences with Fairfield; there was something enticing and generous about her feelings towards him. It occurred to her that, before she had met Lionel, Michael Fairfield was very much the sort of man she might have imagined marrying.

There was one serious check upon her feelings towards the curate, however: Brady did not like him at all, shuffled herself up into a little petulance every time Anna mentioned his name.

'Brady?' she asked one night when her maid had come to tidy up. 'What do you have against Mr Fairfield?'

'Nothing, m'm,' said in a tone too sharp to be true.

'Come now, my love. Be open with me.'

Brady stopped her work and came, like a sulky child, to sit beside Anna on the bed.

'Well?'

'They don't care for him downstairs, neither.'

'Why? . . . what is it?'

'He doesn't belong, m'm, that's what they say. He wants things to be so, and they aren't so, not here, and he worries at them and bothers people.'

'Does he? Is that why you don't like him?'

'I . . . I think he comes here too often, m'm, although I know it's not for me to say.'

'It is for you to say whatever you think, my love. You know that.'

'He's new-fangled, m'm, not like the Major, not like the Major ever could be, nor Lieutenant Harry. He's very clever, but he doesn't understand.'

'What? What doesn't he understand?'

'How things should be.'

Anna wanted to rise against this, to prise it out of her with arguments, but knew that she could not, that Brady was probably right in her way. She felt hurt that Brady could not support her in her friendship with Fairfield, but she took the girl's hand and squeezed it, to reassure her that, if it came to it, she would never betray her with Fairfield, never.

'You think he comes to see me too often, Brady?' she said quietly.

'Yes, m'm.'

She hugged Brady and when, the next day, Fairfield called, she was not at home to him, sat in her room with the fiction of a headache becoming a reality, listening to his voice below, hearing him leave.

. . . twenty-five . . .

There were, of course, his letters. He wrote every day, but the letters arrived often in clutches of three or four, and she had to sort them chronologically before reading the instalments of his war. She kept them entirely to herself, answered her mother's questions about them with a defensive blandness, locked them away lest Brady should find one.

She was wretched if more than three days went by without her receiving a letter; but she did not like reading them. She raced her eyes over the large ungainly writing, read the careful details of army life, the shortages and dreariness, the cheerfulness and camaraderie, his awkward attempts to describe the countryside, the horrible understatement of 'We were in action today'. Each letter disappointed her with a specific bitterness, for she knew they were not real, did not represent even a metaphor of what he experienced. She imagined behind them a manic need to reassure her. She knew that she was being cheated, and at times she wanted to rush off to him and throw them in his face. In the end she settled herself to the comfort of handling them as things that he had handled, of believing in him behind his letters, of imagining the toils of his mind as he struggled for the words, his hand upon the paper. She held them to her face as if she might breathe in something of him. She pressed them to her breasts so that, by proxy, he might touch her.

She found that she was writing back in the same language that he wrote to her, reassuring him, creating a myth of comfort and busyness, relating anecdotes of Lewis that were not strictly untrue, but which embodied nothing of what she really felt, were images of her life as might be seen by an outsider, as she wanted it to be. She read and re-read what she had written, re-wrote again and again, lest any suggestion of her loneliness and anguish should leak into her phrasing; yet, she grew afraid, in her darkness, that somehow this anodyne correspondence, all these sordid, sentimental lies, would become so ingrained that when he did return they would be the reality of their discourse. Then everything would truly be over for her.

Then one day, a real letter did come. She had willed it, and was caught in the black irony of that willing. She knew, even as she opened it, that it would be different and her heart rose, but as it rose it exposed the gulf below it.

My darling Anna,

We have been in action today and have achieved great things, although the scale of this war is so vast that great things individually are small. We have also sustained some terrible casualties and I must be the bearer of grief to you, my love. Be brave.

You have probably heard by now that your brother has been wounded. A shell exploded close to him and he caught the blast of it in his face. I have visited him in hospital and he is as cheerful and courageous as you would expect. He will be coming home to you soon, so you can cherish him back to health and equanimity. I am glad that it is over for him here, although I know he will not settle easily to the life he must now lead, to the necessity of leaving the rest of us here to continue this fearful business to the end. He has lost his sight, my love, irrevocably, and that will be so, so hard for him. Be brave and give him courage.

For many others, there will be no recuperation. James Hartforth fell close to me, and Cecil Lambert, Gerard Lalling, Peter Ford, David Brooke-Angell, so many.

And poor Jack Wilkie. How will you tell Brady? He fell in the first moments, went cleanly and instantly, but that is, I know, bitter comfort.

It is very late and I am very tired, but I had to write this before I could sleep. I ought to have waited until I could have given you this in softer terms. Forgive me. I will write again tomorrow, God willing, when I will be able to say things that I cannot say now. I feel I should have written more, but there seems nothing more to say at this moment.

I love you and miss you and carry you with me every moment of my peril.

Her first instinct on reading this was to be busy. She had gone upstairs to read the letter in private as she always did. She called out at once.

'Mother? . . . Mother?'

She ran into the innocent silence of the house, down the stairs, into her mother's drawing room without, for the first time in her life, even thinking to knock.

Her mother sat in a chair before the window and rose, surprised to be discovered in this attitude.

'What is it?' she said, knowing at once the nature if not the substance of this intrusion.

Anna thrust the letter at her and watched her read it in a terror of impatience. Why did it take her so long? A frightful urgency took hold of her. She wanted to snatch away the letter and run on with it, felt that there were hundreds of people she had to tell, hundreds of things she had to do.

'I will go south at once,' her mother said, apropos, it seemed, of nothing.

'Why?' Anna asked.

'To bring him home.'

'To bring who home, Mama?'

'Harry. For Heaven's sake, Anna!'

'Oh.' She blushed at her stupidity, felt herself beginning to cry. 'Harry. Yes.' She swallowed and struggled, and said, eventually, 'May I come with you?'

'No. You must stay here. You need to make things ready for him. Do stop crying, Anna. We must be practical, above all . . . above all.'

Anna stopped crying. Her mother turned to the window and stared into the pale morning, or beyond it, quickly lost in her own silence, which spread and swallowed Anna too, the impetus lost in a blankness out of which everything suddenly had drained.

A little later, back in her room, Anna waited for Brady to come to the summons she had sent below. Inside, she fluttered, restrained the urge to stand and pace about the room. She sat on the small sofa where Brady would sit beside her. Something terrible inside her told her that she was looking forward to this scene.

'You wanted to see me, m'm?'

'Yes, my love, yes. Come and sit beside me.'

'What is it, m'm?'

'Come . . . oh Brady, Brady, they've killed Jack Wilkie.'

Brady did not cry out, did not turn to her, sat lumped beside her. She had put her arm about the girl's shoulder, ready to draw her weeping to her, but she did not weep. Her arm felt ungainly, intrusive, and she withdrew it.

'Brady?'

'Oh, there're lots more where he came from,' Brady said with a sudden anger that made Anna start. 'Lots more, lots more.'

Anna could not bear this. She rose and moved across the room, wanting Brady to go. She was appalled by her response, but she knew this was only superficial, that in some way it was her fault, that Brady was right to feel this and she was weak and selfish to feel anything other than this.

'The Major, m'm?' Brady said. 'Is he all right?'

'Yes . . . I don't know . . . I don't know . . . no. Oh Brady, help me.'

But there was nothing to be done, nothing more to be said. It was not grief. It was as if they were suddenly all moved apart into little vacuums, suddenly out of reach.

Her mother left that evening for the south. The next morning a telegram arrived. Brady brought it personally to Anna, who had stayed in bed, overcome with an enervation. It seemed as if nothing was resoluble any more, nothing fitted, nothing could be predicted. The telegram cleared all that.

Brady stood beside her bed as she fumbled it open. *Regret to inform you . . . Major Lionel Drewer . . . lost in action . . . missing presumed killed . . . deepest sympathy . . . letter follows . . . Radstock.*

Anna read it several times but seemed to be able to make no sense of it. She handed it to Brady.

'I don't understand, Brady. Is he dead?'

Brady read the telegram and put it down very carefully, within her reach.

'Yes, m'm.'

'But he promised.'

'I know.'

'Then I want to be dead too.'

'No, m'm, no.'

She could not make Brady understand. She did not feel pain, did not want to cry, did not want anything. It was just silence. Everything around her disappeared into the distance, blown away by a small gust of wind that cleared the surface of everything and left only a sheer expanse of flat, cold stone.

'M'm? . . . M'm? . . . Shall I bring Master Lewis?'

'No!' she cried, suddenly afraid, trembling. 'No, Brady, you are not to. I absolutely forbid you to. I don't want to see him. Take him away somewhere. Do you understand? Do you understand me?'

Brady stood and faced her out, her face set, her fists clenched. She's going to hit me, Anna thought and, with a cry, she turned away and buried herself in the bedclothes, expecting the fury of her maid to descend upon her at any instant.

. . . *twenty-six* . . .

Her mother returned home at once, stayed a few days, but there was nothing for her to do there; she returned south. Harry had been moved to a hospital, and she took a lodging close by to be ready to move him north. He had contracted a fever as a result of his wounds, and it would be some time before he might safely be trusted to the care of a rural practitioner.

Anna too was ill, buried herself in a little fever that, whilst not physically serious, was feeding upon her state of mind. She lapsed into the misery of it, but knew as she did so that she was using it as a prevarication. Brady knew it too, and came up to her with a sourness that made her afraid. She preferred the other servants, who treated her like the tragic figure she childishly wanted to be, but was not. Her illness, and the avoidance of grief it embodied, were not tragic but selfish, petty and wretched.

In the silence of her sick-bed, she tried to believe that *missing presumed dead* allowed her some leeway of hope, a distant little light that she could steer by, for the rest of her life if necessary; but she could not believe it. It was dishonest: she was not, finally, of the calibre to set herself to such devotion. He was dead. She accepted it, dinned the fact of it into her, hoping thus to breach the sac of grief that she knew must be swelling within her somewhere; but the repetition of it grew meaningless and tedious. His death meant nothing to her, as he meant nothing to her, as she meant nothing to herself.

In spite of her fierce injunction, Brady brought Lewis to her, stood by whilst she told him that Daddy would not be coming home, that Daddy had given his life for them all, yes, and for everyone else in the whole world, to make the world a better place. That she was managing this was, she supposed, something; when it was over, however, when Brady had taken the uncomprehending infant away again, she recoiled into a nest of self-disgust, for the lies had come foully from her mouth, and it was finally worse that she had been able to give them than if she had been true to herself and had refused. As for the child himself, her initial instinct had been right: she feared and disliked him. Something had been torn out of her and he, Lewis, was a part of that which still lay within her, within the maimed numbness, something before which she would have to go on pretending, which she would have to go on nurturing in the lies, a burden that would, every time she lifted it, remind her of its dead-ness, of her deadness. She would truly have rejoiced if they had come to tell her that the child was dead, was taken away, that she would never have to see it again; and behind the wretchedness of these thoughts came the abiding desire for her own death. Her life was surely over now, in all practical ways; it was cruelty to drag her out through years, decades.

Brady bullied her at last into rising and dressing. She would still not leave her room, but she allowed Lewis to be brought to her, to sit on the carpet before her little fire and play with his toys. She even began to read to him, although she kept losing concentration and coming back from her silence to find his face looking expectantly up at her. She admitted him into her caresses, but held her breath as she did so, set herself. The familiarity of these actions made them easier to achieve as the days passed, but she never overcame the disgust, not finally; she simply became more adept at concealing it, deader on the surface, as if a calloused pad of normality was growing over her.

'There's a visitor to see you, m'm,' Brady said one morning, about a month after the end.

'No, Brady. No visitors.'

'M'm, you must. He's outside now. He's been told you'll see him.'

'Did *you* tell him that? How dare you?'

'It's Mr Fairfield, m'm.'

'No. Not him. No.'

'You must see him, m'm.'

'Who says I must?'

Her dialogues with Brady had taken on this tone of futile aggression recently. The girl had turned spiteful. When her mother returned she was going to rid herself of Brady. Until then, she supposed she was helpless against this further humiliation.

Fairfield entered circumspectly, nodded rather than greeted her, started a little when Brady closed the door emphatically on her way out. Anna did not, after the first moments, look at him, determining to ignore him, hoping that he might have the tact simply to slip away.

'May I sit down, Mrs Drewer?'

'I would be grateful if you did not call me that any more.'

'What may I call you?'

'My husband is dead.'

'Yes. I have called several times. I wanted you to know . . . to have my deepest sympathy.'

'Yes, yes. Thank you, Mr Fairfield. You have done your duty. Now, please. I would rather be on my own. I don't know who told you that I would see you, but I was not consulted and, forgive me, but I find your presence here an intrusion.'

'If . . . if you cannot regard me as a friend, could you, perhaps, regard my presence here as . . . professional? I know that you have refused to see me. I know that I am here against your wishes. But I

98

must persevere, because I have a duty to do so, as a minister of religion.'

If only she could make him understand her weariness, the weariness that piled upon her as she heard his words in all their dull predictability.

He proceeded: 'I cannot begin to comprehend the loss you have suffered, but I believe that I have consolation that might . . . might give you strength. I ask only for your good faith, for your patience.'

'Mr Fairfield, I have no good faith, no patience. I wish only to be left alone. I find . . . I find after all, you see, that I did not love my husband. I wish only to be left alone, for the rest of my life if necessary. If I had a religious faith once, then I no longer have that. I'm afraid that I have nothing in me which might respond to you any more.'

'I . . . I do not believe that you did not love your husband.'

Suddenly she rose to this, faced him, something hardening in her head.

'I will explain it to you then, Mr Fairfield. Whilst my husband was alive, I developed an appetite for sexual intimacy which he fostered and sustained. Now that he is dead, I find that there was nothing behind that appetite, only an emptiness. If I had the courage, the energy even, I would probably set out to satisfy my appetite elsewhere.'

'Mrs Drewer!'

He sat uninvited, was dropped down onto the chair. For the first time since the news she felt an active pleasure, a spurt of cruelty that lifted her and turned her towards him.

'I have asked you,' she said clearly, 'not to call me that.'

'What am I to call you, then?'

'Whatever you wish to call me.'

'Very well, then . . . Anna. I will be as frank with you as you have been with me.'

'Please, spare me your frankness, Mr Fairfield.'

'No, no. You have said things to me that I must and will answer. What you have said is degrading. I am appalled by it, which I assume to have been your intention. Oh, Anna, Anna! Can you not see that this is a desire to debase yourself in the face of the grief that you cannot bear to admit. It is a testament, not to the fact that you did not love your husband, but that you did love him, with an intensity that cannot face his loss. It is a tragedy, Anna, for he is still alive. . . .'

'Don't you dare to tell me that he is still alive, Mr Fairfield.'

'His immortal soul is still alive, and to that you are answerable.'

'Ah, that. His immortal soul.'

'Can you really not believe in that?'

'I . . . I don't think it would be of any use to me if I could,' she said flatly. 'What I have told you about our married life is true, you see, but you will not be able to believe in that. We have reached mutual dead ends, Mr Fairfield. You have done your duty and may leave me now.'

He was silent then, and she felt the complacency of her victory. She wanted to be alone now to consider what she had told him, to work it out in her solitude. Its truth, which she felt now fiercely, needed to be faced.

'Give me your hand,' he said suddenly.

'What?'

'Give me your hand, Anna.'

'Why?'

'Give me your hand, Anna, just to hold.'

'Are you in love with me, Mr Fairfield?'

'Of course I am. I . . . I thought you knew that.'

'This is absurd.' She felt tears prickling stupidly in her eyes. She jabbed her hand towards him and he took it, enfolded it carefully between his in a still caress. 'I need . . .' she began, but faltered, not knowing what she needed; perhaps it was for this man to lie down with her, but the thought of that, in its bluntness, made her writhe, not in revulsion, but in the pettiness, the poverty of it. 'I need . . .' she said again, for she did need something.

She withdrew her hand and rose, moved away from him, willing him to rise and follow her, which he did, coming close behind her. Her hands were clenched at her breast and she dropped them to her sides where he took them; and when he had taken them she drew up his hands and placed his palms upon her breasts.

'You see,' she said.

'What do I see?'

'What I am.'

'I see nothing,' he said, the words warm on her neck. 'I am only here.'

'As my minister of religion, Mr Fairfield?'

'No.'

'As my lover?'

'That is not . . . not possible.'

'Is this wrong?' she asked, stroking his hands upon her.

'I don't know. I want to bring you back.'

'And where do you imagine I have gone?'

'I don't know. I don't know, but you must be brought back, at all costs.'

'Brought back where, or don't you know that either?'

'Brought back to love.'

'If I had loved Lionel, I would not be permitting this. No, don't pull away. Your hands are soft. You touch me gently. He was . . . never still when he touched me. I was never still. I . . . I can't understand it. I can't understand that he cannot . . . is not . . . that I . . . I want that, you see, that moving, that life . . . your hands are warm. Does it please you to touch me?'

'Yes.'

'I'm glad of that. Leave me now. You've done your duty.'

His hands slid from her, but he did not move at once.

'May I visit you again?'

'In a few days. Give me time.'

He brought his mouth to her neck, exhaled a dry kiss upon her and then was gone; and then, at last, the grieving began, the real fever, the burning and turning of her nakedness within the dry binding of her clothes. The physical loss of Lionel was overwhelming, more than anything; and yes, yes, she wanted Michael Fairfield to become her lover, to enter her, to stop up the terrible rent in her out of which she felt herself draining away. She imagined his tenderness, his solicitude, the complexities that he would have to thread his way through to discover the reality of his own desire; she longed to watch him thus, to guide him, to cover his desires with hers. She played out the scene in her mind in a stark clarity of detail that roused her pleasure. She stood in the window-bay with her legs apart, her hands splayed on the shutter-frame, her spine wrenched down.

'M'm?'

She turned in a blaze of shame to find Brady a yard from her. Before one thought could connect itself with another in her head, she had struck out and her hand swelled with smarting, a fierce bloody glow massing on one side of Brady's white face.

'You knock before you come into my room, you damned bitch,' she said. 'You knock and you wait.'

She waited for Brady's fight, wanted her to strike back, wanted to crash about the room tearing at her clothes and hair, feeling her firm little fists drumming against her; she wanted to tear it all open and bloody, here, now, settle it between them. But Brady did not fight; she held Anna's face in her eyes which filled with tears. She did not sob, but the tears streamed down her face.

'I'm sorry, my love,' Anna said quietly, looking down.

'What would the Major say if he could see you like this, m'm?'

'Don't, Brady, please don't.'

'I have to. I promised. I won't give up. I won't.'

'What am I to do, Brady?'

'Whatever you have to do, m'm. I was wrong about Mr Fairfield. He's a good man.'

'I want . . . I don't know . . . I want my lover back, Brady. I want him back so badly.'

Brady then took her in her arms and held her, body to body. She felt watery and nerveless against the strong push of Brady's breasts, in the thick grip of her forearms. The rage was gone now, and she felt the pain of loss in her. She gasped with it, struggled to come to the surface of it but sank again, cried out. Brady held her up, wrestled with her as she twisted and shrieked. But she knew, in the distant still heart of herself, and Brady knew it too, that in the pain was the beginning of her healing; that because there was now pain, there could also be peace, somewhere, somehow, peace.

. . . *twenty-seven* . . .

In the darkness where now he lived, Harry Brand was crowded with incessant noise. It seemed as if, in his blindness, he had become infinitely sensitive to any sound, within or without, but the prodigality of this noise was frightful: indiscriminate rushing and gurgling and clattering, the babble of indistinct voices, one of which often was his own; the roaring of engines and cataclysms; a continuous low whining which was, at times, the spinning of a shell that never fell, the drone of a machine running out of gear, the manifestation of a pain that he could not quite feel, or simply some abstract expression of his own perpetual misery. He lived crouched within this cacophony, blanked out before it. Perhaps it was him, after all.

He came to the surface only when he was touched. It was women who touched him, soft, dexterous hands about his face, guiding his own hands to a spoon, lifting his chin for the rim of a cold enamel mug. A man came once and shaved him and he felt as if the whole of his face was shorn away. He rejected any further such molestations, and began to feel, in the space below his bandages, on cheeks and chin, the growth of a beard, rough at first, then growing enough to be pliant, gaining the wiry pubic spring that it pleased him to touch.

He touched himself elsewhere too, freely treated himself to the little squeeze of pleasure that mustered in his penis. He felt no shame in these indulgences, simply and profoundly because he did not feel himself any more to be a part of a social or moral order. He was over now, nothing mattered, and he grabbed on to any pleasure because it made him feel just that edge more alive.

They told him that he was going home, but that meant nothing. He was put to sleep, woke with new noises, sea-noises, train-noises, fraying at the edges of the abiding roar. He was bumped and jostled and lifted, landing, waking finally, in a cool clear place where the noises were softened, distanced; but after a while it was much the same. He settled to a new, slower pace of things, a quietness. He felt that he had simply been put out of the way somewhere.

Then, one day, a new hand came upon him, female but without the tenderness of the nurses, a hard hand in a cold glove.

'Harry?'

'Mother?'

He knew it was real, he knew he was home, by the smells and sounds of the place. He came back amongst them as if he was putting on an old familiar set of clothes; a certain, peppery dustiness, the carbolic scent of a certain rough soap, the black smell of wet soot in old chimneys, the hours and days of boyhood confinements. The roaring and crashing in his head receded a little, outfaced by the ticking of old clocks, the rattle and hush of the wind, the lifting of familiar latches. He rested here, felt a peace lagging itself around him.

Brady came to look after him. He always knew when it was Brady.

He could hear her moving about his room, tidying things, sorting out clothes. She took his breath away, drew him into a tight space. He could imagine her voraciously. Unlike the others who visited him, she had a substance; they were shadows, presences, but she was pure flesh. His desire for her made him weak.

'Mrs Drewer says you're to get up today, sir,' she said. 'I've run you a bath.'

'Will you . . . will you help me, Brady?'

He was a child in her strong arms, a large, ungainly child who was led down the corridor, undressed on the cold flags of the bathroom, stepped over the enamel barrier into the warm depth of water, soaped and flannelled. He submitted to the procession of sensations, blushing with shame and delight. Much of this he knew he could have done himself, but that was not the point. He thanked her continuously, but was huddled down under her practicality, the desire palpable, but diminished in the context of her busyness, a boyish instinct that made him blush.

She would lead him down into the drawing room where Anna read to him, where Lewis came to sit solidly on his knee, where his mother began to discuss the affairs of the house with him and where he began to find his voice again, began to remember who he was and what he must now become, as far as he was able to; but Brady was his mainstay. He gathered his independence for her, proud of the achievements he made, in cutting and eating his own food, in making his way along the walls and down the stairs, in mastering the stick that would give him further freedoms. He felt her always watching him, tutoring him, ready catch him lest he fell.

When, at last, as she put him to bed one night, he reached for her, touched the starched front of her gown, she undid herself and slotted his hand between her breasts with the certain practicality with which she did everything else for him.

'How is he today, Brady?'

'Oh, he's well, m'm.'

'You won't indulge him too far, will you?'

'I'd do anything I could for him.'

'Has he. . . . ?'

'He likes to touch me.'

'My poor love, is it beastly for you?'

'Oh no, m'm. He's a lovely man.'

'Brady, really!'

They laughed together, Anna and Brady, in the intimacy they had rediscovered, the close heart of the life they fostered in the ruins. They laughed often now, and the shuddering remembrance that caught them in the flow of this laughter was growing less as the seasons warmed again: spring and summer, and autumn and a year gone.

They talked, but never about the past; about Harry and Lewis and the other servants; about the groom who had returned from the war with a hand gone, who had designs upon Brady's virtue, approaching her with a soldier's knowingness which she saw through at once.

'It's not that I don't like him,' she would whisper, 'but it's not simple any more, is it?'

'No. It ought to be, but it isn't. It's the rest of our lives now, isn't it?'

They talked also about Mr Fairfield, who had returned to be with his parents in the grief of his fallen brother. Anna expected him to join up. She missed him. Perhaps one day, in five years or so; but who could know where they'd all be in five years? She saw him a soldier, writing noble poems from the front and dying there with a dream of her in his heart, and this hurt, for she knew that she didn't deserve this, was not worth it.

She spent much of her time with Lewis now. He was, naturally she supposed, a solitary child, needing less of the affection that he had needed a year before, living increasingly in his own world. He could ignore her watching entirely, would play and mumble to himself for hours, and for hours she could watch him, trying to interpret him, trying to form an opinion of him that might help her to help him. She felt that he would have a troubled life, for what reason she did not clearly know. She wanted to absorb as much of him as she could in these crucial years, so that she might, in some way, be there for him when he would need her.

He reminded her of Lionel; not only physically, but in a larger way. Lionel had promised that he would return; perhaps his return was here, in his son, in the continuance of the power of his life and of the command of her affections. This made her afraid for herself, afraid that her love would not be enough for him, that she did not know how to express that love in any way that a child might understand.

She would call to him sometimes, softly. Sometimes he would not hear her, lost in his world. Sometimes he would turn to her and look to her for something. At first she merely opened her arms and he came and received her embrace openly. Later she felt that this was not enough. She tried to engage him in conversation.

'What are you playing, my darling?'

He did not understand this question, had no distance upon his games that might allow him to put them into words. At last, after puzzling for some moments, he said, simply, 'War, mummy.'

'Who's winning the war, Lewis?'

He puzzled again, for this did not seem to be part of his concept of war.

'War where Daddy's gone,' he said.

She could not press him further, felt the knot of feelings block her; there was nothing that she wanted to know, nothing she wanted to tell him. If his war was as quiet and orderly a place as his game appeared to be, then she was happy for him to live in this illusion. She wondered if he remembered Lionel at all, but dared not ask him, for his answer would not belong to the same order of reality as her question. She settled back to marvel at his world, at its innocence and clarity, dreaded trespassing there, afraid of the future, his future, feeling at her weakest and most vulnerable in his presence. If Michael Fairfield were to return, were to ask her to marry him, she knew that she would accept.

. . . *twenty-eight* . . .

Michael Fairfield had indeed determined to resign his curacy and join the ranks. The death of Peter, his twin brother, had filled him with shame. He began many letters to Anna Drewer, but could finish none of them. He loved her with a clarity that made him unable to speak freely to her again of anything. He would keep silent, would not burden her with his own sadness. He would go to war and he would die there. It seemed a fitting consummation to his existence.

He willed himself to one last test. Alec Morton had roomed with him at Oxford and they had struck up a friendship of opposites. Where he had been earnest and studious, Alec had been brilliant and dissolute. As he had carefully clarified his Christianity to fit himself for the ministry, Alec had lacerated him with atheistical cynicism. They had come once to blows, after which, for the only time, Alec got him shamefully drunk. They had parted at graduation with a friendship established through three years of mutual endurance, and an intense knowledge of one another's weaknesses. Fairfield decided to visit Morton, to spend a fortnight having his sentimentality argued out of him, to see at the end if there was a truth left that was clear enough to die for.

Morton was working towards a medical qualification, but had been distracted by the demands of the war to spend his time in a hospital for psychiatric casualties. The hospital was housed in the commandeered town-house of some dead Midlands industrialist, high-walled and hideous.

'For the lads of towns like this,' Morton told him, 'the front line is not much worse than their ordinary lives, and at least they get fed and paid regularly, and indeed find themselves for the first time valued a little, in words at least, by the bastards who pretend they don't exist in peace-time. As for silly young buggers like you, Fairfield, this bloody war is no more than poetic justice.'

Fairfield smiled to find his friend in such predictable form.

'I'm thinking of joining up,' he said, cradling the mug into which had been poured two inches of raw gin.

'I expected no more of you. I'm sorry about your brother, Fairfield, and I'll say no more about your motives. You know, of course, that your chances of survival are not very good out there.'

'Yes. I do know that.'

'Is it Peter?'

'Partly . . . partly Peter. It's also, probably, love.'

Morton laughed.

'Let me guess. A war widow?'

'Yes.' He blushed at his transparency. 'She's . . . intelligent, well-read, open. Her husband was a professional soldier, some years older than she, a very strange person for her to have married, really; the sort of man we would have both disliked, I think; yet the loss of him was terrible for her, devastating. I learnt a lot about the nature of marriage from her, watching her break under his loss. In the circumstances, I was very close to her at that time.'

'He was probably very good in bed.'

'Yes, I believe he was.'

'She told you that?'

'Not in so many words. . . .'

'Ah no.'

'She said she had developed . . . an appetite for sexual intimacy.'

'In those words?'

'Yes.'

'Good God, Fairfield, you have been out in the world. I congratulate you. Have some more gin.'

'No. No, thank you. I admire your constitution, Morton, but have no desire to emulate it.'

Morton laughed, saluted him and drank.

'So . . . you did not feel able to satisfy her appetite, then?'

'Perhaps you are right about me, Morton. Perhaps I have not got the grip on life necessary to do more than surrender myself with as much integrity as I can muster.'

'Do you have any real idea what it's like out there?'

'I can imagine death and pain, and I think I can face them if necessary.'

'No. You have no idea, none at all. The slaughter . . . the blind, bloody slaughter is beyond anything you can begin to imagine, and there's no point to it, none whatsoever. If there were any ideals at the beginning, which I doubt – vague fantasies, schoolboy dreams – now there are none. They're locked into a blind, self-perpetuating carnage that is beyond any rational control. It will go on for years and years, until both sides are exhausted and destroyed. It is the end of our world, Fairfield. Everything that anyone believes in, not only men like you, but rationalists like me, has been proved empty in the face of this war. If you want to die, blow your brains out like a man, don't go out there to add your misery to the misery of the world.'

'I can't accept that, Morton. Even if you were right, I would have to go and see for myself; which, I might say, is more than you have done.'

'I'll show you. Here in this hospital there is evidence enough. Down there are the survivors, the physical survivors, but . . . but something has been done to them, Fairfield. If they were physically maimed, that would be easy, but . . . but it's worse than that. Their humanity has been distorted, mutilated, in some cases literally wiped off. Some of them are no better than animals now.'

'I don't think I'm up to your freak show, Morton. I don't think it would prove anything.'

'Don't you? I think we ought to put that to the test. Drink up that gin. You're going to need it.'

Morton took him down into a comb of white rooms, partitions of larger rooms, each with an iron bedstead and a slice of window. The doors each had small hatches, which Morton opened, offering Fairfield an image of a man. He made no comment, merely showed him: some were asleep; some huddled up in a corner, on the bed or on the floor; some standing in the middle of the room at attention, eyes closed; some looking about as if trying to work out where they were; some standing with heads bowed, too heavy to lift, shoulders slumped, mouths open, turned off; some paced, some evenly, some turning on the spring of some rage or terror; many stood with their faces to the window glass. One alarmed them by having his face at the hatch, great wet eyes ready to devour whatever appeared. There was a ubiquitous pall of disinfectant which never quite managed to cover the stench of corruption.

Fairfield was numbed. He began to believe that he was seeing only one man in countless postures. He had expected to be appalled; but he was not appalled. A vicious tedium possessed him, as if he had been presented with a parade of gross, artless pornography which failed to lift him in any way, stopped him even thinking about what he saw. Morton's propaganda had failed. It was nasty, yes, but it did not mean anything.

'Enough,' he said at last. 'This is pointless.'

'That is exactly its point.'

'I cannot feel pity for these men, Morton, not when so many have given so much more than they have.'

'You still don't understand, do you?'

'Probably not.'

'One more, then.'

'No more.'

'We will go in and talk to him. He's quite harmless, an interesting case. This way.'

Fairfield followed sullenly, wanting this to be over, wanting this

visit to be over, wanting to shake it all from him and to follow his
instinct as he ought to have had the courage to do all along. Morton
had become locked into his old ways of thinking, saw only what he
in his rationalist arrogance wanted to see; there was no longer any
communication between them that was of value. He thought of Anna
Drewer and felt a desire to open himself, if only to death, a desire to
bare himself and to let the world flood in. Here were only locked
pits, wretched invalids driven down into the sump of themselves.
Their fate was pathetic, but hardly tragic. Morton busied himself
here because these creatures embodied the certainties he nurtured;
but they were nothing to him.

They had come to the end of a corridor, and Morton was unlock-
ing a room. Fairfield followed him and found himself in the room of
a tall, emaciated, ugly man with close-cropped grey hair and a grey
beard-growth of the same density, who sat in khaki fatigues on his
bed.

'Good evening,' Morton said cheerfully. 'I've brought a friend of
mine to meet you. The Reverend Mr Fairfield. Fairfield? May I
introduce Major Blank?'

The man scowled at Morton and Fairfield in one sour glance.

'Why don't you leave me?' he said malevolently. 'I'm dead.'

'You're not dead, Major. Hardly a scratch upon him, Fairfield.
They found him wandering about naked. Says he can't remember
who he is, but I think he can remember, not a genuine amnesiac. It's
something else. Something he doesn't want to remember, something
he did. What? Did he run away? Did he commit something particularly beastly that he doesn't choose to remember? D'you believe in
God, Major? Perhaps that's what I've not been able to do for him,
Fairfield. I'll leave you here with him. You can say a prayer with
him, or for him, or on him, or whatever it is you do.'

Fairfield felt a pulse begin to swell at the back of his head, had to
suck at the air to stay stable.

'Fairfield?' Morton had turned to him. 'What is it?'

'I know this man, Morton.'

'What?'

Morton turned to the figure on the bed who was not even looking
at them, was staring at the floor. Fairfield moved past Morton and
sat beside the man. Under Morton's eye, he reached and lifted the
man's hand, took it in his and held it. The man turned his malevol-
ent face upon him, seemed to be mustering spittle on his lips.

'You're Lionel Drewer, aren't you? Major Lionel Drewer.'

'No,' he said, but not definitely, as if it was a move in an argument, a deliberate paradox.

'Yes you are. Anna sent me. Now that I've found you, I'll go and bring her.'

'No,' he said again, as before.

'Oh yes.'

'I died.'

'No. You didn't die.'

'Tell her I died.'

'No. Not for you, Drewer, for me. I don't care about you. I don't even know you. But I want to give you back to her, more than anything I've ever done.'

He felt Drewer's hand tremble, then begin to shake, felt the whole of him begin to shudder as if he were going into a fit. He held on tight, even as the man's strength began to crush his bones together. The pain filled him with an ecstasy and he thanked God that he should have been granted this fulfilment.

. . . *twenty-nine* . . .

Anna travelled alone, forbade even her mother to journey with her. There were complications, formal identifications, military procedures, but Fairfield had offered to come down should she need him. He, at least, understood her need to be alone at first, to come face to face with him with nothing in between.

The wearisome machinery of travel and of establishing herself in a dreary provincial hotel occupied her, brought a screen of petty irritation between her and the gulf which she approached. Only when she slept, which she did fitfully throughout the journey, did the gulf yawn, a blackness full of indeterminate lumps and claws into which she tumbled choking, waking to the gritty discomfort of the train.

She wore her black still, partly to avoid attention on the train, and partly because she did not feel entitled to shed her mourning. She believed that she would surely find him at the end of her journey;

but there was something not right, something uncertain, something that had to be accommodated before she could be as she was, the living wife of a living man. She knew that whatever she found, it would not be the same, not the same man who had left her almost two years before. They had been apart for nearly as long as they had been together. An impenetrable strangeness lay before her, the gulf, the darkness. She clenched herself to her duty before it.

After a wretched night in the hotel, she arrived at the hospital early and was ushered into the office of the senior doctor. He offered her tea, which she declined, and seemed unwilling at first to come to the point, which made her desperately uneasy. I'll go, she wanted to say. I'll come back another day. I'll send my mother, the Reverend Fairfield. I find, after all, that I cannot stand this. She lacked, finally, the courage to say this, followed him mutely and dully.

He had primed her with various hypothetical prognoses of the patient's condition, but she did not attend to any of that, disliked his oily professionalism, the antiseptic reek of him that did not conceal his essential dirtiness. Disliking him helped, she found; had she found him reassuring and attractive, she would have wept, and that would not have been right.

They came at last to the door. The doctor opened a hatch and peered in. She held back, not wanting to peek in on him like that. She had not expected the key which the doctor applied busily to the lock. She was frightened. The door was opened.

He was sitting on his bed. He did not move, nor turn his head as they entered. She thought he was accused of some crime that he should be like this, wanted to rise at once and defend him. His wretchedness was an outrage. She turned to the doctor to find him watching her intimately.

'Mrs Drewer?' he said.

'What?'

'Is this . . . is this your husband?'

'Yes.'

'You are certain?'

'Yes. Please leave us now.'

'Mrs Drewer, that is not permitted, I am afraid.'

'Not permitted? How dare you? Look at him. Isn't what you have done to him enough? Am I to be included in your humiliations also?'

'Mrs Drewer, please.'

'No. You will leave us. Please go.'

'I cannot . . .'

He was close to her, breathing sourly upon her, reaching to her sleeve as if about to pull her away. She slapped his face with all her strength and, when he recovered from the blow, a long wisp of greasy black hair had fallen across his forehead. He reached up to touch where she had struck, then turned and left, with the door wide open behind him.

She clipped up the hatch, closed the door, pulled a chair across to block it and sat down. If they tried to come in, if they peered through the hatch over the subsequent minutes, she did not know. She sat neatly and formally, and regarded him there on the bed. He had not moved, had not even lifted his head. She watched and waited for him, her anger monumental, thumping through her.

At last she called him.

'Lionel? . . . Lionel? . . . Do you know me? . . . You are not to do this. You are not to refuse me like this . . . Lionel?'

This would not work. This was only smacking at a closed door and would go on until she bled. She did not know even if he could hear her but, after another extensive silence, she decided to work upon the assumption that he could, that he knew somewhere who she was.

She tried again.

'Listen to me, then. Listen. Whatever you are now, whatever you have become, whatever they have done to you, once you were Lionel Drewer, and once I was your wife. I will not leave this room until you know this. If you ask me to go, I will go, but only when you say my name, only when you turn to me, face me, tell me, by name, to go.'

She watched him minutely as she said this, but he did not move. She let the silence return. Minutes passed, hours perhaps. She began to understand what they had done to him. When she had first seen him, she had known him at once; that had been easy, much easier than she had thought. Now, in the silence, she began to lose her sense of him, began to imagine that he was not Lionel Drewer after all. He was emaciated and pitiful. Everything that she had desired and dreamed of in him was lost. He was a cipher. It would have been better to have found him dead. An exhaustion began to pull her down, to load her eyes and to bring low aching to her bones.

Something jerked her awake again. She did not know what it had been, whether some move he had made or whether spontaneous. She shook herself and wondered what else he might try.

She did not want to touch him, the thought of it revolted her. She saw the folds of loose grey skin about his neck, could smell the staleness of his flesh, could not bring herself to that; but, even as she articulated this disgust, she knew that she would have to go to him, would have to touch him, to place her mouth if necessary over that rank pit in his face and breathe herself into him. She shuddered but rose from her chair and came to stand before him.

She looked down and saw the bald lumps at the top of his spine, the grey rim of dirt about his neck, the flaking of the skin on his raw scalp. That he was alive at all was an obscenity. She folded her knees and squatted on the floor before his fallen head. She planted her elbows on his knees and clapped her hands over his ears, jerking the head up until his face, for all its watery lack of focus, was a foot from hers.

'Tell me to go,' she said.

'Go,' he said, the sound half-throttled.

She shook the head.

'By name, Lionel, by name.'

'I . . .'

'What?' She shook him viciously. 'What?'

'. . . died.'

'I wish you had,' she said. 'I wish I were free of you. I wish there were a way out of this misery, Lionel, but there is not.'

'You cannot . . .'

'What?'

'. . . touch me.'

'Why not?'

'I have. . . .'

'What?'

'. . . a disease.'

'What disease? Lionel, what disease?'

'I cannot . . . be . . . forgiven.'

Stark tears were running suddenly down his face. She jerked his head towards her and began to lick them off him, felt them metallic and acid on her tongue, felt her stomach rise, her mouth fill with bile. He began to shudder and the bed began to rattle. A trickling came and she moved her hand down to feel the thin running of his urine between her fingers.

114

And in the degradation, suddenly she came clear, the knot unravelled. In the disgust she felt, at last, the deep shuddering of his humanity. Whatever filth possessed him, she would bring it up out of him, would smear it over her. She clung to him now mercilessly.

'Anna, go. For God's sake, go.'

'Never. Never. Never. You'll have to tear me from you in pieces, my love. I've come into the pit to find you and I'll drown before I'll let you go.'

. . . *thirty* . . .

He knew that he had died. He remembered the moment, the face looming into his face, the lips snarled, the blade entering him, the bullet, the light that overwhelmed him. There was darkness then, massive, but which cleared abruptly; after which he continued to exist, but in two discrete registers.

Firstly there was his corpse, of which he was aware distantly. He remembered stripping it naked, laying it out in the mud. There was a grim landscape over which, later, he was wandering. There was pain also, hunger, thirst, but, having died, these did not reach him. He had been recovered from this landscape and sent somewhere for the doctors to explore. He was glad that he might be useful, would have been happier if the hungry wretches who had loomed at him from huddled holes and broken shelters had been able to cook and eat him. He would have been content to be reduced to hot slabs of meat, sliding into pinched bellies; but they had brought him onto this white slab and had visited him and probed him, had operated his body with antiseptic curiosity. He had not minded this, for it was all peripheral to the reality, the other, higher world in which he now existed.

In this other world, he ranged through a world of faces, communed with other ghosts. There were the faces of his own, personal dead whom he saw turn to him with a brilliant second of recognition before the light went out of them. They seared him with the final flare of their light. He saw behind this light the faces of their women, their mothers and sisters and lovers, turning to him with the last question, the last doubt that he resolved, tumbling them off the edge of the world. He reached for them but they were closed to him, closed to everything, keening in chorus, a multiple wailing that filled him with pain that would not be stilled, that would not leave him, that clung to him like filth. He clawed out to them in the darkness but their bodies were empty sockets from which the dead had been torn. They choked him with their suffering as he tried to grapple with them. He gathered from them the moments of lost tenderness: the triumph of birth, the nursing, the summer games, the gathering about tables and hearths, the warmth in bitter weather, the court-ship games, the touch of fingers and lips, the pride of nakedness, the lock of bodies and the intimate aftermaths of copulation, lost now, tumbled off the edge of the world in the terminal shock of incom-pletion. He knew it all, catalogued it, chronicled it, let it drive its nails of suffering into him. If he were a god, he could have gathered it and borne it away with him; but he was not a god and his register-ing of it could bring no relief to those who engendered it. It could only condemn him.

It was the man Morton who began to bring him to the realisation that he was not dead, simply because Morton refused to believe that he was dead. Morton treated him with a cynical humour that insinuated itself into him like needles. He found that, when Morton appeared, his external body acquired emotions, for he truly loathed the man, loathed the way he fingered him and breathed around him. There were moments when he wanted to break out and smash Morton to death, moments when he almost believed that he could do this. When Morton left him, for a few moments, an hour perhaps, an increasing length of time, or a length of time which grew slower and slower, he felt the reverberations of this emotion, felt the sweat on his flesh, the jerk of his pulse, the whole soiled process of life again, from which only slowly, only partially, he drifted back into the shelter of his nightmare.

Then one day, Morton brought another with him who named him, and then he knew he was lost, then he knew there was only defiance, mounting denial, the crumbling refusal to remember or accept anything, to bury himself back into the horrors now as pro-tection. But the final curse had been laid upon him and he could not avoid it. It was coming for him.

It came with the woman. He struggled to keep her away, for he knew that if she touched him she would become as he was. He could not bear to go through that again. She named him, as the other had, but not simply. She dressed his naming with complexities that fitted like keys, that opened him up. He shuddered with disgust at himself, shuddered to shake it from him, but the shuddering itself was a denial of his death. She was relentless and cruel, and it was her cruelty that finally brought him down, for it was an active cruelty, a living personal cruelty that stung him back to life.

She took him away with her, took him on trains, in carriages, into the shadows of a large house where people came to him and touched him, wept for him. He was Lionel Drewer and she was his wife. Her name was Anna. They had a son, Lewis. There was a blind man called Harry Brand. There was a servant girl called Brady. Each fitted themselves around him and made him substantial again, although he could do no more than sit and tremble, or sleep back in his nightmares, or gibber a few sentences. He knew who he was, what he was, what he had been and done, but there was no way in which he might come into that inheritance.

She, his wife, appalled him above all. Her proximity to him made something rip inside him. She did not leave him even at night. She came into his room and slept in a bed next to his, and he woke to hear her there, to hear her breathing and stirring, to feel her closeness blocking every vent through which he might have escaped. Sometimes he woke to find her hovering over him, touching his head with her palm, with her lips, suffocating him with a tenderness like acid.

He knew, as soon as he had any strength of volition, that he must find a way to destroy himself; this time permanently.

. . . thirty-one . . .

The servant girl, Brady, came every morning to shave him. Under the soft warmth of the lather, the blade moved in cold rasps. It would take only the simplest of jerks to slip it into his flesh; but the girl would not have permitted that. There was something vigorous about her, a blustering life that would not have allowed him to escape whilst she was in charge of him. If he were to be liberated, it would not be here.

'There, sir,' she said, swaddling his face in a warm towel. 'You're coming back to yourself again, you really are.' She brought a mirror, but he could not recognise himself within it, saw only a gaunt gargoyle that repelled him.

'Leave . . . the razor,' he said.

She looked at him.

'Oh, I couldn't do that, sir.'

'Leave it.'

'I'll fetch the mistress, sir.'

'No.'

But she was gone and he felt stupid to have asked. He had exposed himself and would now be subject to another layer of humiliation, another unwrapping of bandages that swaddled him.

The servant girl reappeared with the mistress, his wife, who looked at him, at the girl. They exchanged brief words and the girl went quickly, to bring others perhaps. He closed his eyes, retracted, felt the woman's hand upon his arm, his face, heard her saying something that he would not hear. Then she opened his limp fingers and slipped the razor under them, closed them with her hand around his. He opened his eyes then, lifted the razor to look at it. It was shut, the line of its blade hidden in the bone handle. It felt heavy and cruel. He was afraid of it, of the responsibility of it. He reached out and placed it on the table beside him.

'I thought you wanted that?' the woman was saying. 'What is it? You're a coward, Lionel, a coward to want it and then not to have the strength to use it. You're a coward to want to use it at all. But be sure of this: I will not allow you to die alone. If you would do it, then do it now, do it with me here watching you. You have made me suffer everything, and if that has to be suffered, then I will suffer it face to face.'

'You don't understand,' he said. 'You don't understand.'

'What? What is there for me to understand?'

'I died.'

'You did not die.'

'You don't understand.'

'How did you die, Lionel? Tell me.'

'What was . . . done. What I did . . .'

'You were a soldier. What did you do more than that? You taught me to understand that, to respect it. What is it? What did you do that was worse than that?'

'You don't understand.'

'I want to understand. I want you to tell me.'

'I cannot tell you.'

'Why not?'

'Because . . . because it's a sickness. You would become sick. You would become . . . dead.'

She rose suddenly and turned away, walked across the room in a black hiss that drew his breath with it. She turned and came hissing back, down upon him.

'If you had any sickness to give me, Lionel, then you gave it to me when you married me. I am what you made me, and I will not let go of you now. I cannot, not whilst you are still alive, and I will fight to keep you alive with every vigilance I can muster. It is necessary for my own survival. We are together now, and whatever horrors, whatever suffering attends you, attends me also. Whatever degradations you have committed, you have done them to me also. What? Have you killed? Have you taken pleasure in killing? Have you been with whores? I have no judgement of you, Lionel. I am not your God. I am your wife. Your humanity is all that I understand. I understand it because it is the image of my own humanity. Since you have been gone, when I believed you dead, I have felt and imagined things that appeal and sicken me. I have been cruel and lustful, I have despaired and sought to maim those who love me with my despair. I have not been to war; thank God, I have been here in the shelter of those who love me; but I have no moral seniority. I find only that I have more courage than you, more determination, more anger; these are not admirable qualities, whatever they may appear to be. They are the desperation of love, of physical love. I will not leave you. I will stay with you now, after this, night and day, hour by hour. I will live my life within reach of you until you know me, until you accept and receive me, or until you can stand me no longer and shake the life out of me. Oh yes, you are capable of that, Lionel, I know you are; because I am capable of it. When Brady came to me and told me that you wanted to be left with the razor, I thought, right, I'll go back. I'll give it to him, and if he doesn't have the courage to do it himself, I'll do it for him; and I may yet. There is nothing to chose between us, Major Drewer.'

He had tried to shut this out, but she had been too close. She had breathed the words into his face, her presence sweet and noxious, her eyes like splinters, her teeth bared and her body a bulk of dark, devouring flesh. She terrified him and he whimpered. He no longer wanted death because he knew that it would be no escape from her.

She was true to her word. He had to live now with every move he made watched and supervised by her, every function of his life administered by her. They ate at a small table, and when he could or would not eat, she would push her plate away also. At night she came into his bed and lay beside him, watching him as he collapsed at last into sleep, always awake when he woke. As the days passed she consumed him until he felt that he no longer existed except as a function of her presence; had she then gone, for a moment, he would have fallen into panic.

His nightmare, his other world, was by this process blocked from him. When he slept he did so now in absolute darkness, waking to her rankness, the fear of her proximity. He had moments of anger against her, felt that she had deprived him of himself, imagined violence against her, then remembered that she had predicted this and her prediction of it seemed to trivialise it, to reduce the emotions to ashes as he felt them.

How long this stage of siege lasted, he did not know, but the first sign of its change came one morning when he had woken, when she had sat him up in bed and brought him tea whilst she went to the basin to wash herself. It was a bright morning and she stood in the light of the window sponging her nakedness, lifting her arms to wash her breasts, squatting splay-thighed to wash her genitals. He suddenly without realising, became caught on a barb of desire, watching her with a warmth mustering on his flesh. A moment later he became conscious of it and it disgusted him; he turned away, covering himself in anger and violence. She slipped on her gown and came to him, sat beside him and waited until he had mastered himself, until he had put on his mask of numbness to be able to face her again; but he knew something had happened to him that morning, that he had been lured out for a second. For the time being, he could only be afraid of it.

. . . *thirty-two* . . .

There was something going on that he did not understand. The maid
came in with a serious face and spent a long time talking to her.
Whatever it was, it did not directly concern him, but he found
himself curious, involved, upset by it. The maid left and a little
while later returned with the boy, holding his hand. The boy's face
was dark with defiance.

'What have you done, Lewis?' she demanded, in a voice that he
had only heard her use on him before. 'Well?'

The boy was silent. The maid released his hand and went to sit by
the door. She was in her usual chair and the boy stood before her.

'Firstly, Lewis, look at me,' she said.

The boy lifted his face.

'Were you in Grandmama's room?'

The face fell again.

'Lewis! You will look at me!'

He looked up and in his face was now fear, a widening eye, an
uncertain lip, a pallor. Drewer recognised this, knew this scene from
somewhere.

'Were you in Grandmama's room?'

The little head nodded quickly.

'No. You must speak. You must answer me.'

'Yes, Mummy.'

'What did you do there?'

'I was playing, Mummy,' the voice pathetic, minimising itself
before these accusations.

'In Grandmama's room? You know you are not to go in there. You
know that. What were you playing? Lewis? What were you playing
in there?'

'With . . . with the papers . . .' Now tears, wretched, culpable
tears.

'With the papers on Grandmama's desk?'

'Yes. I didn't mean it.'

'You didn't mean it? How old are you, Lewis? You scribbled on the papers. You tore up letters, important letters. Oh, Lewis, how could you have been so wicked? How could you have?'

'I'm sorry, Mummy.'

'Are you? Are you sorry?'

'Yes. I am. I am,' with a pathetic earnestness, desperate to be believed.

'I'm going to have to beat you, Lewis.'

'No, Mummy. No, please, no.' The fear was turned to panic now. He turned to the door to see the guardian maid.

She rose from her chair above the boy.

'You are to bend over this chair. Come along now, Lewis. You have been wicked and you must be punished. When you are punished it will all be over. You must be a brave boy now.'

He writhed and wept and turned and begged.

'Lewis, you have hurt me more than you can know with what you have done. You are hurting me even more by this behaviour, this cowardice. Shall I ask Brady to come and hold you down like a little puppy-dog?'

The child turned to Brady who was implacable. Lionel begged silently for the boy to submit which, at last, he did.

'You won't beat me hard, will you, Mummy?'

'Yes, I shall beat you hard, Lewis, for you have been very, very wicked and I must beat you hard.'

Whimpering and flinching he bent himself over the arm of the chair. He was so thin, so young. Drewer was appalled most of all by his own impotence. He trembled and had to wipe the saliva from his mouth as he watched.

His wife stooped quickly and removed her shoe. For a second as she rose with it, she caught her husband's eye and he saw then not the retributive sadism that her tone had implied, but that she suffered, that her whole face was a contortion, that the humiliation was hers as much as the child's.

Quickly she rose and turned to the boy. Three times she struck him, true to her intention, very hard, the smacks like explosions. He did not make a noise until she was done, until she had stooped to replace the shoe; then the sound of his pain rose, a howling of a simple wretchedness that the world should contain such pain, that anything he might have done should have merited this monstrous violence.

122

Brady came and lifted him, cuddled him against her bosom.

'There, my lamb, you were a brave boy, a brave boy. Go now to your Mummy and give her a cuddle.'

But the boy would not go, would not turn from Brady's skirts, burrowed deep within them.

'Come along now, Lewis.'

'Leave him, Brady,' she said. 'Take him to . . . give him something . . . I will see him before he goes to bed.'

Brady did not look content with this, seemed determined to bring the boy round, but Anna was weeping, stooped over with her balled fists in her mouth and the maid lifted the wretched boy and carried him out.

Lionel watched his wife, saw her pace about the room, saw her strive to contain her tears, to make herself hard again. She seemed to have forgotten that he was there. He had been not only impotent but incidental; and yet he found himself now in a tangle of emotions that the vividness of this drama had run through him and, as he struggled to clear them, or to have them within reach, he began to speak, to push the thoughts out of him with a fluency that he had thought he had lost forever.

'When I was a boy, no older than that, my father beat me, like that, bent me over a chair. I don't remember what I had done. I don't think I ever fully understood what I had done. Something. Something that made them very angry with me. I don't know. He used a cane. He made me bleed. Afterwards he shook my hand and told me that I was a man. I understood that. When I left him, I felt proud of my beating. I examined myself, licked the blood off my fingers, was disappointed when the weals turned black and faded. Do you think he will understand?'

She had come before him, stood staring at him with pity and disgust.

'He died soon after that, my father. I remember his beating of me more than any other memory I have of him. That he was able to do that to me made me feel that he loved me, he loved me enough to hurt me when it was necessary.'

'I will never, never, never do that again,' she said, 'and I will kill you before I allow you to do it. Why, in God's name, didn't you stop me, Lionel? What have I done to him? Do you think he will be proud of me when his pain has gone? Pity me, pity me.'

'How?'

She trembled and wept, clasped herself and turned from side to side. He stood unsteadily before her and, as his shadow came over her, she went still.

'I can't,' he said.

'Coward . . . pathetic, contemptible man. Where are you? Where are you?'

He could not take his eyes off her all afternoon, all evening, and for once she did not face him, not for a moment: the positions seemed to have been reversed. He wanted to say things to her but they died in his mouth. He wanted to feel things for her, but when the feeling came to the surface of his body he retracted and shuddered and forced them down.

Supper came and, whilst they ate it, or tried to eat it, there was a knock and Brady appeared with Lewis, brushed and washed and dressing-gowned. Brady released him and he came to Anna, stood formally beside her.

'Mummy, I am very sorry that you had to beat me. I promise, I promise, Mummy, that you will never have to do it again.'

'And I promise that I will never do it again, my lamb.'

He came then for his embrace. Lionel watched with pity for the boy's submission, and with envy, suddenly, for the affection he exchanged.

'Lewis,' he called when the boy had left his mother and was returning to Brady.

He stopped, looked at his father suspiciously.

'I . . . I'm sorry, my boy.'

That was all he had wanted to say, but the boy looked at him, wondering what he was sorry about. The women watched him too.

'I'm sorry that . . . that the world is such a place,' he said, blushing as he said it. 'Goodnight then, my boy.'

'Goodnight, Daddy.'

Brady took him away and he could not look at Anna. She rose from the table and returned shortly. He did not look up, but her hand appeared under his face with a case of cigarettes. He took one and looked up to see her take one also. They shared a match and faced one another amongst the wreaths of smoke that seemed, at last, to blur the air between them, to make it tolerable.

'I think,' he said, 'I think that I . . . am beginning to become clearer now.'

She did not react at once, considered this.

'I hope so,' she said, then after a while: 'Do you really not remember?'

'I remember . . . I remember . . . yes, I do remember, but that's not . . . not the problem.'

'What then?'

'Everything . . . everything I remember belongs to a place that does not exist any more. The people do not exist. They all died. They lived in a world that was clear, was mapped and covered by roads and towns and names. If you wanted to go there, you went that way. If you wanted to do this, you took that decision. When I was . . . in battle . . . out there . . . when I . . . the whole landscape was destroyed, torn apart, not just the individuals, not just them, the whole of it, everything they . . . everything we belonged to. We lost our names, we lost our nations, we lost whatever it was we were supposed to be fighting for. It just didn't mean anything any more. We didn't mean anything any more, not to them, not to the men who sent us, and then, at last, not to ourselves, not to ourselves. Fighting, killing, fucking. . . .'

He stopped suddenly, looked up at her, for the word had fallen out of him in a trance and he was appalled to have given it to her; but she smiled.

'I know that word, Lionel. I know what it means, and what it implies.' She watched him until he had to look away. 'I am not afraid of anything you have done, nor ashamed. Brady goes and . . . fucks with one of the grooms. She and Jack Wilkie . . . fucked. I envy her freedom. I am not free. Nor are you. Before you went away, we did things that bound us together. We gave up our freedom. You have done things . . . you have killed men, perhaps you have also fucked. . . . I do not forgive you, because there is nothing you can do that I am not bound to accept as part of what I married, what I love. Lionel, this love is a dreadful business. I am a poor mother, an undutiful daughter. There is nothing I can do but fight to have you back, not as you were, because that has gone forever, but in some way that I can feed my love for you, can draw you back into me. Be with me. That's all I ask of you. Be entirely with me. Let us go on together. There is nothing else to be done.'

He was pitiful under this. He put his face in his hands.

'I am not a man any more,' he said.

'I don't know what you mean by that. Whatever you are, you are here. You kept your promise. You have returned and, in spite of everything, I would be nowhere else but here. Lift your face to me, Lionel. Lift your face.'

. . . *thirty-three*

The war ended at last. Lionel resigned his commission. There was little money on both sides and, with care, they might make a frugal life. They rented a small house in a Norfolk village and set up a home there: Anna and Lionel, with Lewis and Brady. They had little society. They lived close together and, within a year, a daughter was born, Helena.

Lewis was nearing the age when he must be sent to school. Money would be provided by the family for this essential and, although neither Anna nor Lionel finally wanted him to go, they could see no reasonable alternative.

'We have not done well by Lewis,' she said one night.

Lionel agreed, was more outwardly optimistic about the natural resilience of boys than she, but it was a subject of which they were both essentially afraid.

Helena became her mother's child. Anna watched Brady and knew that there was something that did not content her, that she did not fit in their new life. She had lost some of her openness perhaps, squabbled with shopkeepers, found the locals too wrapped up in their own righteousness. Although Anna and Lionel had, in their new home, found a new peace, a new pleasure in their marriage, and in their new daughter, Brady missed the north.

They received a telegram. Her mother was ill, and they must journey back. Lionel showed a reluctance to go, felt no real duty there, did not feel that Mrs Brand had ever quite forgiven him for the state in which he had returned from the war. Anna knew that he was right, was glad to release him; so, Lewis being away at school, Anna left her husband to his bird-watching and his books, and journeyed north with her infant daughter in the arms of the blithe Brady, who seemed to glow as the miles were consumed.

'Who is it you're looking forward to seeing most, my love?' Anna asked her on the train. 'One-handed Charlie?'

'Good heavens no, m'm. He was just . . . well, once or twice.'

'Brady! We ought to have discussed this. Is there anything I ought to know? Were there others?'

She blushed.

'Who?'

'I thought you knew, m'm.'

'No, Brady. Who? Tell me.'

'I can't, m'm, not if you don't know. You do know, though.'

'Not my brother?'

'I'm afraid he's quite a one for the girls now, so I hear. Trevis tells me he's put young Deborah in trouble.'

'Oh, Brady.'

'Don't worry about me, m'm. I've seen a deal too much of him now to let him put me into any trouble. He's a good man, m'm. He makes you laugh and he's always kind. He gets low sometimes, with his blindness.'

'Would you . . . would you like to stay in the north, Brady?'

'Oh, I couldn't, m'm, not with the baby.'

'We could find someone else, someone local.'

They looked at each other, friends, held hands, but Anna knew that her instinct was right, that she had to find some way to leave Brady there, that their friendship was past its high season and there were new lives to be made.

Her mother seemed to have aged decades. They had left her, not two years before, a strong woman in the best of her years. Anna found her now collapsed into a terrible dotage, the careful edges of her life frayed with disease and pain; only at the centre the eye still watched.

'I waited for you,' she said. 'I wouldn't let them telegraph before. I don't want you to drag out your time here. Have you come alone?'

'Brady is with me, Mama, and Helena.'

'I have no time for babies now, child. Your husband is not here, then?'

'He . . . thought it best I come alone.'

'I think you might have done better, been happier. . . .'

'Don't, Mama. I am happy.'

'That curate, the one who was here during the war . . .'

'Michael? Michael Fairfield?'

'Yes. He died you know.'

'No . . . no, I didn't, I . . . in the war?'

'Not the war. The influenza. They say that took as many as the war. I don't know any more. I don't know what it has all been for. Can you make sense of it?'

'No. There is no sense to be made of it.'

'Well, I'll soon know, one way or the other. Do you think I'll meet your father?'

'Surely, Mama, surely you will.'

'Do you think he'll approve of how I have spent my life?'

'How can you doubt that?'

'I don't know. When it comes to it, at last, I don't know. I don't have the strength any more to know anything, or even to care very much. This place will be gone in ten years. Harry's a fool. They'll take it all from him whilst he breeds bastards. None of it will last, once the morality, once the sense of duty has gone. That went in the war. Too many died and those who have survived only want pleasure. It's the age of selfishness now. I wanted . . . I wanted you to have this house one day, you and your husband . . . not Lionel Drewer, not him, he wouldn't do at all. Nothing is as it ought to be. If I am at peace now, it's because I have given up. That's what's killed me, child. Thank you for coming. Thank you for your tears. I have tried to do my duty by you, but you were always strange, always restless. I hope you are happy. Bless you. Bless you.'

The tears were as much for Michael Fairfield as they were for her mother; for the man she ought to have married, for the world she ought to have belonged to, this world, the world that she knew was ending here. She felt as if her past was being cut from her finally. A whole world of consolation would die with her mother. She sat beside her long into the evening, clasping her hand in the silence of a love that was only now perhaps revealed in all its strength and honesty. Much of what had been said had hurt her, but she knew the nature of love well enough now to know that pain belonged to it as much as joy; perhaps more so.

She died in the night. The cousins and neighbours and tenants gathered and the funeral proceeded in protracted formality, in condolence and repression. When the last of them had gone, Anna summoned Brady and told her that they would leave as soon as possible.

'Couldn't we stay another week, m'm?'

'No. I want to be out of here. I'm sorry, my love. I will try to find a way to send you back here, I promise. Be with me for a little longer, for I too still have need of you.'

When they returned, Lionel seemed more animated than he had been in years. His sympathy for her bereavement was cursory, but she was glad of that, wanted it to be over. She mourned her mother, but was surprised how quickly that was receding. There was something new here and she wanted to know what it was.

He had been offered a position in the colonial service. It had come via Radstock who had survived the war as a Major-General. It was in Africa, in a country where the regiment had served. He had resisted immediate acceptance of the position until he had told her; but he would accept it, assumed her acceptance of it as a matter of course; which acceptance she gave with all the delight he could have wished for. It was perfect: a new beginning, a new purpose, a new world.

On the back of the euphoria, however, there were complications.

'Will Lewis come with us?' she asked.

'I think . . . I think Lewis will have to stay at school. There is really no education out there. He might be able to come out for the summer. I don't know. It's a long way.'

'But . . . what you are saying is that he will be left here, that to accept this position will be to abandon him?'

'We are not abandoning him, my love.'

'Effectively. Effectively, we would be.'

They looked at one another, shared the guilt of this, for they knew it was not an issue, merely a part of the price; and they knew also that in their darker selves, they would not be sorry to leave him behind them, for he had become a token of their dark time, a memory of their pain.

'Brady will go north,' she said. 'She will be there for Lewis when he comes home for the holidays. It's where she is happiest. She will see that he comes to no harm.'

Six months later, the other side of a thicket of farewells that had snagged at them, hurt them with losses and guilts, Lionel and Anna Drewer were steaming south through high seas and a blinding gale that, out of the shelter of the cabins, out-roared every gesture of humanity that might be raised before it.

They stood together, clinging onto the rail with the rain and spray driving through the flaps of their oilskins, watching the great slopes of the sea shift, lit with an ominous phosphorescence. They loved it, the brute energy of the storm, their own insignificance below it, the small, tight beating of their lives made provisional. Should the sea have risen and sucked them into it, they would have been content, together at that moment, to be lost.

They came from this moment at last and, reeling like drunkards, made their way to the shelter of a companionway and down into the warmth and light of the vessel's pitching normalities, the veneer of luxury here pleasantly subverted by the tumbling of the storm, by the crash of breakage and by the odour of the general *mal de mer* by which, surprised and smug, neither was affected; nor was Helena, whom they visited in the cabin of her new nurse, who eyed her employers with a green malevolence. Helena slept sweetly pink, clutching her toy, oblivious not only to the storm, but to the whole proceeding of freedom.

They returned to their cabin and undressed in a farce of sliding toiletries in a light that pulsed into darkness. She insisted on the adventure of the top bunk, where he joined her and where, against the throb of the engines, matching themselves to the pitch and roll of the storm, they made love with a slow, liquid delicacy, with an understanding that seemed not confined to each other, but to encompass the storm and world; in which they were at once reduced to the puppets of a universal biological purpose, and expanded to a perfection of human significance one with the other. Behind them a world of obligation and death; before them a new continent beginning to writhe into a violent consciousness of itself; about them ocean and storm; between them a bolt of pleasure that held them for a moment quite, quite still.

Book Two

SUBJECTIONS

One . . .

'My father died in the war,' said Collis proudly, an assertion of himself, a definition almost.

'Well, my father came home,' Lewis said with a deliberate insolence that generated the shock that he intended. The others were now firmly with Collis, ranged against him. He felt the charge of his isolation, a definition stronger than Collis's, and dangerous.

'Well, you can't talk, then,' Collis said, looking round to receive the approval of the pack.

'I can talk if I want to.'

'Yes, but nobody's going to listen to you, Drewer, screwy Drewer.'

The others tittered.

'Anyway,' Lewis said, tossing his head, shrugging, 'the war was stupid.'

The heresy of this hit the group of boys percussively; they closed around Collis.

'No, it wasn't,' Collis said, pushing through to him.

Lewis turned his back and resumed his slouch, began to move away, knew they'd come after him, felt the pulse in his neck and shoulders, the places he imagined them grabbing him.

'You're stupid, Drewer,' Collis said, without quite the courage to make a fight of it yet, coming round wide to face Lewis, blocking his path. 'I bet your father was a coward. I bet that's why he came back.'

'At least he's not dead.'

Collis showed his teeth then, and stabbed a punch at Lewis's shoulder, skewed him to one side. The punch was the next logical move in the game, and it had hurt probably more than Collis had meant it to. Lewis righted himself, rubbed his shoulder, then faced Collis squarely, could see the apprehension below the jutted defiance of his chin. Lewis punched his nose. Collis had a pudgy face and Lewis was surprised at the superficial softness of it, the hardness of the bone beneath which hurt his knuckles. Collis, thrown back against the wall, his face screwed up, was bleeding and crying.

Somebody grabbed Lewis's arms from behind and he writhed, lashed out behind with his legs, spun his assailant round to face the rest of them, a phalanx of shoulders closing around him, none of them wanting to commit a blow individually, although as a group they would gladly have beaten him insensible. Lewis put his head down and, dragging the unseen figure who still clasped him, charged into the mass of them. They became a flailing ruck of arms and bodies. Lewis freed his arms and pushed his fists into any bulk he could see, felt the pommel of blows on his arms and back.

'Stop that!'

The voice had come from the other side of the yard, but they obeyed it at once. The ruck dissolved and they stood separate, each trying to edge his way to the periphery of it.

Mr Triller screwed his way across the wet gravel on his tin leg, grunting and wheezing, his gown flapping, his lank hair draped about his ears. Lewis found that he was the only one watching the master, and quickly dropped his face like the others.

'Who did this, Collis?'

The inevitable silence. The wrong question.

'Well? Who hit Collis?'

'I did, sir.'

'Drewer. Very well. And who started it?'

An unexpected silence. Lewis looked up at Collis whose face was pale below the mask of blood and blubbering; if Collis failed to own up, it would be a substantial victory to him.

'I started it, sir. He insulted my father.'

'He insulted my father,' Lewis said fairly.

'Headmaster's study at break tomorrow, Drewer and Collis. The rest of you run round the yard three times. And you, Drewer. Collis, go and wash your face.'

Lewis had not been into Mr Crowland's study since the beginning of term, when his father and mother had brought him here. He remembered the old man's kindly reassurances, but had not been deceived by them; they had been addressed to his parents as if he were not there. He was here now, standing beside the trembling Collis whilst the old man wrote on thick notepaper, sucking on his pipe, making it gurgle disgustingly.

'Stand still, boy,' he said once, without looking up. Both boys braced themselves tightly.

'Right,' he said, pulling the pipe from his lips where it had stuck, rising in an abrupt fluster of his gown. 'Right. Fighting. I will not have fighting. I will not have loutish boys who punch one other like gutter-snipes. Well? Anything to say for yourselves? Collis?'

He looked at Lewis as he said this.

'No sir,' he said meekly.

'Drewer?'

'I'm . . . I'm Collis, sir.'

Mr Crowland took this personally, and Lewis could hear Collis whimper under the impact of the glower.

'Collis. Are you? Are you indeed? Drewer?' said without removing the glower from the wretched Collis.

'Yes, sir?'

'Behind the door, you will find my cane. Fetch it to me, boy.'

This was part of the ritual. He had expected it. He turned quickly and found it, propped alone in the corner, a purposeful bamboo with a curled handle, dark-stained, long and thick. He wanted to examine it, but the moment he touched it it seemed to become active in his hand. The fear returned to him and he felt himself become fragile and loose. As he handed the implement to the headmaster, he felt that he would not be able to hold up against the savage weight of it.

'Please, sir, please.' Collis was coming to his rescue.

'What?'

'Please may I be first, sir?'

'Why should you be first, eh, Collis? Eh?'

'Please, sir.'

'What would your father have said if he could see you now, Collis?'

Collis was weeping, stooped over, wretched.

'Over here then, Collis. I expected more of you. Three strokes.'

Lewis was glad to see how it would happen. Collis's terror fortified him. He was still afraid, but the fear seemed to have settled into a white numbness, a tension that, for the moment, held him. Mr Crowland took Collis by the scruff of the neck and positioned him precisely on the rug before the fire, then pushed his head down, at which his knees buckled.

'Straighten yourself, boy. Legs straight; touching toes.'

Collis tried, wobbling. Mr Crowland stepped back and swished the cane about, limbering it, then deftly swept it back in a long arc and drove it in. It struck with a tight thwack and Collis gave out a startled 'Oh!' Lewis watched as the old man took his time, flexed and examined the cane before arcing it back and down again a second time. He's enjoying himself, Lewis realised: Collis's cries, the way his legs were sagging, the trembling of his lank posteriors, these were a part of the old man's pleasure, punctuating this wretch-edness with the swing and jerk of his cane, grunting as he did so. Lewis watched with bewilderment; and now, suddenly, it was his turn.

'To your work now, Collis. Next time it will be six. Drewer?'

Lewis stepped back to give Collis space to blunder past him, his face screwed tight and leaking. The white space opened and Lewis could feel his heart fighting within him. He took a deep breath and stepped forward smartly, held up his head and met the old man's sweaty eye distinctly; the sight of it shrivelled his bravado at once. He turned and bent over, clenching his eyes shut, feeling himself begin to grow giddy. Quickly, quickly, he wanted to say; I'm going to fall over.

He heard the cane's descent, heard the blow more than he felt it; a bar of numbness came across his buttocks, beginning to glow, begin-ning to heat, beginning to sting wretchedly, to force tears into his eyes. He lifted his head and gasped as the second stroke came pounding over the first. He could not help the sound breaking from his mouth. The pain was multiple, expanding, slashing and throb-bing into his thighs, and the third stroke came.

'That's it, boy. Away with you now.'

It was an effort to lift himself. His buttocks seemed swollen gro-tesquely, stinging, blinding and choking him. He writhed as if he might slough this misery from him.

Mr Crowland was standing there with his hand out. He wants to shake my hand, Lewis thought, and this was appalling. He lifted his hand dumbly and the old man held it tightly, pumped it twice and then let it go.

'You took that manly, Drewer, manly.'

'Thank you, sir.'

He dreaded Collis waiting for him outside, but he was spared that. He hobbled along the dark, empty corridors with the drone of the school at its work about him. He made his way to the latrines, leant against one of the cubicle walls and sobbed with the blind, stupid shame of it. He had a vicious image of finding Collis and taking it out on him, of hitting him until he screamed. He hated himself for shaking hands with the old man. He hated the school and all it stood for, revealed to him at that moment. He saw, in the way the masters spoke to them, in the tasks they set them, in the rules with which they pursued them, in the whole purpose of the school, that ultimate pit of retributive violence which enforced and justified everything, into which they might be tipped randomly at any moment, pushed down by pain and humiliation. He loathed it, loathed it.

A while later, he did not know how long, he pulled down his trousers and examined the hot weals on his flesh. He urinated and washed his face, dried it on his sleeve and walked tightly back to his lesson. The master knew where he had been and indicated him, almost with embarrassment, to his desk. He felt the others sneaking glances at him, but he did not look up from his exercise, set his face and shut himself down.

. . . *two* . . .

The years of his preparatory school passed with terrible slowness. In later years, he recalled most of all feeling cold, feeling hungry and feeling bored. He made few friends, found that he was by nature not a joiner-in, but had the self-reliance to be left alone, brooding about by himself, doing what he was told and minding his own business. He was no scholar, although his mathematics was competent. The reading and writing, and the grind of languages, were purely penitential. He enjoyed the football, and in his senior years played for the school team, although his success was limited by a lack of any real competitiveness, and by his absolute lack of team spirit. He played for the physical exhilaration, for the shove and run and directed aggression that he could release on the muddy fields.

Weekly came the letters with the strange colonial stamps. There were always two pages written by his mother with, usually, a paragraph added by his father.

They lived in a bungalow amongst trees, near a river, where a great plain began to merge into scrub and then into jungle. It was very hot, every day, even during the rains. There were snakes and gigantic insects. The natives were friendly and gentle, but lazy and without any idea of honesty. They were quite a way from town, and had very little society, but they were very happy. Helena was growing into quite a little savage.

Lewis looked forward to these letters. They became the highlight of his week. He came to know his parents, over those years, better than he had done before. He built up a very precise picture of their life and dreamed of going out to join them; but not yet, when he was older, when he was a man. He set himself to his work always with them in mind, bearing himself in relation to them. He found that he could write back more freely and honestly than he had done before. He told his parents about his successes and his failures at school, criticised himself before them quite severely. He told them when he was beaten, told them why. At about eight weeks' remove they answered his letters, and he heard their voices then with an emotion that grew within him. At times, at simple reassurances, at encouragement or gentle admonition, his eyes would fill with tears of love for them.

Be brave, my boy, his father wrote. *Life is strange and we can never quite live up to the standards we set ourselves. Do not judge others by your own strengths, as you would not want them to judge you only by your weaknesses. Know your weaknesses and guard against inflicting them on others. Try to be happy. If our prayers and our love can make you happy, then you will be, very happy.*

In his last year at school, they wrote to tell him that he had another sister, Naomi.

At the end of term he was released from the solitude of dormitory and classroom to the absolute solitude of Uncle Harry's house.

The house had many rooms, each of them with its particular silence, its particular dread. It was a cold house and, as he moved through it, its coldness clung to him. He came to know himself in vast solitudes animated with fears that never quite came out of the dampness.

He began to distrust himself, to feel that his solitude was necessary to protect him from something dark and inimical. He began to know loneliness here, to long for a friend, but whenever there was a suggestion of another boy coming to stay, to play with him, he reacted with instinctive dread, ran off into his secret places and refused to countenance such an invasion of himself. He wanted friendship but did not know whether he would be capable of it, did not know how much of himself he would have to give away for it, had fantasies of something tragic and dreadful happening if ever he were to have to share his life with someone else.

'Aren't you lonely, Lew?' Uncle Harry would ask him.

'Sometimes,' he said.

'Bill Cameron's lad's about your age. Won't you let me ask him over?'

'I don't want to play, Uncle,' he said. 'I like being lonely. Really I do.'

'You're a strange boy, Lew, but then your mother was strange at your age, and your father, of course; he . . . do you miss them?'

'Yes.'

'Have you another letter from them?'

'I read you the last.'

'Yes. Ah, well. If you want to be alone, you shall be. I couldn't stand it if you were noisy. I like the quiet. I hear things very well. I love to sit here and listen to this old house. D'you like this house, Lew?'

'I prefer the woods.'

'Of course you do. That's right. I was never indoors when I was your age, wouldn't be now if I didn't have to be. You must take me out into the woods one day, Lew. I'd like that.'

The woods surrounded the house, beyond ragged parkland; and beyond the woods were purposeful farmsteads where other families lived in a normality that he spied upon sometimes, but which seemed quite beyond his reach.

He came to know the woods well, was easier here than in the house, although the weather too often confined him there. The woods were large and dark, but at least they were alive. He watched birds and came to know their names. He found books to tell him about the trees and fungi. He sought to learn about the woods, although he knew there was something here that he could never learn, that all the names and all the rough botany he learnt merely mapped the woods, but could never explain them.

Sometimes he dreamed of disappearing into the woods, of losing himself within them and never coming out again; but it grew cold, the wind heaved the great trees above him, and unseen animals slithered and rustled amongst the leaves. In sudden panics he would run from the woods into the house, run to find Brady and be safe again.

Brady sustained an island of warmth within the house, without which he might have become lost and strange beyond recall. Brady was normality and ordinariness. Brady fed and clothed and washed him. Beyond Brady there were complexities and the shapes of nightmare: she was his point of sure commonsense, of eggs and toast before the glaring grate, of bathtime and storytime after a day in the wind, of clean, starched laundry that scratched until he had warmed and softened it. Beyond, everything was shadowy, threatening: with Brady everything was to be got on with, tidied up and sorted out. She listened to him whenever he wanted to speak, but only half-heard him, laughed at his seriousness, cobbled odd answers to his most troubling questions. She chivied him and chided his wayward-ness, but was never cross with him; he could not imagine anything that he might do that would make her cross. He suspected that the real world was the world beyond Brady and the nursery, but it was there that he had his thoughtless childhood.

He slept sometimes in Brady's room, when he was ill or fretful. He would watch her from the concealment of bedclothes, perhaps to catch her in some secrecy, some rite, a prayer offered to a hidden power. He saw only the practicality of her flesh, the loosening of her hair. It comforted him more than he was able to say. He slept at peace then, dreamless and sealed in a calm of the quiet seas and warm islands of his favourite stories; and later of the far world of plain and jungle and natives where his mother and father lived, where were the two bright little girls who were his sisters.

... *three* ...

He passed into the public school where Uncle Harry had been twenty years before him. At first it was just a vastness: the dormitories long, stark rooms, the corridors wide and flagged, the classrooms high and full of strange books and symbols that bore the implications of vast ranges of complex knowledge, the whole institution filling houses and halls, by which, in his first days, he was dwarfed, intimidated, scurrying along with the others, trying to find some sort of bearing, some sort of routine that would protect and sustain him. It was more than the size of the place, however. In his dormitory and classes he was amongst other boys, similarly dwarfed; but above them, in the levels into which they would rise, were not boys but young men, powerful, self-assured beings stamped with an individuality that, as he found the safety from which to watch them, daunted him. The solitude he had established would not, he felt, protect him for much longer.

At the prep school, the prefects had been favourites of the masters, their errand-boys and monitors: here, the prefects wielded an authority that seemed at times to be more than the masters; and, unlike the masters, they were not removed from the objects of their authority; on the contrary, they knew the world they ruled intimately, and plied themselves upon it with a cruelty that was precise and intimate. It was hardly a week before Lewis had been identified as a 'sulky little arse' and slippered in full view of his dormitory with his pyjama trousers round his ankles. The pain was tolerable – Crowland had had a far heavier hand – but the coarse public enjoyment generated by this punishment brought him humiliation on a scale he had never imagined. He quickly set himself to conform immaculately, his heart hard within him and a cold viciousness braiding itself through everything he did.

He was never quite a bully, for that would have required him to amass a pack; but he was vicious when crossed. He felt continually cornered by trivial things, by casual remarks, by infringements of his space or rights. To push in front of Drewer in a queue would be to invoke a sharp fist jabbed into the kidneys; to borrow his protractor without his permission earnt an ear twisted into agony; to make a comment about his academic blunders meant a close confrontation in the dormitory or prep room. Once they made him an apple-pie bed, but he knew whose idea it had been and he dragged the fat fool out of his own bed and slapped his head until, a wobbling heap of tears, he went and remade Lewis's.

In some of these aggressions he was brought to task, subjected to the customary punishment; but they knew that he was hardened to it. He played, anyway, a fierce game of rugger, and the prefects began to see in him a wild boy of much potential. His housemaster, however, a sensitive man who had returned from the war with an instinctive disgust at violence, was worried by him, brought him up to tea with his wife and, when she had tactfully withdrawn, attempted to draw Lewis out. He failed. The boy sat on his sofa in a knot of awkwardness, brought to the point of tears by the kind questioning. In the end, the housemaster let him sit there in silence whilst he studied him, saw the hurts and self-contempt that were twisting within him, and was afraid that, before long, something would go seriously wrong.

It might have done. Lewis, as the first term passed, sank into wretchedness. There was something wrong with him. He hated everyone around him with a fury that was never far from the surface. He woke each morning in a sweat of dread. He wondered who he was going to have to fend off today, knew that one day he would go too far, that someone would really break through to him and he would disintegrate into a mess of rage and shame. They would send him away then, and he would be on his own, entirely, lost. He was desperately lonely but had no side of himself that could open enough to admit anyone. At times he wanted so badly to join in with their gossip and their games, felt sick and angry when they moved back from him: at times he despised them entirely, and this was frankly easier. There was something wrong with him.

Then, quite miraculously, he made a friend.

He knew O'Neele, of course, a quiet, soft-faced boy, tall with bright blond hair and large eyes. He was a scholar and musician of impressive quality. Often he wept, huddled over his desk, dropping tears onto his book. He was said to be homesick. There was some shadow over his family: his father, apparently, had not fought in the war, had perhaps been a conscientious objector. He attracted some malevolence but was really too easy a target. Lewis sympathised with him, saw in him another pool of misery, but knew there was little he could do.

Then one evening in the second term, Lewis came into the latrines to see a crowd of boys huddling about one of the open cubicles, sniggering and taunting. He could not see the object of their spite, but as they had not noticed his arrival, he concluded that some plot was being hatched against him. He moved quietly to the edge of them.

Between the bodies, Lewis could see O'Neele squatting on the lavatory, huddled over and whimpering. They noticed him then, and shuffled together.

'O'Neele needs a nappy change,' one of them said.

'You're disgusting, Dover,' Lewis said, moving in on the boy who had spoken.

They fell silent then, looked at one another. They knew the way he spoke and they were apprehensive. Dover, whistling a nursery rhyme, strutted off with his hands in his pockets and the others followed him, leaving Lewis alone in the place with the wretched O'Neele.

Lewis used the urinal and, when he had done, turned to see O'Neele still huddled up. He went to the cubicle.

'O'Neele? They've gone . . . what's wrong? . . . O'Neele?'

'I've had an accident.'

'An accident?'

'In my bloody underpants.'

'Oh.' He understood then. He did not think of O'Neele, but of Dover, wanted to go and find him and punch him. 'Look,' he said at last. 'Take them off. You can wash them in the basin. I'll keep a look-out for you . . . all right? . . . O'Neele? . . . For God's sake, O'Neele, you can't sit there all night.'

At last, O'Neele unlocked himself. Lewis moved off and sauntered about the entrance to the latrine, wondering what he would do if any of the seniors appeared. He did not look back, but heard O'Neele at a basin.

At last O'Neele joined him.

'Thanks, Drewer. Thanks a lot.'

They stood there for a moment, looking at one another.

'Don't you hate this bloody place?' O'Neele said at last, and a smile of fierce mutuality was exchanged between them.

Without ever designing it, he and O'Neele began to find one another's company, whenever the brutal busyness of the routine allowed them to. They could not eat together and were in different forms, but they would meet in the evening, lounge about the prep room together and, on free afternoons, would go up to the music room where O'Neele practised and Lewis sat on the floor and listened to him.

This was what sealed it, listening to O'Neele play, his long body loose and his hands smoothing out the keyboard effortlessly, making the music turn and flow under his fingers. Lewis was amazed at his skill. It was another world which he had never imagined. The music made him swell with melancholy and longing, lifting him out of the squalor of himself for minute after minute.

'How did you learn to play like that?' Lewis asked him.

'I don't know. I practise a lot, but it's just something that I can do. You know. It's the only thing that makes life worth living here really.'

They exchanged information about their homes, a sure sign of intimacy in that place where home might have been on a different planet. Lewis asked him about his father.

'He's a professor of geography,' O'Neele said. 'And his father was a shop assistant. My father was Old Bollock's tutor at college. That's why I'm here, I suppose.'

'Is it true that he didn't fight in the war?'

'He wasn't fit. He has . . . something wrong with his heart, but . . . but I don't think he would have gone even if he'd been able to. He didn't approve of the war. Did your father go?'

'He was a soldier before the war, a regular. He went on one of the first boats. He was . . . wounded, sort of. He went mad. It made him mad.'

O'Neele was silent, under the weight of this revelation.

'He got better,' Lewis said, shaking himself free of the thoughts. 'He joined the colonial service, looking after a whole country of natives.'

Lewis could not understand what the sensitive O'Neele saw in him.

He was gross and brutal and stupid and expected that his friend would pass beyond him, find other more compatible souls. He was afraid of this because his hours with his friend were the first hours of any sort of contentment that he had had in this place.

O'Neele was still occasionally the victim of the pack, but Lewis knew better than openly to fight his battles for him. He cried less now and, after playing the piano at a house concert, he began to gain some respect. Lewis still had troubles, was still regularly beaten, but he felt that he was inviting it less, that it was all becoming easier. He had someone to share it with now. O'Neele would sometimes help him with his prep, explain things that he had failed to grasp in the ache of the classroom; so that side of his life too became easier.

He felt that the relationship was still profoundly one-sided, and this made him uneasy; then one day O'Neele was late for dormitory inspection, very late, came up mumbling useless excuses, and Lewis watched wretchedly as his friend was commanded to bend over the end of his bed and slippered heartily.

'You're never late,' Lewis said to him next day.

'I thought it was time I got walloped.'

'You did it deliberately?'

'I suppose so.'

'Did he hurt you?'

'Not as much as I thought he would. I was bloody scared, Drewer, when it came to it. I nearly piddled myself.'

They laughed and O'Neele lowered his shorts for Lewis to inspect the bruising, telling him that it was worse than it actually was.

He was not entirely easy about this, for he knew that O'Neele had submitted himself to this in a perverse token of solidarity with his wayward friend. He felt a strange honouring in this and felt himself moved into a position of importance that he was not sure he was capable of fulfilling. Where might he lead his friend next?

. . . *four* . . .

In the summer holidays, O'Neele was to come to stay. Lewis was nervous of his arrival, wondering if the friendship that had flourished under the dark pressure of school would be sustained in the empty haunts of the old house and woods, wondering how he would manage the opening of his final solitudes to the presence of another. He wanted O'Neele to be happy here so badly that it seemed ominous.

In the event it all worked wonderfully. O'Neele played his sonatas for Uncle Harry who was much impressed. He was impressively polite to Brady who in turn set herself to bring every sort of delicacy up from the kitchens, to supply and indulge the boys in every way she could. O'Neele found the old house limitlessly interesting, and Lewis took a new pride in the place, showing his friend round, explaining things, learning himself much that he had never known about it to feed his friend's curiosity. They played hide and seek amongst the dusty rooms; they romped and tussled, played games of snakes and ladders with each of them making new rules in the middle of it, both reduced finally into heaps of stupid giggling. They even moved to first names; O'Neele's was Joseph, or Joey. The summer opened around them gloriously.

He was apprehensive about taking his friend into the woods, for here his greatest secrets lay. He dreaded Joey O'Neele brushing them away with his laughter, exposing all his fears and fantasies as the childishness he knew them to be. Then Brady suggested a picnic, and Joey brightened at the prospect so visibly that Lewis had to concur. They set off very early and wandered down one of the larger paths. Lewis felt the trees cluster about them. He began privately to mark his favourite places, the tunnels he knew through to clearings and to steep banks where you could slide. He wanted to go there, to give that to O'Neele, but could not bring himself to suggest it. He tossed his head back to let the clear sunlight fall upon it. When he looked at his friend he found himself the subject of a curiosity.

'These woods scare me a bit,' he said.

'I know what you mean. But . . . but it's really good here, Lewis, isn't it?'

They smiled and Lewis knew then that it was all right, that he understood.

'Come on, Joey. Let's go through here.'

'There's no path.'

'Don't worry. I know the way.'

They made their way through to a little clearing, a space where the sun fell and a patch of soft grass provided a carpet for their picnic. They had both become silent and in the silence Lewis knew that his friend felt what he felt. It was exciting and he wanted to talk about it, but did not know what to say. He felt a longing come to the surface of his flesh.

They shared the bread and cheese, the meat and lemonade, ate hungrily then lay back in the rising sunlight. Lewis relaxed and felt himself drift under the high blue sky, a slow, precise enchantment flowing through him. It was not a detachment, for he was intensely aware of his friend, lying as he lay, looking as he looked. He knew that he was waiting for him to speak.

'Lewis?'

'Yes?'

'D'you ever . . . think about girls?'

'Girls? No. Not really. Do you?'

'Oh yes. I have . . . I have this dream of playing the piano in a big room, with a girl listening to me, leaning on the piano and listening.'

'What sort of girl?'

'A beautiful girl, of course, with long hair, black hair, and big eyes which she closes and opens very slowly.'

Lewis imagined this and it made him suddenly very happy, lifted something in him. It seemed to fit his mood perfectly. He saw the girl, watched her move, lift herself, turn, a loose dress rustling about her. Then the private intensity of this caught him, made him embarrassed. He sat up and looked down at his friend who lay straight out with his hands behind his head, his eyes closed.

'Sex!' O'Neele said emphatically.

'What?'

'Sex. You know what sex is, don't you, Lewis? . . . Don't you?'

147

O'Neele shuffled up on one elbow and looked at Lewis, his face bright and laughing again, making Lewis uneasy.

'Lewis? You know about babies and all that, don't you?'

'I suppose so.'

'Tell me, then.'

'Women have them. Mothers.' Lewis assumed, now he came to think about it for the first time, that babies somehow grew like fruit within the bellies of women, but he knew even as he thought it, that there was more to it than this, knew that he didn't know. He asked.

O'Neele lowering his voice, told him what it was, what men did. As he heard it, although he had no notion of it before, he felt as if he had always known it. He felt himself lifted up and able to see things suddenly from a clear height that made him gasp. He laughed and O'Neele laughed; then he thought and began, clumsily, to try to imagine the act and was perplexed again.

'Have you ever. . . . ?' he asked.

'Good God, no. I'm only fourteen, Lewis,' he said. 'But I think about it all the time. Actually . . . it's bad for you to think about it too much.'

'Why?'

'Because . . . because you end up . . . playing with yourself . . . I do , anyway. And that's bad for you, apparently.'

This required further explication. Lewis was fascinated, understood at once the hardness that came into his penis, often when he woke. He had once even done what O'Neele was describing, had instinctively touched himself and had produced a little semen in a flush of sleepy pleasure. He was amazed at O'Neele's knowledge, roused by it even.

Practical exploration soon became both logical and adventurous. They knelt together side by side, shuffled down their shorts and admired one another's stiffness. O'Neele went first, pumped quickly and efficiently and then held still as the semen bulged and dripped. Then he knelt back and watched as Lewis performed, matching his speed at first, then finding his own, slower rhythm, closing his eyes as he felt the little surge knot and break at the end of his erection.

Afterwards, as they walked back, they felt, not shame, and certainly not embarrassment, but as if they had exchanged something that could not be returned. They smiled complicitly, but did not discuss what had happened.

They felt little shivers of guilt under the eye of Brady and, after they had gone to bed, they lay in the darkness and speculated whether she had ever done it with a man. They felt as they talked that they were entering dark and forbidden territory, the world of grown-ups, and they shivered and giggled into the night.

When O'Neele had returned home, Lewis's solitude returned with a new dimension. Thinking of his friend, dreaming of him, sometimes as a boy, sometimes as a girl, with breasts and that dark genital potential that he could only imagine vaguely, he attended to the erections that came to him nightly now as he dipped down towards sleep. He stroked himself into that moment of bright liquidity and sunk back into the warm clutch of his dreams.

. . . *five* . . .

His arrival at school for the new term was the worst he had ever faced, the atmosphere of carbolic brutality catching him by the throat. He held himself in and kept his head down over his unpacking amongst the excitement and greetings that jabbered about him. He did not want to see O'Neele at once, not until he had become a little more adjusted, a little more certain of himself.

He saw him going into supper and they exchanged a smile. Afterwards, in the half-hour before they had to go to bed, he wandered over to O'Neele's box in the prep room.

'Hello,' he said.

'Hello, Lewis. Have a choc.'

They shared an expensive box of confectionery, pigging themselves before someone noticed and O'Neele was forced to hand them round the room.

'Did your uncle get my letter?' O'Neele asked.

'Yes. I had to read it to him.'

'It was a wonderful holiday, really wonderful, Lewis. God, isn't it awful to be back here?'

'I nearly told my uncle that I wasn't coming back,' Lewis said. This wasn't entirely true, but as he said it, it became true. He did not belong here, could not belong here, would not if it meant giving up one more ounce of himself.

'Lewis?'

'What?'

'I may . . . may be leaving.'

'Leaving? When?'

'Well . . . maybe soon, maybe before half-term. I took a scholarship exam for this music college, you see. I would live at home and . . . and, well, really just devote myself to music.'

Lewis felt something sink inside him.

'You can't go, Joey,' he said. 'I'd go mad here without you to talk to.'

'Oh, you'll be all right. I mean, we'll still be friends. I'll write and you can come and stay with me, at Christmas like we decided.'

Lewis had nothing to say. He stood looking into his friend's face and twisting in a desire to put his arms around him.

They spent almost every spare moment from then on in one another's company, met up at breaks and wandered through wet afternoons out of bounds into the woods and lanes about the school.

O'Neele became franker about his impending departure.

'I actually had an idea that I might be going when I came up to stay.'

'Why didn't you mention it?'

'I thought . . . I thought it might spoil things. I think it would've done, too. I wanted to pretend that it could go on and on. I really wish you were coming with me, but . . . you see, Lewis, we've become . . . friends, proper friends, and, well, that doesn't really work here. I mean, they'll start thinking we're . . . odd.'

'I don't care what anybody thinks.'

'Yes, but you can't avoid caring, Lewis. I mean, the only way you can get by here is if you join in, or if no-one notices you. God knows, you tried if anyone did, and look where it got you.'

Lewis knew this was right, became at once resigned and yet uplifted that O'Neele should know him so well. It burnished his sense of himself, a sense that he was going to need badly in his friend's absence.

As the day of O'Neele's departure approached, Lewis steeled himself to open the one unspoken matter between them. They were in the music room at the time and aware of one another with a particular sharpness.

'Joey? You remember when we went into the woods?'

He laughed. 'Oh yes.'

'Are we . . . queer?'

'Oh, I don't think so. It was just . . . a bit of fun, wasn't it?'

'Might we be?'

'I don't know. Does it bother you, Lewis?'

'A bit. Does it bother you?'

'No. Not at all. I thought it was . . . good fun. Tell me something, Lewis. When you, you know, do it, do you think of boys or girls?'

'Girls.'

'There you are, then.'

Lewis was reassured, briefly, until, running through O'Neele's logic, he knew that he had not been entirely honest.

'Not always girls, Joey. Sometimes I think of you.'

O'Neele was silent then, and Lewis though he had offended him.

'Me too,' he muttered.

No more was said on the subject, or needed to be said. They would meet at Christmas, away from the claustrophobia of school, from the shame and sordidness in which any contact might have embroiled them. There were boys who did such things together, whose behavior became known, who were subjected to sniggering and shame. They could not have borne that. It is better, Lewis thought, that he should go.

He went and Lewis drew back into himself once more.

He muddled through the term. He did his work, perhaps better than before, accepting its drudgery, became immune to it perhaps. He lost his interest in sport, which seemed to embody the spirit of the school, which spirit he knew to be dead for him. He ate and slept and did what they told him. He felt himself dulling day by day.

There was a complication about Christmas. The O'Neeles were going to be away, so the visit was deferred. Lewis was less disappointed than he'd imagined he would be. It seemed inevitable. He knew that he had lost his friend, that his chatty letters were coming from an increasing distance. He imagined Joey O'Neele glowing in a bright world of music and beautiful girls, flourishing in his big, busy family whilst he was lost here in this sterile place.

He even lost the will to masturbate, at least in school. It was a dry pleasure in such a place, a common pleasure and sordid. He needed to be able to dream, and even that was fading. He was tired and listless and fell into sleep with a blank resignation. In the solitude of the holidays, however, on certain nights, he lost himself in extensive self-explorations, turning images through his mind, of O'Neele, of girls, of situations, woodlands, bedrooms, the energy amassing in him until it seemed to crackle with static, charged and dangerous. As he finally took hold and brought himself out, achieved usually by simple, fierce pressure rather than by any caress, his mind filled with images of killing, of throats cut, of the crack of a gallows-trap, of the jerk of a body under a fusillade of rifle fire. When it was done, he lay there in a heavy sweat, his heart thumping, his eyes open to the moving shadows of the night, to the shuffling and creaking of the house. He felt, at these times, that he was capable of anything and it frightened him.

. . . six . . .

Eighteen months later, at last, he boarded a train south and was borne into the heart of London, amazed by its size, by the unimaginable complexity that piled up beyond his carriage window, the unending mill of people who moved through the great station concourse amongst the dynamic exhalations of engines, their manifold cries and hurry echoing into the high girders. He was bewildered and apprehensive, but the busyness and anonymity of the place began to find him, to generate a new excitement. He wished, almost, that he might turn and disappear into the press.

Joey O'Neele was almost unrecognisable. He had grown into lankiness, grown his hair into a blond shock. He wore round tortoiseshell glasses. His face was lean and, Lewis, felt, dauntingly handsome. He wore loose, comfortable clothes, no tie, soft shoes. Lewis was diminished and awkward, but Joey shook his hand and smiled his old smile, led him out to a taxi.

On the way out to where he lived in a street of high terraced houses, he absorbed Lewis in questions about school which Lewis did not enjoy answering for all his friend's laughter. He did not want to belong to school any more. He wanted to be initiated into this world. He glanced out at the passing streets, the shops and the shoppers, the building sites and landmarks. It excited him with a potential that he knew to be erotic.

The O'Neeles were very kind to him. Joey took him round the sights, to cafés and picture-houses, repaid Lewis's hospitality with a largesse that was embarrassing. But it was not the same. Joey was sociable, had a wide circle of friends, some of whose houses they visited; strange boys with musical talents like deformities; and girls, deeply serious, contemptuously intelligent, even to look at whom would have been insulting. Lewis felt claustrophobic within these houses. 'And do you play, Lewis?' they asked him. He shrank back, talentless and inarticulate. He felt himself continually on display here, felt them appraising him, seeing through his emptiness. He was not happy. He wanted to go home.

In the second week of his stay, however, as he sat up in bed reading a novel that Professor O'Neele had told him that he would enjoy, but which he could not understand, there was a knock on his door, and Joey slipped in, closing the door behind him, listening.

'You want a drink, Lewis?' he whispered.

'I had some milk, thanks.'

'Bugger milk.'

He produced a half-bottle of gin from his dressing-gown pocket, collected Lewis's tooth-mug, and decanted half-an-inch into the bottom of it.

'What about you?' Lewis asked.

'I'll use the bottle. Cheers.'

The gin seemed to bore a hot hole down Lewis's throat and into his chest. He coughed and gasped and Joey laughed, swigged from the bottle and smacked his lips.

'Like it?' Joey asked.

'Not much.'

'Drink up, though. It'll make you feel warm and blurry.'

'D'you drink a lot?'

'No. The parents would go berserk if they knew I drank at all, but what can you do, eh?'

'Would you get beaten?'

'No. They don't go in for that. I would get lectured, and lectured and lectured. I'd rather get walloped. At least it's over with then.'

'Don't tell me you'd rather be back at school.'

'No, I don't actually think I would. But . . . but there are things I miss, now I'm not there any more. I miss being the odd one out, being the only one with any music. Everyone's got music here. Lots and lots of it. And I miss you, Lewis. Really I do.'

Lewis was silent. He didn't believe this, could not see how it could be true.

'Look, Lewis, I'm sorry. You've had a pretty grim time here. I wanted . . . I wanted to show you everything, but it's all a load of rot, really. Oh, it's fun and all that, but it's not real. They're all very clever, very talented, but, I'll tell you something, under all that, they're fake, all of them. I wish you lived here. I wish we could share a flat or something. Wouldn't that be great?'

'What could I do? I couldn't do anything.'

'Oh, you could find yourself a job. That's easy. In a year or two, maybe. Think about it, Lewis. I'm serious. I really need you here.'

'Why?'

'Don't you know?'

Lewis felt himself going warm. He put the tooth-mug to his lips but only the last drip was left.

'Because . . . because you're not a bloody musician and . . . and because you're my friend. Because you know what I'm like. Because when I'm with them I'm just as fake as they are, more fake, but with you . . . because, Lewis, there're all these beautiful women here and all they want me to do is to accompany them on the bloody piano, and all I want to do is to touch their tits. Thank God there's someone I can say that to at last.'

He looked at Lewis with a sudden helplessness. Lewis saw him as he had always been, the masks of his sociability and his talent dropped. It made Lewis laugh and his laughter caught O'Neele and before long they were giggling and sniggering together in a sudden access of liberty.

'I'm drunk,' O'Neele said.

'So am I, I suppose.'

'I'll tell you what we'll do tomorrow. We'll go to an art gallery.'

'An art gallery?'

'Yes. To look at the women.'

'In the pictures?'

'Not in the pictures, dopey. Real women. They walk through those rooms in a trance. They look at all that art and it makes them glow with sex. Lewis, it's wonderful, wonderful.'

The art gallery lived up to its promise. They walked together from room to room, not looking at one another because that would have caused them to giggle. They sat on leather benches, but never too long in one place. For the first time, Lewis opened his eyes and filled his head with the shapes of shoulders and breasts and waists and, above all, the faces, the serious, the bored, the languid and the perplexed, each printing itself upon his imagination with a shock of potential. I could step up, he thought, I could speak to her. She would turn and see me. He never came within a remote distance of living out any of these scenes. The women he watched were as unattainable as the women in the canvases beyond them.

They went for a sandwich in a tea room. Joey had suggested a pub, but Lewis wanted somewhere less adventurous. Over sandwiches and milk, they discussed their morning. Joey was animated and openly lascivious, had noted particular girls, a couple of whom he claimed he actually knew.

'Did you see that one in the green, Lewis? On her own. About eighteen. Looked as if she was avoiding someone. Looked shocked at that thing with the satyrs, but couldn't take her eyes off it, kept trying to peer closer to see what was actually going on behind the bushes. We should've tried, we really should've done.'

Lewis couldn't compete with this, hardly remembered any one of them distinctly, was filled with a general desire that now, out of the electricity of the gallery, was grown lumpish and troubling. Whereas Joey's excitement was bubbling out, Lewis felt his turn within him. The distance between himself and women seemed unbridgeable. He felt the darkness gather in him again, wanted to escape, to be back home, alone; but he knew the moment he thought it that solitude was no longer possible. The women in the gallery, and the world they represented, the whole complexity of London and the vast net of lives and relationships that spread about him, was essential to him now. He wanted what Joey had offered him last night: the freedom of this place, the freedom of himself amongst it. It was not an easy freedom, that he knew, for even as he imagined it, he felt its shadow moving in on him: and the shadow was subjection.

He returned, meanwhile, to school to serve out his time. In what was to be his last term, he became a junior dormitory prefect. Towards the end of term, when the head of dormitory was ill, a cocky little boy called Matthews distinguished himself by refusing to run an errand for a sixth-former on the grounds that he didn't see why he should run around after a fat Jew.

Lewis felt himself assuming a strange incarnation as he appeared in the dormitory just before lights-out, the gym shoe hidden behind his back. An irony jagged into him, prodding him cynically, almost making him laugh as he went through the ritual.

'Matthews? Out of bed.'

'Me? Why? What have I done?'

'Abuse. You know what I'm talking about.'

'Oh, come on, Drewer.'

'Am I going to have to fetch some help?'

Matthews began slowly to extract himself from his sheets.

'How many?'

'It's just gone up to four.'

'Oh . . . come on, Drewer. That's not fair.'

'Five.'

'I've got a boil on my bum. Go and ask Matron.'

'Six.'

The dormitory had begun to titter. Lewis grew nervous, did not know whether the tittering was directed at him or at Matthews.

'Look . . . please, Drewer. . . .'

Lewis grabbed his fat arm and yanked him out into the middle of the dormitory. He gave a small squeal. Lewis turned him and shoved him over the end of his bed, pulled at his pyjama trousers which were tied tight. Matthews squealed again and fumbled at the knot.

His buttocks were large and white. They revolted Lewis. He swung the gym shoe at them ferociously three times, driving his anger and disgust out into the boy's flesh; then he had had enough.

'All right, Matthews. Get into bed.'

The boy bunched his trousers up and shambled, not into bed, but down the dormitory.

'Where are you going?' Lewis roared, but he did not turn.

'He's piddled himself,' someone said, and the laughter broke out in a storm about him.

'Shut up!' Lewis bellowed and was obeyed at once. 'I'm in the mood for it tonight,' he added as he walked to the light, 'so if there's any noise, I'll be back.' There was no more noise.

Back in his own study, Lewis felt suddenly sick. Beating Matthews had given him an erection.

. . . *seven* . . .

It had always been understood that, on completing school, Lewis would sail out to join his parents, at least for an extensive vacation during which he might contemplate the shape of his life before him. After his holiday with Joey, he knew that he had to be in London. He wrote to his father with as much resolution and determination as he could concoct.

If it is what you want, his father wrote, *then it is what you shall have. You know yourself better than we do now.* This was his ticket to freedom.

He became a clerk in a small bank in the City. He took lodgings in the house of a retired schoolmaster and his wife, friends of the O'Neeles, had his own room, but ate with his hosts, a pleasant, quiet couple who made a fuss over him. Their own son had died in the war, and Lewis was perpetually uncomfortable under their sentimental regard for him. He retreated behind a mask of politeness and dared not, for the first two months of his stay, even miss supper. The erotic lure of London was as far away here as it had ever been, although he did not mind that yet, needing to settle and establish himself. He read a lot, went to bed early and rose at dawn, his favourite time, with the smoke of the city lingering over the rooftops and everything settled into its own quiet. He experienced a loneliness at these moments, but it was resonant and romantic.

The work was mundane to the point of tedium. He filled in forms and copied columns of figures into ledgers. He visited other banks and public institutions with bundles of papers to be signed or stamped. He ate his landlady's thick sandwiches but washed them down with half a pint of ale in a smoky, noisy pub, soaking up some of the brashness of the commercial world, beginning to acquire a taste for it. He didn't mind the work, became intrigued by the whole mercantile structure. He took books from the library and began to teach himself how it all worked.

Mr MacBlaine, the junior partner, took a liking to him. He had served with Lewis's father and with Uncle Harry, and Lewis was embarrassed by the vicarious prestige this gave him. He struggled to justify himself on his own merits and did so. Within a year, he had been given a promotion and a pay rise. He began to be given access to the accounts, began to meet the smaller clients, began to feel that he belonged here. It was secure and certain and progressive.

His first evening engagement was to the MacBlaines' for dinner. MacBlaine had two daughters, a year older and a year younger than Lewis respectively. Mrs MacBlaine was consumptive and lived abroad, so Lewis ate dinner between these two girls under their father's paternal smile. They were of a different mould to O'Neele's musical girls, giggly and spoilt and both rather stupid, brought up to be so, Lewis thought. They flirted with him in competition, made him nervous for, although he did not find either of them specifically attractive, they gave off a bland sexuality at which his inexperience lurched. He drank more than he should have drunk and left in a blushing blur, lapsing, once he had achieved the safety of his bed, into a shamelessly pornographic fantasy featuring the combined Miss MacBlaines, as if deliberately to smear them with filth so that he might not think of them further.

At weekends, he met up with Joey. On Saturday they would go out, to a music hall or club, sometimes with a crowd of Joey's fellow students, often alone; never, in those first months, with girls. Their sallies were ostensibly erotic quests; they did a lot of watching, a lot of fantasising, but satisfied themselves usually with getting drunk. They discussed the possibility of tarts, but neither had the stomach or the courage for that. Joey, anyway, was developing a relationship with a girl called Candida.

'It's pure lust,' he told Lewis. 'She knows what I'm after and knows that once she gives it to me, that'll probably be that. But she puts up with me.'

When Lewis eventually met Candida, he was surprised. She was certainly not as stupid as Joey advertised her to be. She was languid and sarcastic and fond of his friend, treating him like a tiresome little brother, whilst Joey, in her presence, beamed with a pride and delight in her. She did not approve of Lewis at all. Joey told him later that she thought him a bad influence.

Roberta, the elder Miss MacBlaine, was married and Lewis was invited. There were a lot of their friends there, rich young men and women whose combined shallowness depressed him. They seemed, as he drank champagne and watched them laugh and chatter and touch, to inhabit an easiness that made him uncomfortable, first in its exclusion of him, but soon in its evident superficiality. None of it meant anything.

He tagged along with them when they went dancing, became attached to Georgina, the younger Miss MacBlaine, who clung onto him and told him she thought he was lovely, that he shouldn't be so lonely, that he should enjoy life more. Taking her home in a taxi, both of them drunk, he hauled her against him and kissed her, smeared his lips over hers and felt, through the blur of alcohol, the softness of her body pressed upon his. She was passive and compliant in his arms but then grew afraid of him suddenly, pulled away and began to cry under Lewis's cold consideration.

Eighteen months into London, he moved to his own small flat. He learnt how to cook simple food, bought a gramophone and listened to music. He went to bed early and rose to walk the three miles to work through the park and along the river embankment. He went to the opera house occasionally, dined in a small club twice a week, took a newspaper. He grew a thin moustache and smoked, after his dinner, an expensive cigarette. He lived neatly and regularly.

He would go drinking with Joey O'Neele now and then, but that whole world was fading from him, drifting away. Candida, whose dark contralto voice Joey accompanied on an increasingly regular basis, quite abruptly admitted him to her bed, after which he became her puppy-dog, amazed at his good fortune, stupidly happy. He and Lewis had nothing much to talk about any more.

Lewis inhabited a hermetic masculine world of the bank and his bachelor flat. He had a circle of acquaintances, but no friends. He felt his world closing around him and was glad of its security and certainty. He realised that he had set a course for himself that could well last him the rest of his life. The darkness and desires of his adolescence seemed to have become domesticated, dulled, unimportant. Occasionally he would see a woman who would stir something in him. He would watch her, be pleased by her, but he never crossed the gap.

A month after his twenty-first birthday, MacBlaine called him in to discuss the Bratley account. Sir Godfrey Bratley had inherited a small provincial engineering firm from his grandfather thirty years ago. During the war, he had moved into armaments, made a very great deal of money, acquired a knighthood and a society wife who had given him four daughters. Since the war, he had made attempts to diversify, but times had gone hard and the speculative imagination which had made him his fortune faltered. The problem was simply how much could be salvaged from the wreckage of the business, which was terminal, to allow the family to live.

MacBlaine had known them a long time. Their various accounts had been one of the stand-bys of the bank, and he found the whole business extremely sensitive. He brought Lewis in to show his hard, professional face. Sir Godfrey himself had retired to a nursing home to cultivate symptoms appropriate to a broken man. Lady Bratley arrived at the bank with her four handsome daughters, the eldest of whom was eighteen, the youngest ten, to throw herself upon MacBlaine's mercy. She emitted a continuous, dignified sniffing, patting the mousy head of her youngest child, who peered around the room with myopic incomprehension, fidgeting with boredom.

Lewis found the scene distasteful and farcical. MacBlaine explained categorically that the house in the country would have to go, that the town house would have to go, that the exclusive schooling would have to be replaced by something more functional, appealing at every injunction to Lewis.

'There's no alternative, my dear Lady Bratley. We've spent hours, haven't we, Drewer? Hours and hours.'

'Indeed, sir.'

'Mr MacBlaine. I beg you . . . simply . . . simply leave the address of the workhouse with Celia. They may expect us tomorrow.'

'Come now, Lady Bratley. Really, you do yourself more harm . . . giving way like this. I think we can, if we are very, very careful, secure an income of . . . of something approaching two thousand pounds per annum.'

'Two thousand pounds! Mr MacBlaine, when I married Sir Godfrey I had twenty thousand pounds, of my own money. . . .'

'Slightly more than that, Lady Bratley, if I remember, but . . . but capital, Lady Bratley, capital and that . . . that has been progressively eroded. I will explain it once again. . . .'

Two thousand a year. Lewis held his lips straight but could not keep the malicious gleam from his eyes. His salary was two hundred and fifty pounds. And what, he wondered, would be the salaries of those who lived out their lives in the terraced streets that clustered about the dead factory, whilst Lady Bratley went to the workhouse on two thousand pounds a year. He despised these people, was glad of their degradation.

As MacBlaine once more, in the simplest terms available, explained to Lady Bratley where her dowry had gone, Lewis was imagining them having to shed their fine clothes here and now, having to leave their fob watches and strings of pearls in a heap on MacBlaine's desk. He considered suggesting that they might take that one on as a secretary, enjoyed visualising her breaking her fingernails on sealing wax, watching her wilt with the fatigue and tedium of work.

'Might my mother have a glass of water, please?' the eldest girl said, turning to Lewis abruptly.

He did not move at once, blushed as if she were able to see what he had been thinking. Her strong face glared at him and he went cold.

'Please,' she said again. 'Mr Drewer?'

Lewis turned and left the office.

As he filled the glass, his hand trembled. He called to one of the juniors and told him to take in the water, could not go back in there, could not bear to have that girl look at him again. He locked himself in the lavatory and found tears of an inexplicable hurt filling his eyes.

When he emerged, they had left the bank and Lewis returned to MacBlaine, apologised, a small digestive problem, he said.

'A sad case, the Bratleys, Drewer,' MacBlaine said, 'very sad.'

'I liked the eldest girl,' he said, sorting out the papers on MacBlaine's desk. 'She'll do all right, find herself a husband within six months, although he will have his work cut out for him.'

'Nonsense, Drewer. Really. You worry me sometimes, you know.'

'Would you care to put a pound on it, sir?'

'Certainly not.'

. . . *eight* . . .

Celia Bratley had been betrayed. Her parents had brought her up with the certainties of wealth and social advantage, only to have deceived her. She blamed her mother more than her father: she knew nothing of the business, had only once in her life been in the town where the factory was situated, and never within sight of the works itself; but she had been brought up entirely within the grandiloquence of her mother's living, had taken as a fundamental truth that there was nothing she might do, no, not even commit murder, that the funds might not be found to cover. She regarded her father, in the aftermath of the disaster, in his illness which was developing from nervous collapse into something darker, as a kindly, foolish old man. Her mother would survive him and blame him thereafter, as she had always blamed him, for every dissatisfaction, every mote that lay in the languid path of her existence. Celia hated her mother, for her spineless profligacy, for the tyranny she exercised over her and her sisters, a vicious tyranny of spirit whilst their surfaces were pampered and neutralised by money; and she blamed her for the sudden abyss which the absence of money opened before her.

Money was the nourishment of her life; it had made her proud and distant, had given her the security of her selfhood. She had enjoyed the trimmings of wealth, but had not been extravagant. She had spent less than a quarter of her allowance, had preferred the weight of the money more than the pleasures it might purchase. Now the weight was gone and she felt loose, vulnerable, fragile; she hated this feeling with a fury that made her impossible to live with. Her mother and sisters avoided her. Her friends no longer called, no longer included her in their social designs. They had run from the family ruin, afraid of its contamination. She could understand that, accept it; they were right to drop her. But she knew, underneath this fiscal surface, that they avoided her because of what she had become now, her wounds open, the bitterness streaming from her at the slightest contact. She hated what she was becoming and sought only to have someone close enough to exercise that hatred upon; and then, late at night, after a day's loneliness, shut away avoiding the dirty little men who paced about their home measuring and valuing, she felt the hatred dissolve and reveal the emptiness that it covered, the emptiness of her life and the emptiness of herself, the stale uselessness of everything she had ever done.

Lewis's instinct had been right. Within two months of the family's acceptance of their penury, she realised that, for her, the only way out was marriage. She did not visualise married life in any detail at all. It was just the way out, leaving them all behind to rot in their own self-pity. It was essential. She began to swallow her bile and to become social again.

They had moved, by this time, rented a house in the suburbs amongst doctors and solicitors. The MacBlaines lived two streets away. She did not for a moment feel that she was enjoying herself at the musical evenings, the river picnics, the visits to dreary concerts by second-rate orchestras; but it was necessary.

She began to consider the young men, to turn her mind towards the reality of a marriage; and at this she felt a slow panic. She could not imagine one of them approaching her without a flinch of revulsion. She knew that she was, if not beautiful, at least striking. They came near, often, chatted and made stupid attempts at flirtation; but she froze them out, could not help doing it. She did not see how she would ever manage it.

She had always hated being touched, had shrunk even from her father's whiskery kisses. She had been told the facts of life by a schoolfriend when she was thirteen, and they had disgusted her. As she grew older she began to understand a little more of it, watched and saw how such a thing could be possible; but not for her, not for her. The idea of being naked, of being entered by a man, filled her with anger and disgust. That, she knew, would be the end of her. She had heard of marriages where an agreement was struck that there would be no physical intimacy. This had become her ideal: an older man, perhaps, who had been married before and had got all that out of the way. Now, in the biting air of her new reality, she knew that she was simply not rich enough to fund this ideal.

She began to watch Mildred, the eldest of her sisters, now seventeen, the prettiest of them, the most outgoing. Mildred found it easy, liked to have the boys clustering about her, laughed with them, went dancing, played games with them that Celia knew, even if Mildred didn't, were rehearsals for an adulthood that she would achieve without a murmur.

'You know, Mildred,' she said to her one day, 'you're turning into quite a little tart.'

Mildred had blanched and then burst into tears.

'At least you have the grace to be ashamed of yourself,' Celia said, wondering in a cold chamber of her mind why she was doing this.

'You know what they call you, Celia?'

'I don't give a damn what they call me.'

'They call you "The Curse", because you're such a permanent bloody pain.'

Celia left quickly, because she too had to cry, because she wanted to cry with Mildred, to put her arms about her and become her sister; and because she was incapable of this.

. . . *nine* . . .

Mr Drewer from the bank had somehow lodged himself in her mind. The experience that afternoon had been the most hateful of her whole life, and he was a part of it. She loathed MacBlaine, but that was easy to understand; he had made money out of them for years and then had foreclosed on them. Mr Drewer had been different, however: he was young, not part of the ubiquitous hypocrisy of adulthood; but this made it worse. There was something cold and cruel about him, unlike the squirming MacBlaine: it seemed as if he had been enjoying their degradation.

She had turned to him about to unleash her contempt upon him, but his look had stopped her. He had seemed for a moment frightened of her, frightened not of what she might have said to him, but of something that he had seemed to see in her. It was a passing thought, a moment's flash and jump that had sent a small shudder through her. He had left the office and she had waited restlessly for him to return. He had not returned. She did not see him again before they left, and this activated a disappointment in her that was quickly dispelled in the mounting practicalities.

She did not brood upon him thereafter, but she remembered him, a face, a moment, that had jumped out of the quotidian and sunk back again. She did not think further than that. When he appeared in her life again, however, she felt that she had somehow been expecting him.

She was at a concert with a group of friends. It was a charity concert and someone had given them tickets, a fashionable occasion at which Celia saw several of her old acquaintances who smiled at her with a faint condescension that made her angry. The programme consisted of interminable masses of loud orchestral tissue and, by the interval, Celia was bored and dreading another hour of it. She sat at a table in the crush bar whilst her escort went to fetch her a glass of wine. She poised herself vacantly, assumed an abstracted statuesqueness that usually deterred the casual trawlers.

Shortly, she became aware of a man standing beside her, and she intensified herself to drive him away. He was not driven away. He spoke.

'Miss Bratley?'

She did not turn at once, incurious as to his identity; then, slowly, she lifted her eyes, heavy with ennui, and found herself looking up at Mr Drewer.

'Are you well?' he asked.

'Yes. Thank you. Mr . . . Drewer, isn't it?'

'You remember me?'

'Oh yes. And how are things at the bank?'

'Oh . . . dull and prosperous, I suppose. Are you enjoying the concert?'

'Yes. It's quite splendid, isn't it?'

'Well. I can't say I'm enjoying it much. They are a very dreary orchestra. Have you heard them before?'

'I really can't recall.'

'You're not fond of music?'

'I really don't have an opinion.'

'You surprise me, Miss Bratley. Good evening.'

And he had moved away seconds before her pallid escort arrived breathless with the remains of a glass of wine, most of which had been spilt in the journey from the bar.

Again there was a sense of incompletion; as if he had come hurtling towards her and had deflected at the last moment, spun off somewhere else. She decided definitely that she did not like him, but this seemed too simple. She needed to have a clearer picture of him to dislike him. There was something that frustrated her here. It stacked onto the sum of her many dissatisfactions.

About a month after the concert, she was in one of the big stores collecting a package of toiletries for her mother. It was a hot day and she did not like shopping, did not like the continued extravagance that these purchases embodied. She handed the list to the assistant and sat to wait for their preparation.

'Excuse me, Miss Bratley?'

It was one of the senior assistants, not the one who had taken her order.

'What?' she said.

'Excuse me, but might I ask how you were . . . intending to pay for these purchases?'

'My mother does have an account here.'

'Ah. The point is, Miss Bratley. . . .' The voice was lowered to a tacky intimacy. '. . . There is quite a substantial amount outstanding on the account and we wondered if we might expect a settlement in the near future.'

A fierce discomfort came over her flesh.

'I will speak to my mother,' she said.

'Yes, well . . . well, we have written to her about this . . . I think . . . I think we would not be happy were the account to be extended any further at present. This is most distressing, most distressing, but you must understand. . . .'

She wanted to rise and leave at once, sweep away, but a surge of humiliation weakened her, brought tears to her eyes. This finally was the depth. About her the shop was busy, mahogany and plate-glass, the gleam of brass fittings, the assistants bobbing obsequiously and the customers with large, casual gestures making their purchases. It was a world of wide financial arrogance and she had just fallen out of the bottom of it, sat hunched on her chair leaking tears of misery and shame, about to be shown out by a side entrance, her right to be here revoked. She wanted to be dead.

She could hear them fussing about her. Any moment, one of them would touch her arm, would raise her and lead her away. She would scream, could feel it building up within her.

Then someone placed a parcel on her lap.

'Please, Miss Bratley, please. I am most terribly sorry. Consider . . . consider the matter closed.'

She jerked up her face. Did they dare to patronise her thus? Then she saw Mr Drewer a pace behind the assistant. He stepped forward, took the parcel and offered her his arm.

'I'm . . . I'm quite all right, thank you,' she said.

'I will see you to a taxi, Miss Bratley.'

She submitted, for it was the only way she could have left with any dignity. She could hardly breathe for the mortification of it. The sweet air of the store choked her.

Only out on the street did she begin to attempt to reassemble what had happened, to realise who was on her arm, leading her to the kerb.

'Mr Drewer,' she said.

He turned to her with a deep concern that made her shudder. He released her arm and she stood back and breathed deeply, smothered a cough, shook her head.

'Are you all right now?' he asked.

'Yes. Thank you. A little faintness. Nothing to. . . .'

He handed her the parcel. She had forgotten it, wondered how he came to have it, wondered why they had relented so swiftly; then she knew.

'Do I . . . do I owe you money, Mr Drewer?'

'Certainly not.'

'You did not pay for my mother's shopping, then?'

'It is of absolutely no consequence. Look, there's a taxi.'

'Wait. I will walk. Please.'

'Four miles? Please, Miss Bratley.'

She had begun to walk but he kept up with her, seemed to be parting the crowds before her. She wanted to be alone. She wanted to cry so badly that it hurt her.

He took her arm again and propelled her gently to the kerb, opened the door of a taxi and handed her inside. She could see him, through her tears, give directions to the driver, drop a pile of coins into his hand. She wanted to stop him, but the taxi was moving away and she submitted to her wretchedness.

She felt as if she had been sold to him for a parcel of scented soap and talcum powder.

. . . *ten* . . .

Lewis supposed that he was in love. It was not at all what he had expected, but then he had expected little. Love, he had supposed, was a softness, a melting, the way certain music made him feel. This was a restless, brutal longing that permeated his thinking, that made his days long, his motivations ragged and provisional.

She had disturbed him that first day in the office, but that had happened before with women; perhaps not quite as intimately as that, but then perhaps he had never before been as close to the source of the disturbance. Then, when he saw her at the concert, had engaged there with her languid arrogance, he found himself made angry by her in a way that he could not quite accommodate. He began to think about her, to find tentacles of fantasy adhering to her. They frightened him and he suppressed them.

He had seen her in the store, had followed her, watched her, seen her difficulty, and had stepped brilliantly forward to rescue her. He had not enjoyed doing anything in his life more than that. Later he thought it had been her humiliation that had stimulated him; but it was not that. It was simply that he was in a position to help her, to throw himself down in the path of something that was threatening her. Her humiliation was important in that it made his triumph the more absolute.

As she drove away in the taxi, he felt an extravagance of childish joy at the back of which, when he was alone, he knew was the possibility of her, the eroticism of her pride and her strong, angular body. He wanted not merely to possess her, but to lose himself within her, burrowed deep and drowning in the sensuality that she kept clamped within her.

Two days later a letter, marked *Personal* arrived for him at the

168

office. In it was a five-pound note and a covering letter, five lines of decorative scrawl.

Dear Mr Drewer, I hope this covers the expenses you incurred on my behalf yesterday. I must apologise for the state that you found me in, and must thank you for assisting me. I know that I can rely upon your discretion. Yours sincerely, Celia Bratley.

He wrote back: *Dear Miss Bratley, I am almost offended that you should need to remind me of my 'discretion'. That I was in a position to be of assistance to you was a matter of considerable pride and pleasure to me. I return your note, which is outrageously more than you owe me. Please consider the matter closed. Yours sincerely, Lewis Drewer.*

He had to wait excruciating months before he saw her again. He heard from MacBlaine, although he never actively sought information, that her father had died, that her mother seemed incapable of taking any sort of command of her finances, that they might have to move into the country, that Celia was doing something, was going to a day college to try to improve her languages.

'You would have lost your pound, Drewer. She's taking over, taking on the responsibility. A fine girl, that.'

Lewis could not see her as taking on any responsibility apart from for herself, suspected that she was merely escaping. He dreaded hearing that she was engaged, but expected to hear it, and not hearing it, he began to grow dangerously hopeful. She was, after all, formidably desirable, practical enough to bolt for the first comfort that opened for her. Up until then, he admitted, it had all been fantasy; now he asked casually which college she attended.

She sat in a small tea room across the road from the commercial college for an hour after her classes, every evening. She had a mug of tea and a dry scone which, sometimes, she did not even bother to eat. A pile of her books lay on the table beside her, but she did not open them. He sat at a table within sight of her for several evenings, watching and waiting. She did not notice him there, did not notice anything.

MacBlaine's image of her as purposeful and practical did not hold up against her reality. She looked tired and unkempt, drawn and nursing an anger that she did not seem to have the strength to articulate. Once he saw an oily young man sit himself at her table, push his attentions towards her, but she hardly noticed him. He reached across and touched her arm and she looked up at him with a flash of fury that sent him away. He watched her and waited for the moment, for the courage, for the power to approach her.

'Miss Bratley?'

She looked up through heavy eyes, as if naming her had caught her out.

'Oh yes. I was wondering when you'd reappear, Mr Drewer.'

He did not ask if he might sit, sat anyway.

'How are you?'

She did not bother to answer this.

'I was very sorry to hear about your father.'

'Yes. I expect you hear everything. Tell me, Mr Drewer, is this another chance encounter, or have you tracked me here?'

'I . . . have tracked you here. Forgive me.'

'I am in your debt,' she said with resignation.

'Oh no.'

'Your gallantry is frankly offensive. Tell me how much I owe you, then we can be settled. I want . . . everything to be settled. It is important to me.'

'Two pounds, twelve shillings and eight pence, then. I hope you will allow me to waive the interest, at least.'

She took out a purse, but he knew it would be beyond her present cash.

'I will have the money on Monday, Mr Drewer.'

'May I take you to dinner tomorrow evening?'

'I . . . I have a previous engagement.'

'Of course. I'm sorry. I want . . . what I ask has nothing to do with your circumstances, nothing to do with anything that has happened. I think you are a remarkable woman, Miss Bratley, and for entirely personal motives I want to have dinner with you. I have offended you, I know, but this needed to be said. I will come on Monday so that you may pay me the money you owe me, so that everything might be settled. Forgive me for imposing upon you in this way, for taking advantage of you. Good evening.'

He rose and put his chair back carefully.

'I think you are despicable,' she said.

'I think you are probably right,' he said, smiling, filled with excitement.

She was not there on Monday. He walked boldly in, looked round, then left. He was out in the open now and did not want to lurk any more. He expected nothing more than rejection. It stung him like a lash, but he was braced to it. He had no idea of subterfuge, no plan beyond seeing her again, collecting the money and disappearing.

He went every day to the tea room, but it was Thursday before she reappeared. She looked worse, darker and trembling. He came to her table, waited until she looked up, and then sat down.

'You're not well,' he said.

'I have been . . . a little unwell. I'm afraid I do not . . . have your money, Mr Drewer.'

'It is of no consequence at all. It was you who wanted to give it, far more than I wanted to receive it. We will consider the matter closed, then, as I had already considered it. Please . . . please don't be upset. I will leave you now and will not return. I wish you the very best. Goodbye.'

'What is it you want of me, Mr Drewer?'

He had no open answer to this question. She spoke still as if he had some hold over her, that she had some debt to pay.

'If you were to buy me dinner, would that cancel the debt?' she asked.

'There is no debt.'

'Yes, there is.'

'Very well. Yes. The debt would be cancelled.'

'Saturday, then?'

'Saturday.'

. . . *eleven* . . .

The moment he stepped from the taxi, the front door opened and closed, and she was coming down the small path towards the gate. She wore a dark cloak which flowed about her. She approached him in a bolt of hard beauty that left him helpless. He opened the taxi door and, without a word, without even a glance at him, she stooped and entered. He gave the driver directions and slipped in beside her.

For several moments he had nothing to say to her.

'I hope I didn't keep you waiting,' he managed eventually.

'No.' Later she said, 'Where are we going?'

'Er . . . Jones's. In Deverill Street. Do you know it?'

'No.'

'I should have asked. Is there anywhere you would prefer to go?'

'No. I thought . . . I thought we might be eating at your . . . your flat. You do have a flat, I assume?'

'Yes, a small flat, but . . . quite unsuitable for entertaining.'

'You live alone?'

'Oh yes.'

'I envy you.'

She was silent then. He had not remotely considered taking her back to his flat. Perhaps she wanted that, perhaps he had missed an opportunity. If he had done, it was an opportunity that he was by no means ready for.

He had no expectations of the evening. He assumed that she would be silent, if not directly rude, would order expensive dishes and then fail to eat them, would ask to be taken home within an hour. He inured himself thus to the humiliation he felt certain that her acceptance was primed to deliver. He would be immaculate, however, as detached as he could be, so that her rudeness would have no visible purchase. But he would watch and wait for any slight opening that he might take advantage of. Her mention of his flat had perhaps been such an opening; he had missed it, anyway. He tried to avoid looking at her as they entered the lit streets, as the taxi slowed amidst the clotting traffic. He did not know if she was looking at him, did not expect her to be and did not want to know that she was not.

They arrived. Jones's was a quiet, superior sort of place, most of the diners solitary men. Released from her cloak, she revealed a dress of dark crimson, cut tight, lace at cuffs and collar, a single string of pearls. She moved through the tables to the cubicle he had reserved, creating a wash of attention. Lewis, daunted by her magnificence, felt that he was out of his depth.

It was a pleasant meal, which was not what he had expected. He had foreseen humiliation, hoped for revelation; but he had not counted upon sociability. She ate well and drank quite a bit, was hardly confidential with him, but, if it was a duty to her, if it was merely paying him off, she performed it with grace. She asked him about himself and he told her about his family, his work, his life. At times, as he spoke, she seemed not to listen, to drift into her own thoughts. When he tried to turn the conversation upon her, she was evasive.

'You know all there is to know about me,' she said.

After the meal had been cleared, she accepted a cigarette and they sat for the best part of an hour.

'You haven't once used my name,' she said.

'How am I to address you?'

'My name is Celia. You know that. And you? Do you prefer Lewis or Lew?'

'Oh, Lewis.'

'Foolish of me to ask, really,' she said. 'Lewis Drewer. You are not what I expected, not at all.'

'What did you expect?'

'I don't know . . . someone older, I think, someone more . . . sophisticated. Does that offend you?'

'Not at all.'

'Are you in love with me?'

'I . . . expect so.'

'Poor boy. Silly boy. I'm sorry. Perhaps you'd better take me home now.'

As they drew through the suburban maze towards her house, her tension returned, her solitude. He was drunk enough to ask her to come back to his flat; but her silence stopped him. He made a vague offer of next Saturday and she gave him a vague refusal.

When the taxi halted at last, she said:

'Please don't get out. I would rather go in alone. Thank you for this evening. I hope it hasn't been too much of a disappointment for you.'

'The reverse of a disappointment. . . .'

He was about to elaborate, to reach for her to achieve at least a formal physical contact, but she had opened the door and was moving away before he could organise himself. He watched her go inside, sat silent and still for a few moments, until the driver turned round and asked him for directions.

He assumed that her hurried disengagement was due to a need to conceal him from any prying eyes. He was surprised, therefore, when, on Monday morning, MacBlaine knew of it.

'A private dinner with Celia Bratley, Drewer? It surprised me, I must say. Come to dinner on Friday. Miss Bratley is coming and you can be her escort.'

He was nervous of how Celia might take the presumption of this pairing, but he gave nothing away to MacBlaine.

It was a dreary evening. Georgina had a young man now and was showing him off. He was South American and rich, oily and arrogant. Celia seemed content to be escorted, but in the ostentatious formality of the evening they were together only as pieces on the social board. She paid little attention to him, or to anything, seemed at her customary distance.

He was permitted to walk her home, however, two paces behind her sister and mother. He made a clumsy attempt to take her arm, but she shrugged him away. The embarrassment of this bridled, but she was not thereafter unfriendly.

'Thank you for coming this evening,' she said.

'It has hardly been a chore.'

'It was my idea that you should be invited.'

'I didn't know. Thank you. I thought MacBlaine was playing games.'

'He wouldn't know how to play games. He's a disgusting man. I wish . . . Lewis?'

'Yes?'

'My mother will ask you in. Please don't accept.'

'Very well.'

'Take me dancing next week.'

'Dancing?'

'You don't have to.'

'I'd love to. Friday? Saturday?'

'It doesn't matter. Friday.'

He had no more idea how to dance than he did how to fly. He telephoned Joey in a panic and he and Candida came round with a pile of gramophone records. They drank gin and had a bizarre afternoon with Lewis dancing Candida about the confined space of his drawing room under Joey's tuition. It did not seem as difficult as he had thought it would be, but then Candida was not Celia, was as clumsy on her feet as he was, was small and comfortable in his arms, laughed a lot and threw glances across at her lover. After two hours, he had just about enough confidence not to make a complete imbecile of himself, although he later realised that much of this confidence came from the gin bottle.

He had to pay a price for this tuition: when Candida had disappeared to the bathroom, Joey asked if they might borrow his bedroom for a couple of hours. When she returned, Lewis invented a dinner engagement and left them to it. He went to a concert, stood in the gallery amongst the students, but could not enjoy the music. He went to a cheap restaurant and ate enough to blot up the quantity of beer he drank.

He returned home after midnight, entering circumspectly, but they were long done and gone. He could smell them on his sheets, her dark scent, Joey's hair oil and the rankness of their copulation. He did not change the sheets, but slept in the smeared and rumpled nest of their pleasure, in a sweat of prurient envy.

Next Friday he would take her dancing, would at last touch her.

Joey had suggested the place. He should have reconnoitred it. It was loud and modern, full of vivacious garishness, of kissing and laughter, and girls who jigged and shook and wobbled their breasts under sheaths of shiny material to the blare and beat of a jazz orchestra. Celia's cloak revealed tonight a lighter dress, yellow, loose at the sleeves and across the bodice. He noticed that she was more heavily made up, had bracelets that rattled and a string of bright glass beads about her neck.

They took a table near the dance floor, ordered drinks and surveyed the menu. She seemed uneasy tonight, restless, glancing quickly about her, then turning to his concern and smiling forcefully at him.

'D'you like this place, Lewis?' she asked, abruptly leaning across the table towards him.

'I don't know. I don't really know what I'm doing here.'

'You've brought me dancing. Come on, then. Dance.'

He had his hand on the small of her back, his other hand extended with her fingers locked in his. The side of her body was pressed into his chest. He moved through the dance steps with a breathless concentration. It felt like handling a dangerous machine for the first time. She stared into his face throughout, her lips edging into a smile then pursing, a frown breaking the surface of her forehead. The music jerked and jittered, the drums skittering and the brass punching repeated figures that roared into him. It made him feel drunk, the movement, the intensity, the presence of this hard, unyielding woman. Below the waist they stepped and twisted in a rigid formality; above the waist they were static, locked, staring at one another.

At a break in the music, they disengaged and returned to their table. He called a waiter. They lit cigarettes.

'Well?' she said.

'Well what?'

'Enjoy it?'

'Oh yes.'

'You're good. You dance well. You don't . . . cling. You move well. I'll bet you were good at sport at school.'

'Sort of.'

'I know people who were at school with you, Lewis.'

'Who?'

'Jeremy Carver.'

'Oh yes. He was a couple of years below me.'

'He tells me you liked to beat little boys on their bare bottoms.'

'I didn't like it.'

'But you did it.'

'Only once. It was done to me often enough. It was the way things were done. I hated school.'

'I would have liked to have gone to a boys' school. No, don't laugh at me. I mean, I would have liked to have been a boy.'

He wanted to pursue this, but by the time he had thought of something to say, she had gone silent on him, was looking around the dance floor.

Drinks came, then food. She had little appetite this evening and, after a couple of selective mouthfuls, moving the food about her plate for a while, she gave up. He refilled her glass, but she did not drink. He too lost the will to eat and, when he put his knife and fork down, she said, without looking up:

'Take me home.'

In the taxi, she wept. He reached for her and she took his hand, perhaps, he thought, to restrain it. He asked her what was wrong, but she shook her head.

'Nothing will come of this, Lewis, you know that,' she said eventually.

'I don't want anything.'

'Yes you do. Don't bloody well lie to me. But you won't get anything. I . . . I can't. . . .'

He let her lapse back into her silence.

As they neared her house, she let go of his hand and took a handkerchief from her bag, attended to her face, breathed deeply, restored herself.

'Can I see you again?' he asked.

'We're going away. Into the country. We'll have to give up the house.'

'What about your studies?'

'They weren't really serious. Nothing is really serious.'

'Can I give you my address?'

She sighed. 'All right, but don't expect anything. Don't lie awake waiting for me, Lewis. I couldn't stand that.'

He wrote out his address and she tucked it, without looking at it, into her bag.

As before, the moment the taxi stopped, she was gone.

. . . *twelve* . . .

She had hoped that the country would be better; it was worse, and she had been a fool to have hoped. They were in a small house in Hertfordshire, on the edge of a large estate. Her mother had fantasies of their being absorbed into county society, but no-one called apart from the vicar. Mildred had friends in London with whom she went to stay as often as she could. The younger girls, Amelia and Prudence, were away at some grim little school. Celia was incarcerated with her mother, therefore, through long, long weeks of dismal weather, damp, fires that smoked, poor food poorly cooked. They hardly spoke.

Her mother's life was becoming progressively dormant. She would spend most of the day in bed with some lassitude or other. When she came down, she would sit with a handkerchief, leafing through albums and still, Celia knew from the few words she occasionally dropped into the afternoon, expecting something to happen, someone to come and make everything right again, Mac-Blaine to write and tell her that the money had returned, that they could all go back now. She was also, Celia noticed, beginning to smell, to abandon that first of decencies and dignities. If all her breeding hadn't taught her that, then there was surely no point in any of it.

Their bathroom was certainly primitive, the hot water system giving the barest six inches of warmth which cooled within minutes. Celia mortified herself there every morning, becoming, in the desolation of her life, aware of her body in a way that she never had done when there were hovering maids and fine clothes to neutralise all that lean whiteness. She wished that she'd been a man, wished that she might be rid of the encumbrances of her large breasts, hated the flaw between her legs with its ugly hair. In the chill of the bathroom she explored these parts of herself, these external manifestations of her sex that would not, it seemed, allow her to be what she wanted to be; which was free.

And at the worst moments, she imagined Lewis Drewer looking at her thus, imagined his arousal, not as any image, but as a sudden noxiousness that would bleach her in an instant. It was the image of her death. And in terrible moments, she imagined going to him and exposing herself to him, finishing herself off; for he would surely want to kill her, surely that was what he wanted finally.

She thought of him often: at times with a softness, a nostalgia of something that had been possible once but which was not so any more, imagining that she had liked him, found him serious and kind; at times with fear and disgust, for below his good manners, she knew what lay in wait for her: a sexual possession which she could not approach in her imagination without becoming breathless with fear. At times she felt that this was what she deserved, that she was cowardly not to go and accept her punishment, that to resist it would be to subject herself only to a long withering. Better to have done with it at once, to be over; to be free of everything, especially herself.

Her mother moped herself into illness soon enough and Doctor Turnbull became a regular visitor to the house.

Doctor Turnbull's wife had died of the influenza. He had a sickly son of whom he was greatly fond. He had been in the war and had come home with profound social concerns. He was forthright with

Lady Bratley, admonishing her indulgence, recommending exercise, regular diet, cold douches, mental stimulation. He took no account of her social standing, or lack of it, which made him a novelty. She sobbed under his strictures, but was too frightened of him to resist and made an effort, a real effort. Celia was impressed with Doctor Turnbull.

And he with her. They sat and talked after his attendance upon her mother, and she was glad of his reading, of the positive practicality with which he viewed the world, even though she found his socialism and pacifism beyond her particular stomach. She went to dinner with him and to concerts, had found at last a friend. She had plans to become a teacher of French and German and he advised her, found books for her. She had not known that men could be so civilised and decent.

She ought to have known better, ought to have seen it coming. One day her mother, who had been particularly good, particularly attentive to Amelia and Prudence who were home for the holidays, asked for a moment alone with Celia.

'Doctor Turnbull has spoken to me about you,' she said. 'He asks if I would have an objection to his proposing marriage to you . . . well? You have no reaction to this? . . . Celia? . . . I wept, I'm afraid. It is not what I had always planned for you, but . . . but he is a very good man and, so he tells me, not without either substance or connections. We would be able to live in his house, which is far too large for him. We would . . . be settled. I have always known that there would be an end to this penury. You have done very well, child, very well.'

Had she simply delivered the proposal, it might have been different; but the crude calculations that followed spoiled it. Marriage, if it were to give her anything, would, she had always imagined, release her from the clutches of this woman, from the rest of them; from Mildred, who she knew, although her mother didn't, had become the mistress of a married man in London; from her ugly little sisters whom school had turned dull, spiteful and mean.

'You will accept this proposal?' her mother asked; it was only just a question.

'I am certainly not in love with Doctor Turnbull,' she said, 'or do you not consider that of any importance, Mother?'

'If you put your mind to it, you might quickly come to have affection for him. You know that as well as I do. Does he not deserve your affection? I know that you think I do not, but I thought you liked him, Celia. I really thought you liked him.'

'Certainly I like him. This does not mean that I wish to share his bed. I will talk to him.'

'You have responsibilities, Celia, to others than yourself. Please remember that.'

He was almost apologetic when he came into the drawing room where she sat alone, waiting for him. She had been very angry with her mother, and after their conversation had determined to refuse the offer out of hand, as contemptuously as she could. As the hours had passed, as the night had come and gone, however, she had become resigned to what seemed like an inevitability. She did like him. She didn't believe in love, not as it was commonly understood. In bed she could close her eyes and trust him to be at least efficient in whatever he needed to do to her.

He proposed to her with reasoned humility, sitting beside her and taking her hand. His hands were warm, moist, his proximity made her clench; she could not help it. The simple acceptance would not come to her lips.

'I need more time,' she said. 'It is not easy for me, Ronald.'

'Of course, I understand. There is no urgency. May I ask one question?'

'Certainly.'

'I asked your mother . . . I asked her if there was any other attachment. She assured me that there was not, but I . . . I need to have your assurance. I would not for the world bring you any shame or unhappiness.'

'No,' she said quickly, 'there is no other attachment.' As soon as she had said it, she felt herself blush as if she had lied.

'Thank you,' he said.

'But . . . but I am not a virgin,' she said.

'That . . . that is of no concern to me,' he said. 'In fact . . . forgive me if this is offensive to you, but I am glad you are not. I think we might find much happiness together, my dear Celia.'

'Please,' she said, as he leant himself towards her. 'I need more time. I need. . . .'

When he was gone, she was appalled at herself. She had told him a bald truth which felt like a lie; and a bald lie which felt like the truth; both of which could only come back at her, shamefully, as lies always did to those who carried the crucifix of honesty, as she did, as she did. She must go to London. She must go to Lewis Drewer. She must make both the truth that felt like a lie, and the lie that felt like the truth, become truth. Beyond this terrible penance, she could return, become ordinary, marry Ronald Turnbull and become the mother of his children.

. . . *thirteen* . . .

When she stepped from the railway terminus into the dark streets, a few snowflakes began to fall from a thick sky, orange with the glow of streetlamps. There were no cabs and her restlessness would not permit her to wait for one. She set off along the streets urgently, and the snow began to tumble down about her, lifted and turned on bitter swirls of wind, massing as grey slush on the streets and pavements, covering everything that was still and dark and silent with a sharp white benediction. She put her head down and drove into it.

It was all right whilst she was moving. She dreaded having to stop, arriving there. If only it would be quick, if only she would hardly have to pause before it was upon her and over with, then she could cope with it. At last she was in his street; sober, quiet houses with lights aglow in high windows against the thick flicker of the snow.

In the lobby of his house, she felt bitterly cold, felt the snow melting upon her, turning her clothes sodden, her flesh like dough. She ascended the stone steps to his floor breathing in the harsh air. She knocked fiercely at his door. She heard him at the latch, felt the weight of him behind the door. She closed her eyes, felt the door open.

'Hello, Celia,' he said simply, as if he had been expecting her.

She glanced briefly into his face, felt a shudder of undefined familiarity, then walked past him, seeking a source of warmth, finding a small gas fire, kneeling down before it and chafing her hands, trembling, the edges of her teeth dancing in the cold. First she must get warm; one thing at a time.

'Would you like a drink?' he asked.

'Water. Thank you.'

When he stooped over her with the glass, she used it as a point of focus to rise, to look about her for a seat, to perch on the edge of a chair at a distance from where he lay, loose-limbed, without a jacket or tie, in a low chair, watching her. An old instinct was a little affronted by his informality, until she remembered how she had come here, until she remembered why she had come.

'Is your mother well?' he asked.

'I'm engaged to be married,' she said.

She watched this hit him, watched his eyes close for a moment. What am I doing here? she asked herself. For pity's sake, what am I doing here?

'Congratulations,' he said. 'Do I know him? No, I don't suppose I do. When is the . . . happy day? Am I invited?'

She glared at him until he had stopped this nonsense.

'I'm sorry,' he said. 'I'm . . . a little drunk.'

'I know you are. Actually, it's a lie. I'm not engaged. I just wanted to see how you'd take it.'

He dropped his mouth open, blinked, then said simply, 'You bitch.'

She laughed quietly, sadly, glad to have brought him out like this.

'Yes,' she said. 'Poor little Lewis. Can I have a cigarette?'

As he held the match for her, she saw his face clearly for the first time, saw a ferocity in the depth of his eye that frightened her. She stood up and moved away, went to the window and pulled aside the curtain.

She watched the falling snow, great white tatters of it lifting and turning in the wind. She felt him, after a while, rise and come to stand behind her. She felt a sudden solitude against the quiet obliteration that fell out into the night. A cold despair came over her, like corruption. She felt his hand touch her shoulder, but she had no reaction to it.

'For God's sake, Celia, come and get dry.'

She did not respond until he reached beyond her and closed the curtain; then she turned and his proximity rose up at her. She shuddered. He unfastened the catch of her cloak and pulled it away from her, draped it over a chair. It was sodden and weighted. She stood in a thin blouse which adhered wetly to her skin. He moved her chair to the fire, turned the fire up, brought her back to it, knelt down beside her.

'I'll run you a bath, a hot bath.'

'Thank you,' she said simply.

He left her whilst he busied himself running the bath. She stared into the bars of heat in the fire. I'm not here, she told herself, not really. I don't exist. Whatever happens won't matter in the slightest.

He returned, stood before her and took her hand, raised her and led her into his neat little bathroom where he had laid out a towel, a dressing gown, a pair of his pyjamas. He left her there.

She went to lock the door, but realised the futility of that. She shed her wet clothes in a heap on the floor and slid into the beautiful warmth of the water, lay back and felt the cold ooze out of her, forgot everything, slipped her head under the surface and felt the pressure of the warmth on her eyelids and nostrils, rising as if this had in some way cleansed and cleared her, ready for anything now; but the simple comfort of the bath was too much and she dozed.

She was roused by a small rap on the door. She pulled herself quickly up and crouched over, waited. The water had cooled and she began to shiver again.

'Celia?'

'What?'

'I just wanted to know if you were all right.'

'The door's not locked.'

There was a pause.

'I was just worried that you'd fallen asleep in there or something.'

'I'm all right.'

In the clammy silence, behind the drip of a tap, she could hear his breathing. She imagined his hand hovering on the doorknob. She clutched her knees and held her breath.

'Don't get cold,' she heard him say, heard him moving away.

Quickly she rose from the water and became busy, drying herself systematically, slipping into the loose flannel of his pyjamas, feeling her flesh tight and warm within them. The masculinity of these garments made her feel odd; the tightness of the jacket across her breasts, the open flap at the crotch, the roughness of the material, a certain scent below the starch of their laundering. In his nightwear, she felt that she already belonged to him, that it was in a way done, the basic decision taken and accepted. The rest would be a formality. She breathed easily, did not think about him closely. He was a functionary, necessary to her. It was simple.

When she returned to his sitting room with her wet clothes bundled, he was standing waiting for her.

'Where can I put these?' she asked.

He took them from her and spread them over a small clothes-horse. She watched how he handled her silks and linens, delicately, attentively, like a shop assistant, she thought; but that was not it. He was reading her from them, carefully spreading out her intimacies. She did not look any further, sat before his fire and began to tease out her hair in its heat, bringing it to life again, the bright length of it, making it shine again.

He offered her food which she declined, but accepted now a gin and tonic, another cigarette, sat with her legs curled under her, cosy before his fire. He was an attendant shadow in a chair to whom she began to talk now, speaking out the clauses of her contract clearly, riding over the catches of her breath that were like glimpses down from a precipice up which she toiled with a blank resolution.

'When I said I was engaged, it was not completely untrue. There is a man . . . he has asked me . . . to marry him. He's a widower, with a small son . . . in the country. I . . . I haven't given him an answer yet. I am . . . I am expected to accept him. He . . . he has money. It will be a good thing if I marry him. It will settle everything. And I do like him, Lewis. He's very kind . . . a strong man, a good man . . . I will accept him. It seems inevitable . . . it seems right . . . but I have this difficulty . . . I told him that . . . I had no other attachments, and . . . and that is not entirely true . . . and I told him that I was not a virgin, and that is entirely untrue. It will cause . . . misunderstanding, shame. I don't know why I told him these things. I don't understand. I don't want to understand. I want . . . I want to play out my little melodrama. I want you to sleep with me and then we will be settled, all debts cleared. Then I can get on with my life and you can get on with yours.'

There was a pause for which, at first, she was grateful, imagined his tacit concurrence; then, as it grew, she became afraid, aware of the dryness of her mouth, the weakness of her limbs.

'Lewis?' Saying his name was a mistake. She bit her lip.

'You don't know what you are asking,' he said slowly.

'Yes, I do. Of course I know.'

'Why me, Celia?'

'Because . . . because you . . . because you're in love with me.

Aren't you? Isn't that what it means? Isn't that what you want?' His attitude irritated her. She could not comprehend his difficulty.

'It isn't all I want.'

'Well, it's all I can give you.'

'Do you like me, Celia?' he asked.

'What?'

'Do you find me attractive?'

'That doesn't matter.' It was frankly not a question she was prepared to consider.

'It matters to me.'

'All right. Yes. If that's what you want me to say.'

'I want more than that. I want you to make me believe it.'

She felt herself becoming drawn into complexities that brought tears into her eyes.

'What do I have to do?' she said.

'Come here.'

There was a moment of panic, then she steeled herself, rose and stepped into the shadow where he waited, stood before him. He rose. She closed her eyes and tried not to breathe. He untied the dressing-gown cord, unbuttoned the jacket, pulled at the bow of the trouser cord. The trousers slipped down her legs and flopped over her feet. The warmth fled from her. His eyes were upon her like lamps; she felt their movement, felt her nakedness prickle under them. It is necessary, she said. It will soon be done. His hands were warm and dry, reptilian, moving over her. It is not me, she said, not me, but her nipples were delicate under his fingers, a hard pulse ached in her thighs when he pressed upon them; and then, appallingly, he applied his mouth to her, breathed closely upon her mouth, tasted her breasts, her navel, parted her legs and opened her vagina with his tongue. Tears streamed from her clenched eyes, the gasp of her repressed weeping jolting through her. Under his touching she was different: she had never been like this before. She wanted to scream and flee, but what she wanted to flee from was what he touched, the quivering, liquefying mass of her. She cried out.

'Do you like me, Celia?' he said. 'Do you like me now?'

She broke from him, gathered herself together, and threw herself into a chair, bunched up, her back to him, contorted, disgusted, weeping.

He came and knelt beside her, touched her shoulder.

'I can't. . . .' she said.

'I know,' he said kindly. 'I'm sorry.' He rose and returned to his chair. 'You see,' he said. 'You shouldn't have come here. I'm not your man, Celia. I want more than you've got to give.'

She surfaced into anger, shook herself and faced him, hated him, hated herself; but something was in her blood, something was incomplete. She failed to understand and she had to understand.

'What do you want?'

'Go to bed, Celia. We can talk in the morning.'

'Tell me what you want, Lewis.'

'What I want isn't important to you. There's no point in discussing it. If we leave it here, at least . . . at least we might be able to part on civilised terms, and that is important to me, Celia. Go and marry your doctor. You don't want to get involved with me.'

'Why not? I am involved with you. That's why I'm here.'

'Are you?'

She felt she'd been tricked into this, trapped by it.

'Apparently I am,' she said.

'Yes,' he said. 'We're alike, you know, very alike. That's the danger.'

'What are you talking about?'

Her tone was brusque and practical, but it was a lie. Below the thinnest of surfaces, she felt mad, felt within her a horrible complicity. It occurred to her that, as he had touched her, as she had quivered and wept, there had been a pleasure, a need for it, a child's pleasure in its own excrement, a need to drown in flesh, the spasms of disgust that would bring her to life.

'Tell me, Lewis.'

He lit another cigarette, inhaled it deeply, his head thrown back against the chair-back.

'Being touched disgusts you, doesn't it? I disgust you. And yet here you are, asking me to . . . to fuck you. What you want from me is a degradation. You want me to degrade myself and you, to fuck you like an animal, without tenderness, without desire, without affection. The whole idea is disgusting, but, because it is disgusting, because of your disgust, I want it more than anything in the world.'

When he had done, there was a silence so pure that it hurt.

'Is that . . . is that *love*?' she said.

'Love?' He laughed. 'I don't know about love. I don't think I . . . I don't think either of us would be very good at love. Go home to your doctor, Celia. He'll give you love, I expect; or at least affection, tenderness, consideration.'

'I thought you loved me,' she said, not with any sentimentality, rather with an amazed curiosity.

'I think I do.' Another pause, then he said, 'Go to bed, Celia.'

She conceded, but did not move, did not speak. What if he were right? She didn't want him to be right, but felt that he was right. She thought for the first time that evening of Ronald Turnbull. His complete irrelevance appalled her. And then she knew that, one way or the other, she had to know.

'You have to do it, Lewis,' she said.

'Go to bed, Celia.'

'You have to do it. I need to have it done. Can't you understand?'

'Leave it, leave it,' he said, his voice tired.

'Are you afraid now?' she said, feeling suddenly that she had taken the advantage. 'All that talk. Haven't you even got the courage of your own perversion?'

She came at him, opened herself, thrust out her body at him. It seemed easy, a defiance. He laughed, but nervously, shifted, shrugged.

'Let me see you,' she said. 'Come on, come on.'

'There will come a point,' he said quietly, 'beyond which I will not be able to stop. Just as long as you know that. Just as long as you really do want to go through with this.'

He watched her for a few moments, then lifted himself up, moved round her, began to clear a space on the floor, spread cushions and a rug down. She began to feel isolated, bewildered.

'Don't you have a bed?' she asked.

'You're going to need somewhere to sleep. I think . . . I think it will be better here.'

This seemed, she supposed, logical. She wandered into the space he had cleared. He fetched a towel and folded and laid it down.

'What . . . what are you going to do?' she asked.

'What you want me to do, Celia.'

'Do you need to . . . to hurt me or anything?'

He stopped, turned to her. He was angry and she drew back from him.

'No,' he said shortly; then, an afterthought, 'Yes, one thing.'

'What?'

'Kiss me.'

It was difficult. She came to him and he put his arms about her, but she was restless, could not settle herself, wanted only that he should take what he wanted quickly. He put his hands to her head, held her still, then put his mouth upon hers. She retracted her lips, the skin on her face taut.

'Kiss me,' he said.

She tried to relax but only trembled, achieved it at last with a sob that made her mouth open. He covered her mouth with his, took her breath into him. She strove to regain control of her lips and, in doing so, found herself engaged with his lips, moving and sucking, a slither of tongue entering her, an image of molten flesh pushing her back into her head.

When he drew back, she felt exhausted. Quickly she turned and folded down onto the floor, propping herself on one elbow, rolling her head to loosen the muscles. She brought saliva into her mouth, licked her lips, trying to recover herself from his possession of her, the taste of him sending jerks of recoil into her stomach.

She had lost touch with him as he moved about the floor; then suddenly he knelt down in the cusp she made with her body. He was naked, his hands cupped in his lap. She looked at him with watery eyes. His flesh was pale, boyish, with a discreet dark down on his thighs and in the centre of his chest. It was not a strong body, not aggressively masculine. So far, a reassurance. He moved one of his hands and took her hand, placed it on his thigh, held it there. Meat, she thought, a weight of lean, anonymous tissue; and then he moved his other hand, brought from behind it his phallus: dark, bloated, disgusting. She turned away quickly but he had her hand, would not let her loose, held her until she stopped straining, whining. He drew her back although she would not face him, took her hand and touched himself with it. Under her palm she felt it urging, slippery, with a cruelty pure beyond negotiation.

She wrenched herself away and balled up tightly, dragging the clothes and blanket about her. His face came close to hers.

'Tell me to stop,' he said. 'Tell me, for I won't take pity on you.'

'Isn't it over?' she said. 'Why isn't it over?'

She felt his hands about her clearing away her coverings, setting her legs out, tucking something under her, tucking up her knees. This is all right, she told herself. This is what I expected. It is being done to me. I have no part in it. I am safe. But he was touching her with his fingers, perhaps his tongue, until she felt her vagina swell,

188

open, felt it a hole that went deep into her, a terrible stunned rawness. She whipped her hands across her to cover herself, to hold herself in, but he caught her hands, held them back. Then he entered her and she shrieked. Then he flattened himself upon her and she writhed, lifted and strove and kicked into space as he pushed and pushed against the hurt inside her and she felt, not pain, not after the first moment, but a rushing of fluids, a flood of herself pouring into that wound to staunch it. Something had liquefied within her, disintegrated. Then suddenly he was still and she was still twisting, and he slipped from her and left her with the coldness setting upon her.

'It's over now,' he said.

She curled over again, grabbed at the blanket, wanted to be nothing, but a process of catastrophe was gibbering at her belly and thighs. He returned to her, tried to put his arms about her, but she shook him away, lay squirming in her mess; until he became practical, lifted her up and took her through to the bathroom. He sponged her thighs and she wept at the humiliation, submitting to whatever he did until the moment, the instant she felt his touch was attempting to console her, to show her affection; then she shook him away, struck at him.

He took her at last to his bed, slipped her helplessness into the consolation of clean sheets. As she tussled with sleep, she tried to tell herself that that was it, that it was done now, that she had succeeded; none of these was true. She did not, at that moment, feel even remotely human; and even if she had been, she had given herself to Lewis Drewer, belonged to him now, part of the processes of his body as much as of her own.

In the morning this hysteria was gone, but so, effectively, was everything else.

. . . *fourteen* . . .

In the morning, hobbling about in his shirt and soiled trousers, making tea, he felt dispossessed of his flat, of his life. He wanted to go in to her, but dared not. He felt that he knew her now less than he had ever known her, that he had come so close to her that she had disappeared. He moved about, cramped by her silent presence, scurrying, longing for her to call him to her, ready to do anything, make any concession. He wanted to be able to shut her in here, to keep her forever. He wanted what had happened not to have happened and yet he wanted it to happen again, to go on happening. There was a fever of pleasure whenever he thought of it.

Sitting at the kitchen table with a mug of tea, the paper open before him but his mind still saturated with her, he did not hear her. Suddenly there was the slightest catch of breath and he turned to see her in the doorway, his dressing gown loose around her, her face drawn, the bleared eyes upon him. When he reached her and touched her shoulder she winced, then sagged against the doorframe. He drew back, for she had reacted as she might have done had he hit her, and he was afraid. He spoke her name, softly. She nodded her head, shook herself briefly and moved to the table, sat where he had sat. She helped herself to a cigarette from his case which lay on the table. He sat down opposite and struck a match for her.

'What will you do now?' he asked.

She looked up at him.

'What am I supposed to do?' she said.

'Well,' he said, 'you could stay here.'

She glanced about her, faced him suddenly with a look of bitter contempt.

'Is that what you've made me now?' she asked.

'What?' he said. 'What have I made you, Celia?'

He liked this. He preferred her fighting to her subservience. She did not answer him, crushed out her cigarette.

'I must. . . .' she began, then puzzled as if she could not complete the thought.

'What?'

'Go home now.'

He paused, sought to find a way through this, but carefully.

'May I see you again?'

'I suppose you may whenever you want to, Lewis. I've become your prostitute now, haven't I?'

'No,' he said. 'Celia, there is no . . . obligation here. Go home, back to your doctor. . . .'

'My doctor? Is there something wrong? Do I need to see a doctor?'

'I thought you were going to marry a doctor.'

He could not fully believe that she had forgotten but, watching her register it, seeing it turn within her, he began to be afraid again.

'That,' she said. 'Well. That's sorted out at least.'

'You'll marry him?'

'How can I? How can I now?'

'I don't see . . . I don't see why it should make any difference.'

She did not speak but looked clearly at him, showed him her face as her disgust quivered about the clench of her teeth, the clench of her whole body. It filled him with a sick desire for her and, although he was man enough not to translate that desire into any word or action against her, he could not tell her any more that she was free, that she should go back to her doctor, that she should never see him again. It was too much for that.

Shortly she went for her bath, dressed and left through the snowy streets for Hertfordshire. They did not speak beyond immediate practicalities; she did not want him to come to the station with her; they made no plans; they did not touch, even in parting; but it had begun. He knew that he had taken possession of her, exulted in it, felt strong and cruel; would have died for her at a whim.

His previous sexual encounters had been trivial: a girlfriend of a girlfriend of Joey O'Neele's; a stenographer he had taken to Epsom. With them he had blundered through intoxication to pleasure, to release and subsequent disgust; not at them whom he pitied, at himself, at his failure to do more than ejaculate, his failure to make them happy or real or proud, only ashamed. He had sought, sexually, for a lyricism, an emotional deliquescence: it had never lived up to his masturbatory imaginings.

What of this, then? He did not clearly know, in the slump that followed her departure. There had been no lyrical blur, rather a squealing, shrieking concentration; the physical had not melded gracefully into the emotional, but had revealed a new proximity, an intensity that was, as he thought of it, starkly biological. The softness that he had imagined he knew now to be a lie, an evasion. He felt that he had touched the rawness of sex and, after the stun of it faded, he delighted in it, longed for her to come to him again, began making plans, opening his life to admit the possibility of her everywhere. He imagined her aggressive, he imagined her mad, he imagined her punitive and humiliating, each variation rising with a certainty, a force, a liberation within him.

. . . *fifteen* . . .

'Well? Where have you been?'

'I have been to London, Mother. To see a friend.'

'Oh? I didn't know you had friends in London. It wasn't that awful Lewis Drewer, I hope. I won't invite that man to the wedding, Celia, nor Mr MacBlaine. They are responsible, you know. They have brought us to this.'

Celia sat on the edge of her mother's bed, gave herself a little time to be calm.

'There will be no wedding, Mother,' she said simply.

There was a moment of the iciest silence.

'I suppose,' her mother said, 'it is because you know that it will resolve our wretchedness that you will not bring yourself to it. I suppose it is because I want it. You merely want to spite me.'

'I will not marry Ronald Turnbull because I am not fit to marry him,' she said, knowing that this would not be understood but needing to say it, needing to make this statement of herself that she would never be able to make to him.

'This will be the death of me,' her mother said.

In the event, perhaps it was. Certainly, within a month she had died, of what Doctor Turnbull called a seizure. Celia had found her one morning rigid with spite and contempt, and death. She had wept at her own shame, at the relief she felt of being rid of this selfish, indulgent woman. I am more like her than I have ever admitted, Celia said to herself at the funeral.

Doctor Turnbull was marvellous, organising everything, having Amelia and Prudence to stay. He had been marvellous over her refusal of him, so marvellous that she had sickened of him. Had he fought her, hit her, denounced her, even now she might have accepted him. He receded from her thoughts where, in truth, he had never been much of a presence; at least, not since her return from London.

A month after her mother died, she rang Lewis.

'I saw it in the paper,' he said. 'I'm very sorry.'

'Don't be sorry. I'm not.'

After a pause, he said, 'When can I see you again?'

'I need a break, just a couple of days. Not London.'

They met in London, and he drove her into the country. She slept and, when he woke her, it was dark, and they were turning into the forecourt of a small riverside pub. He took her hand and slid a wedding ring onto her finger.

'Lewis, no. Not this.'

'It's expected. It's all part of the hypocrisy. Mr and Mrs Lewis. Try not to forget.'

Their room was small and, in spite of the summer, smelt musty. A little window looked out over the river which glinted in the darkness, a heavy, moving mass slapping the banks with a small echo. Moths battered themselves on the grimy glass.

Lewis closed the curtains, switched on a small electric light by the bed. She watched him as he moved about the room, looking in cupboards, opening the door and peering both ways down the corridor, closing and locking the door, testing it. He did not look at her, moved as if she was some sort of hole in the floor which he had to avoid. He lowered his case onto the floor and unbuckled it, took out a bottle of brandy and two tumblers which he had wrapped in a towel. He poured two small bolts of brandy into the tumblers and came to her at last.

She drank the brandy in one, shuddered, handed him the glass. He took it, placed it beside his, which he had not drunk from, on the bedside table. He returned to her, held her arms to her sides, closed upon her, kissed her mouth.

'You must try. . . .' he said. 'You must try to give.'

'How? Tell me.'

'I can't. I don't know how. Hold on to me.' He lifted her arms and put them around his neck, then moved his hands down, slid up her dress, grasped her between her legs. 'Try to be . . . be proud of yourself. If you are weak, I can only hurt you, only . . . hurt you. . . .'

He edged her back against the wall, unbuttoned himself and entered her abruptly. She trembled and writhed to hold herself still, had to cling onto him, had to co-operate. He reached down and pulled up her thighs, lifted her feet off the floor. She ground her teeth and hissed, clawed her nails into his neck, pushed herself up to straighten her spine.

'Where are you, Celia?' he said. 'Where are you?'

He felt suddenly something twist in her, heard her breath catch, looked to see her lips peeled back from her teeth, her mouth open, felt her at last push down upon the careful, regular slip of his penis, felt her coil and lift, a tiny choking cry pushing up her throat. Her weight became enormous, her body a sack in which something struggled to escape. The muscles in his neck and arms cramped and his back felt as if he would never be able to straighten it. Every point of naked contact between them was slippery with sweat. He pressed her back and drove it out of her, all of it, exultant in her delivery, in her discomfort, in the absolute animality of it.

At last she grew limp, lolled, and he lowered her legs carefully, extracted himself. He had not ejaculated, but then he had not been protected. He was proud of his self-control. He stood her against the wall and her dress slipped back into place. He unknotted her hands from his neck and pressed them together between his. Her head lolled, her eyes were closed. He moved his face to hers and ran his mouth over the scorched surface of her skin. She shivered, shook her head, and he drew back, turned to ease himself back into his trousers. He sat heavily on the bed and drained his brandy, refilled his glass, hers too.

'Here,' he said, offering the glass.

She limped across to a chair. With her back to him, she drew up the dress and examined herself, winced, then pulled the dress over her head and shook it out, brushed it, laid it on the back of the chair. She unbuckled her shoes and rolled down her stockings, then, running her hands through the black shock of her hair, straightening the sheen of her slip, she came and sat beside him, took the glass and drank. She asked for a cigarette and watched as he fetched it, found an ashtray. He stood before her as she smoked, watched her attention close upon the burning end of the cigarette, shaping it into a cone on the rim of the ashtray.

'I brought you off,' he said. 'Didn't I, Celia? Didn't I?'

She looked up briefly, then, before he could stop her, had driven the cigarette into the flesh between her thumb and forefinger, screwed it in.

They were three nights at the riverside pub, after which they returned to their previous lives. They made no plans to meet again. They emerged blinking from a cave and fled from one another into the safety of themselves.

Over those three nights and two days, they had struggled to reach some sort of sexual balance, some form of the act that would embody gentleness and consolation, that would release them. In this, they failed; but in failing, they learnt.

The initial posture was his desire and her disgust, his need to inflict and hers to submit. He sought always to push her to the point where she would break, driving at her with a gargantuan appetite that was only briefly staunched by protracted and withering ejaculations. He never lost sight of her, however, never reduced her in his mind to a mere function. She was always necessary; her compliance, her disgust, her vivid consciousness was essential. His ejaculations were intervals, the precursors of hours of rest, of sleep, of small excursions into the normality of the inn and the surrounding countryside; but the point, the focus and justification of it all, was hunting her out, driving her deeper and deeper, taking hold of her and wrenching her up into orgasm.

She hated it, and he had to watch her closely every time, for her instinctive reaction was to cause herself pain, to provoke him into hurting her; but, although she hated it, all of it, she never drew back. Her passivity was nominal and he became inventive in out-flanking it, catching her unexpectedly, forcing her to react against him and, in her reaction, to engage her.

She did not, for those three days, want to be left, did not ever give the slightest indication that she needed to be alone. He knew, and every encounter confirmed it, that as she was ministering to his desire, so he was ministering to a need in her that was as perverse as his. It was he who became disgusted, with himself obviously, but also with her, with her relentless accommodation of everything he did to her. At times he spilled over into an overwhelming tenderness for her, taking her in his arms and soothing her soiled flesh; she was never more monumentally removed than at these moments.

. . . *sixteen* . . .

'What will you do with yourself?' he had asked her over what passed for dinner in the dingy pub dining room.

'Oh,' she had said vaguely, 'I suppose I might persuade someone to employ me as a teacher.'

'You'll be a good teacher.'

She had looked up to see what he meant by this.

'Marry me,' he had said again.

'No,' she had said. 'I couldn't . . . I couldn't manage that. This is . . . isn't this enough for you, Lewis?'

He hadn't pressed her.

'My parents are coming home,' he had said. 'My father's retiring. I've been looking for a house for them. There's a place in Norfolk that I think will be what they want, just outside a small town called Framling. You could . . . well, I've been up there and there's a girls' school nearby. I was looking out for somewhere for my sisters.'

'I didn't know you had sisters.'

'I must have told you. Helena and Naomi. Helena is sixteen, Naomi fourteen. I've never even seen Naomi and only saw Helena when she was a baby. The point is that . . . that you might apply for a job there.'

'Are they looking for a French teacher?'

'I understand that they're always looking out for teachers.'

'Is it a good school?'

'Not . . . not particularly, I think, but . . . but you ought not to be in London. You'll be safe there. I don't want you to be out of reach.'

He had become awkward saying this, and she had smiled.

'Very well,' she had said. 'Do you have the address?'

As soon as she returned to Hertfordshire, she wrote to Miss Naomi Dachet, MA, Headmistress of Manfield Academy, and was promptly summoned for interview. Miss Dachet, impressed by her resolve and by her intelligence, by her apparently fierce independence, employed her at a salary of fifty pounds per term, board and lodgings provided.

The girls detested her and she applied herself to them like a purge. She enjoyed the work, parcelling the languages into neat, progressive sections and delivering them with precision and control. The girls scribbled in their exercise books, stood in order and read their lessons, went quietly from her form-room with a weight of learning to be mastered before tomorrow. She was scrupulously fair, had no favourites, did not have individual apprehensions of them at all: she simply expected them all to acquire the knowledge she transmitted. She was here to drill them into learning, to give them intellectual strength. Most of them, she knew, would be lost, would drift from school into marriage to farmers or solicitors, buried in rural domesticity and dull cycles of procreation. She wanted to give them at least a little strength, a little sharpness of mind before they disappeared into the darkness of their maturity. It was a losing battle but she never underestimated its importance.

She could forgive dullness, even idleness; took a perverse pleasure in their resentment of her. Miss Dachet had equipped her with a short cane as part of her equipment, but had cautioned her against using it as a substitute for thorough teaching, or to shore up any weakness in her own discipline. She understood these injunctions clearly and, although several of her colleagues regularly lined up the idle and incompetent and made their palms sing, Celia despised them for it. For her first term, she never even touched the implement, although it hung darkly from its hook on the side of her desk. They wondered what it would take to provoke Miss Bratley to beat them. They found out.

'Gillian Ford, stand up.'

This was spoken from the rear of the class. Heads turned briefly, but quickly returned to their exercises.

'Are you wearing scent?'

'No, miss.'

'Go out to the front of the class. Stand facing the blackboard.'

The girl obeyed with a foolish jaunt, glancing about her.

'Face to the front!'

She was left to stand there for some minutes until she became restless, then Miss Bratley was moving quickly through the desks, had taken her place at her high stool, had opened an exercise book and had begun to mark it with a sequence of neat corrections.

'I will ask you again,' she said quietly. 'Are you wearing scent?'

'It's not . . . scent, miss.'

'What then? Eau de Cologne?'

'Yes, miss.'

'You are aware of the school regulations? . . . Well?'

'I was at a party last night, miss. There's no regulation to say you can't put on perfume at a party.'

'How old are you?'

'Fourteen, miss.'

'You're a slut, Gillian Ford, a slut.' She slipped from her stool. 'You must be taught discipline. Hands out, if you please.'

Afterwards, in the common-room, smoking one of her strong cigarettes, she recognised clearly that she had enjoyed beating that girl. She had enjoyed the fear she had generated, the performance she had given, the swing and snap of the cane, the charge that had sprung up her forearm. There had been a fire of righteousness in her reducing the girl to misery; she had felt that she was squashing something repellent, scouring it out with pain. Afterwards, she had made the girl open her clawed hands, made her show the weals she had put across the plump pinkness of her flesh, had noted them with professional curiosity. She had demonstrated herself, had caught the first emergence of corruption and had shrivelled it with her physical strength. An elation filled her until, later, she remembered the tales she had heard of Lewis's schooldays, of his beating boys on their bare bottoms, and something shivered inside her at this connection.

On Sundays, it was her duty to help shepherd the girls the mile and a half into the town where they attended Matins, filling the rear pews of the stony church and sitting stunned in chilly tedium through psalms and intercessions, and a sermon of wearisome predictability. She had been through this at school, and knew what the girls must have felt, subjected to a tedious lump of traditional respectability that was meaningless and irrelevant. There seemed to her no challenge here. Faith was offered as an enormous, archaic discomfort.

In her solitude, however, as the months passed, she began to listen to the service, to attempt to imagine what it all might mean. She found herself gradually drawn into it. She would not have said that she believed in God, and certainly not in virgin birth and resurrection of the body; but it began to seem right to her that there was some sort of destiny, some sort of design; and she understood with merciless clarity the meaning of sin, the idea of retribution and suffering; that human beings were essentially weak and corrupt, and answerable for their frailty. It made her afraid to think like this, but the fear was stimulating. It made her quiver with thoughts of death, hold herself tightly into her flesh, aware of its transience. She began, during the services, to lock herself into the rubrics, to submit herself to their penitences and thanksgivings. She began to attend services on her own, during the holidays, began to take communion which she had not done since school, accepted her attendance at church as a duty to herself, a cleansing submission to a power beyond her, although she would still have been coy of naming that power, even to herself.

She began to want more than this, began to want something to come to her from without, some vision, some answering of her submission. She did not expect an angel, or even a shaft of light; but she did expect something to touch her mind, to open within her, to assure her that she was real and that it was real in relation to her. She walked the wood-paths and fields, she sat in the church alone. It trembled about her; she could feel it there, perhaps, just beyond her. She tensed herself for it. She relaxed herself almost to hypnosis. It would not come. Sometimes she would turn and there would be someone else there, the vicar or verger, or the woman who did the flowers. They would nod at her respectfully and she would hurry away. Perhaps it would come late at night as she sat reading or preparing her work for the morning; perhaps it would come in the classroom.

'Are you all right, miss?' one of the girls would say.

'Get on with your work. Raise your hand before you speak in my form-room.'

What would come to her, what was waiting to repossess her, was not God. In her cold moments she knew this. It was Lewis Drewer to whom, for no reason that she could clearly articulate, she belonged; either to him or to anybody, anybody who happened to stumble across her secret; anybody, everybody. She would rather, on balance, that it was only Lewis.

. . . seventeen . . .

On a flat plain below a hemispherical sky in which the sun was a gigantic whirlpool of heat, two girls raced on lean horses past scrub bushes and dry creek-beds. They wore polo helmets, jodhpurs, white shirts that flapped loosely. They did not race to win, to reach any destination, for there was no destination before them; they raced rather to keep up with one another, to urge ahead a little to provoke one another. Unravelling skeins of ochre dust behind them, they rode with mouths clamped aggressively, although their eyes were bright with pleasure, their cheeks glaring with sweat and energy.

Spontaneously, they slowed, reined their horses and, turning them, brought them to a standstill. One of the girls swung adroitly down and stroked the dark flank of her animal, removed her helmet and smeared her face across her sleeve. The other, the elder, stood up in her stirrups and peered back along the sinking dust-trail they had made.

'Can you see Abraham?' the younger asked, unstrapping a water bottle from her saddle.

'We left him miles back.'

The younger girl untucked her shirt, unbuttoned it halfway and trickled water onto her breasts.

'Naomi, for God's sake!' the elder girl said.

'They bloody well itch, Nell.'

'You just want to make sure they're still there.'

'They're so . . . so stupid. I'm going to have them cut off like Mrs Forbes.'

'You're horrible sometimes.' She, Helena, jerked up her horse's head to stop it nosing at some dry stalks, urged it a little way forward.

Naomi strapped the water bottle back and, slotting her foot expertly into her stirrup, hoisted herself in one gymnastic spring back into her saddle. She walked the horse forward to her sister's, leant across and put her head onto Helena's shoulder.

'I'm sorry, Nell,' she said.

Abruptly, Helena's horse jerked back, forcing her to pull hard to control it. Naomi looked and saw a patch of dust begin to uncurl, to change from dirt into snake with effortless precision. She watched the head lift, the black-bead eyes animate, the mouth open to release the long, venomous hiss of itself. Both girls stooped low, gripped their reins, held down the fear of their beasts as the reptile, slowly and evenly, lowered its head and wound its perfect progression of ribs into a weaving track of departure, disappearing, blending back into the nature of the earth.

'I hate those things,' Helena said.

'They're beautiful. I'm going to catch one and take it back to England with me.'

'You're full of plans, aren't you?' Helena said as they shook their horses into a walk, heading back, the sun now falling flat upon their shoulders.

'Aren't you?'

'Me? No. England will be very dreary. Plan all you like, Naomi, no-one'll let you do anything there.'

They fell silent, following their shadows which spread out before them. Both were possessed of a sense of something ending, of this strange inimical landscape in which they belonged now, alone, together, giving them up, sending them back to a reality of which they were both, in different ways, afraid.

Anna Drewer sat on the veranda reading her son's latest letter, trying to imagine the house he had found for them, trying to imagine England, trying to think the best of it, the best of everything. She looked up often into the glare of the setting sun, an involuntary concern catching her. There was so much to be afraid of here; she felt it more now that they were to leave. She felt as if this place would not let them go, that they were defying some fate in leaving, returning. A small breeze touched her face, the weight of the day lifting a little at evening. How good it will be, she thought, to feel rain again, fog, snow, to come out at last from under the flagstone of

201

heat that pressed their lives here, month after month, flattening them into enervation. That would be good, at least that.

She heard the horses before she saw them, a distant dry rattle of harness, the sound carried in the stillness. She looked up at once to mark the three riders against the haze of the dusk, the easy pace of their approach reassuring her, settling her back to a comfortable fussiness of small concerns: dinner, packing, letters to write, people to see, the girls to chivvy.

She could see them now, her tall girls on their tall horses, distinguish them clearly from Abraham who rode behind them, although she could not, at this distance, tell them apart. Watching them contented her profoundly; they were the sum of her achievements here, fine strong girls, independent: Helena with her grace and sensitivity, Naomi fierce and spontaneous; her wild colonial girls, brought up in freedom such as they could never have had at home.

They were coming down the small escarpment now, dipping into the shadow, their white shirts strong against the dark. One of them raised a hand and waved: Naomi, it would be Naomi. Anna would not rise, would not betray her concern, would wait for them to leave their horses. Helena would see them stabled, would give Abraham instructions, examine their flesh for burrs and ticks; whilst Naomi would run up onto the veranda and flop in a chair, scratch herself and shuffle under Anna's admonitions.

'Why must you always leave Helena to look after your animal?' she would say.

'Oh, Mummy,' would be the reply. 'Oh, Mummy.'

The predictability of this, in the context of their final days here, brought a sudden strength of certainty to her, a sudden awareness of love as something real and physical and strong. It did not matter that there was so much weakness elsewhere, that she was a frail white woman who had outstayed her energy in the irreducible absolutes of this continent. In her girls she was strong, and she was taking that strength and was going to fling it at England.

'Are you awake?'

'Of course. Light the lamp.'

'No. I'll be with you in a moment.'

Anna heard the creak and flap of his holster straps as he slipped from the bedroom. She heard him through the thin wall in his dressing room. She imagined him too large for the room, knocking against its walls, struggling out of his dusty uniform, growing larger naked, more substantial, long-boned and thick-sinewed, dry, bristled skin, shedding the Englishman in a heap on the floor. She shut her eyes as he came in to her, as he lifted the net and ducked himself under it, as the hard unevenness of the bed shifted to his weight. They lay silent, separate in the cooling darkness.

'Did you read Lewis's letter?' he asked.

'Yes. He's been to a lot of trouble.'

'Well, I should hope so. If he's made a nonsense, Anna, we're in queer street.'

'Don't you trust him?'

'Oh yes, absolutely. He's very good at that sort of thing, dogged and meticulous. God knows where he inherited that from.'

'I don't think we gave him very much at all.'

After a while, he said, 'I'll tell you something about Lewis's letter that worries me; no, not worries me exactly. . . .'

'What?'

'When did he last write to us about his social life?'

'There was that friend: O'Neele.'

'Yes, but that was months ago. D'you think he has a social life?'

'Of course he does.'

'But not one he can tell us about.'

'No, well, if it's at all interesting, I'm sure he can't tell us about it. Things are very different for him than they were for us. He probably has a mistress.'

'And would you be happy if he had?'

'Lionel, I don't think I have any right to come back after fifteen years to a country I hardly know any more and tell a twenty-four-year-old man how to conduct his private life. What do you intend to do? Sit him down and tell him where babies come from?'

'Do the girls know?'

'Lionel, of course they do.'

He was silent for a while, but she could sense something uneasy working its way in him. She turned to him and touched his face.

'What is it, my darling?' she said.

'What if. . . .'

'What?'

'What if Lewis doesn't like girls?'

'Then he doesn't like girls.'

'No, what I mean is, what if he prefers . . . men?'

'That's stupid, Lionel.'

She dropped back from him, angry. The thought had never remotely occurred to her; it entered her now like an infection, like something that, thinking of every dire eventuality to forestall it, she had neglected, the one thing she had missed slipping under her guard. She did not know, did not know how she might have known, did not know how she would ever know, or not until it was too late. She had a secure image of her son, carefully constructed over the years, an instinctive intimacy with him that she had felt across the miles. Now, suddenly, Lionel had wrecked it, casually, cruelly. She thought of her lost son and a darkness came over her, darker than the tropical night, sharper than the predators that howled in the nakedness of the plain. She wanted to be home.

. . . eighteen . . .

The night before the boat docked there had been a dance. It had been a dangerous time for such a function: Helena, who had formed a friendship with a young subaltern slowly and cautiously over the weeks of the voyage, had, on that last night, slipped with him onto the open deck and, against the cold buckling of the wind, had allowed him to kiss her, to smother her with his strong body and to dart his tongue into her gasping mouth; Naomi, meanwhile, had celebrated the approach to England with most of a bottle of champagne that had made her feel as lithe and light as a leopard, at first. When Helena had rushed into their cabin, slammed the door behind her and burst into tears, however, Naomi was dumped over the lavatory bowl in a miserable vomit, with a headache that was screwing her eyes back into her brain. There ensued a furious row between them which had ended in bricked-up silence, with both girls burrowed into their bunks in exhaustions of wretchedness and spite. The boat docked before dawn and excited plans to be up to see the day break over their new world were lost.

Naomi was awoken by a sharp rap at their cabin door. She resisted the knock in her aching sleepiness for a while, before waking to realise where they were, to note the silence of the engines. They had arrived and she had missed it. She rolled from her lower bunk, found her travelling-clock and reached up to give her sister a shake.

'It's gone eight, Nell. We're here. We missed it.'

Helena shuffled herself deeper into her bunk and Naomi was considering a wet flannel when the knock came again.

Assuming it would be their mother, she went as she was and unbolted the door, alarmed to find a young man there: thin, a dark, watching face with pronounced features; ugly, she thought; typical bloody Helena. She gripped her nightdress at her neck, her elbow covering its front, and closed the door to an inch.

'I'm afraid my sister's not up yet,' she said loftily.

'Naomi? . . . You're Naomi?'

'Yes, yes, I'm Naomi. And who are you?'

'I'm your brother.'

Helena did not hear the exchange. She too had assumed it must be Tom Rawlings. She burrowed deeper and deeper, burning with shame, terrified of what she had done, what she had let herself in for. She heard Naomi shriek, laugh, bring him into the cabin. This was too much. She rolled herself over, pulled herself up and saw, appalled, her sister embracing a strange man, hanging round his neck and kicking one foot back behind her.

'Stop it!' she cried. 'Who is he? Get him out of here at once.'

Naomi turned and laughed at her.

'You stupid cow, Helena. It's Lewis.'

For a second she didn't know who Lewis was. He stepped clear of Naomi, a little nonplussed by the effusion of her welcome, smiled up at Helena, who gave a little cry of recognition.

'Hello, Helena.'

'Well?' Naomi said. 'Get down from there and give him a kiss, then.'

Helena wasn't sure. She wasn't as free as Naomi was, dancing about in a nightdress in front of a strange young man, whoever he might be. She felt herself blush, smelt the rankness of the previous night in the cabin.

'Look. I'll come back when you're dressed,' he said.

'For heaven's sake, Nell,' Naomi said.

'Hello, Lewis,' she said at last. 'Have you seen Mummy and Daddy yet?'

'Actually, no. I thought I'd surprise you two first. I'm sorry. I've caught you out. I'll go and see if they're up.'

'No!' Naomi cried. 'I want to take you to them. I'll just pull some clothes on.' And she actually began to unbutton her nightdress.

'I'll wait outside,' he said.

'Lewis,' Helena said. 'Just a minute. Naomi, stop. She's quite impossible, Lewis. I'm sorry.'

She began to climb down from her bunk, aware of his watching, aware of the material of the nightdress caught between her buttocks, of her breasts dangling. She turned on the ladder and he was holding out a hand to her. She took his hand and landed abruptly on the rough carpet of the cabin floor. He took her shoulders and placed a neat kiss on her cheek.

The formality done, she stood back and looked into his smile, blushing of course, but opening, filling at last with pleasure. She could see their father in the angles of his face. She had imagined him so differently, imagined him tall and open, with a bright confidence of masculinity; he was slight almost, and his watching of her was complex, involving, as if he knew her very well, as if he knew things about her that she didn't. My brother, she thought, belonging to me, and I to him. Suddenly she began to want him to be proud of her, wanted to be able to say something to him that would assert her in his admiration. But there was nothing; there was only what had happened last night and, remembering that, she burst into tears.

'Hurry up,' Naomi said irritably. 'I want to get dressed.'

Lionel Drewer had not gone to bed. He had dozed in a chair, changed out of his dinner jacket and gone up on deck to watch the glow of England sharpen into distinct lights, to see the shapes of the shipping through which they were drawn, to see the warehouses and wharves, to hear the cries of the stevedores, his native tongue worn smooth by men who used it in the brusque familiarity of manual work. There was a smell of damp and coal-dust and the sweat of a northern sea. The familiarity of it all fell upon him with a certainty that made him feel that he was waking after a long, long sleep, returning to a crowded, demanding world from which he had been hiding.

After they had docked, he returned to the cabin and woke Anna, shaved and packed up his things, helped her pack and sort the cases out.

'It's light now,' he said. 'Come out on deck. Come and have a look at it, at least.'

'No,' she had said. 'I want to be finished here, first.'

'We're home,' he said simply.

'I know.'

She looked at him then so pitifully that he couldn't bear it. He held her briefly and then returned to the deck to watch the unloading, but that seemed so cumbersome, so inefficient, activating all his official instincts. Rather than make a fool of himself by shouting down at their incompetence, he removed to the other side of the ship and stared glumly out along the grey sea-lane that had borne them here. The sky was leaden and factual, the sea-birds mundane and raucous. The liner, which had seemed so exotic when they had boarded it, was now streaked with weather, foul water trickling from its orifices down into the oily surge.

He absorbed it all blankly, felt a monumental uselessness fill him, blotting out all the resolution he needed to re-enter this new world, this old world. He felt as if he had come back to a place that had not changed, that was waiting for him with all its miseries and darkness. We will go back, he said to himself. I will buy a small farm, find a job in a company, grow tea or maize. The rightness of this straightened him. Yes. They would return. There was nothing here, worse than nothing, everything they had freed themselves from. They would return. He turned to go quickly and present this decision to Anna.

As he turned, he heard a cry behind him.

'Daddy!'

He turned back and saw his two tall daughters, one either side of a thin young man, clinging on to him, propelling him forward. They advanced upon him with a cluster of laughter. Three yards from him, they stopped, the girls disengaged themselves, and the young man stepped forward and offered his hand.

'Hello, Daddy.'

Lionel took the hand, grasped the boy round his shoulders and gripped him to his breast with a rage of shame.

... *nineteen* ...

They spent a week in London before going to open up their new home. Lewis reported every afternoon at their hotel to take his sisters out. They seemed, to their parents, to idolise him, were fractious and lethargic through the morning's routine, brightening up only when he arrived with some new delight. They did the museums and galleries, ate pastries in expensive restaurants, went to the theatre and the cinema. He spread before them a cornucopia of treats which intoxicated their colonial hearts. He did not take them back to his flat, and he did not introduce them to anybody.

Anna was invited out with her children, but she always found an excuse not to go. They did not press her, did not have a conscience at leaving her. She was glad of this, wanted the young people to get to know one another. London tired and depressed her. She wanted to be in her own home, to have a regime to her life again, to put the girls into a fixed context. She was happy for them in their new-found liberty, for the time being.

Their rooms at the small hotel were never going to be big enough to contain Naomi. She had to be given lectures on modesty and decorum which made her pout; nor was Anna sure about the way she approached her brother, the kisses and embraces and frank talk about her physical complexities. Lewis was perfectly mannered, raised an amused eyebrow now and then, accepted her entirely and passively on her own terms. Helena, who had always seemed to define herself against her sister's effusions, became more like her in Lewis's presence than she ever had been; not that she was ever loud or sulky or immodest; these were not in her; but she laughed a lot, became busy with plans and enthusiams, seemed blindly happy, open to anything, her quiet and poise suspended before the social operations of her brother. It was almost, Anna thought, as if she were in love.

By the end of the week, Anna had transferred her unease from her daughters' behaviour to her son's. There was something not quite right about him, something cold and secretive. In the few moments of solitary conversation she had with him, he seemed to present so smooth an exterior that her inquiries slid off him.

'Why don't you invite a friend to dinner, Lewis,' she ventured once. 'We'd like to meet your friends.'

'I'm not sure you would, Mummy; anyway, there'll be enough time for all that. I have a lot of time to catch up. You'll be sending them off to school soon, making them dull and English. I want to enjoy them before that happens. They're wonderful girls. I hadn't imagined they would be so much fun. You don't mind me giving them a good time, do you?'

'Just look after them. They're not used to all this.'

He laughed and kissed her.

She didn't like his kisses. They were firm and adroit, confirmations of himself upon her and upon her relationship with him. They assumed things that she did not feel could be assumed. It was as if they had never been away; but they had been away, there was a fifteen-year space between his affections for her now and the affections of an eight-year-old boy.

'What is it with Lewis?' she asked Lionel one evening as they sat up waiting for him to bring the girls home.

'I don't know.'

'There's something, though, isn't there?'

'Yes. I think there is. I don't know. We've lost touch with him. He's been on his own too long. There's something we've missed. I don't much like him now, I'm afraid. Is that a terrible thing to say?'

She felt it was a terrible thing, but it did not shock her as it ought to have done. It silenced her, drew her in, made her afraid to say what she felt.

'We must get the girls into school soon,' he said. 'We must keep them busy, find them friends of their own.'

'We've lost him, haven't we?'

'Oh yes. It was sentimental of us to assume that it would be otherwise.'

At the end of the week, they piled into Lewis's car, the women in the back and Lionel beside him as he drove. It was a bright autumn day, the car was warm, and Lewis drove with confidence and care. Naomi and Helena sang songs in the back as they had done on the long drives along the dusty roads of Africa. Their parents sat quietly.

Lewis, at carefully spaced intervals, reminded them of certain details, outlined what arrangements he had made for the delivery of basic groceries, for the transportation of their trunks and tea chests. Lionel turned to Anna at times and exchanged glances which said, Let us be there soon. Let him let go of us quickly.

'Will you be staying, Lewis?' his mother asked.

'No, no. I must be back in London tonight.'

'It's Saturday tomorrow,' Naomi said. 'You don't have to go to work, surely.'

'Nevertheless, I have to be in London.'

'Why?'

'I have things to do.'

'What things?'

'Naomi, be quiet,' Anna said. 'You have taken up quite enough of your brother's time for the moment.'

'You won't abandon us, will you?' Helena said.

'Of course I won't abandon you.'

'Will you come and stay next weekend? He may come and stay whenever he wants to, mayn't he, Mummy?'

'Of course he may. It will be his home too.'

'I'll telephone you when I get back to London,' he said. 'We'll be there in ten minutes now. You're on home territory now, girls.'

They were quiet then, looking at the low, hedged fields and the patches of woodland, damp and glistening under the brittle sunlight.

'It's so . . . so cramped,' Helena said.

Lewis laughed, looked at his father to share his amusement but found his father also looking grimly into the landscape.

Empty of all but basic furniture, uncarpeted and smelling of new paint, the house was large and echoey, and cold. The girls ran off and explored for themselves, their frights and enthusiasms ringing down. Lewis, meanwhile, took his parents on a systematic tour.

'I wasn't sure,' he said. 'I knew you'd want somewhere of a decent size, but I didn't want you to have too much bother with maintenance.'

'You've done very well,' Lionel said. 'Very well indeed. We're very, very grateful.'

He stayed and ate a rough supper with them, having lit the kitchen range, showed them how to do it. Lionel and Anna thought he would never go; even the girls were subdued, tired and overwhelmed by the newness. Lewis continued to be endlessly helpful until they fell into silence around him.

'Stay the night, Lewis,' Anna said. 'You'll not make it back before the early hours.'

'No, no,' he said. 'Thank you, but I must go.'

They followed him through to the hall to bid him farewell, to thank him for everything.

'I hope you'll be happy here,' he said. 'It is wonderful to have you back at last; wonderful.'

When the sound of his car had at last disappeared into the thick night, they went mutely to bed, as if there were nothing more to be done in his absence. A dispiritment clouded them all. They felt abandoned in a chill, dark space that was too large for them, and yet, at the same time, enclosed, limiting, a capacious cell in the solitude of which they would learn more about themselves than they wanted to know.

Lewis drove straight from his parents to a small lay-by within sight of Manfield Academy. He turned off the lights of the car, lit a cigarette and viewed the hulk of the school with its few lights glaring like yellow carbuncles. He did not know where her room was, but he could sense her out there, moving, restless, turning in the coils of herself.

Not an hour passed when he did not think of her, even during the busyness of the preceding week. Even when he was with his sisters he thought of her; especially then. They gave off, each in their individual way, a fierce sexuality, innocent and open, that he related to the toils of his relationship with Celia, putting it into a perspective that cleared it, made him feel that it was part of a bigger world, part of the multiplicity of humanity. He had felt, with Helena and Naomi, brilliantly normal again, stabilised. He had found the other life he had lacked and from its bastion he would be stronger for her. He yearned for her with this new strength, sat at the wheel of his dark car and filled his mind with her, set his pulse to her.

He would call her tomorrow, make arrangements, take her home to meet his family. He started the car, gunned the engine for a while, then switched the lights on, almost expecting to catch her in their beam. She was not there, not yet. He reversed and opened the miles between them rapidly.

... *twenty* ...

He stayed away a month, although he telephoned them regularly. The sound of the telephone, jangling through the house, made them stop, held them. Lionel would step quietly through their watching and answer. Yes, things were going very well. The vicar had called, and Colonel Jexly. They had a girl from the village now, not living in, but coming daily. They were looking for someone for the garden. They would manage, were managing, were still sorting out really, still settling in. Then he invited himself down for a Saturday night. Naomi expected him to take them out, wondered what treat he would have for them. Helena spent a long time deciding what to wear, unpinning and repinning her hair.

He blew back into the house just as he had been before. Lionel and Anna felt diminished by him, hated the fuss the girls made. He brought them fine shawls from London, a bottle of whisky for his father, a couple of new novels for his mother. But there was something else, some other surprise that he had for them, and at dinner he presented it.

'I was thinking of coming up again next weekend.'

'Fine, Lewis. Of course,' his father said.

'May I bring someone to dinner?'

'Of course you may,' his mother said. 'A friend, Lewis?'

'Naturally. Don't sound so surprised.'

'We'll have to clear out the spare room, girls,' Anna said.

'Oh no. That won't be necessary. She's . . . she's someone local, actually; well, not exactly local as such. She's a teacher at Manfield. I knew her in London and suddenly discovered she was living up here, working.'

The implications of this were substantial. Each of them wanted to ask him questions, but none of them knew how to phrase the question they sought to ask. A silence ensued. Lewis smiled at them, much pleased with the effect he had created.

'Well?' Naomi said at last. 'Tell us her name, at least.'

'Her name, Naomi, is Celia Bratley.'

She did not know why she was here. She did not want to meet his parents and his sisters. She struggled against it, but did not know how she might have refused him, could not now have refused him anything. She despised him, but could not keep away from him, came away from every contact with him unsatisfied, angry, tearful. She lived the rest of her life wrapped in a tight skin, hardening over her. She did not know how it would ever be resolved. Perhaps he would drive her mad, kill her even; perhaps this was what she wanted.

'Mummy? This is Celia.'

'Hello, Celia. We are so glad to meet you.'

'And my father; and Helena; and Naomi.'

She shook their hands in turn, found it difficult to meet their eyes, which registered her intently. She felt their solidarity, the exchange of questioning glances, their first impressions of her locking her. She looked back at Lewis, wanting to know whose side he was on. He was observing the situation curiously, her before his family, as if this were an arrangement that interested him, as if he wanted to move about and consider its various angles. She hated it.

Over dinner the formality barely covered the hostility. Mrs Drewer made the conversation; her husband seemed to have removed himself to a distance; the girls plainly glowered at her, the younger one breaking into stupid chatter with Lewis or her sister as if deliberately to exclude her; whilst Lewis leant forward, watching every exchange, apprising it subtly.

'Do you enjoy your work, Celia?'

'It has its satisfactions, Mrs Drewer. I must earn my living, however.'

'Yes, of course. You have family?'

'Three sisters, but we . . . we were never really close.'

'Tell us. Lewis has warned us off Manfield. I mean for Helena and Naomi. What would you advise?'

'Oh, it's a very ordinary school, really. I would have thought you would want something a little more high-powered. We do our job there, but girls need more than that nowadays, I think. They need to be doctors and civil servants. I wish I had had a better start.'

'What would you have liked to be, Celia?' his father asked abruptly.

'I don't know, Mr Drewer. I think I would have liked to have become an academic, perhaps. I like the discipline of knowledge.'

She ought to have given something back to them, to have asked them about their time abroad, to ask them how they found Lewis after all these years, but she had no stomach for this. She endured their questions, but did not want to be involved with them any further than she had to be. She did not want them to like her, did not like them, with their smug solicitude, the wealth of mutual emotions that she felt moving between them; she did not want to belong to that. She responded to their questioning with a sharp, defensive clarity.

She knew what they really wanted to know, the sisters particularly. She could sense it on their open mouths, in their restless evening dresses. She looked at them occasionally: the older one was always staring, always dropped her face when Celia turned; the younger faced her out, her nose lifting, her lips opening to reveal uneven teeth. She knew what they wanted. She would have enjoyed telling them. Your brother and I copulate like dogs. They were both virgins in a way that she had never been: their virginity was clean and true, whereas hers had always been a mask, always a hypocrisy, always a denial of herself. She was bitterly jealous of them.

She removed to the drawing room with Mrs Drewer and her daughters, whilst Lewis drank port with his father. The younger girl did not stay long, said she had a stomach-ache and retired to bed. The elder served coffee, but not to herself, sat despondently whilst the petty chat proceeded between Celia and her mother.

'Go and see if Naomi's all right, will you?' her mother prompted soon enough.

There was a silence then.

'Tell me about you and Lewis, Celia.'

'What would you like to know, Mrs Drewer? We are friends. We knew each other well in London. He's been very . . . very kind to me. As you know, I had some trouble with my family. He's helped me find my feet again.'

'I find it very hard to know what he feels about things,' said his mother.

'Do you? I've always found him . . . very direct.'

'Ah well,' she said, closing the opening she had made. 'Ah well.'

'Well?' he asked as he drove her through the gates and turned onto the road.

'I don't want to talk about it,' she said, lighting a cigarette.

He wanted to talk about it, though. He said nothing, but drove her to the place from where he had watched the school, on many occasions, his vantage point. He turned off the engine and waited for her. She sat silent beside him, hardly registering where they were. It was a blowy night, with a drizzly swirl beading the windscreen. The trees heaved and crackled above them, and the distant lights from the school flickered and blurred.

'Well?' he said at length.

'What?'

'How did you like my family?'

'How do you think they liked me, Lewis?'

'I have no idea.'

'You liar.'

'I don't care what they think about you.'

'D'you mean that?'

'Yes. They're a game I play, Celia. It's fun. They don't know who I am. I keep them guessing. You were wonderful tonight, really wonderful.'

'Fuck me, Lewis,' she said abruptly.

He wanted to laugh, felt a sheer, cold silence come between them.

'What, now?' he said.

'Now, yes. Here. Just do it.'

They went into the back of the car. He made her sit astride him, made her do it. She was remarkably quick, twisting it out of her, made a noise as if some long thorn were being pulled slowly out of her flesh. They sorted themselves out and returned to the front of the car.

'Shall I take you back now?' he said.

'In a moment.'

Then she did something extraordinary. She leant across and placed her head on his shoulder, reached her arm around him and lay for some minutes cradled against him, and he soothed her hot face, kissing her hair, told himself that this must be it, love, this must be love, this beached aching, this floating, motiveless tenderness, this wonderful stupid joy that he felt in her, every second a perfect replication of the one before, his heart toiling manfully within him towards her.

. . . *twenty-one* . . .

Lionel waited up for Lewis's return. Anna could not bear to wait, had gone straight to bed, had not even been in to see the girls. Lionel sat at the dining-room table, drank brandy and waited.

Helena appeared at the door in her dressing gown.

'Daddy? Is he going to marry her?'

'Go to bed, Helena. Go to bed.'

She went.

Lionel did not stir when he heard the sound of the car, did not move when the front door opened, closed, locked. Lewis would see that the light was still on; he could come in if he wanted to, if he had anything to say.

He could not think about that woman with any clarity. Had he met her in any neutral context, he would have labelled her the typical spinster schoolmistress, full of the cold repressions of her profession. Against Lewis, however, he did not know. He had known women like that, in the army and in Africa, women who should never have married, whose hurts had turned to spite and cruelty. And he knew something more about his son now; that under the superb confidence he operated amongst them, there was a wound of weakness and ignorance with which he had turned to this woman for consolation. He had watched Lewis closely whilst she had been there, had seen his complacency and knew that it had gone a long way, too far to stop now probably. He waited, poured himself more brandy and wondered whether he really wanted his son to come in to him.

'You weren't waiting up for me, were you, Daddy?'

'Come and have a nightcap, Lewis.'

He accepted, sat down, lit a cigarette, smiled, eased back in his chair and undid his tie. He smelt unmistakably of semen.

'Did you see your guest home all right?'

'Oh yes . . . well? Tell me what you think, then.'

Lionel shrugged; various platitudes occurred to him, but he could not bring himself to any of them.

'How well do you know her, Lewis?'

'Oh . . . pretty well.'

'Are you lovers?'

Lewis laughed, raised his eyebrows, gave a little whistle.

'How much do you want to know, Daddy?'

'Only what you want me to know.'

'We're lovers, yes. Does that upset you?'

'No. Nothing to do with me. Will you marry?'

'I don't know. I've asked her to marry me, but . . . but, it's not simple. She's . . . not a tremendously happy person.'

'And what about you, Lewis? Are you happy?'

'Oh yes.'

'Give me one of those cigarettes, would you? Thank you . . . there's talk of another war, you know.'

'I thought you'd fought the war to end war?'

'Apparently we didn't. Don't you read the newspapers, Lewis?'

'Only the financial pages, and the music critics; oh, and the odd murder.'

'If there were to be another war, would you fight?'

'Would I have a choice?' Then, after a pause, he said, 'You didn't like Celia much, did you?'

'I really have no opinion of her. She didn't give much away, did she?'

Lewis laughed and refilled his brandy glass.

'No, She gives nothing away. You have to fight for everything with her. She's wonderful.'

'Lewis? How would you react if . . . if I said I thought she was using you.'

'Using me? Well, of course she is. And I'm using her. Isn't that what it's all about?'

'I'm not sure. Perhaps. It's nothing to do with me. Well, I think I'll go up now. Turn off the lights, would you.'

Lionel left him with the decanter amongst the remains of the dinner table. Anna was asleep, or pretending to be. Even the girls were quiet. Only Lewis could be heard, moving downstairs. Lionel listened and realised that Lewis was cleaning up, washing the dishes, making himself useful, bright and cheerful, dumbly pleased with himself. Is that it? Lionel thought. Is he really just stupid?

He sat in his dressing room, staring at the floor, half-undressed, lacking the volition to proceed to bed, afraid that Anna would turn to him, would ask him questions he did not want to answer, did not want to think out. What Lewis had said to him returned to him indigestibly: fighting for everything, using each other, that's what it was all about. He refused to understand any of this. It was an emotional, psychological language that he did not speak.

Things were different now; and it was not just Lewis. He had seen it on the streets of London, had read about it in the papers, seen it in a repulsive exhibition of modern art that Lewis had recommended and which he had taken himself secretly off to see. He had seen it then; but now he felt it, knew it and, seeing it close-up for the first time, he began to understand.

Before the war, when he had courted Anna, things had been clear. There had been ways of doing things, predictable social forms into which you had fitted yourself, however ungainly you might have been, clear boundaries of what was proper and what was not proper. Now it seemed that what had once been completely off-limits, whole dark sides of people that used to be closed down, locked safely away, were being opened up. It didn't matter whether Lewis was stupid, whether his mistress was a manipulative bitch, whether they loved or respected one another in their intimacies. People had become their own gods; people in themselves, as they were, not as they were expected to be, judged to be. They had come out from the protection of formality, revelled in their individuality, explored and pursued themselves into the darkness, curious, laughing, prodding at being alive; celebrated themselves in all the cynicism of their ugliness and perversity. It appalled him and terrified him; he wanted only to hide his head from it, from the shame and anarchy of it.

He thought of what was happening in Europe, the gathering triumphs of tyranny, which seemed to him a direct reaction to what Lewis embodied, a return to brutal, murdering certainty. He understood that now and knew that Lewis and his generation would have no possible answer to it.

He thought of his daughters and the world into which they were about to set forth and he shuddered.

. . . *twenty-two* . . .

Celia recalled her visit to the Drewers with miserable shame. She knew that they despised her, saw her for what she was. She knew what she was, and Lewis knew; but she could not bear that to be shared with others. Lewis rang her from London the week after and seemed entirely pleased with the evening, and with the effect she had made. Remembering how she had behaved afterwards, she understood that her humiliation had been designed by him to draw her into a new sexual complicity. She loathed it.

He reassured her, however, that she was unlikely to run into any member of his family over the next few weeks, as they were all going north to visit his blind uncle. She was resentful that Lewis should be a part of a complex family, a family that was not only wealthy, but established, gentry with tradition and history. She felt he had cheated her, had come to her alone, a solitary figure with only his own inadequacies to play against hers. She was alone still; he was revealing his own belonging to her, stage by stage, drawing it round her, a net that he would pull tight about her. She would become his wife. She would become a part of it. She would disappear.

She had entered her second year of teaching with every instinct and foible of her first year hardened. She was becoming a caricature like the rest of them: the ferocious Miss Bratley with the withering eye, the little shudders of revulsion at them, the pitilessness of her knowledge of their weaknesses. She longed to put her cane to use again, came to the edge of it on several occasions, but moved back from the edge in a confusion of motives, never finally certain that if she let that rage out of her it would ever be satisfied.

She wondered how many of her colleagues had the devastations of another life below their masks; began to watch them, to imagine them obscenely, tending their genitals like pets, dreaming of farm-lads with penises like overripe fruit, or of the pallid, plumping flesh of the little girls in their classes. She felt the lurch of a communal madness waiting behind every closed door, a rank stench below the carbolic and cabbage of the school corridors, the stench of menstrual decay.

She prayed at night, in long vigils, but her God told her only that this was the burden of the flesh, that it must be endured. She begged for pity, for release, for death even; but there was none of that available. Once, after a particularly intense and restless hour upon her knees on the carpet beside her bed, when the words had ceased to fire in her head and had left only the blunt shoving to bring out the pain, she suddenly surfaced to find herself coiled down over a small but fierce sexual climax. After this, things became very clear. She got into bed and lay there quite empty, not knowing whether she had reached a new depth or whether, in some way, she had been subject to a revelation.

'Hello, Celia!'

She turned from the bank counter to find Mrs Drewer standing close behind her. She nodded her head and turned back to finish writing her cheque, to wait for the man to count and re-count her money, to slide the pile of coins across on the note. As she slipped the money into her purse, she found that her hands were trembling. That woman was still there, waiting behind her, watching her.

'Are you well?'

'Yes, quite well, thank you, Mrs Drewer.'

'I'm sorry we haven't been in touch before, but we've been staying with my brother in the north.'

'Yes. Lewis mentioned it.'

'Is this your afternoon off? Come to tea, why don't you? Lionel's in town, but the girls would be very glad to see you.'

'I have some . . . some things that I must do. Thank you.'

'Do come. Please. You've been on my conscience.'

The dingy little bank was the wrong place for this exchange. Had they been out in the street, she could have walked away; but the eyes of the clerks were upon her, the eyes of the other customers, greasy eyes before ticking little brains.

'I'll be just two minutes,' Mrs Drewer said, moving to the counter and handing over a money order.

Celia moved aside, composed herself, tried not to think of those girls, his sisters. She took a succession of strong breaths and listened to the heavy tick of the bank clock, the muffled talk, the scratch of pens, the shifting of bodies from desk to desk as this little outpost of the great financial machine went about its functions.

'Right, then. I've a little car now, so I can drive you out and back to Manfield. Come along.'

The house looked different in daylight. It was a bright, naked winter's day, and the rooms were wide open to the sunlight. The furnishings and ornaments were spare, but with a burnished, personal quality that suggested to Celia that any object she might care to select would have a history, a story, a meaning. In her days of affluence she had had many fine things, but none of them had meant anything to her; now she had almost nothing, nothing of value, nothing that she would not have been quite content never to see again.

The drawing room was warm; a lavish coal fire roared up the chimney and spread a heavy heat.

'We cannot get used to the English cold,' Mrs Drewer told her. 'Warmth is our great extravagance. Do make yourself comfortable, Celia. I'll fetch the girls and set the tea in motion.'

In her hostess's absence, Celia listened to the noises of the house: the daughters being called, doors closing, voices. She leant back in her chair and, closing her eyes, felt suddenly very tired, the heat from the fire blurring her.

She roused quickly as the door opened and the sisters came in together, the younger going straight to the fire, kneeling before it and consuming its heat greedily, whilst her sister came and shook Celia's hand.

'Hello again,' Celia said.

'Hello, Celia. Stop pigging all the fire, Naomi.'

Naomi withdrew with a surly toss of herself and plumped down on the sofa beside her sister, glowering at Celia.

'Have you seen Lewis recently?' Naomi asked.

'No. Not since he was last down. Have you?'

'We don't see him here,' Naomi said. 'I thought he was your . . .'

'Naomi!' Helena said.

'You thought he was my what, Naomi?'

'Your boyfriend.'

'Naomi!'

'Well, I suppose he is. Does that upset you?'

Naomi opened her mouth to respond but her sister jabbed her side and she restrained herself. Celia began to enjoy this.

'It's French you teach, isn't it?' Helena asked after a pause.

'Yes. French, and a little German, and games: hockey and lacrosse. Are either of you two games players?'

Naomi snorted contemptuously.

'Well, not really,' Helena said. 'We used to ride a lot.'

'Have your parents decided on a school for you yet?'

'Yes,' Helena said. 'Dovebridge. It's near London. D'you know it?'

'I know of it. It's a very good school. You'll enjoy it there.'

'Well, I won't enjoy it,' Naomi said. 'Schools are prisons where they lock you up and stop you from being yourself.'

'Of course they are,' Celia said. 'But that's necessary. Don't you think? If everyone was entirely themselves, the world would be a very nasty place.'

'Speak for yourself,' Naomi said.

'For heaven's sake!' Helena said. 'I'm sorry my sister's so rude, Celia. You're quite right. She does need to go to school, to learn some manners at least.'

'I don't mind.' And really she didn't mind, preferred Naomi's aggression to the constipated politeness she had expected here.

'Go and help Mummy with the tea,' Helena said.

Naomi jerked up from the sofa and left without a word, banging the door.

Celia smiled at Helena who looked at her closely.

'She's a spoilt little bitch,' Helena said. 'She's been poisonous ever since we arrived.'

'It's not just me, then.'

'Good heavens, no.'

'I thought it might be something to do with Lewis and me.'

'Oh no. Why should it be?'

Celia watched the lie flushing on her face.

'I'm not in love with your brother, Helena,' she said quickly. 'I don't even like him very much. We share . . . some secrets about one another. That's all.'

'What secrets, Celia?'

'You wouldn't want to know them, even if I could find the words to explain them to you.'

'Are they . . . about sex?'

222

'If they were, how could I tell you?'

'I know about all that. Honestly.'

'No you don't,' she said sharply.

Helena then began to cry, and Celia took pleasure in that. Helena was the one member of this smug little family whom she could reach, the one she could mark. Like the rest of them, Helena loathed her, loathed what she did to Lewis, but she was too old for the active hostility of her younger sister, too young for the social command of her parents. Making her liberal effort here to come to terms with her brother's mistress, she was particularly vulnerable. Celia watched her struggling with what she had told her so far, wanted to go on. You're in love with him, she wanted to say. You want to know what I know about him, don't you? You want the intimacy of that knowledge to fill your fantasies of him. What shall I tell you, then? What?

She stood and moved across to stand above the weeping girl, the implacable schoolmistress before the snivelling slut she would shortly brace up with a little medicinal pain. Helena fumbled with a handkerchief and snuffled into it.

'I'm sorry,' Helena said, then, before Celia could respond, sprang up and wrapped her arms around her, was hugging her. 'I only . . . only want him to be happy,' she said. 'I only want him to be happy.'

Something tore within Celia at this response. She clasped Helena to her tightly, and in a bleak instant she understood the nature of love, felt it pour from this wretched girl and knew its absolute lack within her, knew the nature of what replaced it within her, shuddered with revulsion.

'It's all right,' she said. 'It's all right. Please, Helena, please.'

She lowered the girl back onto the sofa.

'Tell your mother that . . . that I felt ill, that I had to be back. Apologise for my ill-manners. Look after your brother, will you? He deserves better than I could ever give him. Really. Really.'

As she left, running out across the hall, through the front door and down the slopping gravel away from the house, she trusted Helena to forestall any attempt at pursuit; anyway, by the time she reached the road, she was moving too fast and too far for them.

. . . *twenty-three* . . .

Ringing Celia was a complex process. He could ring her only between eight and half-past on Tuesdays and Thursdays, and then usually had to negotiate with some hard-voiced woman who begrudgingly went in search of her. Their conversations lasted no more than seven minutes; he timed them.

'Might I speak to Miss Bratley, please?'

'Oh. Ah, yes . . . a moment, please . . .'

He had to wait longer than usual listening to the crackle of the machine and hearing the echoes of heavy-shoed feet, the prurience of muffled voices.

'Hello?' It was not Celia.

'May I speak to Miss Bratley, please?'

'May I ask who is calling?'

'It is a personal call,' he said.

'Miss Bratley is not here at the moment.'

'Not there?'

'Excuse me. I am Naomi Dachet, Headmistress. May I know, please, to whom I am speaking?'

Lewis felt a sudden premonition, a darkness into which he was moving.

'My name,' he said slowly, 'is Lewis Drewer. I am a close friend of Miss Bratley's. May I know, please, what has happened to her?'

'Are you, Mr Drewer, the young man who rings her regularly?'

'I do, yes, occasionally ring her. What is this about?'

'Well, we were hoping that you might tell us.'

'What do you mean?'

'Miss Bratley has absented herself from her duties here without so much as a word. We thought that perhaps you would be able to furnish us with an explanation of her . . . her absence.'

'No, Miss Dachet. I have absolutely no idea where she is or why she has gone. I will be travelling down tonight. Have you informed the police?'

'The police, Mr Drewer? What are you saying?'

He rang home and learned that something had happened, that Helena had been with her, had said something, that Celia had left abruptly. Helena was not available to come to the telephone, had gone to bed, wasn't feeling well. Lewis set out after her, after them all.

Driving down through the night, his anger kept him awake. It did not make him reckless on the empty roads; it was a hard anger that he applied in his mind to all of them; to that dismal headmistress woman; to his family, to Helena of all people, who had turned upon her and driven her away; to her, silly bitch, tumbling off into the darkness to some squalid little suicide somewhere. The thought of that, which seemed a high probability, made the rage jump up in him; the stupid waste of it, the obscene self-indulgence; as if she had cheated, finally, in the game that he was playing with her. Only with himself was he not angry: a fist of righteousness was rammed through him.

He arrived at dawn and was waiting in the kitchen when his mother appeared to make tea. He had already made the tea. He told his mother that he wanted to speak to Helena, didn't care how ill she was.

Helena appeared looking sheepish and sickly, gave him little information, had not really understood what happened. Naomi had gone off in a sulk. They had talked about him, yes. She, Helena, had become upset.

'She was so . . . so cold about everything, Lewis. She frightened me. She said . . . she said that I was to look after you, that she wasn't good enough for you, then she left. I . . . I didn't really think. Lewis? Have I done something dreadful? Have I?'

He kissed Helena and told her that it was all right, that he would find her, that it was not her fault. She had had a serious fright, though, a sexual fright, and the nature of that disturbed and intrigued him. He must set off in search of Celia at once.

He rang the bank to tell them that he had a family crisis that would detain him for a couple of days. Next he went to the school. He arrived at the front door, made an impression of himself, and was shown into Miss Dachet's study. He took a somewhat aggressive tone, suggesting obliquely that if anything had happened there might well be a scandal, that Miss Bratley was very well connected. Having put the headmistress on the defensive, he had little difficulty in persuading her to allow him to search her room.

The woman stood in the doorway as he searched, which he did not like but could think of no way of avoiding. There was nothing there of any value, no correspondence, no address book. The harsh impersonality of the room depressed him, suggesting that there was a blankness to her life that perhaps he had not fully accounted for. The religious books also disturbed him. There is quite a lot, he thought, that I do not know about her.

He returned home for lunch without the first clue of how to proceed. His mother suggested ringing the police, but he did not want to admit that what had happened might fall into their jurisdiction. He had lunch with them, but was so wrapped up in his speculations that he surfaced to find them watching him, waiting for him, not daring to suggest anything. Even Naomi was silent.

After lunch he drove to the coast; it was not that he hoped she would be there; he merely wanted to be alone to think. He parked on the esplanade of a dingy and deserted seaside town and watched the windscreen of his car become obscured by spray from the futile, heaving sea.

He came then to a standstill. The energy of his anger had driven him throughout the day, made him purposeful, had created a certainty or progress within him that here, now, was emptied. He began to admit the possibility that he had lost her, that whether she was dead or alive, she had gone, that he would never know why or where. And he began to grieve for her, began to know the truth of her as he felt her torn from him. Then it was only himself that he blamed: for not knowing her, for his abuse and cruelty, for plunging himself into her in search of himself, always himself, never her, driving her always into reactions to him, feeding on those reactions, developing himself against them. He would never touch another woman. He would search for her for the rest of his life if necessary, never give up, never be satisfied until he had found her; and if she was dead, then he was dead; and if she was alive, whatever his life became would be in her gift; and if that gift was merely what he deserved, then he was finished anyway.

He returned to Framling late and tired, took a little cold supper in the kitchen, made a point of being pleasant to Helena and abrupt with Naomi, who wanted to burst out and tell him she wasn't worth it but did not dare to. He could sense that this was developing into the most serious rift that his sisters had ever known. Good, he thought. They needed to grow apart. Helena needed the strength of independence from Naomi.

In the morning, he woke with an idea.

'Mummy? You said you saw her in the bank. What was she doing?'

'Withdrawing money, I assume.'

'How much money?'

'Really, Lewis. I don't peer over people's shoulders in banks.'

'A hundred pounds? Five pounds? You must've had some idea. It's important.'

'Not a hundred pounds, certainly. I don't know. There was a note, some change. Not even five pounds. Why?'

The local bank was a branch of one of the big banks and Lewis rang through to London to their head office to speak to Bill Naylor who owed him a favour. Quite a lot of people owed Lewis favours.

'What can I do for you, Drewer?'

'I want to trace one of your customers. A girl. Purely a personal matter, but very important, very urgent. The name is Bratley, Celia Bratley. Have you got that?'

'Celia Bratley. Right. What d'you want? Her address?'

'No. I want to know if she has drawn out any money today; not yesterday, today. And I want to know where she drew it. Or any cheques she has written in the past twenty-four hours.'

'Drewer, that could take a week to find out.'

'I know. But it's important to me. I'll be at home or at the bank. Ring me the instant you find anything. Please.'

He returned to London and waited, went back to work, twitched telepathically the second before a telephone rang, had to rouse himself from a moment's blankness after each disappointment. He was more ruthless than usual that week, and even MacBlaine kept clear of him.

After ten days, he could wait no longer and rang Naylor again.

'Oh, Drewer. Yes, there was something. I meant to ring you, but you know how it is. Where are we, now? Ah yes. Blackwell. Does that make any sense to you?'

'None at all.'

'Somewhere up north. Industry. Hymn singing and hunger marches, that sort of place, I believe.'

'What is it, Naylor?'

'Well, that's it really, old man. She drew out fifty pounds from a branch in Blackwell. They had to telephone through for confirmation.'

'When?'

'Let me see. Wednesday. Last Wednesday. Any use to you?'

He went in to see MacBlaine at once.

'I'm afraid I shall have to take a few more days off, sir.'

'This personal business again, Drewer, is it?'

'Yes, sir.'

'Well, it's not very convenient, you know.'

The old man could hardly be blamed for his moment of spite. Lewis took his punishment meekly.

'It could be a matter of life and death, sir.'

'Indeed. Not . . . not a member of your family, Drewer?'

'No, sir. A young lady of my acquaintance.'

'Really, Drewer? A dark horse out in the paddock, eh? Nothing . . . nothing scandalous, I trust, young man. Anyone we know?'

'Celia Bratley, sir.'

MacBlaine dropped his mouth abruptly. Lewis had not meant to tell him; five minutes ago would have endured torture rather than tell him, but the delight of winding him like this was worth it.

'Celia Bratley? Good Lord, Drewer. Are you still in touch with her?'

'Oh yes, sir, very much so.'

'Well . . . well, you'd better . . . take a few days then, but . . . but don't . . . don't be any longer than . . .'

'No, sir, of course not.' And as he turned to leave, he had another thought. 'Where did the Bratleys have their factory, sir? Can you remember?'

'In the north somewhere.'

'Blackwell?'

'No, no. That was where their house was, or just outside. Went there once. Rather a grim sort of place. Why d'you ask?'

. . . *twenty-four* . . .

It was a long drive north. During the drive, he rehearsed his strategies. He imagined visiting methodically all the lodging houses in Blackwell. The tedium of this prospect made him decide that he would not actively search for her, not for a couple of days. He would simply visit places, make himself obvious in the sort of places she might visit. Her old house, of course. Then where? Churches? Yes, he would begin on the vicars. He wanted ideally not to see her, but for her to see him and step out from wherever she was hiding; he did not think that she would, but he wanted to give her a chance to.

As he moved into the clustering conurbation, the dead factories and clumps of idle men on street corners, the urchins who watched his car with pinched malevolence, he began to feel absurd, even considered turning back, leaving it. He had come too far for that, however. He would make the gesture, but knew he would fail; knew that he would have to come to terms with failure, the central failure of his life. He had come to realise that, below the clever shams he inhabited for his family and for MacBlaine, all that he had come to value in himself depended upon her. He did not know how he was going to begin again on the other side of her. This journey was a penance, then, a ritual futility, the last stone to be turned before he went away and found, God only knew how, some other motivation for himself.

He arrived late in Blackwell, booked into a commercial hotel, rose early and went off to see the house she had lived in for the first years of her life, the years of her affluence. He had located the house on the map, but was not prepared for the thick screen of trees, had expected to be able to see it from the road. There was a gateway but no gate, a lodge that did not look inhabited. He stopped the car on the road before the gate, then, constructing some fiction for the occupants, he turned in and drove up the narrow, twisting drive.

The trees opened suddenly to a small stretch of unkempt lawn beyond which the house stood. It was smaller than he had imagined, a heavy, squat building with mock turrets and pinnacles. It was boarded up, deserted, decaying. He drove the car slowly up to the front of the house, stopped, and wondered whether it was even worth getting out.

He glanced round, intending to reverse the car to face the way out and, as he did so, he saw her sitting on a bench on the far side of the lawn, quite alone, quite still, watching.

As he walked towards her, she did not look at him, stared at the house with a sad, serious face, as if everything were now at an impossible distance.

'Celia?' he said, when he was by her.

She looked up then, noted him briefly, looked away again. He sat beside her on the stone bench.

'What are you doing here?' he said quietly.

'Oh . . . just looking. I grew up here, you know.'

'Yes. Everyone's been very worried about you.'

'They had no need to be.'

'How long have you been here?'

'Not long. Half-an-hour or so.'

'What have you been doing, since you left, I mean?'

'Coming here. I arrive here as early as I can. I sit here until dusk, then I make my way back into town.'

'Did you . . . did you expect me to come and find you?'

'No. I just . . . I just wanted to be here, away from it all. Yes, I suppose in a way I did expect you. When you drove up, I knew I was expecting you, but I hadn't thought about it before then.'

'Will you come back with me?'

'Where?'

'Well, to Framling, to London, to Manfield. Just back, Celia.'

'I don't think I can really.'

'Why not?'

'Because . . . because I don't really belong there. I don't really belong anywhere. Except here, and this . . . this is all over. I thought someone was living here. I'm glad they're not. I hated the thought of someone else having a life here. They're going to pull it down, you know.'

'Come back with me, Celia.'

'No, no.'

'Not to that bloody school. Come back with *me*. Come back and marry me.'

'That's quite out of the question, Lewis. You know it is.'

'I know nothing of the sort. What are you going to do?'

'I don't know. I haven't thought. Come out here, I suppose.'

'And when your money runs out?'

'I thought I might become a nun, but I don't think they'd have me. Do you? I mean, I'd have to tell them everything, wouldn't I? Perhaps I'll be a prostitute. D'you think I'd be any good at that?'

'Is that a serious question?'

She shrugged and sighed vaguely.

'Celia, come and get into the car. We'll go and pick up your things . . .'

'I don't have any things.'

'So much the better. We'll be in London by morning.'

'I can't, Lewis. You know I can't. Please. Don't be a pest.'

'Why can't you? Do you want just to stay here, to sit here?'

'It's not a question of what I want. It's just how it is.'

'Explain to me how it is. I don't understand.'

'It's no good. That's all.'

'Why?'

'Why must you keep asking about it? It's no good. It's just no good.'

'What's no good, Celia?'

'I am no good. You are no good. None of it's any good at all.'

'Was it something Helena said to you?'

'Helena?'

'My sister. You ran off after speaking to her.'

'Oh yes. I remember. Yes. You see, Lewis, she's in love with you and I am not.'

'She's my sister, Celia. I love her dearly, but I can't marry her, can I? I can't take her to bed with me. I can't have children with her.'

'No. You can't, can you. Poor Lewis.'

She paused here. He felt for the first time since he had arrived that he had made her think, had caught something within her.

'Is that what you want out of life, then, Lewis?'

'Yes, it is.'

'I'm sure you'll find someone soon.'

'I've found you, Celia.'

'Yes. That was clever of you. You've always been clever, too clever for me, made me do things I don't want to do. That's been the problem.'

'Has it? Has it been a problem?'

'I think it has.'

'Very well. I concede. I will leave you in a little while. I will go back to London. I will tell no-one where you are. I will not make you do anything.'

'It will be for the best.'

'For you, perhaps, although I doubt it. For me, it will be . . . a kind of death, but I will not fight you. I will not impose myself upon you. If you want your freedom, then you shall have it, although you will not have freedom here, only this nasty little pit you have dug for yourself in which, my love, you will drown. I cannot bear to see you like this, but I am weak and helpless before it.'

'Do you love me, Lewis?'

'Yes, I do.'

'I don't love you, though.'

'You love no-one, least of all yourself. What you're doing here is to commit a mindless act of spite against yourself. Come back with me, Celia, marry me, have my children. I will teach you about love. It begins, it always begins, with an act of surrender.'

She was silent then. For ten minutes they sat in the silence of the afternoon, with a fine, bitter rain blowing across the lawn upon them. Then at last he rose, looked down at her, then began to walk slowly across the lawn to the car. When he turned back for a final image of her, she was walking across the lawn towards him. He waited for her and, when she came to him, he opened the car door and she got in.

. . . *twenty-five* . . .

It was too late when they left Blackwell to make London in one run. He stopped at a roadside hotel and booked them into separate rooms: he did not want to complicate things, felt her to be tremendously fragile now; he wanted only to bear her safely south where he could look after her.

Over dinner he found her entirely practical, entirely acquiescent.

'I'll ring your Miss Dachet tomorrow,' he said.

'Yes, please. If you would.'

'I'll fetch your things next weekend. We must find you somewhere to stay in London.'

'Fine.'

'You could stay at the flat, if you would prefer it.'

'No, probably not.'

'You'll be all right on your own?'

'Yes.'

'We'll meet in the evenings. There'll be lots for you to do.'

'I'll make myself useful.'

'I . . . I've been looking at flats.'

'Good.'

'I . . . I was assuming that we *are* to be married.'

'Yes.'

'Church? Registry office?'

'Oh . . . whichever is the easiest. A registry office?'

'Fine. May I ask . . . my family?'

'Of course you may.'

'Will you ask your family?'

'My family? My sisters, you mean? No, I don't think so, really.'

'Celia?'

'What?'

'It is all right, isn't it?'

'Oh yes.'

'It's what you want?'

'It's what . . . I want. Yes.'

'To marry. To have children.'

'I . . . it's all right, Lewis. I've been stupid. You'll look after me, won't you?'

'Oh yes.'

They parted at her bedroom door with a quick embrace. He held her but, feeling her tremble, released her, kissed her, saw her slip inside, and went to his own room.

He did not sleep well. The sheets seemed soiled and the radiator clanged through the night. He did not know what he had done, what he was doing, wanted to go through to her but knew that he must not.

At last he did sleep, woke late and hurried into his clothes. He knocked at her door.

'Come in,' she called.

She was still in bed, but wide awake, waiting, lying on her back, her clothes scattered on the floor. He closed the door and came and sat beside her.

'Did you sleep well?'

'Yes, thank you.'

'We're late. I'm sorry. I overslept.'

'Right,' she said, and began to pull the bedclothes from her.

'Wait,' he said.

She paused, closed her eyes.

'Give me your hand.'

She withdrew her arm obediently from the covers and he took her hand, pressed it to his lips.

'Talk to me,' he said.

'What about?'

'Tell me what you want.'

'I want . . . whatever's for the best.'

'Tell me that you want *me*.'

'Yes.'

'Tell me that you can go through with this.'

'Oh yes.'

'Tell me that you want to be my wife, to have my children. Tell me, Celia.'

'I want . . . I just want it to happen to me. Please don't push me.'

'I must have your freedom in this, Celia. I will not ask for your love, or your happiness, but your freedom . . . that I must have. D'you understand me?'

'You have . . . my freedom. There is nothing else left of me, Lewis. Whatever there is, is yours. If it's not enough for you, then you must say so.'

He drew her face to his, touched her eyes, her cheeks with his lips, breathed into her, then shaped his lips over hers, felt her turn herself towards him, mustering herself to his kiss. It was enough.

They found a small unfurnished flat and he gave her the task of furnishing it. She took no decision without his concurrence, but he

234

gave that automatically, watching her begin to become involved. She stayed meanwhile in a small family lodging house, but, as he had promised, they spent every evening together, sometimes dining out, or at a theatre, mostly sitting in his flat, talking about the practicalities. She remained subdued, a dutiful student of his life. He became infinitely solicitous. They spoke quietly as if there was something listening, watching, waiting for them to make a mistake. He felt at times that he had merely defeated her, at times that he had broken down her shell to reveal a terrible vulnerability and tenderness that it was his pride to possess and his honour to protect. Sometimes he watched her and felt that she had disappeared, and he wanted to cry out, to grab and shake her back into her fear, the fighting revulsion of their first days.

He did not take her to Framling, rang them when she was not there, kept them informed. He seemed that he was hurting them by his refusal to bring her down; but he would not subject her to their scrutiny. They would come to the wedding. When it was all settled, there would be time for the rest of it.

The wedding was to be in February. He told her that he wanted her to look beautiful, to be as she had been; he wanted that very badly, although it was an effort for her. He wanted her to have a bridesmaid, but there was no-one she was prepared to involve; her past was all gone now. She would not even write to her sisters telling them.

'Would you like me to ask Helena to be bridesmaid?'

'If you like.'

'No, my love, if *you* like. It's not important, but if you wanted her . . .'

'All right, then; Helena.'

When Lewis asked her, Helena was very happy. She hugged him and burst into tears. He sat her down on the sofa and explained exactly what she would have to do: spend the night in Celia's lodgings, help her dress, bring her to the registry office.

'Have you asked Mummy and Daddy?'

'Oh yes.'

When he had gone back to London, Helena's initial joy was blurred, firstly by Naomi's jealousy, and secondly by the reserve that her parents obviously felt about this development. The effect of this negativity made her feel that the duty she had undertaken was momentous. She had been trusted with the care of the person her brother loved. What would she do if Celia wept, if, at the last moment, she could not go through with it? What qualifications did she have to deliver this woman to her brother's bed? These worries burnished and strengthened her.

The day came and she was delivered to Celia by her mother. Celia was formal and practical, not remotely like a woman in a flutter of nuptial expectations. They had tea, her mother trying to generate conversation, and Celia seeming distracted and frankly bored.

When they were alone, Celia took her to her room. A camp-bed had been put up for her. She was to sleep with Celia.

'You won't mind that, will you, Helena?'

'Oh no. Celia?'

'What?'

'Thank you for asking me.'

'It was Lewis's idea.'

'I know it was, but . . . you don't mind me being here.'

'Not at all. Thank you, Helena.'

'I am very happy for you, really I am.'

They embraced, smiled. Helena asked to see the dress, showed Celia what she would be wearing, discussed the plans.

They went to a neighbouring restaurant for dinner and Helena watched Celia drink more than she ate. The conversation was one-sided, Celia asking her about her life abroad, how she found England, what school was like. Helena would have told her anything, did betray all sorts of family confidences that, afterwards, she blushed to have done.

They went back for an early night. Helena, who had herself drunk a little more wine than she was used to, caught herself prying on Celia's undressing, wanting to see what she was like. Celia sensed this and became a little nervous.

'Don't keep looking at me,' she said.

Helena, mortified apologised extensively, at which Celia came and sat beside her bed, touched her hair.

'It's all right,' she said. 'Really.'

When she was in bed and the light was out, Celia asked if she minded if she had one last cigarette. Helena lay and watched the glow of the cigarette in the darkness of Celia's face.

'This time tomorrow,' Celia said, 'I shall be in bed with your brother.'

236

'Are you . . . nervous?'

'No. You're a virgin, aren't you?'

'Yes.'

'Lucky you.'

'Tell me.'

'What? What do you want to know, Helena?'

'Does it . . . hurt?'

'Yes.'

'Why . . . why do women do it, then?'

'Because they can't help it. It's what they're made for.'

'My mother told me . . . that it was beautiful, if you love your husband, that it was the most beautiful thing in the world.'

Celia was silent then. Helena heard her shifting about, heard the small crunch of the extinguishing cigarette.

'Celia?'

'What?'

'You do love Lewis, don't you?'

There was more silence then, and Helena began to be afraid.

'Come here,' Celia said at last.

Helena quickly crossed the darkness. As she approached the bed, Celia opened the covers and Helena slid in beside her, wrapped herself in her arms, wept against her body into which the breath was drawn in deep, driven out, drawn in again, by lungs that were determined and purposeful.

'There is only this,' Celia said at last. 'Clinging onto each other through the night, knowing every hurt, every fear, clinging on and fighting through.'

. . . twenty-six . . .

In August, he drove her north to visit Uncle Harry, to show her where he had been brought up. She admitted to herself that she was curious, although not to him. She remained entirely under his authority; this was what she had taken on when she had married him. It was not a posture, if it had ever been one, for she could see

237

no way out of it. Between her inner and outer life there was an absolute division: she moved her body through the pattern of days, watching herself closely from within curious, bewildered at times, but never actively unhappy.

He was the model of consideration, as she had known he would be, delighting in everything she did, every detail of her. She might have found that cloying, but she accepted it, lived within it. She did what she had to do, felt there was no credit in any of it, was not motivated by his pleasure except insofar as it kept life easy and pleasant. She fitted herself into his life and found that it was comfortable and undemanding. Perhaps this hermetic security was what she had always lacked: the security of a devotion in the shelter of which she could hide, where the complexities of her former life, if not resolved, were made irrelevant. She had begun methodically to learn cookery, had bought a sewing machine, and these domestic occupations filled her days, involved her completely. She played Lewis's records throughout the day, not really listening to them, but glad to have something going on in the neat rooms of their flat. She could imagine that the music was the most important thing, and that she was merely moving round on the edges, tidying and sorting, being useful and quiet.

By the time they went north, she was pregnant. Lewis was not yet aware of this, and she wondered how she was going to tell him, felt that to admit it would be to give herself away. She had thought sex was going to be a difficulty for her, but she found that she could settle herself to his physical possession of her with an easy competence, could move and lift herself nimbly; felt afterwards, in the wash of his tender gratitude, that she had done well, very well. The act itself pleased her in a way that she had not imagined it could: it had a comfortable intensity within which she could contain and direct herself. Although she knew that it was essentially done to her rather than with her, she liked to feel his urgency working out within her, his labouring at her, the silent simplicity of it all. And after it, she felt free, relaxed, completed, dropped into calm, dreamless sleep.

Only once, since their marriage, had she achieved a sexual climax. This had happened at Framling. They had drunk rather a lot at dinner and had gone to bed rather merrily. Lewis had hushed her, reminding her that the girls were asleep just over the corridor. In bed, Lewis had seemed, unusually, a little reticent, said he was tired; but she was not going to let him get away with that. She had touched him a little, set him going. He had laboured over her and she had gripped him, pushed herself forcibly up against him, had thought of Helena tucked up in her innocent bed with the reality of the world contracting about her, breathing closely over her. She had come with a violence that had made her twist and bellow, a sudden bodily madness that had risen against the whole cloying reticence of this house, of him, of the life that she had submitted to. Afterwards there had been a silence of shame within which their hearts had drummed. He had slithered from her and lain apart from her. She had turned to him and apologised. When they had returned to London, life had gone on as before, the incident unspoken, the days and weeks and months unfolding in their quiet certainty.

'We're nearly there,' he said.

She roused and looked, for the first time, at the landscape. There were hills, green and brown in the sunlight, with outcrops of jagged rock, the lines of stone walls tracking unevenly up the slopes, the flecks of browsing sheep. The muscularity of it took her by surprise, brought her a distinct pleasure; she felt herself lift to the hills, wanted to be on top of them, looking down. Their boldness made her bold.

They turned west, away from the high hills, through steep-banked side roads with woods coming down close, with the sun shut out above, flickering through the foliage. She lay back and let the light play on her face through the car's open roof. She closed her eyes.

She felt the car turn sharply, slow, felt the surface of the road roughen. She sat up and looked about her. They were travelling down a long drive through thinning trees into parkland. Before them, through the trees, was a large country house built in soft stone, with ranks of windows that caught the setting sun and sent it back in sharp splinters of brilliance.

'Is that the house, Lewis?'

'Yes. Is it what you expected?'

'No. Not at all.'

But she had, somewhere, expected this. In a dream, a girlhood fantasy, she had imagined just such a place, imagined belonging here, liberated from the constrictions of the world here. She felt herself open with a sudden gratitude that, at the end of it all, he should bring her here; and the incredible truth that he himself belonged to such a place made her feel a tenderness for him of which she had perhaps never before been capable. For all her submissions he had rewarded her with this.

When at last he drew the car to a halt before the steps that led up to the front door, she leant on his shoulder and wept.

. . . *twenty-seven* . . .

'I hope you won't be upset by Uncle Harry,' he had said.

'Why might he upset me?'

'Well, being blind, you know, he likes to touch people, women particularly.'

He had watched her shrug, as she always shrugged. He knew that in truth he wanted Uncle Harry to subject her to his customary explorations, wanted to see how she took it. He wondered if that might break the surface of her calm. He was looking forward to their arrival.

The front door was open. Her moment of emotion in the car he had not understood. She had mastered it quickly and they stood in the empty hall holding hands. The familiarity of the place enveloped him, excited him. He felt very strong here, felt that he had returned independent, able at last to take this place on his terms, to belong here as he had always wanted to.

'Hello?' he called loudly, bouncing the echoes about the stone and dust. He felt her hand grip his in the expectant silence that followed his call.

A door opened somewhere above them.

'Lewis? Is that you? Come on up, my boy. Come on.'

They saw Uncle Harry on the landing as they ascended the stairs. He stood in his usual patched tweeds, holding on to the edge of the door. His beard was greying slightly and he had grown a little stout. Both Lewis and Celia were taller than he but felt progressively slight as they approached him, a small bolt of a man with a peppery distinction.

Lewis took his hand and he slung his arm about his nephew's shoulder.

'Splendid, my boy, splendid.'

'Uncle Harry? May I introduce my wife, Celia?'

She stepped forward and offered her hand, then blushed as she realised that she would have to make the first contact. She took his hand but, Lewis noted, held herself back a bit.

'How do you do, Captain Brand.'

'Celia, is it? Welcome. Welcome indeed.'

He disappointed Lewis, shook her hand briefly and then released her.

'Well, come on through. I'll get some tea.'

They sat in his parlour, a bare room that needed cleaning. Having located a bell-pull and tugged at it vigorously, he found his way to a high-backed armchair that was positioned in front of the window. There was a sofa close by to which Lewis directed Celia.

'I get the sun here,' he explained, 'sit like some damn lizard. I'm learning to read, you know, these finger-book things. A woman comes in once a week. Miss Schlieff. A bloody Boche, would you believe. She terrifies me. I don't know whether it's worth the bother, but it keeps me out of mischief.'

'Don't you have someone within earshot, Uncle Harry?' Lewis asked.

'No, no. Prefer to be on my own. Hate to be fussed over. Retley's here most of the morning. D'you know Retley? No, you wouldn't, I suppose. He's my steward, or secretary, or whatever it is. Good enough sort. A bit fussy. Your mother didn't like him much, and your damn sisters made fun of him, or at least the younger one did. Naomi. I like your sisters, Lewis.'

'Yes, I thought you would.'

A servant girl arrived.

'Which one of you is it?'

'It's Dora, Captain.'

'My nephew's here, dammit. Get someone to bring their bags in, and let's have some tea.'

She disappeared with a slovenly flounce that entertained Lewis but which made Celia nervous.

'How's Brady?' Lewis asked.

'Brady's fine. She's the housekeeper now and keeps them all in what little order there is down there.'

They talked about the house and the estate, the servants and the neighbours, until the tea arrived. Uncle Harry did not once direct a question at Celia and Lewis began to wonder if he had forgotten that she was there.

'Celia,' Lewis said, indicating the tray, 'would you mind?'

She seemed glad to busy herself pouring, cutting the heavy fruit cake.

'So,' Uncle Harry said, taking his mug in both hands. 'How d'you find married life, then, Lewis?'

'I find married life delightful. We wanted to ask you down, but . . .'

'No, no. I don't travel any more. No point. At least I know my way about here.'

There was a pause then. Lewis glanced at his wife, who smiled briefly.

'I must go and find Brady, find where we're sleeping. May I leave you to entertain Celia, Uncle Harry?'

'Delighted, my boy. Off you go.'

He touched her shoulder as he rose, stooped and kissed her neck, which felt hot. He closed the door behind him.

Harry Brand was uneasy in the presence of this strange young woman, Lewis's wife. He had not the slightest conception of her, did not know whether she was young or old, tall or short. His basic response to women was disgraceful and he could not operate that now. She was a dark space that he could not begin to map.

'Would you like more tea, Captain Brand?'

'Er, yes . . . that would be very kind.'

He felt her approach, withdraw, heard the trickle of tea in the mug, felt her returning, the warmth of her body, the rustle of her dress. She settled close to him, where Lewis had sat, put his mug down on its mat.

'Is this your first . . . first trip north?'

'Yes,' she said. 'Your house is very beautiful.'

'I . . . I'm most terribly sorry, but I've forgotten your name.'

'Celia.'

'Of course. Celia. How stupid of me. May I ask . . . how old you are?'

'I am twenty.'

'Have you known Lewis long?'

'About two years.'

The open clarity of her answers daunted him. He could think of nothing else to ask her.

'I can't get used to this damn blindness,' he said.

'Lewis mentioned that you liked to touch people, to get to know them. If it would be a help to you . . .'

He did not answer, was terrified of this boldness, felt her moving, kneeling down by him, taking his hand and placing it on her face.

'Please,' she said. 'I want you to know me.'

Her features were smooth and cool, her nose straight, her chin strong. He brought up his other hand and curved the symmetry of her cheek-bones, of her ears, which were long, felt the clean fall of her hair.

'You're beautiful,' he said. 'Aren't you?'

'Yes,' she said. 'Perhaps I am.'

She touched his forearms lightly, rose slowly, and his hands moved down the length of her. He had not known how tall she was, how substantial; the delicacy of her face had not prepared him for the broad, full breasts, the span of her hips, the lean strength of thigh.

'Thank you, my dear,' he said, weakly, the hurt of his emotions clotting in his throat.

She laughed a little, with pleasure.

'Is Lewis good to you?' he asked.

'Yes.'

'You know, don't you, that he will inherit this place when I am gone.'

'I . . . I hadn't thought.'

'Oh yes. I am so glad that he has found someone . . . found you. I hope you will be happy, very happy.'

'I think we might be. Yes.'

He heard footsteps and tried to withdraw his hand, but she retained it as the door opened. He heard the footsteps stop and then Lewis's laugh. He did not know what sort of laugh it was and he blushed, old fool that he was, to be caught like this.

. . . *twenty-eight* . . .

Brady did not like Master Lewis any more; perhaps she had never really liked him. His strangeness had always, finally, defeated her. Now that he had returned, now that he was married, she did not know him at all.

He visited her in her room, took her in his arms, so tall now and she a little old woman, feeling this for the first time, shedding big, wet tears. He sat her down and chatted to her, told her about his journey, about his parents and sisters.

'Let me fetch Celia, Brady. I left her with Uncle Harry. How is he?'

'Oh, he's just as he always was.'

'Still misbehaving himself?'

'Oh, I don't know about that any more.'

'I'll bet you do, Brady. I'll bet you do.'

And he left her sitting on her little armchair. Flies buzzed on the window sill. The scents of rose-water and linen filled the little room. On the mantelpiece were faded postcards from Anna Drewer, a drawing of a snake done by Helena when she was six, a framed postcard of a young soldier, Jack Wilkie, twenty years dead now: the fragments of her life, left in the slip of the years. It had been ten years, more, since she had made the journey to her master's bedroom. She had watched him rouse to the younger girls, and had slipped out of the habit of her visitation. 'Why don't you come to see me anymore, Brady?' he had asked. 'I'm too old for all that now,' she had said. 'You don't go lonely, do you, sir?' He had puffed a bit, but how could she not have known about it? She knew it all, knew who they were and what they did, how mostly he liked to touch them now, to suck at their big new breasts. She was past that now. A long time ago she had known the energy, the delight of it, the lock and grunt and tussle; now it came back to her only in half-dreams, far away. She mothered the young girls, made sure they did nothing they did not want to do, taught them caution and cuddled them when they wept. It seemed that she had lived her life through others and the cruel truism was that they outgrew her, one by one, Anna and Lewis, Harry Brand and the girls. Poor Jack Wilkie: she loved him now more than she had ever loved him alive.

There was a rap at the door and Lewis was back with a tall, shapely girl, hard-featured, southern and proud, in a short, sheer dress.

'Brady? This is my wife, Celia.'

'I'm very pleased to meet you, Mrs Drewer.'

'Please. Call me Celia.'

'Oh no, m'm. I'd rather not.'

What she had expected, exactly what she had expected. It depressed her. He had got himself a girl from the magazines, haughty and sterile, a London girl. They did not stay long with her, went to change for dinner. They had come to peer into the past, to tour the museum of his childhood, to smile and bring presents to the pensioners. She ground her teeth in anger. You don't belong here, she cried in her head, in her heart. You don't belong. You have no rights. Go away. Go away.

Celia made an announcement of her condition at dinner that day. The Captain was delighted, was delighted with her and with his nephew; but then he was blind, he did not see what Brady saw, how they moved about with their cold London looks, imagining the house in their own way, coming to claim it. The new Mrs Drewer looked at Brady, whenever they met, not with a smile, for that would have been too obvious, but with a private look, a question, asking for her concurrence. She could not have given it.

'And what d'you think of her, then, Brady?' the Captain asked her when she went to see he was comfortably in bed. She did not always go, but felt that he might like to talk tonight.

'Oh, she's a fine-looking woman, sir.'

'She'll do, Brady, she'll do. I bet she gives him a good time, eh?'

'I wouldn't know, sir.'

'You don't like her, do you?'

'She's not one of us, sir. But, then, I suppose Master Lewis wasn't one of us, not once he'd gone away to school.'

'Tell me something, Brady. I've always wanted to know.'

'What, sir?'

'Did you . . . did you make a man of young Lewis?'

'Oh no, sir, not like that.'

'I always imagined you had done.'

'I think it might have been better if I had.'

'What d'you mean by that, Brady?'

'Oh, I don't know, sir. Let me take that pillow.'

She did know, of course. There was something soulless about him, something hard and superficial, and cruel; she had always known he would be cruel. She imagined that woman ministering to his cruelty, copulating with mirrors and lights, opening it all out, driving away the dreams. She should have taught him to dream, to know that moment when pleasure spread into sleep and the whole world had meaning, life like a fish plunging into the depths, smooth and perfect, in its absolute element.

She did not like having them in the house, avoided their room, afraid of what might be going on there. When they left, she was glad, felt the house breathe again, as if it had been constrained by their presence. She knew they would be back, grew afraid of them.

. . . twenty-nine . . .

A fortnight or so after they had left, an incident happened between the Captain and his teacher, Miss Schlieff, the German refugee. Brady had been expecting it, she supposed; not that Miss Schlieff was the Captain's type at all. She was hard and correct, rather masculine in her manner. There was a feminine side to her, which came out in moments of sadness that occasionally overcame her, particularly when people were kind to her; and they were generally kind to her. She was strange and different, cautious and interested, and they became rather proud of looking after her, showing her the ways of the house.

The Captain had asked Brady about her.

'She's a sad article, sir,' she had said, 'lost here like some stray.'

'What sort of stray, Brady? A pussy cat?'

'Not a pussy cat, sir. Not that at all. More . . . more a fox.'

'She'd better watch out for all those damn bitches down there, then, hadn't she?'

'Oh, they like her, sir. They fuss over her. She cries a little sometimes, when they are kind to her.'

He had thought about this, then had said, 'She smells strange. You English girls all smell of plants – roses and honeysuckle if you're lucky; mallow and turnip and old cabbage if not. She smells . . . I don't know. It catches me sometimes . . . spiced beeswax, maybe. Something almost religious, although I don't think she's religious.'

'No, sir. Not religious.'

'What does she look like, Brady?'

'Oh, not . . . not pretty, sir. Big eyes and a little mouth. She could disguise herself as a boy, easily.'

'No tits, eh?'

'I didn't mean that, sir. Her face, I meant. She's thin, but quite full-figured.'

'Does she tell you anything about herself?'

'No, sir. Nothing.'

This conversation had alerted Brady. He was beginning to become intrigued by Miss Schlieff. When it happened, therefore, Brady was ready for it.

Miss Schlieff found her in the linen cupboard amongst the starch and hot pine slats. The door was open, but still she knocked, waited until Brady had turned and had taken off her spectacles.

'Miss Schlieff?'

'Miss Brady, I . . . I am not able to come here any more.'

'Oh no,' she said. 'Don't say that.'

Miss Schlieff bowed her head. 'It is not possible,' she said.

Brady came close to her. There *was* a strange smell to her, a trembling heat that she gave off. Brady took her hand.

'Has the Captain been misbehaving himself, dear?' she said. 'You mustn't mind that. He's a sinful man, but . . . but there's no harm in him. I'll speak to him. He won't do it again.'

'I must go now,' she said.

'Come and have a cup of tea. Before you go. Please do.'

In Brady's room, she sat and drank tea whilst Brady explained her photographs, took her through the family. She was quiet, but attentive, following Brady's tour, pausing occasionally to dab her eyes.

'And who is that, please?' she asked at last, as she was supposed to.

'That's Jack Wilkie. He was my sweetheart. He died in the war. D'you have a sweetheart, Miss Schlieff? Back in Germany?'

She shook her head, began to say something, but the words would not come in the way she wanted them to come and she frowned.

'What's brought you to these parts, then, Miss?' Brady asked.

'I . . . I was here one time when I was young,' she said. 'I must leave Germany. I have come here where I remembered . . . remembered when I was young.'

'Tell me about your home,' Brady said, 'your parents.'

'My parents are . . . are taken away. My brother also. They are dead now, I think. In Germany now many people are taken away, many people are dead. My . . . sweetheart also. His name was Michael. There was a camp here, in Stonefell, for socialists. I came to Stonefell with Michael. We went out onto the hill at night. We had sexual relations in the shining of the moon. It was very beautiful. It is gone now, all gone. I will be sent back. I also will be dead. There will again be a war, like the war that was before but worse than that war, worse.'

'Why will you be sent back?'

'Because there will be a war. German persons will not be permitted.'

'We'll look after you,' she said. 'The Captain won't let them send you back if you don't want to go back.'

She was silent then, heavy.

'What has he done to you, my dear?' Brady asked.

'He is my enemy, Miss Brady,' she said.

'Your enemy?'

'Yes. Oh yes. He is my class enemy. I am a socialist. It is the high bourgeois like he who have brought the war, who profit from the war. This is why the war is fought. This is what the war is to keep. But in my country now is something that is worse than that, worse than anything. We have all failed. There is only now despair.'

Brady didn't really follow all this, felt that anyway it was a diversion.

'Did he touch you, my dear?' she asked.

248

'He . . . yes, a little. He held my hand. He . . . I sat on his knee and I permitted him to touch my breasts.'

'I'll give him a good telling-off,' Brady said. 'He's a wicked old man.'

'No,' Miss Schlieff said. 'I have permitted it. I have wanted it. It is I who am wicked, Miss Brady. I think, if I become his sexual mistress, then they will not send me back to Germany. He is my enemy, Miss Brady. I am a coward.'

Brady expected her to be crying, but her face was set hard, a defiance behind her assertions. Brady smiled, could see something else there, began to know where all this was going.

'And . . . and do you like the Captain, Miss Schlieff?'

She dropped her face briefly. 'He is very kind to me,' she said.

'But d'you like him as a man, that's what I'm saying.'

Again the pause, the mind working at the words, determined to be clear. 'I cannot speak of such things,' she said. 'It is not right that I should speak of such things.'

'When I was . . . your age,' Brady said, 'and younger too, I used to like the Captain; and he used to like me. I used to go along to his bed sometimes when he got lonely and I got lonely. He's a lovely man, Miss Schlieff. You've not got to be ashamed of that, not with me.'

Miss Schlieff looked at Brady hard and close, but could not find any words to say. At last she looked at the wristwatch that she wore.

'I must go then, Miss Brady. It is late. I have to be back at my lodging house or they will wonder what has happened to me.'

'We'll see you next week, then, Miss Schlieff?' she asked.

'Yes. I will come next week. Thank you, Miss Brady, for serving me tea and for showing me your photographs. I am grateful to you.'

. . . *thirty* . . .

They did not go north for Christmas; her condition precluded that. The child was due a year, almost to the day, after they had married, and it arrived on time.

She remembered little of the process of birth. She woke in the night in hoops of pain. Lewis drove her to the hospital. They gave her dulling drugs and, from a far distance, she felt herself opened by a great disburdening, as if at least half of herself was dislodged and breaking from her. And then she was the mother of a small, ugly daughter.

In the hospital, blue and white, with the cloyment of too many flowers, with an antiseptic pall over the under-reek of urine and night-sweat, the infant cried and was brought to her breast where it lay and guzzled at her. Lewis came and beamed at her, peered down at his child, exuding a smugness that wearied her. Lionel and Anna Drewer came cheerily, wanting to make her feel that she belonged. Naomi came and was silenced by the enormity of what her sister-in-law had undergone, had no argument against that. Helena came and held her hand and asked her the one question that meant anything to her.

'Was it terrible?'

'It was . . . it was nothing to do with me, in the end.'

They agreed on Susan, for no other reason than they both seemed to like the name, and it had no associations for either of them. Lewis suggested Helena as godmother, which was easy, and Joey O'Neele as godfather, which was more contentious. Celia did not like him, greeted him when he called with a frosty formality: much, Lewis thought, as she treated me when we first met. O'Neele always spoke of her with an almost exaggerated respect.

O'Neele was doing well for himself now, was writing music for the films and making a good living. One of his tunes had become very successful and could often be heard on the wireless sung by a sentimental Scotsman. He cultivated eccentricities, lived in a large, chaotic flat and entertained a succession of casual girlfriends, most of whom littered the edges of the film studios. 'They end up with me when they've failed to bed a serious producer,' he said. 'I play them tunes and stoke up their little fantasies. I might've married Candida, but I'm glad I didn't. We wouldn't have been happy. I never took life as seriously as you, Lewis. You were made to marry and be a father and all that, but not me.'

Motherhood and domesticity affected Celia in strange ways. She became more sociable, outward, more outspoken, harder, bleaker.

She began to articulate political opinions that shocked him. She was for capital punishment, thought trades unions should be banned, and did not see why they had to pay taxes to support people who had not taken care of their own old age. She once went so far as to assert that unmarried mothers should be prosecuted.

'What if we had . . . had been careless?' he asked.

'If I had become pregnant, then I would have deserved punishing. I am not very proud of the things we did before we were married, Lewis. I was very ignorant, but that is no excuse.'

Lewis did not know that he had political opinions until she began to express all this venom, and then, rather surprisingly, he found that he had sympathies that, the more he thought about them, the more his work in the bank seemed to compromise. He looked at the world around him and saw so many things wrong that seemed so obviously easy to put right. He looked at what was happening in Italy and Germany and Spain, and began to feel that they were living in a neat little bourgeois eggshell that was being subjected to dangerous pressure.

They moved from the flat to a small detached house in the western suburbs, quite an expansion financially, but Uncle Harry helped, and Lewis was now in a senior enough position at the bank to begin to lay out a bit. Celia, whilst never extravagant, required more money than he had ever anticipated that she would; but he was glad to spend his money on her, glad to build about her such comforts of affluence as he was able to.

He found her strange, at times. Socially she could be arrogant and cruel, and he would watch her, at dinner parties, and be alarmed by her presence, afraid that she would say or do something outrageous, slap the face of some simpering little kitten or some patronising man who tapped a hand on her rump; but below that alarm, he was still intensely proud of her, proud that he had brought this madwoman into his life, let her loose amongst his constipated colleagues; wanted her at times to bring the tedious gentility of it all down around their ears. He would watch her across the table. She never looked at him. See that beautiful, cold, hard woman, he would say to himself. In two hours' time I am going to fuck her until she whoops; a fantasy he never entirely fulfilled.

At a private dinner to celebrate a promotion that Lewis had achieved, Celia told him that she was again pregnant.

'Are you happy about it?' he asked her.

'It is as it should be, Lewis. Yes. I am happy.'

'I don't know how anyone can bring children into the world at a time like this,' Naomi said to him once, Celia being out of the room, otherwise she would not have had the effrontery for such a statement. Lewis smiled patronisingly at her, but her accusation made him uncomfortable, nevertheless.

Naomi was seventeen now and clever, going to university, going to be a doctor, going to return to the colonies and work amongst the natives, 'to give something back for all this country's sucked out of them.' Her energy was turning to a fine social anger as she became a woman, and Lewis wondered if any man would ever be brave enough to reach her.

She certainly had a high contempt for any male of her own age, and for her elder sister who, now nineteen, was usually in various depths of love. Helena was strikingly beautiful and, having left school, was busy at home, drawing her family into the social life of the county. The young men with whom she was involved were, Lionel told his son, depressingly similar: good-looking, well-mannered, immature and shallow.

'Is it true she turned down an offer of marriage?' Lewis asked his father.

'Yes, indeed she did. Poor little Edward. I think it took her completely by surprise. I mean, I don't think she gives twopence about any of them, although she indulges herself in romantic moods now and then. She's enjoying herself enormously. I won't believe she's truly in love until she starts becoming miserable about one of them.'

She was always very glad to see her brother and sister-in-law, turned down all invitations for the duration of their visit, was not at home to any of the young men whom Lewis rather wanted to meet, but of whom Helena, when pressed, seemed rather ashamed. There was a project for her to come up to London to undertake some sort of study in the fine arts, but it was more for something to do than through any binding vocation. Lewis invited her to come and spend some time with them, and she leapt at the idea; their parents were not sure about this, however.

'They think we'll corrupt her,' Lewis said to Celia.

This had been meant flippantly, but Celia considered it silently, seriously.

'D'you reckon she's still a virgin?' he asked.

'Oh yes.'

'How can you tell?'

'She told me.'

'Would you like her to come and live with us for a bit, Celia?'

'I would, yes, very much.'

'You ask, then.'

'All right. I will.'

And she did, clearly and unambiguously, over the dinner table. His father hemmed and said they'd have to think about it, but his mother, quite suddenly, said yes. Helena leapt up and gave her mother a kiss, and her father. Naomi said nothing, but it was plain what she thought her sister would be getting up to in London.

Lewis spent time when he was up at Framling talking to his father, with whom he found he had far more in common than he had imagined, particularly now that he was discovering the political articulation of his mind. They discussed the international situation, and agreed that there would be war before the decade was out.

'We didn't get the peace right,' his father said. 'Perhaps there was too much pain for us to see clearly. Too many people had died, too many were crippled in one way or another.'

'It won't be the same, though, Daddy. It's not the old aristocratic officer corps who are in charge there now, but gangsters. And last time no-one knew how to fight the new warfare. They tried to fight old wars with new weapons. They've learnt a lot since then.'

'I've asked you this before, Lewis, but will you fight?'

'I don't think there'll be that sort of choice this time. I don't think there'll be soldiers and civilians any more. I think everyone will be part of it, the front line on our doorsteps.'

'Then God help us all, my boy.'

'Perhaps that's why pleasure has been so important to us, to my generation, I mean. Perhaps we knew what was coming and were determined to make the most of it while we could. There's not been much to believe in since the war.'

'Well, there's always socialism.'

'Socialism? You shouldn't use such words to a banker, Daddy.'

'You know Uncle Harry's become a socialist?'

'Uncle Harry?'

'You may laugh, Lewis. I'll give you his letters. That girl, the refugee who's teaching him to read those books for the blind, she's educating him. He wants to set up some sort of camp for refugees, up in the house. God knows what's going on up there. He's been sitting on his backside for twenty years, interfering with servant girls, getting odder and odder. Your mother and I are going up to see him when Naomi's back at school. We were going to take Helena, but she'd hate it. You will look after her in London, won't you?'

'Of course we will, Daddy.'

'Celia and she get on well. She and Naomi have come to blows about your wife before now.'

Lewis smiled, poured himself more port.

About a fortnight later, Lewis came through to the drawing room where Celia was reading a magazine, curled up on the sofa about her belly, feeling cow-like and imposed upon.

'Did you hear the telephone?' he asked.

'The telephone? Yes. Was it important?'

'It was my father. Uncle Harry's getting married.'

'What?'

'To a German refugee girl called Hanni Schlieff. He has to marry her, apparently, to save her from being deported as an undesirable alien.'

She folded the news inside her, struggled to say something that was both true and honourable, as her bright northern dream flickered out.

'I'm very happy for him,' she managed at last.

He watched her but said nothing; came to her and touched her but she flinched and shrugged and he went away.

This was it, then. The restless weight of the past months, the tedium of marriage and maternity, the sour staleness of it, setting about her. Tears of anger and self-pity came. She had been cheated of herself once more.

... *thirty-one* ...

Helena found staying with Lewis and Celia awkward. Celia, heavily pregnant, spent much time in her bedroom, emerging watery and ill-tempered. Lewis was the prince of charm, as always, but would spend a brief ten minutes with Helena here and there, before going through and shutting himself in with Celia. There was Susan to be played with, of course, her bright little god-daughter who burbled and romped energetically. She tried to make herself useful in the nursery, but the nursemaid had tight regimes and was not happy at Helena's improvisations. After a week, Helena admitted to herself that she was bored; or, if not bored, at least surplus to the daily business of the household.

Her studies were to begin in a month, and she had a pile of very dull books to read and a paper to write the subject of which she did not even understand. The weather was rainy, and she stood at the window of her bright little bedroom and looked across at the similar houses opposite, waiting, as patient as she might be, but feeling always that the days of her youth were leaking away.

Joey O'Neele came to dinner. Helena, who had only met him briefly at the christening, took to him at once; flashily handsome and fashionably casual, he was at last a genuine specimen, London man. He devoted his entire attention to her and she felt herself flush and laugh at his manipulations. They had an upright piano and he played pretty tunes, popular melodies which she recognised, and was then much impressed to learn that he had composed. He played effort-lessly, a cigarette jutting up from the corner of his mouth, his silky blond hair drifting over his closed eyes. Celia had given her warnings about him, and the prim schoolgirl in her could clearly see his super-ficiality; nevertheless, she enjoyed being charmed, feeling the lift of her beauty coming off him as he watched her.

Over dinner, Joey and Lewis drank three bottles of wine between them, less the two-and-a-half glasses that she was permitted. Celia drank milk. The conversation moved to politics, the certainty of war, the horrors of Europe.

'Well,' Celia said suddenly, making her first contribution, 'if you ask me, the Jews have only got themselves to blame. They belong nowhere, and make money out of everyone.'

'Do you know what's being done to them?' Lewis said, suddenly angry, angrier than Helena had ever seen him.

Celia smiled at him sourly. 'I know what your bolshie journalists would like me to believe is being done to them, Lewis.'

'You know nothing. You have the monumental complacent bloody ignorance that has allowed those bastards to get away with whatever they want to get away with for years. Whose side will you be on when the war comes, eh?'

'The people of this country are far too sensible to go to war for the Jews.'

'The people of this country will do what they're told, as they've always done. They'll go to war with anyone, waving their little flags and feeling smug and patriotic. But you're right. They would never go to war to right any real injustice. In a year's time, Celia, you and all the other smug bitches will wake up in the middle of a bloody nightmare and wonder what you did to deserve it.'

Celia rose, monumental, knocking the chair over behind her. Lewis and Joey rose also. Lewis stepped down the table straight into his wife's glare.

'Sit down,' he said. 'We've got guests.'

She slapped his face with substantial force, turned and went out, slamming the door behind her. Lewis strode immediately after her, opened the door, slammed it behind him too. Footsteps could be heard on the stairs, voices raised, doors crashing.

Helena, in the breathing-space behind the stun of this, stooped over and wept. She did not want to be here any more. She forgot Joey was still there until he reached across and refilled her wine glass.

'Don't worry,' he said. 'Marriage gets like that sometimes. They'll be upstairs now kissing and making up.'

She looked up at him, very glad of him, trusting his reassurance completely, needing to trust it. She apologised, wiped her eyes, smiled at him. He asked if he might smoke, asked if she would like a cigarette. She accepted, puffed inexpertly. It made her feel a little giddy, but the narcotic eased her. She straightened herself and then wondered what was going to happen next, whether Lewis and Celia would re-appear and, if they didn't, how long Joey would stay, what would transpire. She was a little drunk, and alone with a man of considerable experience in seducing young girls.

He chatted to her about her course, about her family, easy talk as if nothing had happened, as if it were all the most natural thing in the world. He asked if she'd like him to play something for her before he left.

'Perhaps you'd better not,' she said.

'No. You like music though, don't you?'

'Very much.'

'Let me take you to a concert tomorrow night. There's a wonderful American band over here at the moment. You'll love it.'

'Yes. Thank you. I'd like that.'

They arranged a time and he rose to leave. She followed him through to the hall and accepted a small kiss from him before he disappeared into the rain.

She had not decided whether to go to the concert wih him or not. She was quite prepared to stand him up, but it had been pleasant to accept him openly and clearly like that. She would have to consult Celia in the morning; and, remembering Celia, she became nervous again, listened up the stairs, but the house was in silence. She made her way quickly to bed.

She slept later than she had intended, came down to find that Lewis had already left for work. Celia was in the kitchen, tidying things up for the woman who came in to clean and wash. The nursemaid was there also, giving Susan her breakfast. Everything seemed the pattern of normality.

Helena, who had the edges of a hangover, took a cup of coffee upstairs and went into the bathroom to soak. Celia rattled on the door and told her to hurry up, to leave the water if it wasn't too dirty.

'I'm just getting out now,' Helena called and got out. 'The door's open.'

Celia appeared and tested the water, drained some off and topped the bath up with hot.

'Are you all right?' Helena asked, when her sister-in-law had lowered her belly into the water.

'Of course. Why shouldn't I be?'

'After last night.'

'Oh, that was nothing. Marriage is like that sometimes.'

'That's what Joey said.'

'Did he?'

'He's asked me out to a concert tonight.'

'Oh? Did you accept?'

'Yes, but that doesn't mean that I'll go.'

Celia looked at her sideways, uncertain of whether to approve or disapprove.

'Do you think I should go?'

'If you want to.'

'Do you think he'll . . . try and seduce me?'

'I'm sure he will.'

'You wouldn't object to me going, though?'

Celia pondered, soaped herself, sighed and shifted the blubbery mass of herself about in the narrow tub.

'Helena,' she said. 'If you want my permission to go to bed with Joey O'Neele, then you will not get it. You're certainly old enough, however, to make that sort of decision for yourself.'

'Would you advise me not to go?'

'Go if you want to. He won't do anything to you that you don't let him. Just be clear what it is you do let him do.'

Helena moved about a bit, tried to find some other way of approaching her.

'I won't go,' she said eventually, defeated by it.

'You do like him though, don't you?'

'Oh yes. He's . . . great fun.'

'Then go with him.'

'I don't understand you sometimes, Celia.'

'What don't you understand?'

'You don't like him at all, do you?'

'Joey O'Neele? No. I think he's loathsome. He brings out the worst in Lewis, every time he appears. You, however, are easily a match for him. You want to go, I know. Then go. Lewis is probably right. There will be a war soon. You may have little enough freedom.'

The jazz band was loud and the hall where they played the roughest place Helena had ever been. The men all looked like gangsters or homosexuals, the women varieties of prostitutes; not that she had any idea what these exotic creatures really looked like. Everyone knew Joey, and he was called up to play the piano, which he did, winking down into the darkness to the table where she sat. He bought her drinks, but she was careful; the atmosphere was intoxicating enough. She smoked several cigarettes, which seemed to stimulate her nervousness.

They left early, with the music still swinging out, but she had not really taken to it. It lacked the sentimentality that she liked in popular tunes. It was music of cities: assertive and sophisticated, articulating a world of easy pleasure that she did not trust. She thought often of her parents, of Naomi, was a little homesick, a little bewildered. He understood this and was very gentle, very attentive, warming her, distracting her, making her laugh.

She accepted his offer of a final drink without a qualm. His flat was dominated by a large room in which a large bed, a large piano and great rugs were spaced out under a sloping glass roof through which the frosty sky glittered. There was much untidiness here, but it was the untidiness, not of disorder, but of creative abandon; clothes and papers tossed here and there in the rush of ideas and passions. She felt, nevertheless, as she sat in the middle of the room on a small, hard horsehair divan, that it was all a little calculated. She cradled her brandy globe and sat up against the back of the divan, her legs along its length, her body taut and posed. He spread himself across his keyboard and played the sentimental tunes that she had desired.

How easy and fine it all was, after all. She loved this place. He was a beautiful man. She felt herself slipping, not down some terrible slope of depravity, but into a clarity, a strength. Before, there had always been complications, a seriousness demanded of her to which she could never commit herself, although she had made herself unhappy at times trying, wrestling with herself, asking herself if this or that were love, what she really wanted, what she could really give. Here, suddenly, it was all easy, a delightful fizzing of freedom in her blood.

He brought his playing to a crashing finale and spun on the stool to face her. She applauded, tapping the fingers of one hand against the palm of the other. He stood and bowed to her, then sat down again and fiddled with something, with some sheets of music, scanning them distractedly.

'Now what?' she said.

He eyed her. 'You scare the life out of me, Helena Drewer,' he said.

'Do I? Why?'

'Well . . . well, firstly, because you are so beautiful that it hurts. Secondly, because you're coming on over there like a blast-furnace. Thirdly, because if I laid a finger on you, your brother and sister-in-law would have my testicles cut off. Fourthly, because really, Helena, really, I could not spoil you for the wonderful husband you are going to find to live happily ever after with. Fifthly, because you are still so beautiful that it hurts.'

This made her laugh, giddy laughter that brought tears to her eyes.

'I'm not going to get married,' she said. 'I'm going to have lots of lovers. I'm going to learn about beautiful pictures and beautiful furniture and beautiful music and beautiful men.'

He gave a little whistle, leant back and kicked his heels together in mid-air.

'In that case, dear, dear Helena, may I take you to bed?'

She arrived back with the milkman. Lewis was waiting for her, came to the door as she appeared. He was wearing a dressing gown, had been sleeping in the drawing room, waiting.

'What the hell have you done, Helena?'

'Oh, Lewis, Lewis. You know what I've done. Don't start all that.'

He glowered at her, indicated the drawing room, and she went through dutifully, sat down and lit a cigarette.

'And what do you think the parents are going to say? Have you thought of that?'

'Lewis? You're not seriously going to. . . .'

'I don't know. I ought to. They'll find out, you know.'

'How? How will they find out? Anyway, I don't care. I won't be ashamed of myself, not for you or them.'

'Oh, you stupid, stupid little tart.'

'Lewis!'

Celia was there. Helena had begun to cry, not from shame, but from anger, and here was rescue. She leapt up and ran to Celia, flung her arms around her.

'All right, all right. Be careful of me, will you. Go on now. Go and get into the bath.'

In the bath she fell asleep, and was woken by the rattle of Celia on the door. She had locked the door, as she always did when Lewis was in the house. She pulled herself out and admitted her sister-in-law, returned to the tub which was cold and scummy now.

'Well?' Celia said, lowering herself down on the lavatory lid.

'I'm fine.'

'How do you rate the experience, then, Helena?'

'Wonderful.'

'Are you in love with him?'

'I could get a taste for it.'

'What? Love, or sex?'

'Love. I already have a taste for sex.'

Celia was silenced.

'Celia? . . . I'm fine. I'm nineteen and mad and happy, and I don't know how long I've got. Say something kind to me.'

'I envy you. Is that kind?'

'Oh yes. Oh yes.'

Lewis fled from his house that morning feeling outnumbered, outmatched and irrelevant. His life had been devoured by a conspiracy of women: there was his wife lugging her belly about, prodding it at him as if it proved his uselessness; there was his daughter over whose tight little existence he hovered with a limp redundancy; there was the nursemaid, trim as a joint of meat, but with as much sensual apprehension of the world as a clockwork duck; and now there was Helena, the bright and beautiful image of all he could ever love without spoiling, now opening her legs with the aplomb of a gymnast to accommodate something as trivial as Joey O'Neele. He had been angry, but when he stood on the suburban platform and waited with the familiar suited dummies he saw every morning, a dummy amongst them, he found it absurd, farcical.

Sex makes fools of us all, he thought. Once the monster is domesticated, there is only the absurdity, the lolling idiocy of the fat prick and its silly little spasms. He regarded the bodies about him; the neat, capacious trousers that covered hairy thighs and itchy genitals; the bowler hats that put a black dome over darker fantasy, the briefcases and umbrellas that were clutched in claws. How many of you, he wondered, are at this moment thinking of sex?

In the cold morning reek of iron and cement, with the curving rails running their parallels into the mist, sex was at most an after-dinner aperitif remembered pleasantly, briefly, in the blank of reality. Sex belonged to women. After all, they did most with it, lived their lives in softness and cultivated their sentimental little nests in which it was important. The perspective of the waiting platform brought these clichés, trussing him up for the world that lay before him. With Helena's deflowering, he no longer had any interest in sex. He felt he had come out of its maze of possibilities now and, like a puzzle solved, it had no point any more.

With a squeal and clatter the train rocked down the rails. The dummies leaned forward, but did not step out until the very moment before it stopped; then they were bustling and elbowing their way to favourite seats, opening newspapers, lighting pipes. Lewis too, Lewis too.

. . . *thirty-two* . . .

He took shelter from the contradictions and failures of his domestic life in his work. They were not crucial contradictions, nor terminal failures; simply, he had lost touch with the powerful intimacies on which his marriage had been founded. He fed his home with his time and his money, did his duty in all conscientiousness, but ceased trying to make things happen there. He was settled, had taken all the important decisions that were to be taken as far as his personal life was concerned; the future was clear and predictable. Celia would have her baby; perhaps there would be more babies; the babies would grow and need to be provided for, would, in their seasons, provide new delights, new problems; perhaps they would move to a bigger house; he would be sociable and civic. He had a working marriage that was at the least companionable. He belonged to the world and it all seemed to work.

Above all these bland calculations loomed the war; but he would not think about that until it happened; perhaps it would not happen. He came to understand the smugness of those who ignored its approach. Life had to be lived in the belief of a predictable future, however blindly, however ignorantly; not to believe in that led to rage and despair, and these were luxuries for a man with responsibilities.

After the vicissitudes of the past decade, business was beginning to perk up, and the bank, which had weathered the economic hurricanes prudently and quietly, was well placed to prosper. Lewis loved his work for its abstraction: a balance sheet was real and assessable, its deviousness, unlike the deviousness of the human heart, palpable and demonstrable. He cultivated his hard heart and his sure eye, could tell from a pattern of erratic withdrawals the extent to which an account was going out of control, could skim a portfolio and slice the redundancies from it in minutes, could tap a statement of collateral on the precise point where it was hollow. The counterbalancing of columns of figures was an object of perfection to him. He took genuine, almost musical pleasure, sitting at his desk with a cup of tea and holding a set of figures under the light, running up and down them in his mind, matching and playing with them, testing them, delighted when they rang true, the unflawed diamond of financial immaculacy.

Outside the office there were doubts which, had he admitted a personal register to his work, might have undermined him entirely. He read the papers. He knew that the decisions he and the others of his profession, great and small, took in the privacy of their offices could mean suffering and disgrace for real people, in real houses. He had seen it, at least once, too closely ever to be complacent. The financial universe might have been certain, logical and, within its own terms, honest; but it was not just, not on any human level. His abstraction within the world of his work, he knew, protected him from the reality of its injustice. He imagined, one day, the tide of outrage, black-booted and thick-sinewed, streaming down the streets of the city on the surge of its pain, tearing open the offices, dragging out the toiling black ants of the financial universe and crushing them under the heaps of tumbling masonry. 'We are men, as you are men', they would cry against their murderers; but they would be lying. He would step out to his destruction with a shrug of inevitability.

Helena took up her studies and seemed to find a purpose in them. She was out more evenings than she was in, at concerts, lectures, parties, rolling home often a little drunk, grey with tiredness, but always with a little brightness left for them if they were still up. Meanwhile, her affair with O'Neele proceeded. She would disappear for nights, for a weekend once, never with any pattern. Sometimes she would not see him for weeks. She would always tell them.

'I'm seeing Joey tonight, so don't wait up for me.'

On their father's reckoning of her not being truly in love unless she was miserable, she was not in love. He wondered if she had other lovers, imagined her sometimes flitting from bed to bed, at others working out an intensity of sexual understanding with O'Neele; neither speculation seemed to match her reality. O'Neele himself kept clear. Lewis rang him a couple of times, but he was evasive, never able to meet, even out of range of Celia.

Occasionally Lewis would find a moment with her alone.

'Are you happy, Helena?' he would say.

'Oh yes.' And then would come the pangs of guilt. 'You don't want me to find my own place, do you? I could, you know. It would be much easier for you.'

He put this idea down firmly, found that he dreaded her going, losing touch with her. He told himself that it was a desire to keep some check on her licence, but really it was because he did love to have her there, did find her beautiful and so full of life, so unpredictably, unquenchably happy.

He had been hurt by her sexual liberty, but he knew that feeling for what it was. He viewed her at a deliberate distance, alert with a forbidden prurience that he would have died rather than have expressed. He liked her best of all when she arrived back in the morning, shuffling under her clothes, giving off a radiant completion, yawning and scratching and stretching.

The week before Christmas, Lewis arrived home from work to find Celia sitting with a suitcase.

'There's no hurry,' she said. 'I've telephoned. They're expecting me.'

He arrived back home at one, having stayed for the customary cradling of his new child, another daughter, Celia by that time being fast asleep, buttoned down with as many tablets as they would permit her. He closed the front door carefully and went to pour himself a sedative whisky. Susan's birth had excited him; this one failed to. It was only waiting and waiting in cold corridors. Next time, he told himself, I'll leave her to it like most men do. She wouldn't know, anyway.

'Well?'

'Oh, hello, Helena. Another girl. Seven pounds something or other. Mother well; well out of it, actually. Want a drink?'

'Oh Lewis, congratulations!'

And she sprang forward and threw her arms about his neck. Her body met his hip to hip, her breasts loose under a thin nightgown and, before he had time to dress himself in any sort of considered reaction, he had dropped his hands to her buttocks and was amassing an erection that was both fierce and obvious. She laughed and dropped her face onto his shoulder.

He turned away at once, let her go and put three quick yards between them, stepping back from the edge of a sudden emotional anarchy. He turned and dropped himself into an armchair before daring to look at her again.

She stood with her head on one side, on tiptoe, hands behind her back, the laughter still in her face.

'Help yourself to a drink,' he said.

She did so, took a small glass of aperitif, brought him his whisky and sat before the fire, stoking a little heat out of the embers.

'Well,' she said, with a sigh that was almost resigned. 'What are you going to call her?'

For a moment, he did not know what she was talking about.

After this night, things deteriorated; not dramatically, but perceptibly. The new baby was fractious and opened black spaces in the night, night after night; and Susan, now two, reacted to the division of her importance with strident assertions. Celia brought the lethargy of pregnancy back from the hospital with her new daughter, developed migraines. The doctor became a regular visitor. She seemed to develop hypochondrias and to extend them to her daughters, in whom she began at last to take an interest; Lewis, having wanted this, was now caught in its contradiction. He moved into his dressing room, the thought of exercising a little sexual comfort with his wife seeming irrelevant and wearisome.

The dissatisfactions of home began to leak into his work, not distracting him or dulling any of his edges, but making him decidedly more unpleasant. He could feel it, but did not know what he could do about it. Everywhere he looked he saw incompetence and muddle, compromise and the failure of nerve; moral nerve, financial nerve, emotional nerve. Everyone seemed, one way and another, to be ducking out of everything, hypocritical, dishonest at layer after layer of themselves. It made him angry, because he knew that he himself was touched by this sickness.

One night, on a whim, having dined in town, more than a little drunk, he had pounded the streets until he had convinced himself that he was looking for something, for someone, for Helena, or even for Celia, the old Celia. He had met this girl, couldn't remember quite how, had bought her a drink, chatted to her. At what point he had realised that she was a prostitute he could not have said with any honesty. She took him back to a room, asked him for five pounds, then asked him what he'd like. 'Beat me,' he said, which she did, with practised professional thoroughness. The pain and humiliation might have been cathartic, had it not provoked a dismal arousal, with which she also coped efficiently.

By the time he arrived home, hearing the howling of his child as he touched the latch of the gate, even the shame had dulled.

When, a month later, the war at last broke out, he felt it like a liberation.

. . . thirty-three . . .

In the first months of the war, when nothing seemed to happen, Lewis found the atmosphere of fear a stimulant. Everyone seemed to be rushing about looking up at the skies, huddling over wireless sets, tearing open newspapers. He took on an affected indifference to it all, went on with his work, striding through the surrounding nervousness with his chin straight.

They wanted Helena back at Framling, and were suggesting that Lewis move Celia and the girls into the country. He was not against this, but Celia did not want to leave her doctor. Lewis himself could not, of course, contemplate leaving. Helena, also, had no intention of submitting to some dull rustication. Naomi had abandoned the idea of university for the duration. She would study nursing so that she could be useful. After the war, she would become a doctor, but there was no time for that now.

It came closer, month by month. London became a great junction: people with strange clothes and stranger accents walked bewildered through streets in which the traffic had thinned, past shops which were echoing with the loss of their abundance, stared into the windows that were hatched with tape; at the railway termini clusters of labelled children stood bewildered by a world that had suddenly begun to spin too fast for them; men in uniform loitered in groups, cheerful, reckless, proud, afraid; in restaurants, people huddled together in tight conversations. At night a new darkness filled the city which lay open to skies that had become malignant, part of the machinery of history that had gone out of control.

Huddled in her overcoat against the prevailing current of humanity, excited by the fear, riding on it, Helena made her way through the troubled streets to Joey's flat.

They used one of the lower rooms now, the big studio being impossible to black out. They would talk, but not seriously, the casual chatter of acquaintances with other things on their minds. They would eat out of tins, a dwindling stock of extravagant food, exotic soups and the pressed breasts of little birds, the creatures of distant oceans and sickly fruit in vivid colours. Then they would make love.

Most of all she liked to kneel down, her head in her hands, her elbows clamped into her breasts, curled over and clenched as her lover entered her from behind; not deeply, probing her slowly and sending precise quiverings of exact pleasure, electric into her rigid muscles. His steady hands were at her hips, the silk of his dressing gown folding upon her legs, and the liquids of their pleasure flowing. The triumph was in locking it out for as long as she could, holding herself against its completion, feeling it fracture her control, biting her knuckles to keep it back, the rage in her thighs, twisting it down, grinding her teeth and squeezing her eyes shut to keep in the tears.

Perhaps they had heard the sirens, perhaps not. There was a rumbling that rolled in like thunder but, unlike thunder, did not stop, rolled and rolled until the building shook about them. Glasses tinkled. Something in another room fell and smashed. The world trembled.

They disengaged, suddenly practical. They exchanged concerned glances, looked about them. Helena stepped from the bed and began to find her clothes, to dress quickly but without panic. It was too close for panic. The world was coming in upon them.

They heard then the explosions, a sequence of them, not immediate, but near enough to shake the building into a palsy of falling dust. The light went out. They stood apart in the darkness.

'Where are you, Nell?' he called.

'Here.'

'Are you all right?'

'Yes.'

Independently across the pitch they reached out their hands, found one another, locked their fingers. The world went still again, suspended about them. No, she said to herself, I don't mind dying here like this. It'll be all right. Her heart beat cleanly. She pulled at her lover, drew him to her, put her arms about him as he put his arms about her. She was cold, she realised, but he was warm. She clung to his warmth, to the solid humanity of him. It's love, she thought, after all. I've been so stupid.

Something whistled, high and close, as if it were actually inside their heads; then there was tremendous light and they were flung about in it as if they had leapt off into a sudden infinity.

How long it took, she did not know; perhaps she had been unconscious, perhaps it had only been an instant. She found herself in a heap of breakage: clothes, splinters of wood and glass, the powder of plaster. She thought she was dead, thought she was trapped, but she moved and found that her limbs were free, that bits of what she had thought were debris were parts of her. It was completely dark and the rumbling and roaring were so continuous now as to create an illusion of stillness within them.

'Joe?' she called. 'Joe? Are you all right?'

'I don't know.'

'I'll find a match.'

'For God's sake, don't strike a match, Hel. Can't you smell the fucking gas?'

'Where are you?'

'Here.'

'Find me, Joe.'

'I've peed myself.'

'Oh God, so have I.'

At which they broke into hysterical laughter, scrabbling bleeding and filthy across the black wreckage in search of one another, weak and stupid with laughter at the grotesque joke of being alive.

Lewis arrived at the cordon across the road, saw the smouldering cavity in the building where his sister had been staying, saw the fire wardens and police and ambulance auxiliaries struggling with the human debris they pulled from the building, holding back from it those who wanted to throw themselves into its pain. From the cavity poured out a terrible disorder that the wretched officials, black-faced and puny, strove to contain. He watched and he knew, the certainty entering his heart like a cancer; and as he knew, he felt as if a black bag had been pulled over his head and he had to fight to clear it, smearing at his eyes and hitting the side of his head. A weakness and cowardice filled him and he turned away. He did not want to know, would pretend that he hadn't seen. When they told him the news, he would act properly, but now he could not.

He walked the streets, saw what the bombs had done, felt the triviality of any emotion in the face of it. The worst of it all was that it was not personal, not an act of spite and rage that could be understood as from one human being to another; its inhumanity was literal. There were no people any more, just nations, cities, alliances, military capabilities in the context of which all suffering was relative. Human intercourse was suspended for the duration. The damage was sustainable. The bombs had fallen. The bulk of the city was still standing. Retaliation would be made. There was a fight on now all right.

He turned into streets that had been untouched this time, where it was possible to imagine that nothing had happened. But he could not sustain this fantasy, any more than it was being sustained in any face he passed. The whole city was now provisional, every solidity of building and institution had become hazy, lost in the shadows of what had happened. He preferred the wrecked streets, preferred stepping through the thoroughfares of broken glass, the snaking of fire hoses, the wreathes of damp smoke. This was real, the city broken down to its brute elements. The human fictions that had sustained it, that had been piled up into situations and meanings, had been called down. There was fire and there was death. There was the scrabbling out of the wreckage into a morning that would turn into a long afternoon that would turn into another night that

269

would bring the bombs again and again and again until there was no more morning, until the night fell finally.

When he arrived at the bank and found it gone, rubbled into nothing, he was glad. He could not have returned to work there. He hoped, with a sudden viciousness, that MacBlaine was under that mess somewhere. He was, somewhere; his old life was. He turned and made his way home.

'I'm back,' he called as soon as he had closed the door.

'In here, Lewis,' Celia called.

He went into the kitchen and found Helena and O'Neele sitting huddled over mugs of tea, filthy coats over their filthy bodies, dried blood on their faces, their eyes wide and white as if startled open.

He went to Helena and took her in his arms, shuddered with cold emotion.

'We were there,' she said.

'I saw it. I thought. . . .'

'We were making love. . . .'

'You stupid, bloody bitch.'

'MacBlaine rang,' Celia said.

'Bugger MacBlaine.'

He released Helena who sat limply, took her lover's hand and gripped it.

'We're going to get married,' she said.

'Don't be so fucking stupid, Helena,' he said. 'O'Neele, you'd better go.'

'Lewis, calm down,' Celia said, coming to him, taking hold of him firmly and drawing him through into the hall.

'And you're going to Framling,' he said. 'You, Helena, the children. . . .'

'All right. All right.'

'I'm joining the army.'

'Yes. I know. I know. Calm down now. It's all right, it's all right.'

... *thirty-four* ...

Lewis became a soldier then, entered the purgatory of basic training. He slept in a bunkhouse with thirty other recruits. They spent great tracts of time scrubbing and polishing and bringing everything to a regulation spotlessness, but they never, Lewis thought, managed to make an impression on the essential dirtiness of the whole institution, a spiritual dirtiness of men brought down to a uniformity of function, foul mouths and bloody minds the only margins for individual assertion left.

The food was tasteless, and he was ashamed of the hunger which drove him to consume the mounds of stale potato and gristly, watery stew, the pints of stewed tea. He slept through brief hours of dull itching, became constipated, caught a bad dose of foot-rot. One or two of the others were, as he was, better educated, and used their free hours to read; he, however, vegetated, found he had no discipline, felt himself becoming duller and duller.

The training was rudimentary and stupid. He knew the efficiency of their enemy and could not believe that anything they did here would be of any use whatsoever. They drilled and drilled, charged about with unloaded rifles through contrived assault courses, went on night patrols on which they got lost and cold, incompetently led, dredged of personal initiative and only surviving by treating everything as some cynical farce. He was a poor shot and woefully unfit. He was isolated and miserable, hated the NCOs for their bullet-headed pettiness, despised the officers for their spineless superciliousness. He wanted to be in battle where this interminable play-acting would make sense, if it made sense anywhere; but when he thought about this seriously, he knew that they were completely unsuited for any sustained act of combat. They could simply stand up and be shot, he supposed, and tried to believe that this would be of some use to someone somewhere.

On their weekend passes he went along with the lads into the local town and got drunk, blended in, came to moments of comradeship even, standing by some ex-butcher's apprentice and pissing into someone's hedge. There were local girls whom some of the others achieved, briefly and perfunctorily, but it was talk mostly. The object of the sharpest fantasy were the nurses who, it was alleged, were game for anything. Lurid stories were circulated by the more experienced, lighting up the eyes of the younger ones, making their mouths wet with imagination. My little sister is a nurse, Lewis thought with a shudder.

He had determined to stay in the ranks, to go to war and to fight as his father had fought; but the basic training taught him lessons about himself that disabused him of this simplicity. When he was told that he was being recommended for the commissions board, he conceded. It was a compromise, but it was at least a chance to put his abilities to work for the war on a real level.

The commissions board seemed satisfied that he had completed his basic training without complete incompetence, and that he had been to a decent school. He was the right type, and was given travel warrants for officer training college: Second Lieutenant Drewer.

It seemed that he was destined to be that form of soldier that his father despised most of all: the staff officer, the army administrator, responsible for transport schedules, for requisitions, taking the decisions of the military command and breaking them down into figures and practicalities. His was to be a quiet war; his chances of hearing a shot fired in anger, with the non-arrival of the invasion, were becoming more and more remote. At least it was work he could do, handling things he understood. He was not, he found, without authority; but he knew that he would never have been able to lead men into battle other than stupidly, blindly. Anyone could get them- selves killed. He was efficient and self-contained, his existence monkish, living in a small room in a divisional headquarters, with a soldier-servant to minister to his needs, going to his office early and leaving late, handling the paperwork, telephoning, making reports, attending briefings, taking small responsibilities and smaller initiat- ives.

He drank in the mess with other men drawn like him from comfortable middle-class existences for the duration, doing their bit. Their conversation was about the work they did, about the progress of the war. None of them talked about their families, their other lives; it was bad form to do so. The war, the actual war, the fighting and dying, was happening miles away. They felt neither safe nor comfortable about this; all felt more shame than relief at their home postings, yet dreaded having to go abroad. Malaya and North Africa, to which they dispatched troops and equipment daily, were burning wounds upon the maps they kept in their heads.

He took leave now and then, went to see how they were getting on. They were sitting out the war, growing inward, growing strange to him. He found that he had little to say to them, and the concerns of their domestic world did not mean much to him. Susan and Margaret had to be reminded who he was.

On his leaves, he took particular care, even if it meant spending an extra day travelling, to avoid London. He knew what was being done there, and he could not bear to see it.

It would be over in time. A victory looked possible, but he did not long for it, did not dream of a time when it would all be as it had been, for he knew that it would not, that the years of his life were being consumed here in dullness and, when peace came, there would only be a world of dullness to return to.

. . . *thirty-five* . . .

'Hanni! Hanni!'

She looked up the garden and saw him standing at the kitchen door. What now? she thought, driving her spade into the soil and glancing briefly at the work she had done, the work she still had to do, the squares of lawn she had dug over, the lines of cabbage and potato she imagined.

'Hanni!'

'Here I come,' she said as she strode up the path. 'What is it now?'

'There's someone at the door, woman. Can't you hear? Move yourself. Where are you?'

She took his arm and he settled against her with a grumpy sigh, permitted himself to be led back into the cottage, to be sat down.

'Go and answer the bloody door,' he said.

'In time, in time. Either it is important and he will wait. Or it is not important and he will go away. Don't be an old fool, now.'

There was a sharp rap.

'You see,' he said. 'You see.'

'I see, yes. In time, in time.'

She wiped her hands on her apron and went into the dark hall, began the complex process of unbolting the door, opening it at last to a rush of bright autumn light in which an army officer stood, young, tall and handsome; the worst kind. She closed the door to a crack and peered through it.

'What is required now?' she said.

'Mrs Brand?'

'I am she, yes.'

He smiled, shifted himself as if he were about to tell her good news.

'Er, you are my aunt, I believe. My name is Lewis Drewer.'

She could argue with the authorities, could outface their stupidities, felt strong when they came to trouble her; his family, however, she could not match; of them she was most afraid. Against their cold politeness she had felt their judgement of her, a conniving whore who had come to steal their birthright.

She did not look at this young man as she led him through.

'It is Lewis Drewer, your nephew,' she said. 'I will return to my work.'

'No,' the young man said. 'Please don't go. I have been longing to meet you . . . what shall I call you? Aunt Hanni?'

The old fool laughed.

'Auntie Hanni!' he said. 'I like that. I think I'll call her Auntie Hanni.'

'Be quiet,' she said.

The young man was embarrassed too, smiled at her sympathetically.

'Where are you then, Lewis? Come here and give me a hug. Have you brought your wife?'

'No, no. She's at Framling. I'm staying at the Hall. It's chance, really. There's a conference on up there and I'm fetching and carrying.'

'What? You're a soldier now?'

'You know this,' Hanni said. 'Your sister has written to you about this.'

274

'Not really a soldier,' the young man continued. 'A clerk in uniform. How are you, Uncle Harry?'

'Blind and stupid as ever. They've kicked me out of my home, not that it makes much difference to me. Hanni looks after me, don't you, lovely?'

The young man looked at her, saw her vulnerability and looked away. She went to her husband and took his hand, held it to her stomach.

'Tell me, Mr Drewer,' she said. 'Will the war soon be over?'

'Please call me Lewis.'

'Very well. Lewis.'

'The war?' he said. 'I think it will be a while yet.'

'Hanni says we've brought it on ourselves,' Harry said. 'We being the rich and comfortable. The beastly bourgeois.'

'She's probably right,' Lewis said. 'But that doesn't mean it shouldn't be fought.'

'Of course it must be fought,' she said. 'But the problem is not the making of war, but the making of peace. Perhaps the war is necessary. Perhaps only when there is nothing left of Europe something new can be built.'

He was looking at her, this young man, with sharp eyes, smiling. He understood, perhaps he agreed even.

'May you stay for supper, Lewis?' she asked.

'Yes. Thank you. I'd like that. I've a box of stuff outside, American rations, a bottle of brandy, even. I'll just go and fetch it.'

Whilst she made the supper, trussed the chicken and put it into the pot with the vegetables and herbs, Lewis and Harry talked. She could hear the flow of their conversation and she became nervous again. She did not like people to talk to him when she was not there. She suspected them, knew that he was too good, too open, too easy. Her paranoia told her that this young man was sent to spy out what was happening here, to send lawyers up to part them, to have her sent away. She had liked this Lewis Drewer, but then that was how they worked, the English, flirting with you with their charm and their good manners whilst they betrayed you.

She fetched a bottle of the good wine, for she knew Harry would ask for one. She would hide the brandy; it was not healthy for him to drink brandy. Her devotion to him was total, a physical and moral loyalty that she would have thrown her life away to protect in an instant. She had come to him despairing and exhausted and he had brought her to life, teasing her with his gruffness and his lechery, below which, when she had taken him at his word, she had found an honour, an honesty, that had made her weep. She had always believed in the essential nobility of man, but had never found a man in whose circumstances that nobility could stand free; not until she had met Harry Brand; and she was terrified, day by day, hour by hour, of having him taken away from her.

By the time she served supper, she was sulking, intensely jealous of this young man and his easy access to her husband, jealous of the family they shared, the big family to which she could never belong.

'We have something to celebrate, Hanni,' Harry said as she set down the food. 'Lewis is a father again.'

'My felicitations, Lewis. A boy-child or a girl-child?'

'A girl. Our third. Three girls, Hanni. Susan and Margaret, and now Jane.'

'Hanni won't have children, Lewis.'

She blushed. 'This is private, Harry, if you please.'

'Oh, sorry, sorry.' He reached out his hand for her, but she was busy hacking at the fowl with a knife.

'That smells wonderful,' Lewis said; then, a little later, 'I saw Brady up at the Hall.'

'Yes. They let her stay and caretake the place. She comes down once a week and has tea, doesn't she, Hanni?'

'She was the servant of your mother, I think, Lewis.'

'Yes, and my nanny. She's a strange old bird now.'

'She and Hanni get on famously, you know,' Harry said with a pride that made Hanni blush again.

She handed Lewis his plate. 'You know, of course, that she was your uncle's mistress for many years?'

'Bloody hell, woman!' Harry said.

Lewis laughed. 'I . . . yes, I suppose I did know. It wasn't something we discussed, but I think I knew. Hanni? Why won't you have children?'

She sat down and regarded her food, then lifted her face to him.

'It is private, Lewis,' she said.

'I know. I'm sorry, but . . . but if it's to do with me, then. . . .'

'Why should it be to do with you?'

'Because, you dumb Boche,' Harry said, 'if you have children, they'll inherit the estate. If you don't, then Lewis will inherit it, or his children will.'

276

'I will have nothing to do with this inheritance,' she said. 'I do not believe in it.'

'Just so long as that is not why you don't have children, Hanni. I only wanted to say that, as far as I'm concerned, the place is yours. I have no claim to any of it now.'

'I do not have children because it is not the time to have children, because children are being murdered in this war, because you must believe in the future to have children and I do not believe in the future, Lewis.'

'We'll win the war, Hanni. It may take us five years, but we'll win.'

'But what will be your victory? How many children will you kill to make your victory? No, thank you kindly.'

'D'you think it wrong of me to have children now?'

'I have no opinion of you, Lewis. You must do what is right as you see it.'

'Forgive me then for expressing my opinion of you. Uncle Harry?' he said, turning. 'Don't you want a child?'

'Nothing to do with me, my boy. I do my stuff.'

'If you talk like that, Harry,' she said, 'firstly I will cry, and then I will go into another room.'

'Forgive me,' Lewis said. 'And the food's getting cold. I just wanted to get that clear.'

After the meal, when she was washing up, he came through into the kitchen.

'Hanni, I must go. I'll try and pop over to see you again before I return south. Thank you for the meal. I am so glad to have met you at last, and I'm sorry to have pried into your private life like that.'

'You are honest, Lewis. You are an honest family, I find. That is to be commended.'

'If you think I'm honest, then believe me when I say that what you've done for him is wonderful. He's so happy.'

'I too am happy.'

'I'm not sure about that. Have his child, Hanni. Be brave.'

He kissed her cheek gently and took her hand, then slipped away, and she returned to her suds, listened for the voices in the other room, for the door to open and close.

'Hanni! Hanni!'

'What?' she yelled back.

'Where've you put that bottle of brandy? Leave that for the morning. Come on, woman, let's get pissed.'

She dried her hands, took off her apron and folded it across the back of a chair. She fetched two glasses and reached the brandy down from on top of the cupboard where she had stowed it.

'Hanni! Hanni!'

'Be quiet, you old fool!'

. . . thirty-six . . .

Of course it must be fought. But the problem is not the making of war, but the making of peace. Perhaps the war is necessary. Perhaps only when there is nothing left of Europe something new can be built . . . I do not have children because it is not the time to have children, because children are being murdered in this war, because you must believe in the future to have children and I do not believe in the future . . . We'll win the war. It may take us five years, but we'll win . . . But what will be your victory? How many children will you kill to make your victory?

He had seen them again, had taken a leave up there. Hanni had conceded. She was pregnant and as happy as her defiance could make her. Harry loved to fondle her big belly. It was, he heard, a difficult birth; a son and heir: Maximilian Brand. 'Makes my bloody surname sound kraut,' Uncle Harry had said. 'I have colonised you, Englishman,' she replied, 'colonised but not civilised, not yet.'

Susie, seven years old, Maggie, five years old, Janey, just two, coming out of their shelter into a world that, after just a few more spasms, a few more devastated cities, would be at peace. They will grow into their lives, will hear the chronicle of these years, or a version of it, but it will not belong to them. They will have survived, the debts of history paid for them so that they can be set free.

The night he returned from the camp, he wrote the first words of a letter. *I have betrayed you . . .* He could write no more, because that was all there was to say. He wrote it for his children, but they would not want it, would not understand it. He wrote it for Hanni, for whom it was literally, utterly true; but he could not bear to send it, could not bear to make the admission made in the privacy of his billet open. His shame was absolute. To belong now to the human race was a degradation.

He had travelled into Europe in the trail of battle, had done his work amongst the ruins of cities. He had seen the dead in ditches, huddled in doorways, spread across streets, one even hanging from a balcony as their jeep drove through. The sight of the dead had laid a cold hand upon him; but he had nerved himself to look. I am a soldier, he had told himself. This is my profession. There can be no judgement made here. Provided I am willing to offer myself. This war must be fought. Afterwards there will be time for doubt, for recrimination. He had set his teeth and done his work.

There had been rumours, there were always rumours. He was surely under no illusions as to the savage criminality of their enemy; he had known of that clearly when others had shrugged it off. Nothing he had known or seen, however, no aspect of his understanding of humanity, had remotely prepared him for the camp.

Something important, so important that full resources are to be sent there immediately, precise documentation, an organisational structure to co-ordinate massive and imperative relief. What? A camp. For civilian prisoners, dissidents presumably, socialists and misfits; and Jews, of course, but they exaggerate: confiscate their fat assets and they tell the world they're being exterminated. Don't get me wrong. I've nothing against the Jews. They've had a tough time, but so has everyone else.

An untroubled, pastoral landscape here; the war passed quickly through, or passed by on the other side; the odd wreck, the odd building bombed for the hell of it probably, but a landscape of white churches and green pastures, of trees and little rivers, and fat burghers trying to hide their swastikas before we see them, locking their wine and their daughters in the cellars.

A heavy sky, rain coming, snow even, washing the world, white-washing it; then, coming close, something else; a black underglow, not of smoke but of something else; a blast of foul air, neither organic nor chemical, something else. Something else. A line of wire fencing outside another line, breached, torn open. Gates, guard towers, a complex of low huts, comprehensible, almost reassuring, almost. The convoy slows, but does not stop. It rattles over iron tracks laid in thin grey mud, past soldiers who do not salute, who ought to have saluted. What the hell's going on here? Who the fuck's in charge of this shambles?

Then.

At first ghosts, desiccated forms who move slowly towards them, many, so many, but not a crowd. It is not possible to see them as a crowd, for a crowd has substance, if only in the mind of the beholder. These have no substance, are whittled down to a uniformity, a minimalism, one by one, belonging to no other, connected to nothing; striped, flapping rags hung on bones that have outgrown the bodies they belong to, outsize heads, outsize eyes that cannot focus, mouths that are toothless, stoppled by great dry tongues.

First an animal disgust. These are not human. Then a terror, for they are human. Recognise them. Once Jew, Gentile, man, woman, now nothing, only human, only human. Recognise them and know what to be human means, finally; and in that recognition is the last terror of all, the black space at the end of the world.

But this is not the end, or if it is the end, then there is something beyond it. Behind the ghosts, between the huts, crammed within the huts, silting up the camp, the dead, the less-than-dead; dried skin stretched taut on long bones, organs and muscle turned to water and drained out in filthy dysenteries; faces that register neither pain nor fear nor even despair; faces that register only a final humanity that has not been enough, will never be enough.

The worst of it, Lewis Drewer wrote in another fragment of another letter he could not send, *was the genitals which, in the emaciation of the thighs and bellies, gained a hideous prominence, pubic hair in vigorous tufts, vaginas bulging open, penises long and supple. To see them was obscene and shameful. To look at the corpses like that was to degrade them.*

And so many of them. To count them is meaningless; to reduce them to numbers, to try and bring some objective account of them is to avoid them. But it must be done, something must be done. Corruption and infection are abstracts that can be confronted. Immense blocks of the hard ground are opened by bulldozers which then tumble the mounds of the dead into the holes, clattering cartwheels of stick-limbs, a tumult of seething, stinking corpses. The bulldozers pull back, come forward, drive the mounds of earth over them. Disinfectant, fire, scouring the place to death lest anything should grow here again, anything at all. Nothing shall grow. Nothing shall begin here. Nothing. Nothing.

We did not speak whilst we were there. I suppose there must have been words, there must have been decisions taken, orders given; but I cannot remember words. I can only remember the silence.

When we got out of it, then we began to talk. There was terrible anger, a power of retribution that filled us. It was natural, I suppose, at the time. I wonder how many of us were later ashamed of what we loudly demanded to be done that evening, emptying those smug little villages, burning, butchering, death for death. I was ashamed, although I never wanted retribution. It sickened me as I listened to them; but not because I was better than they were, more moral; and certainly not because I was filled with any forgiveness for what had been done. Retribution was a way of coming to terms with what we had seen, and therefore of avoiding it.

I remember a fat little man, a prisoner, one of the guards. We made them carry the dead out, their dead. He didn't seem to mind that, didn't seem to notice what he was doing, did it as he had done everything else. Someone had told him to do it, someone with a gun, someone who took his decisions for him. I saw him later trying to cadge a cigarette off one of our men. Our man looked at him, then jabbed his face with his rifle butt, and when he was on the ground spat on him. He crawled off and pulled himself up, didn't bother to dust himself down, didn't bother to wipe the blood or spittle off his face, just shuffled off. He made me weep. Life was just something that was done to him, or that he did to others; there wasn't much difference finally.

I wept, Hanni. I wept to have seen what I had seen, to be what I was, to know myself in that place, to lose the last innocence. In the face of what I saw there, and God knows we did not see the worst of it, I knew, I know that love is a delusion, the fancy dress we put over our cruelty, the little light we burn in our minds as we devour one another, looking the other way even as our hands catch and tear, making music and poetry, speaking of love, even when we hear the screaming and the terror; for there we had come upon a place in which the denial of love was absolute; and there, Hanni, I knew myself. I recognised myself.

I am guilty of whatever was done in those camps. I am human and therefore I am guilty. Forgive me. I betrayed you.

... *thirty-seven* ...

Celia travelled up to London alone, as he had asked her to. She hadn't known when he would be coming back. He had telephoned and told her that he had been back a week, that he was at the house, that they ought to talk. She had been worried for months, for he had stopped writing. The war was over in Europe, but in the chaos of victory anything might have happened. When he telephoned there was relief at Framling. His call had been brief and Celia could not answer any of their questions. She only knew that she must go to him.

She did not go joyfully, did not know whom she was going to meet. They had been apart for over half their married life. Their children would be strangers to him. As she sat pressed into the corner of the railway carriage, her mouth dry and her eyes swollen, as the train slowed into the terminus, she knew that what she dreaded most was that he would want sex from her.

He did not meet the train, although she had told him which one she would be on. She caught a taxi which made circuitous progress through the blitzed streets. She gazed at the damage with horror and pity, felt that she was entering a world which she had only imagined, the world of the war; the world he now belonged to.

The house looked deserted, curtains drawn, path overgrown. A window was broken and rubbish had been thrown into the garden. The wooden fencing had gone. I am going to have to bring my children here, she thought.

Her key still fitted the lock but there was a chain across the door. She tried the bell, but it did not work. She knocked on the door and called, tried to peer in. The drawing-room door opened and she could see his shape approaching, unlatching the chain.

'Hello,' he said. 'Come in.'

He did not look at her, turned away as if he did not want to see her face.

In the drawing room, the dust sheets still covered the chairs, but he had lit a fire which burned nakedly in the grate, dispersing a leaping yellow glow about the subdued room.

'The, er, water is back on, but not the gas, nor the electric. Sit down.'

She drew back the dust sheets from one of the armchairs and set up a cloud of dust and moths, which made her start. He was stooping, feeding the fire. When she was seated, he went and fetched a chair, sat on it and stared down.

'How are you, Lewis?' she asked.

'Me? Oh, glad it's all over. You know. How are the girls?'

'Passing round chickenpox at the moment, but all right. Your parents send their love. Naomi and Helena are away, but . . . but they'll be relieved to know you're back. Are you still a soldier?'

'Yes. Technically.'

'Will you go back to the bank?'

'I don't know whether there is any bank. You knew that Mac-Blaine was dead?'

'No.'

'A stroke. Last year sometime. I thought . . . I thought I might go north for a bit, once I get demobbed.'

'To see Harry?'

'Yes, and Hanni, and the child. I was up there, you know, before I went . . . abroad. Will you be all right at Framling for a bit?'

'I expect so.'

'Susan'll be at school now.'

'And Margaret.'

'Yes . . . I hadn't thought.'

'You think we should stay on at Framling, then?'

'Well, yes. I thought . . . I thought that would be best. For the moment.'

'You don't want us back here?'

'Here? Well, if you'd rather. . . .'

'Where will you be?'

'Well, I'm going north. I told you. I really don't have any plans. You're all right for money? I'm sorting something out, an account for you. . . .'

'Will you be coming to Framling?'

'Oh yes. I expect so. Eventually.'

They were silent then for a while. She would not have recognised him if he had met her train. This was a business meeting.

'You don't. . . .' she began. 'You don't envisage us . . . living together, then, Lewis?'

'Well,' he said quickly, 'not immediately. There's a lot . . . a lot that has to be sorted out.'

She had begun to cry, perhaps from relief. He watched her helplessly, quite unmoved.

'You see,' he said. 'I'm just not sure of things at the moment, not of what I'm going to be doing. I just want you to be all right, Celia. I'll get this place back into order. You can bring the girls back here.'

'No,' she said, through her weeping, keeping the conversation up in spite of it. 'We'll stay where we are. What . . . what shall I tell your parents?'

'I don't know. Is there a problem there?'

'No. No problem. They'll be concerned, of course.'

'Yes. Well, I'll write to them. Tell them . . . tell them, I'll be writing in a week or two. What time's your train?'

'My train?'

'I'm sorry. I thought you'd be going back to Framling.'

'I . . . I didn't make any plans. I didn't know what you'd want, Lewis.'

'Ah, no. Of course. My fault. I should've . . . well, you could stay here I suppose. I've spent the odd night. It's not uninhabitable. There are some lamps, some tins in the kitchen: bully-beef and that sort of thing. I'll fetch you in some bread and milk.'

'Where are you going?'

'I've . . . there are some people I have to see in town. I'll stay at the club. You've got the number if you need anything.'

And that was about it. He pottered about, being practical, like an estate agent, then left her.

She was afraid of the house. Being there animated memories of things that, in the cold dust and staleness, she knew to be dead things. She wanted to be with her children. She wanted to be safe again. She slept in her underwear, in a damp bed in a brick of silence that, in a dream, she imagined setting about her, locking her in.

She left for Framling early the next morning. She did not see or hear from Lewis, did not want to. As she approached her sanctuary, however, she began to worry what she would tell Lionel and Anna, began then for the first time to try and defrost her memories of their meeting; knew then what she had missed at the time, that something had happened to him which had changed everything.

284

As she walked back through the town in the bright sunshine, she knew that she had lost him.

. . . *thirty-eight* . . .

She didn't see him again for eight months. He wrote her letters, factual letters, saying where he was, where he had been, making arrangements, financial arrangements, but no plans were made for any sort of future. He promised to come for Christmas, then wrote and said he was staying in the north, helping Harry and Hanni move back into their house.

Helena had sailed at last to join Joey in America. Naomi had begun her medical studies, in Edinburgh, and could not, or did not want to, get away. The house, in spite of the girls' giggling and squabbling, seemed empty, melancholy.

Celia sensed Anna, and behind her Lionel, watching her closely, monitoring her moods, building up a pity for her, a sad, slow realisation of her state. She herself did not feel down, busied herself with the girls, with their clothes and with their reading books. She had begun to speak French to them and delighted in their quickness of apprehension, Susan's particularly.

She had come to see her in-laws as the paragon of marriage: the tall man and his small, slight wife who lived together in an immaculacy of mutual deference and understanding that was both formal and intimate. She had never once heard them disagree. Whenever they spoke they spoke for one another. They had a pride in their children that was generated by a love that could have embraced them at whatever depth they fell, but which was never silent in the face of anything that did hurt. In the early years of her marriage, Celia had resented the Drewers and their smug appraisal of her, had felt excluded. When she had come as a refugee, with their grandchildren in tow, she had found that she was included, felt that she always would have been if she had allowed it. Now they had become a standard of goodness before which she attempted to dress herself in duty. More than that she had not, did not, feel capable of.

Did she miss Lewis? At times perhaps she did. During the war, his absence had been comprehensible, acceptable. But the war was over now, and the lack of him was a numbness. She began to wish that it might be settled. She was troubled by memories of his pleasure, of her pleasure, of the conception of Janey one weekend leave when suddenly something had broken through the clouds. She remembered Helena's first pleasures. If she grieved at all, she grieved at these memories, for they disrupted her from the dogged endurance of life that she was so good at, the finding of pleasures in small things, the slow beginning of a life lived through her children that she could foresee ahead of her.

'Where is he, Celia dear?' Anna said at last, one afternoon when they were sitting alone before the drawing-room fire.

'Oh he's . . . still with Harry,' she said smoothly, not looking up from the magazine.

'Why isn't he here?'

'I don't know.'

'I'm sorry, my dear. Does it upset you to speak of him?'

'No.' She had meant it as she said it, then the tears came to betray her.

'Oh, Celia. What's to be done?'

'Well,' she said, shaking herself clear of the emotion. 'I suppose I'd better go and see him, hadn't I?'

'We'll come with you.'

'No, I . . . I would rather leave the girls, if that's all right?'

'Yes. Of course. Lionel can go with you, though. Would you like that? He could drive you up.'

'No. I'd better go on my own. I'll take the train.'

Had she been manoeuvred into this? Perhaps, but it was the thing to do, obvious as soon as the words had fallen out of her. It would have to be settled. She would go and force him to a decision.

She stepped from the sleeping compartment onto the early-morning platform of the provincial station. It was bitterly cold. She had not taken account of the northern winter. A sharp blast tunnelled through the station and invested her thin clothes, her thin flesh. A few railway officials slouched about their work, clouded in their own breath. If he hadn't come to meet her, then she was stranded. The house was thirty miles away. She pulled her case through the barrier, had to remove her gloves to find her ticket, shivered and fumbled under the curious, fat eye of the ticket collector.

Beyond the barrier he was waiting for her, standing beside a small, old-fashioned car. She was at once afraid of him, for he seemed to have gone wild. He had a ragged beard, wore filthy trousers and a ripped jacket, a large cap pulled down and a garish scarf wrapped round his neck. A moment after she had seen him, she considered refusing to acknowledge him, turning back into the station; but it was too late. The moment of recognition had happened. He walked forward and, giving her a small, nervous smile, took her suitcase, and she was following him mutely to the car.

'You're going to be frozen,' he said. 'There's a blanket in the boot. It's a bit grubby, but it'll keep you warm.'

He handed her the blanket and she tucked herself into it. It smelt of dogs.

'You don't mind my coming, Lewis?' she said when they were on the road, passing through the outskirts of the small city into the cold, snow-streaked countryside.

'I've been expecting you, I suppose,' he said.

'We must sort something out, something permanent.'

'Yes, of course. I'm sorry, Celia. This is all a bloody mess, but . . . yes, we must get it sorted out.'

His tone was abrupt and, although what he said sounded purposeful enough, she knew that he did not really want to face it, that he would accept anything she said.

He was not living in the house, but in a cottage; the cottage where Harry and Hanni had lived out their exile. He saw them occasionally, but was living on his own mostly. He talked about what they were doing, how Hanni was a wonder, resourceful and dynamic, making everything work again, learning about farming and management. He did their accounts for them as his contribution. Brady was well, reviving with a new baby to look after, although Max was hardly a baby now, had never been really, a precocious little thing.

She was envious as he told her all this, resentful that he had abandoned his own family for this. Let him stay here then, she said to herself. Let him give me a divorce. Desertion. She must be careful, then, not to let him revive their marriage in a moment of sentimentality. That he had not touched nor kissed her when they met, either before or now, did not make her feel safe: she knew him too well for that.

'Where am I going to stay?' she said. 'Or are you expecting me to catch the sleeper back again tonight?'

He laughed. 'Oh no. Stay as long as you want. I . . . you can stay in the cottage . . . I could arrange for a room up at the house, if you'd prefer it. Actually, they don't know you're coming. I thought . . . I thought you might not necessarily want to get involved with that.'

'Will you be in the cottage too, Lewis?'

'Well, yes, I suppose I will; but don't worry, I'm not . . . I mean, I'll keep out of your way, I promise. I'm sorry, I didn't think. Would you rather I wasn't there?'

'I don't care, Lewis. Provided you understand clearly that I have no intention of sleeping with you.'

'Of course not.'

This was not a reassurance. Perhaps she would be safe from weeping, drunken knocking on her door; perhaps.

The cottage was small, damp, draughty and cold. There were two bedrooms next to each other up a tiny staircase, with a fragile lath-and-plaster wall between them. The lavatory was outside the back door, and there was no bathroom. The place was also a mess, dirty, sordid. The loss of his fastidiousness disturbed her. She would not stay long.

He rummaged about, made a pot of tea, lit a fire in the living room, moved some things about to make space. They sat opposite one another at the table, she still in her coat. She offered him a cigarette which he took, but refused a light, said he would smoke it later.

'I'll give you another cigarette later,' she said.

He laughed, shrugged, offered her the cigarette back. She took it and put it down on the table between them.

'Well?' she said.

'Well. . . .'

'What exactly are you doing here, Lewis?'

'Well . . . not much, really. Just . . . just being on my own. You see, I need that after . . . I thought, just a few weeks and I'll have it sorted out, but it's taking rather longer than that. I'm glad you've come, Celia. I mean, I came and found you, fetched you back, and now . . . now you've come to find me.'

'You expect me to fetch you back, do you?'

'Well . . . I don't know. I assumed that you'd . . . I don't know. What . . . What d'you think?'

'I had assumed that I was here to talk about a divorce.'

'A divorce?' He sounded as if this was a completely new idea, to which he had no definite reaction. 'That would be one option, certainly. Is that what you want? Have you . . . found someone else?'

'No, Lewis, I have not "found someone else". It just seems to me rather pointless being married and living three hundred miles apart. I mean it's not as if you have to be here. I assume you are here because you don't wish to live with your children and me any longer. And if that is the case, then I don't think that we still have a marriage. I find your whole attitude so simple, so naïve that . . . what? Have you had some sort of breakdown? What is it?'

He darkened, frowned, began to try to say something, then lost it.

'Would you . . . would you like me to return with you?' he said.

'I don't honestly know. If you are keen to return, if you want to make another start, then I'll do my bit. But if it doesn't really matter to you, if you'll come back just because you feel you ought to, or because you don't really mind where you are or what you're doing any longer, then I think we'd be better off calling it a day. Well? What do you think?'

'Perhaps.'

'Perhaps what, for God's sake?'

'Perhaps we'd better . . . end. . . .'

She watched him come at last to this, saw that, in spite of his lethargy and off-handedness, it depressed him, brought him down.

'Don't you want to see your children?'

She had assumed that this was an important card. She did not know how she wanted him to react to it, only that she wanted, expected him to come up in response to it. He did not. If anything, it pushed him further under; and this made her angry.

'Well, if that's all the response I've come three hundred miles for, it's been a waste of time, hasn't it? Perhaps you'd better drive me back to the station. I'll need to book myself a sleeper.'

'You know,' he said, 'my father had a breakdown during the Great War.'

The inconsequence of this exasperated her. She picked up her cigarette case and lighter and rose from the table.

'I'll go and get my bag. If you could get the car . . . Lewis?'

He reached across and picked up the abandoned cigarette, toyed with it, examined it as if he had never seen one before.

'Lewis?'

He didn't even know she was still there. She began to be seriously afraid. She would have to go up to the house, face those people there, ask for a doctor, see him into hospital, have him transferred south, have him looked after, nurse him back to health. She loathed it, the whole process, the stink of weakness and morbidity; the character flaw that she had always known he possessed now opening into a chasm.

'Sit down,' he said, with a sudden decisiveness that made her, after a moment, obey.

She waited, took another cigarette, offered the light to him. He took up the cigarette, leant his face forward and drew the smoke ferociously into him, tipped back his head as he did so, let it out of his lungs with a rasp through closed teeth.

'Did you know about my father's breakdown?' he asked.

'I knew he'd been ill. He was wounded, wasn't he?'

'They found him wandering naked on a battlefield. They didn't know who he was for two years. He knew, or at least I think he knew, but he didn't let on. He closed himself down completely. For two years. My mother thought he was dead. They all did. I was . . . three, four. I remember something of it, vaguely, the pain, the tears, the terrible weight in the house when they brought him back. He never talks about the war, couldn't talk about it. That's why they didn't want me to be a soldier. I wasn't really a soldier, didn't kill anybody, not personally, didn't even fire a gun at anyone. Someone took a shot at a lorry I was in once, but that was probably by mistake. And it wasn't like the Great War. All wars are cruel and futile, but this war perhaps less so than any. What we discovered when we liberated the occupied areas . . . how much do you know about all that?'

'I read the papers. There were some pictures, from one of those camps. I read a report, or your father read it out. It was terrible.'

'I was in one of those camps, you see. We had to go in and sort it out, or try to sort it out and that . . . that's what's happened, really.'

'What d'you mean?'

'I don't think I've had a breakdown, as such. I mean I know who I am, what I am, all that, but . . . but we went into a nightmare there and I haven't really come out of it; to be honest with you, I don't think I can come out of it. The reason that I'm here is basically because I can't stand to be with people any more, particularly . . . particularly people I care for. I think really I want to die, and I suppose I'll do it one day. I've come quite close to it, but it always seems, I don't know, melodramatic. I think if I could do it without disturbing the surface of the world too much, then I would do it. Otherwise, generally, nothing seems to matter any more. I don't expect you to understand this, so please don't feel in any way obliged. I wasn't going to tell you, perhaps I shouldn't have done. I'm sorry, Celia. I'm sorry I married you. I'm sorry that your children have a father who's no good. I'm sorry I ever touched you. Don't try to forgive me, or anything like that, or feel sorry for me, or grieve, or whatever; because none of that means anything.'

'What did you see, Lewis?'

'I saw . . . the dead. I saw the dying. I saw . . . something I recognised.'

'What?'

'Myself, obviously.'

She had nothing more to say. All her truculent assertions were lost now, in the face of this. She stared into his eyes and saw there, at last, what she had always known, in the depth of her; the disgust and terror of life; the very things he had sought in her and fought in her. Everything fell back from this revelation, from this sudden new understanding that she had of him. It was as if they had gone back to that first moment, that first time that he had touched her, as if they had struggled and writhed, and bred children even, and had at last arrived back where they had begun. She felt a rush of triumph enter her.

'Go and fetch your case now,' he said, fumbling in his jacket for the car keys.

'I'll stay,' she said. 'A few days.'

'It won't make any difference, you know.'

'It will to me, Lewis.'

... thirty-nine ...

She tidied up his kitchen, found some eggs and scrambled them for lunch. He went out, but only briefly. When he returned he drifted round her, not sure of what he wanted, of what she was doing. She didn't know either, kept busy to stop thinking, or to try to. She was full of a sharp energy, a proud anger, a need to confront him. She found her thoughts coming on robust and practical. She would get him out of here, get him back to Framling, get him back to London to work.

Over lunch she put these plans to him as forthrightly as she could, giving him a small margin of refusal. He did not refuse, but nor did he concur.

'You haven't understood,' he said at last.

'I have, Lewis, better than you think, but that is not the issue. You said that it didn't matter any more. Well, I'm not going to leave you here to get around to blowing your brains out. The sheer stupidity of that appals me. I need you to give your daughters some sort of home, some sort of social base from which they can make their own lives. We will have separate rooms, live separate lives, if that's what you want.'

'I'll need to think about this.'

'Fine. Think all you like.'

In the evening, when he had closed the shutters and lit the lamps, as the fire began at last to fill the living room with a cloud of warmth, when they made more tea and opened some tinned meat for their supper, he began again. She had watched him, had almost felt the twistings of his thoughts in the closeness of the cottage. She was ready for him.

'It won't work, Celia.'

'You won't try to make it work, you mean.'

'I'll give you a divorce. Find yourself someone who'll be some use.'

'I don't want to find anyone else. I can't go through all that again.'

292

'All what?'

'Sex, Lewis.'

'Find someone who . . . whom you can come to an understanding with.'

'God, you are naïve, aren't you?'

'Probably.'

'So. This is a rejection, is it? Be clear, Lewis. I don't want a divorce. I want you back. I understand how you feel. I accept all that. If you won't come back, then it has to be a positive decision. Don't trick yourself into believing you're only doing it for me and for the girls.'

'You don't begin to understand how I feel.'

'That too is a self-deception. Yes, I do understand how you feel. Oh, but I do, Lewis, I do.'

He gazed at her wearily, began to shrug, to look away.

'Lewis? You remember how you always wanted me to be happy? I told you. I told you time and time again that the only way I could have been happy would have been if you had left me alone, if everyone had left me alone, if I had been allowed to shut myself away, like this, like you're doing now. But no, you would not let me be alone. What did you believe? That you could make me happy by giving me orgasms? Lewis, I hated you touching me. When we had sex, I felt humiliated, degraded, filthy. I came to put up with it, eventually, after we were married. It was just something we did, part of the contract. I'll be honest with you, at times it was pleasant, but . . . the worst times were before, when you forced me . . . forced me to come. Oh I came all right, shuddering with revulsion, with pain. D'you understand me, Lewis? Do you believe me? No, you think I'm making some ploy. You see, you still have your bloody masculine pride after all. What then? What now? You learnt in the war that human beings are capable of the final depths of depravity, that you are capable of them. Lewis, I've known that since the day you met me, before. I always knew it. You were the confirmation of it. But, the point is . . . the point is, that is why I married you. Listen to me, Lewis. Listen to me. That is why I married you. That is why I came to you, why I wanted you to do what you did to me. I tried to hide in myself, but you would not let me hide. And you were right. You can't escape it. You can avoid it, pretend it doesn't matter, lock it inside you, turn it into disgust at others, jump up for castration for rapists and whipping for unmarried mothers, but that's a lie, a bloody lie; so is turning it into disgust at yourself, crawling off to die under some stone. Listen to me, Lewis. It's how we are made. It's what we are. And the only hope for us is to know that, to be true to it, to each other, to become torturers and victims, my torturer, my victim, and me yours, not to stop, to watch each other's humiliations and shames, to know them, to love them, to take delight in them, to offer in exchange your own humiliations and shames. That is what we are, Lewis, you and I. You've come down to it now. I feel like I've been set free at last. At last you understand me, know me, know yourself, know what I know about you. Welcome to hell, Lewis. Thank God, you made it at last.'

When she had finished, she found that she was trembling, her whole body palsied and blurred. She did not want him to speak, did not know what she would have done if he had laughed, or come out with some triviality, or just shrugged. She did not look at him. She rose from her chair and made her way through to the kitchen, out of the back door, into the lavatory where, as she pissed into the darkness, the icy air tightened about her until she could hardly breathe.

When she returned he was gone. She sat back at the table and lit a cigarette, waited blankly as if it were a game and it was his move, as if the board lay before her. When, after an hour, he had not returned and she had smoked the last of her cigarettes, she considered going to bed, but could not face that small, icy box up there. She cleared an armchair of books and clothes and papers, tipped them onto the floor, dragged it before the fire which she banked up with a couple of fresh logs; then, finding an old coat, one she recognised from London, she curled up in the armchair and fell asleep.

She awoke to find him in the room, moving about, doing things. She was a little afraid, disorientated, her head aching and her bones cramped. She had no idea of the time, but the logs had burnt down and the fire was a mound of grey ash in which a couple of embers glowed like jewels. The lamps were still alight, the shutters still closed.

'What time is it?' she said.
'I don't know.'
'Morning?'
'After midnight, before dawn.'
'Where've you been?'

294

'I went up to the house. I had to see Hanni. I've been getting drunk with Uncle Harry. Have you got a cigarette?'

'No. Could you make some tea?'

'The kitchen range is out. I've got some gin somewhere, but you'll have to drink it on its own. Or with water.'

'No gin, Lewis.'

He sat at the table. She shifted herself round to look at him, but did not want to let the cold under the coat.

'Have you got the curse, at the moment?' he asked.

'No. Why?'

'You smell as if you have, that's all.'

'You bastard,' she said, the invective buzzing in her. 'You fucking bastard.'

'You know,' he said. 'I've always had a secret terror of being hanged. I used to have nightmares about it. For about an hour last night, I suddenly thought that was it, get myself hanged.'

'What? By killing me?'

'That was the idea.'

'What stopped you?'

'The girls, I suppose.'

'The girls? You could always have dodged down and taken care of them too. No-one would have found me for a week or two.' I can play this game too, she thought, as well as you can.

'Are all women like you?' he asked. 'I mean somewhere deep down?'

'God knows. I hope not, but I suspect there's something there, somewhere deep down, some little horror. All men are like you, that's for sure, on one level or another.'

'I don't believe you.'

'What? About men? Or about women?'

'About women.'

'Please yourself.'

'What about Helena? What about Naomi? What about my mother?'

'Your mother is . . . I won't talk about your mother to you, Lewis. As for your sisters, well, they're lucky. Helena lives on the surface, bright and happy with it, and that's all right. Naomi, she thinks there are much more important things in life than sex, like saving the world. They're lucky, unlike us. We know too much, think too much, have been too much alone, know ourselves too well.

We are the damned, the obsessed. We have to get out of this place, go back, make a life for our children, live with it. You know we have to. You are going to come back, Lewis.'

'Yes.'

He began to cry a little later. She had never seen him cry, nor any man. Watery eyes, perhaps, but this was great wet tears that plopped onto the table shamelessly, great humping, wretched sobs. She went and held his hands at last and he gripped her until he hurt, weeping his shame out. It's best that we get this out of the way, she thought, although he'd better not make a habit of it. When all this stuff was out of the way, they could get going. It would be all right. They would watch each other too closely now for anything to come loose again. In time he would come to hate her again, to know that hate for what it was; then he would fuck her. She almost looked forward to it; not, of course, physically, but as a vindication of their world, a re-pledging of the last secrets that they had come to, a renewal of their marriage.

. . . *forty*

'It's a progressive school, Uncle Lionel, not a public school. I will learn science and languages and, when I'm older, politics, economics and philosophy. I will not be beaten and I will not have to learn dead languages.'

'Max, it sounds splendid. Are you looking forward to it?'

'No, because I will have to leave home, leave Mummy and Daddy. But I must go to school, mustn't I?'

'Yes, if you want to get on in the world, Max.'

'Off with you now, old man,' Harry said.

The boy offered Lionel his hand to shake, then left the room quietly, closing the door behind him. Lionel watched Harry listening closely for the boy to be gone, as if he might have lingered outside the door. When he was satisfied, Harry laughed.

'I don't think he's mine at all,' he said. 'Far too bright. A prodigious child, eh?'

296

'Oh, he's yours all right,' Lionel said.

'The women have had too much to do with him, I know. It'll be good for him to be at school, although God only knows what sort of place it is. Hanni found it, went down there for a whole week. I'll miss him when he's gone. He makes me laugh, Lionel. I suppose it's Hanni, but he sees the world so strangely. Sometimes he sounds about twenty-five, sometimes . . . sometimes it's like he's just come out of the egg. I started all this too late, you know. I'll not live to know much of what he makes of life.'

'Oh, come on, Harry. What are you? Sixty-five? You've got five years on me.'

'Ah well, all yours are grown and flown now. What is it? Five grandchildren now?'

'Six. Lewis's four and Helena's twins.'

'And Naomi? What's she up to?'

'Not marriage. Far too busy.'

'They've done well for you, Lionel, made their mark on the world, came out of their war better than we came out of ours.'

'Yes, I suppose they did.'

Two old soldiers sitting in the sunlight in a country house, drinking whisky with too much soda in it; two old men, life grown slow within an accelerating fall of days, the pull of the clay about the flesh; the pleasures now of rest, of calm, of sleep, small intimate pleasures that can be shared less; wandering the landscapes of memory, the sad detachment, playing the game now from a fixed position, incapable of change; opinions, perceptions, that one had seemed certainties, now stiff with obsolescence. What have you given to the world? More than you took from it? Such demands have no meaning. It was. It is. I had little to do with it. I was there because it was there and I was who I was born to be.

Perhaps, after all, love is the most important thing, the process of love, the giving and receiving; but that will end with death, will disappear in an instant as if it had never been. Only, he thinks, out of it sprang our children, leaping out from between our closeness; enormous, unaccountable things, generating their own worlds, leaving us beached on the shores of our drying seas. They owe us nothing any more, or if they owe, then the debt is repaid not to us but to those they love, to those they themselves give birth to.

Lionel Drewer considers his children:

Naomi, Doctor Drewer, head down into the mess of the world, trying to find the place to plunge the needle; angry, intolerant, with a hard intelligence that will not accommodate the stupidity of others. Love? Well, men, yes. A night off, a plate of sandwiches and a bottle of scotch, shaking out the tensions with a man inside her. Love? Tenderness and pleasure for a while, indulgences of a self too large, too restless to take the time for more; hard in a hard world.

Helena, Lady Graves, beautiful bird-woman, flying to California to find her lover married; the breakdown, suicide attempt, histrionics in a world where such things are merchantable; emerging, for a season, as Helena Forsythe, film actress; the diabolical embarrassment in the cinema watching one's own daughter flaunting through some cardboard hotel lobby in a backless dress, seeing her thin pretence at acting in a turgid comedy of morals produced by an industry of limitless commercial promiscuity. It was O'Neele himself, apparently, who had persuaded her to come home, on the pretext of learning acting properly. And it was Lewis who had introduced her to Freddie Graves, Sir Frederick, a house in Berkshire, a flat in Belgravia, and twin daughters, her picture in the society pages, disappearing into newspaper cliché: the lovely Lady Graves, hostess, mother, greeting you, even her own father, with a smile so oiled, a kiss so professional, laughing with an open lewdness that is alarming until you realise that it is also practised, coached, honed to the point of suggestiveness, pornographic.

Lewis. Lewis Drewer. Mid-to-late-thirties. Merchant banking. And Celia. A stable marriage. Four children. The girls of course, then a boy, an afterthought or accident, although it is hard now to see Lewis or Celia being guilty of either. Once, a young man so charming and fluent that you had to keep stopping, taking your bearings; a dangerous young man once. And in her, once, a hardness that edged by sudden jumps to the lip of neurosis. When they had appeared together, in those first years, they had inhabited a thin formality below which it was always possible, unavoidable, to sense something hurting, something torn, something bloody. We were afraid for them, Lionel thought, afraid of them; afraid of what she was doing to our son, and of what our son was doing to her. The terrible secrets of marriage. Then the war and he had not come back, as I did not come back; and she went and brought him back, as Anna went and brought me back. And life goes on. The merchant banker with the house in Holland Park, and with four children, the eldest now almost the age Naomi was when we came to Framling, the youngest a baby, the post-war generation. And the parents stiff and correct, smiling now privately to themselves as if at some secret irony, occupying a mutual urbanity, a prosperous formality.

Are they happy? Are any of them happy as we were happy, as still we are, forty years into marriage? Is that the point? Yes, I think it is the point, for happiness is the outfall of love, its ambient heat. None of them, perhaps, are unhappy; but that's not enough, that's merely the toleration of life; happiness is finding a common cause with life. And if we have not given them the means to be happy, then we have failed them; or if that is too harsh, if it is, as it is, probably nothing to do with us, then we have lost them. That, yes. Lost.

And love remains in its sad privacy; Anna and I, the comfort of aging bodies. And if things were left undone, then it is too late, having come through so much, living in the sad nostalgia of survival, for it is sad to have survived, wandering about like ghosts in a world too new, too fast, remembering what might have been done, what was done, what can no longer be done, not by us; and not by our children who have no time for that now. Lost.

'How are your eyes, Brady?'

'Not so good, m'm. They say there's an operation that I could have, but I think I'm too old to be going through all that.'

'Nonsense. We'll book you into a clinic in London. Lewis will arrange it. Will you let us do that?'

'I don't know, m'm. I can live with it, be like the Captain before long.'

'You're a stubborn old woman, Brady.'

'I've earnt the right to be that, m'm.'

'How's Mrs Brand?'

'Haven't you seen her yet, m'm?'

'Oh yes. She was there when we arrived, but had to dash off somewhere to see someone about some fruit.'

'Higley. He's been deducting money for the weight of the boxes. He ought to have known better than to try to pull that one on her.'

'Are things all right, though?'

'Oh yes, m'm. there's a terrible soft side to her, you know. She sings lullabies to the Captain, treats him more like a child than she does the boy.'

'He's an odd little thing, isn't he?'

'He's strange, but then we've had that here before.'

'D'you mean Lewis?'

'I hear he's got a little boy too now.'

'Yes. Henry. But that's old news. He ought to bring the children up here. I'll tell him.'

'We've not seen him since he was living in the cottage that time.'

'We left him, Brady, should've taken him with us. Was he always strange?'

'I don't know m'm. Some belong and some are strange, and he was strange, grew up strange, didn't know who or what he was, didn't know why he'd been born.'

'Good Lord, Brady, do any of us know that?'

'Oh yes, m'm. Most of us do. Most of us belong: Mrs Brand with the Captain, you with the Major, me here. He didn't belong, not when he was here, not when he came back with that wife of his. He'll die not knowing.'

Book Three
LIBERTIES

One . . .

The first fact of Henry Drewer's childhood was that he had three big sisters. His parents always seemed a long way away, Daddy always away at work, Mummy going out to dinner, going to a concert or to Paris for the week; but Susan and Maggie and Jane spoiled and fostered and loved him. They brought him treats, they organised his birthday parties, they took him to the zoo and to the cinema. They busied his life and made him important and happy in a world that otherwise might have ignored him.

Susan was always untidy, always leaving everything half-done, but that didn't matter because she was very clever and was going to go to university. Maggie had red hair and played the violin, was going to be famous, was already calm and important. Jane was just happy, neat and pretty. She was not quite old enough to be clever, or to be important. Jane was the closest, however, and Henry loved her the best.

He was not going to be clever; that was plain enough. He found it hard to remember which letter went which way round, went for special lessons with a woman who was a doctor, but not a doctor who made you well. Nor was he musical; nor could he make his sums add up right. He liked to draw with crayons, fill sheets of fine paper with whirls and rainbows, could lose hours doing that.

He was not going to be sent to boarding school, and that was something, he supposed.

'Oh, it doesn't matter,' Susan said. 'There's more to life than school.'

'I hope that's not a personal statement, Susan,' Daddy said.

'Well. . . .' she said, teasing, her scholarship in a month's time.

'I couldn't bear it if he had to be sent away,' Jane said. 'It's stupid. All the boys I used to know when I was Henry's age who went away to school have become louts.'

'But you all spoil him so here,' Mummy said.

'Make sure you send him somewhere where there's an art teacher,' Maggie said, 'because he's got a talent. I'm serious, Mummy; ask them if the art teacher also teaches games, and if she does, then don't send him there.'

'Do I have to go to school?' he said. 'If I'm no good at it, why do I have to go at all?'

They laughed but it was the sort of laughter he didn't like.

They went for a holiday in France, all of them together. Well, Susan was in France already; they would meet up with her. She had been spending six months with a French family, having passed her scholarship, going to Cambridge University in the autumn. Susan was now nineteen, Maggie seventeen, Jane fourteen, and Henry eight. It was to be the last sustained time that they would all be together.

They took the boat-train to Paris, stayed in a hotel, hired a big car, with their luggage loaded onto the roof, and drove for hours and hours, heading for the sea; Mummy and Daddy in the front, with Henry squashed against the door beside his sisters, gaping in the sticky air to contain his car sickness.

The sun shone and everyone was in loose clothes; even Mummy and Daddy. The girls wore sunglasses. Long straight roads with blinking trees; dust and strange road signs and hoardings that baffled Henry's tentative reading skills. Nor could he feel comfortable about driving on the wrong side of the road: the world seemed inverted, strange, exotic. The ice-creams were different, and the bread, and the air and the fruit. Mummy and Susan, when they stopped for petrol and drinks, poured the strange language out of their mouths fantastically. Henry kept very quiet, frightened and excited. If he had become lost here, he would have been lost entirely. He clung to Jane and would not even go to the lavatory unless she promised to wait for him outside.

They arrived at a small house in a small village, two miles from the beach. There were three bedrooms in the house. He was to share with Jane. He liked this. She would have a shower and come up to put on a dress for the evening when he was going to bed, would chat to him, tell him stories about Joan of Arc, about the Normans, about the French Revolution, thrilling him with gore.

'Don't look now,' Jane would say as she undressed, and he never looked until she told him he could, was terrified of seeing something that he shouldn't see. He would wake sometimes when she came to

bed, bury his head and lie absolutely still as she got into her nightdress, lowered herself into bed, shifted and turned in the heat. It was
very special being allowed to sleep in her room, to wake and peer
across at her sleeping face, her open mouth, the profusion of her
freckles, the tangle of her hair which the sun was streaking with
gold.

One night she woke him coming in by colliding with a chair,
sending it clattering onto the floor.

'Bloody hell!'

He had never heard her swear before. Susan often said 'bloody
hell', sometimes even when Mummy was there; but not Jane. He
turned involuntarily.

'Are you awake? Shush! Go back to sleep.'

He turned over and heard her blundering about.

'Henry?'

'Yes?'

'You won't tell Mummy and Daddy, will you?'

'No,' although he had no idea what he wasn't to tell them.

With a heavy grunt she hit the bed and groaned, then lay still,
then groaned again and turned over. Then there was silence. Then
she farted. Then there was more silence, and then they were both
giggling like idiots.

During the days, there were expeditions to famous places; churches
and museums and battlefields. Daddy led the way, Mummy took his
hand and showed him things; the girls sauntered idly along behind,
hot and dreamy together. They preferred the days on the beach and,
after a while, Susan asked if they could they go to the beach instead,
on their own.

'We'll take Henry,' she said. 'Maggie's promised to teach him to
swim.'

Mummy and Daddy exchanged glances and agreed.

It took an hour to get to their special beach, which was through a
wood and down a steep little path into a hidden bay: two hundred
yards of pure sand with big cliffs on either side. They were not
always alone on the beach, but mostly they were, and it didn't
matter anyway. In the morning it was sheltered and cool and they
built him sandcastles, played football, took long swims.

Maggie, with her confidence and her patience, holding him on her
chest as she floated, lowering herself down and leaving him floating,

305

fulfilled her promise. He strove and fought and gasped, but swam, bobbed about on, or near, the surface, came up spluttering to the singing cheers of his sisters. They played water-ball, Maggie and he against Susan and Jane, not that anyone won or anything.

After lunch the sun moved round and began to fill the little bay with heat. The girls then spread out their towels, pulled the straps of their costumes off their shoulders, and lay oiled in the sun. Henry kept guard, dozed a little himself, drew in the sketch pad that he always took with him. He drew the ups and downs of their bodies as they sunbathed.

'Let's see,' Jane said.

He never minded showing them his drawings; he hated Mummy and Daddy seeing them, because he was never sure they were any good; but the girls were different. The girls were different to anything.

'You've made us look like a mountain range,' Maggie said.

'You ought to be flattered,' Susan said, and Maggie threw sand at her.

'Can I have it?' Jane asked.

'Will you do me one, Henry?' Maggie asked.

He tried, but the next one didn't come out right.

One day a middle-aged couple, not English, came down with a loud dog, stripped stark naked and went swimming, all scrubby hair and floppy bodies. The girls giggled.

'For God's sake, Jane,' Maggie said. 'Don't stare like that.'

'Well, if they prance about like that, they must expect to get stared at.'

'Is that legal in France?' Maggie asked Susan.

'Probably not. But it's like adultery, no-one really bothers.'

'Not in front of the little ones, Sue,' Maggie said.

'I hope you're not including me as a little one,' Jane said. 'I wish I had the courage to strip off.'

'Well? What's stopping you?' Susan asked.

'I will if you will,' Jane said.

'Don't you dare, either of you,' Maggie said. 'I'll take a photograph of you, if you do.'

'Can you imagine them in the chemists' when you went to collect your snaps?' Susan said, and they laughed.

'Take a photograph, I don't care,' Jane said.

'No, Jane,' Susan said, 'not with Henry here.'

She looked at him and smiled. He was relieved, did not want to see his sisters like that.

There were nevertheless secrets that he hadn't to report back on. Susan smoked reeking French cigarettes, and Jane was allowed to have one once. Susan had a book that she had bought in Paris that the other two took turns reading, which was buried deep in the bottom of Susan's bag before they returned.

'What's the book about, Susan?' he asked.

'Grown-ups,' she said, 'and the wicked things they do.'

'You can tell it was written by a man,' Maggie said contemptuously.

'I think it's all made up,' Jane said, uncomfortable.

'Of course it is, dear,' Susan said. 'It's a novel. Novels are only dreams, the hopes and fears of lonely people. But don't worry, it's not really like that at all, I promise you, Jane.'

Maggie snorted, Jane went dark, Susan took her hand; then they simultaneously remembered him, turned and looked at him, sitting with his arms about his knees five yards away, puzzled and alert, not missing a moment, rushing through a forest of inexplicable secrets that filled him with a warmth of loyalty to them.

'One last swim, chaps!' Susan said, leaping up, taking Henry's hands and swinging him up, and he was racing head down amongst the strong legs of his sisters, crashing into the silky water, shrieking with their shrieks, lifted and spun by Maggie's strength, catching her courage, seeing Susan's long body floating on the water with her arms spread out, upset suddenly by Jane swimming through his legs.

In the evening, they would clamber back up the pathway to the wood, where Maggie would give him a piggy-back, would sing a French song which the others would join, wandering home with the sun a great red blob going down into the sea behind them. Sometimes he would fall asleep against her hot neck, on the cushion of her thick, red hair. Sometimes he would ask to be put down and they would wander arm in arm, along the road, singing. Sometimes he would linger back a little, shaking a stone from his sandal, so that he could watch them walking into the gloom, stepping together, knowing with a sudden pride that they were not children, but grown-ups, feeling the world before them opening up, a pathway that he would be able, in time, to follow. They made the world safe and the ladder to the future without trepidation: Susan and Maggie and Jane.

. . . *two* . . .

They had friends, some of whom were girls and some of whom were boys; and they had boyfriends. There was a critical distinction between friends and boyfriends that, aged about eleven or twelve, Henry began to appreciate. Boyfriends brought disturbance, division of loyalties, began to bring the world outside in through the back door.

It was, predictably, Jane who caused the most noise. By this time she was in her final years of school, Maggie being away at music college and Susan having done terribly well at university, staying on to do even better. Jane, it was assumed, would also go to university. Mummy was very keen that she should do so, but Jane was not working as hard as she ought to work. There were complicated arguments over meals which Henry never really followed, and which were never really settled. Mummy and Daddy spoke calmly and persuasively, with all the clear moves of authority; and Jane snarled and snapped and sulked. Henry was alarmed by this rebelliousness, did not know whose side to be on.

One evening, coming in from school and going into the kitchen to grab something to eat, there was a thin, rat-faced youth there with long sideburns and a horribly orange jacket.

'Hello,' Henry said, assuming he'd come to mend something.

'Well, hi there.'

'Oh. Are you American?'

'No such luck.'

'Are you delivering something?' he asked, for the man did not seem to be doing anything else.

'Not delivering, collecting.'

'Oh. Does Mummy know you're here?'

'No, and . . . and I think she's not supposed to know, so keep the old lip buttoned, eh?'

Perhaps, then, a burglar. Henry didn't feel that he could ask this. He went to the larder and fetched a loaf of bread, began to make himself a peanut-butter sandwich. The young man watched him. He wore a bracelet which jangled as he took a comb from his back pocket and ran it through his hair. Henry eyed him as he made the sandwich. He was making a little jigging movement, as if he were humming a tune. Henry began to find him funny.

'Would you like a peanut-butter sandwich?' he asked.

'Er . . . yeah. Great.'

Henry cut his sandwich in half and offered the stranger the larger half.

'Great,' he said through the first mouthful.

'By the way, I'm Henry.'

'Tone.'

They shook hands, smiled at one another, whilst munching through their sandwiches.

'Sorry,' Jane said as she slid into the kitchen. She was wearing a violently coloured skirt, lots of it, making it stick out from her thighs; a blouse that was too tight; eyelashes that flicked up her brows; lipstick the colour of tomatoes. She skipped across the kitchen, leant herself against Tone and imprinted her lips on his nose, whilst he put his hands on her sides, close to her breasts, touching them. 'Oh. Hi, Henry,' she said, turning and seeing him, although she must have seen him before. 'Have you two met?'

Tone indicated his sandwich.

'Oh, leave that,' she said. 'We're late enough as it is. Henry? If Mummy asks then tell her . . . you haven't seen me.'

'Or him?'

'Of course not, stupid. Go and do your homework.'

'Ciao, Henry,' said Tone, waving.

He assumed it was a game, fancy dress or something; he wasn't sure. He wasn't sure that he liked it. Certainly, he would not have dreamt of betraying Jane to Mummy and Daddy, but seeing her dressed up like that made him thoughtful, seeing her touched like that offended him. It seemed rude.

Next morning, Saturday, whilst he was eating his cereal alone in the kitchen, he heard Jane shouting. He thought there was something wrong with her, and, as Mummy and Daddy were unlikely to be up yet, he went at once to the door, intending to run upstairs. From the foot of the stairs, he heard Daddy's voice and he stopped.

'I'm seventeen! I'm seventeen!' he heard Jane screaming.

He could not hear what Daddy was saying, only the tone, heavy with insistence. Doors were slammed and Henry crept back to his cereal which had gone mushy. He tipped it away and went upstairs along the silence of the landings from which, in their room, he could hear Mummy and Daddy talking, arguing, loudly. It terrified him. He scampered to Jane's door and tapped frantically.

'Go away, Henry. Go away.'

'Please, Jane, please . . . please.'

At last she came and unlocked the door and he flung himself round her and cried at a world that suddenly had thorns and traps. Jane held him and they cried together, perhaps for essentially the same reason.

Tone was never seen again, and Jane went round in a haze of dullness and ill-temper for a couple of weeks, only brightening when Henry came into her room. He never asked about Tone, did not want to know.

Susan appeared next with an identifiable boyfriend. His name was Charles and he was a doctor, another doctor who didn't make you well: a doctor of French. Henry speculated why the French might need special doctors, but was old enough now to keep such thoughts to himself. Charles was horrid. He was short and tubby. His hair was too long and very greasy, covering his ears but not the top of his head, which was glassy; as if his brain had worn away that bit. He wore dirty glasses through which he peered at everything, dropping open his mouth, then closing it with a pout of his lower lip as if he had understood it and swallowed it. He talked fast, particularly when he was eating, and Henry could not understand anything he said.

Henry came into the drawing room once to find them sitting together on the sofa, Charles holding Susan's hand and patting it as he jabbered away at her. He did not notice Henry, who was making a quick departure; but Susan saw him and winked her wink at him. This made it all right. Susan was clever and everything Susan did would be all right.

This business of touching troubled him. He could understand why boyfriends would want to touch his sisters; he wanted to touch them, although he was too old for that now. Why they wanted to be touched, however, was beyond him. It was Maggie who explained it to him.

Her boyfriend was much more the thing: a young man called Maurice who was tall and smart and very polite, who stood up when Mummy entered the room and talked to Daddy about money and sport; who was also very attentive to him, asked him about school, about his friends, about stories Maggie had told him when he was young. Henry wasn't sure about this, felt it was altogether too much of a good thing.

Jane and he were asked out for a picnic in the country with Maurice and Maggie in Maurice's car, which was a sports car. At the last moment, Jane went into a sulk and wouldn't go, so Henry had the back seats to himself, which was lucky as there was little room there, and Maurice drove very fast.

They went out into the woods somewhere, close to the river, Maurice paying more attention to him than he did to Maggie, who lay back in the sun and seemed sleepily content. She was always the quietest, the strongest one: Susan, the clever one; Jane, the quick one; Maggie, the quiet one. He would watch her play her violin, see the tight smile, the precision of fingers, the firm cut of the bow. For Susan, life was to be understood; for Jane, it was to be consumed; for Maggie, it was to be controlled.

After the picnic, he wandered off to the river and watched the light flickering as the slow turbulence of the water lifted planes briefly into the angle of the sun. The water was green, metallic, smooth and strong, its moving inexpressibly natural, beyond understanding, magical. He loved it. It made him happy just to watch it like that.

When, having lost track of the time, he wandered back into the woods, he came upon Maggie sitting neatly on the rug, her legs tucked under her, her back straight, posed and perfect, and naked to the waist whilst Maurice, whose back happily was towards Henry, touched and kissed her small breasts. She saw Henry appear, but did not move, held his eyes for a second, then raised her eyebrows and smiled him a tight smile. He retreated into the woods, returning fifteen minutes later to find them packing up the picnic.

'Where've you *been*, Henry?' she snapped.

'Sorry, Maggie. Sorry, Maurice,' he said.

She came to see him when he was in bed that night, curled up with a comic-book, sat beside him. He had been expecting her, put his book on the bedside table.

'You weren't upset this afternoon, Henry, were you?'

'Oh no.'

'Only I felt bad about you seeing that.'

'Maggie?'

'What?'

'Is it nice to be touched by your boyfriend?'

'Are you speaking generally, or just about this afternoon?'

'Oh . . . generally, you know.'

'Generally, yes. Yes, it is nice. It's complicated, though. You'll understand in a year or two, I promise. It's to do with being close to someone, someone you might marry; not that I'm going to marry Maurice, not necessarily. It's like learning to swim. It's exciting and a bit dangerous.'

'Why is it dangerous?'

'Because you can drown.'

'No. I mean the touching.'

'Yes, the touching. You'll understand. You're going to be very good-looking. You're a lucky boy, Henry. Give me a hug now.'

As he hugged her, and she hugged him, he became aware of the pressure of her breasts beneath her thin summer blouse. When she had gone, he felt that he did understand, although what he understood he could not have said. He lay on his back as the last light of the day came through the curtains of his bedroom, in the warmth of a hot summer's day, easy in the comfort of his flesh, life before him a long slide into warm water which, as he fell asleep, he felt himself beginning, felt the air rush up at him, the speed catch him, his body braced and balanced for the moment of contact which he imagined as an explosion of light, a tumult of easy joy.

. . . *three* . . .

Maggie did marry Maurice, but not until almost two years later. It
was to be a very big wedding and Henry kept out of the way of it as
much as he could. He kept out of the way of most things now, spent
his time, when not at school, occasionally lounging about a coffee
bar with a couple of schoolfriends, or up in his room. He had a
drawing-board and spent his time mapping out complex patterns
and filling them with colours. He had stopped trying to draw the
things he saw, because he could never get them right. He had gone
through a stage of drawing monsters with many heads and tentacles
and teeth, slashed open and bleeding with their rib-cages on display;
but now it was just patterns of minute complexity, swirling rivers of
colour that blended and clashed and dissolved. The week before the
wedding he had, for the first time, tried to draw a naked girl, but it
hadn't worked; he had enjoyed doing it, planning and imagining it,
caught up and driven along in it, but it had not come out right at all
and, in a flush of sudden embarrassment, he had shredded the picture into fragments.

He had a new suit for the wedding and was to be an usher. He was
dreading it, dreading being told how he'd grown, what a good-
looking boy he was becoming, asked what he wanted to do when he
left school. He was looking forward to seeing Susan and Jane again,
who rarely came home nowadays. Susan arrived three days before
the day, still with the hideous Charles: 'Well, we don't actually see
the point of marriage,' he overheard her saying in the drawing room.
Charles's bald patch had crept over most of his scalp, and what
remaining straggles of hair he had were grey and mouldy-looking,
but she had managed to tidy him up a bit. She was a doctor of
French now too, wore her hair as short as his, and had taken to
wearing dark clothes with bright scarves round her neck which,
Henry thought, were an invitation for someone to strangle her.

Jane arrived late the night before the wedding, had a row with the
parents, and then came up to see Henry, hugged him, burst into

tears, then lit a cigarette and looked disapprovingly through his records. She was very strange now, all in black with badges and filthy boots, smelly, jangly with bracelets and with make-up that seemed grown into her face.

'It's time you listened to some jazz,' she said. 'Apart from which, you're the only decent one in this bloody house. There's smug little Maggie marrying that pervert. There's that smug cow Susan with her bloody professor, the little gnome, with her "sex is all in the mind, you know" . . . d'you know what sex is, Henry?'

He did know; Maggie had told him last year.

'Well, here's something Maggie hasn't told you: this bloody house is so full of hypocrisy, and it's all about sex, Henry, all about sex. Oh Henry, Henry . . . have you got a girlfriend yet?'

'No.'

'Know anyone you like?'

'No.'

'Promise me something?'

'What?'

'When you do have a girlfriend, then . . . then there's only one rule. Don't tell lies.'

'All right.'

'Not to her, not to you. Just don't lie.'

'I won't lie.'

'God, I'm smoking too much. D'you want one?'

'No.'

'Got any pictures to show me?'

He hadn't really understood what Jane had said. It made him unhappy, nevertheless. He looked at her, and at Susan and Maggie, and at his parents, with a dubiety next day, the wedding day, when they were in their very best, all of them. Even Jane had put on a pretty dress and done her hair properly. His parents glowed in the generosity of their affluence, smart and smiling, proud of their children, all of them on this day. Lying? What had she meant about lying?

Granny and Grandpa Drewer came up from Norfolk, so frail and old now. He was asked to look after them especially, but they frightened him. Mad Aunt Naomi came wearing a brown suit that didn't fit. She spent most of the reception talking to Jane, the pair of them chain-smoking and getting drunk, Jane looking glum and defensive whilst Aunt Naomi interrogated and lectured her. Uncle Freddie and Aunt Helena flew in from America specially, and they brought the twins with them: Rosalind and Miranda.

Rosalind and Miranda were identical, absolutely, each one a copy of the other, the ultimate extravagance, to be two rather than one. They were a year older than Henry. He had not seen them for some years and his memories of them were not good. He remembered standing in this room with them looking dismissively around, picking up things and putting them down again with sighs of tedium. He remembered conversations that went, 'Our Mummy was a film star, you know . . . who's your favourite film star, Henry? . . . Oh, we've met him, he's horrible . . . have you ever been on a yacht? . . . On an aeroplane? . . . Skiing?' His sisters had taught him to laugh at all this, but he felt that he had more to be sensitive about now. Aunt Helena was always asking his parents to let him come and stay with her, but he had put up a quick and solid resistance.

Had they not been identical he would not have recognised them as they stepped from the car and came out of the sun into the portico of the church. They were tall, with perfect black hair that hung down their backs, with soft eyes and mouths and cheeks fluffed with flesh, with long white legs and short, identical dresses, with bottoms that strutted and breasts that surged.

'Henry?'

'Hello, Henry!'

And they leant up and kissed him, breathed on his cheeks, one either side, symmetrically.

'Rosalind. Miranda.'

'Oh well done, Henry.'

'You got us the right way round.'

He was not able to take his eyes off them for ten minutes throughout the day. He was quite dazzled. Whenever he saw one of them without the other, he could not rest until he had paired them. He did not approach them because he did not know what he might say to them. Whatever he said would have been terribly important, and he had nothing important to say.

They found him towards the end of the reception, came up and massaged him in smiles. He was a little drunk.

'Where've you been hiding, Henry?'

'We wanted to see your room again. D'you remember taking us there?'

'We've got to go now; Mum's a bit pissed and Dad's getting ratty.'

'Come and stay with us. Do. Mum's going to ask your mum.'

Their confidence astounded him, the way they moved and touched, brushed something from the other's shoulder, took one another's hands and leant together, tilting the head back in a laugh exposing a white throat, setting their bodies in postures one against the other, profile and full-face. And, at the end, two more kisses like buds on his hot face.

He didn't know whether he wanted to go and stay with them or not; but when the question was put to him, he felt that he had no choice but to say yes; it was a terrible temptation that he had no will to resist.

'Don't let them hurt you,' Jane said. 'They're a pair of nasty little bitches.'

He thought about this, and concluded that they could only hurt him if he expected things from them, if he expected them to feel about him as he felt about them; and he did not remotely expect that. He just wanted to be able to watch them for a few days, a tourist in an exotic country whose language he would not speak, who would see the sights and drink the wine and come home again to school and reality.

They lived in the Berkshire countryside in a large house, an ancient shell full of the most up-to-date magic: a little cinema where they could watch films; a room of refrigerators where they could concoct messy feasts of extravagances; complex record-playing equipment that filled rooms with orchestras and pop groups; a swimming pool in a conservatory; a bathroom so big that it could not have been imagined for solitary use.

He stayed a week and for that time he had their undivided attention. Aunt Helena was somewhere in the house, would be met occasionally, would smile and laugh and ask if the girls were looking after him properly. Uncle Freddie even appeared once, although he did not seem to remember who Henry was and was anyway not much concerned. Henry was pampered and entertained continuously by his two laughing cousins; he could not, finally, have been happier.

He kept Jane's warning like a sign pinned up in his head and, for the first days, it led him to be passive and a little suspicious. He brought himself to feel that they were merely showing off to him, spoilt children patronising and teasing him, watching him and slipping away at night to compare notes on his crassness and clumsiness, edging him day by day to make a fool of himself, tempting him. He knew, on reflection, that this was unjust: they were perfect to him, every moment of the day. The problem was, of course, in him. He found them so overwhelmingly beautiful, caught himself lurching towards them, pushed by something at the back of his mind, catching himself and pulling back, feeling the blood blossom on his face, laughing it out; and they would laugh with him, catch his pleasure and join in with it. After a few days, he could cope with this, could relax and accept that this was going to happen, to enjoy it even, to watch without shame the way they sat back in a chair, the way they moved, the way their clothes obscured, revealed, responded to the shape of their long, taut bodies. He wondered if they knew how he was reacting to them. They seemed, on the surface, wonderfully innocent. There was no talk of love, or boyfriends or girlfriends. Their clothes were fashionably skimpy, but there was never a moment's immodesty in anything they said or did. They laughed and smiled and skipped, dropped like dolls into low chairs, sprawled and stretched on sofas and floors, swam like torpedoes in red bikinis with their hair streaming out behind them, pulled themselves from the pool gasping clear of the water which poured from them. How could they not be aware? Henry sat hunched over his lump as they lifted their arms and waved at him, and the nipples showed through, and the clefts of their buttocks when they turned, and he leapt forward to plunge into the water whilst they weren't looking.

Rosalind and Miranda. Miranda and Rosalind. He never really learnt to tell them apart, never really wanted to. Their duality was a protection. He was outnumbered, confused, never knew to which one he had said what. Even if you ever managed to catch one of them on her own, you never knew who she was, and even if she told you her name, she might not have been who she said she was. By the end of the week he began to suspect that they themselves didn't know which ones they were. It was a constant game of mirrors, constantly funny.

Over that one rainy week in the summer after he was fifteen, he received from his two cousins an exhaustive, exhausting course in eroticism. He dreamed of them, of course, imagined in detail that they would knock on his door in the darkness and slip in either side of him in the big bed. Sometimes he dropped into sleep and the dreams followed him freely; sometimes he could not sleep and pursued the dreams through to their conclusion, then had a quick wash before sleeping clean and sweet, rousing bright and following the sound of their laughter down to breakfast, or an early swim. Such indulgences began to shadow him a little with guilt. He felt that he was, albeit in the absolute privacy of himself, offering them deep insult, abusing them as much as himself. He became, towards the last days of his stay, a little unhappy, felt as if he had spoiled his time here, was nasty and sweaty and smelly.

On his last evening, as they sat and watched television before bed, they said quietly and meaningfully that they had a present for him.

'Henry, you've been so sweet.'

'You must've been so bored here.'

'Listen now, and don't breathe a word, not a word, or . . .'

'What?' he said.

'You know the balcony?'

'Yes.' They meant the small balcony that overlooked the pool.

'Be there at one.'

'One a.m.'

'Don't let anyone see you. If anyone's awake, it's off. Okay?'

'Okay.'

'And Henry, when you're there, don't make a sound, not a single sound, whatever happens.'

'And promise us, promise us that you won't move off that balcony. Promise.'

'I promise.'

'And never tell anyone, never even mention it.'

'Not even to us. It never happened.'

'All right. All right.'

At the appointed time, huddled in the darkness above the dank chlorine reek of the pool, he waited. The pool was lit from within and gave off a ghostly green glow. There was the thrum of the motor that cleaned the pool. There was a steady drip of water. There was the tight pull of his breathing. He sat in his dressing gown, his arms about his knees, the ache of sleep nagging at him, the chill of the night, the adventure that had propelled him here beginning to detumesce when, with a patter of feet and simultaneous slicing sounds, the girls ran from the darkness and buried themselves in the pool in a silent explosion of phosphorescence, naked and white as angels, triumphantly beautiful, impossible, glorious, liberated.

For ten minutes they swam up and down, dived down, trod water with their breasts floating before them, lay back on the water spread out, open to his amazement, although never once did either of them look up at him; not until, quite suddenly, they climbed out of the pool, turned to him and, holding hands, waved.

He did not know what to do then, nor how he might do it. He waited and shivered and whistled through his teeth for a few minutes; then the lights in the pool went out and he hobbled back to bed.

In the morning, as he was packing to be taken to the station by Aunt Helena, Miranda suddenly appeared in his room. He hadn't known he could tell them apart, but this was definitely Miranda.

'Roz's in the loo. I know I shouldn't, Henry, but I had to.'

'What?'

'Where you there last night?'

'Yes.'

'Can I ask you something secret?'

'All right.'

'Did we . . . did we make you come, watching us?'

'Come?'

'You know . . . orgasm . . . you know.'

'Oh, that.'

'Well?'

'Yes, actually.'

'Brilliant, Henry, brilliant! Was it . . . was it good?'

'Yes. It was . . . brilliant.'

She laughed, kissed him.

'Not a word, not a single word to Roz, now, promise-promise.'

He promised. And when she had gone he laughed with the pleasure of it all; the tangles and the greed, the need and the nastiness, melted into games played by children who had managed to keep the wonder and the magic of it.

He returned home older and clearer and stronger than when he had left; wanted above all to tell Jane; but then, as he thought about telling her, knew that she would not have understood, that this was his now, secret and intrinsic, his, and it was going to be all right.

. . . *four* . . .

It was an awakening. The world was full of girls and Henry began to watch them, talk to them, know them. What had been roused in him, which was not only sex, now seemed to be blossoming in the wide world about him, a multiplicity of becomings, possibilities like bubbles bursting in the air all around him.

This was London; this was 1964. The streets were bright and busy with an arrogant innocence, full of music and clothes, and young people making gestures at their parents, at the whole world their parents had made; not gestures of defiance, although they were interpreted as such, but gestures of freedom; not that anyone seriously knew what that meant, but they knew what it felt like. Suddenly no-one owed anything. Things could come out of nowhere and be right and true and good: a song, a mood, a face, a way of walking down the street, of meeting someone and knowing them in seconds. And if it was all ephemeral, trivial, disposable, going nowhere, then that was its strength, its beauty, its simplicity, its freedom. Henry was suddenly at the age of the time.

He grew his hair long and wore loose clothes. He had been given a camera by his parents and he set out on rambles through the West End taking photographs of people, of girls, catching them at bright moments before they saw him and turned to pose or to tell him to fuck off. He set up a basic dark-room in the house and loved to watch their faces come out of the white, floating in the tray of fluid. He would pin the photographs around his room, which was chaotic on every surface, but lit by these glimpses into other lives, into which he sent his imagination wheeling and turning.

He was also becoming sociable, hanging around with a group of friends from the boys' school he attended in a coffee bar into which girls from a local girls' school came. They played the juke-box and smoked cigarettes and spent an hour over a cup of sweet, frothy coffee, prodding a sub-sexual banter across the barrier of their genders. He was quiet here, watching, smiling and relaxed, never even wanting to join in the communal lechery of his friends, which he found pointless, nor even the verbal forays made against the girls, the purpose of which seemed to him merely to embarrass them, to draw them from blushing to a giggling complicity.

He watched the girls intently and found them all, every one of them, beautiful and desirable. Not for him the classifying contempts of his friends, larded with the latest American slang in which the girls were graded on broad scales of sexual attraction and disgust, availability and frigidity. For him, quite honestly, every girl had potential, beauty, grace, waiting to be opened to him. There were too many of them. He fell in love, or whatever it was, two or three times a month, followed some girl, found out her name, where she lived; but the more he knew about her, the more he thought about her, the less attainable she became; as if moving close to her, imaginatively, she would become monumental, beyond his puny powers; and anyway, he usually found out that she had a boyfriend.

At a dance at the house of the son of a friend of his parents', steeling himself to ask a tall, black-haired girl to dance, dancing with her all evening, fetching her drinks and food, learning that her name was Jennifer and that she lived in Tooting and her father was in the BBC, realising that she was as nervous of him as he was of her; then holding her hand across a table; then dancing with her, the slow dance, finding her mouth, open, kissing her and clutching the awkwardness of her body, obscured by a lot of dress, against his body; just buried in the proximity of her, whoever she was, darting his tongue into her mouth, holding her face against his; and when they unclinched at last and returned to their seats, finding a mutual embarrassment, looking at her as she looked at him and wondering what they had been doing together and why; both complicit in an act the implications of which, at the distance they now sat, seemed monstrously beyond them.

There were other parties where the music was loud and the parents away; and everyone got pissed and someone smoked pot and the adventurous ones went all the way then came down to tell their friends; and Henry usually found some girl, or some girl found him, to kiss and tussle about inside one another's clothes, and achieve unspoken arousals and at times even sudden private climaxes; and they were all fifteen and sixteen and the music was hard and simple, catching you in the gut and flooding up into the brain with promises of love, raw-voiced and long-haired, celebrations of youth in urgency and lubricity, the chunk of guitars and the smashing and smashing of cymbals, and the dark nights and the warm bodies, easy and aching, never quite fulfilled, but becoming, becoming.

And out in the night, walking the cold streets home, he came out of the electric blur into which he had sunk, and felt that he had missed something. He wanted to go back and find the girl he had been with, but already he couldn't remember her, and anyway, he would have nothing to say to her. He didn't know what he wanted to be, didn't know what he was. He wasn't anybody, not yet. Around him the houses were dark. He imagined the sleeping people, imagined the girls in their beauty, in their dreams, in all the complexities and perfections of their bodies; and he wanted to stand still and shout, to bay like a dog until one of them woke and came down, and knew who he was, knew him, told him, set him moving, set him free.

. . . *five* . . .

He left his boys' school and went to a local college to retake his basic exams, scratching forward to some sort of qualifications that he might do something with. He would muddle through, then someone would give him a job somewhere. Life was easy, undemanding, although he felt his parents' eyes beginning to focus upon him more seriously. He was seventeen and time was running out.

He lost his virginity in Greece that summer. They stayed in a smart hotel on one of the smarter islands, his parents relaxing in the sun, bathing away the cold, grey English winter. He fell into friendship with a girl called Pen, staying there with her divorced mother who was not much in evidence. Pen was blonde and bronzed, and moody. Henry watched her for a morning, caught her eye and offered her his smile which, in time, she returned. He went over at last and cautiously introduced himself.

It was firstly a companionship. They swam together and went

for rides in pedal-boats, ate greasy cheese pastries and drank bitter orangeade. In the evening they went to the disco and ended up kissing comfortably, lapsing into quietness and calm.

'This isn't going to lead to anything, you know,' she said.

'That's all right, Pen,' he said, beginning to feel that it might.

In the afternoons they sunbathed, enduring the heat, watching one another, just looking, edging out smiles, beginning to say things then stopping.

After about a week, he decided to make a move. 'You know what I'd like now?'

'What would you like now?'

'A cold shower.'

She laughed.

'Do you need a cold shower, Henry?'

'Yes. Definitely.' He got up and dusted himself down. 'Back in twenty minutes.'

'Oh . . . I'll wander up with you.'

The water was lukewarm, but cooler than the sun. They kept their swimming costumes on and stood back to back under the jet, gasping and groaning and giggling, then just stood still, leaning together. At last she turned with a quick slither and grasped his middle, placed her face against his back.

'D'you want to make love?'

They proceeded circumspectly, dried themselves, discussed contraception, and slipped into his bed. It was a considerable success. He had expected awkwardness, physical and emotional, but it proceeded with a natural logic, careful explorations, explanations, manipulating, adjusting, fitting themselves together at last like parts of the same machine. His limbs softened and glowed, all their strength drawn into the tight strut of himself that she worked within her.

They spent the afternoons thereafter in his room, usually but not always making love, playing, talking, soaping each other in the shower. She had sadnesses in her life that made him afraid for her, afraid of her at times: her parents' divorce, mother's boyfriends, running away from school. He knew that, back in England, he could not keep hold of her, that she knew this too, that these were moments of calm, of rebuilding, a clinical relationship that, for a few days, might allow her to see how it might be, to give her a pride in herself, to learn how to give sex, not merely to have it taken from her, which she had done often, living in a mess of relationships in which her sexual compliance usually ended up as the easiest option. Some afternoons all she could do was weep for him, and he would wrap her up like a child and let the day slip by in a tenderness that was beyond sex.

On the last day, he gave her his address and made her promise to come and see him if she needed somewhere to escape to.

'Escape is the last thing I need,' she said. 'I've tried that. Don't think you've seen all of me, Henry. There's a lot of poison still there, and you're so young, you know. I don't think you've really lost your virginity at all.'

There were other relationships over the next couple of years that followed something of a pattern. They always began as friendships, often with girls who were involved with other boys. Sometimes these friendships, almost experimentally, would move into a sexual phase; but never for long, sometimes only for a night or an afternoon. Something never managed to happen and, calmly and mutually, they would move back into friendship.

He was beginning to take the photography seriously, something at last. Money was provided and he converted the attic into a studio, had it painted black, lit, draped, took friends up there almost as a matter of course to pose for him. One of his girlfriends had offered to model nude for him, but he hadn't wanted that; did not feel he could have controlled it. Behind his camera he was very happy, purposeful, fussy and assertive even. He sought always the perfect moment, a certain triangulation of shadow, a certain tilt of the head, the placing of a finger; and with all this precision he sought to find an absolute spontaneity. He would describe what he wanted and position his subject with infinite care: the moment was a fraction of a second before they hit the pose, or the second they lost it. It was almost mathematical, the pose a turning-point on a curve, a fixed, still point, a dead space, either side of which were potential or loss, something perfect in its minute imperfection. Not that he could ever have put that into words, which is why he became angry when they couldn't understand or wouldn't exactly comply with his inarticulate and dictatorial demands.

How good he was, he didn't know. The pictures he thought were perfect, or as near perfect as he could make them, invariably did not please those he showed them to; they always wanted likenesses, or sentimentality of one sort or another. He reduced a girl to tears with

324

his bullying once, and the shots he took of her weeping, of which he was ashamed, were, he was told, the best things he had ever done, by far. Even the silly cow herself thought they were wonderful.

Then Miranda and Rosalind came to spend a night, before joining a party for Switzerland. They were back from America, the house in Berkshire was closed, so they came to stay with Uncle Lewis and Aunt Celia; and with Henry.

It was now over three years since he had stayed that summer. They were taller, fuller, more alike and substantially more sophisticated. He had seen them a few times, at Great Uncle Harry's funeral, at the christening of Maggie's son, at the dismal civil ceremony where Susan had finally made a husband out of Charles who was, it was generally thought, quite mad by now. Anyway, they arrived out of a taxi with a great amount of luggage, and filled the house with chatter and laughter that Henry, and his parents, found rather exhausting. They talked a lot about their boyfriends, who were going to be with them in Switzerland, without, it seemed, any adult supervision. Henry watched his mother's lower lip go hard. As for himself, he wondered how the boyfriends managed, whether it was done as a foursome, whether they swapped on alternate nights; no-one would have known.

After dinner he took them up to his studio.

'Nude, Henry?'

'No, thank you.'

'D'you remember the swimming pool?'

'I remember the swimming pool. Shut up now and do what you're told.'

He couldn't get them at all. They were too aware, all the time, of the camera, pouting and shaping themselves.

'Fucking relax, will you,' he said. He only ever used that word in here and it usually had a stun effect.

Rosalind and Miranda giggled.

'If we lit up, it would help.'

'Then light up.'

They huddled on the floor and took rolling papers and cigarettes out, and a little bag of hashish. They rolled the joint together, a combined operation of evident experience. They lit up and the swathes of sweet smoke rolled about the studio, spoiling his pristine light. He sat down with them and took his turn, abandoning the photography. He quite liked to smoke this stuff, and this particular stuff was predictably very strong and very good. His head fluttered pleasantly and he felt a soft flow of warm liquid running in his spine.

'Let's get back to work then, Henry.'

He concurred, but had no real idea what he was shooting. They seemed more relaxed, certainly, lolled against one another dreamily, playing with each other's hair, blowing into ears, touching with a light sensuousness. He reloaded his camera and, as he did so, they continued to play, becoming rapt in each other in a way that he began to find disturbing.

Suddenly they began to kiss, open-mouthed, a lovers' kiss that he found himself photographing with a voracity that, at the back of his mind, appalled him.

'Fucking hell, girls,' he said.

'But isn't it? Isn't it just?'

What happened next he could not believe, next day, had actually happened. They undressed one another and performed for his lens hard-core pornography that he remembered, would always remember, in a sequence of grotesque images that were so far beyond beauty that they acted as acid on the plates in his head where he developed his most profound fantasies. Female sexuality, which he had appreciated as delicate, sensitive and mysterious, was here presented in comprehensive, brutal animality. They contorted and writhed, jammed their bodies together, slithered about in one another's secretions, gasping with exertion and wincing with pain. As he watched he felt himself falling forward into it, then rushing back from it, his dope-primed brain lurching. It was the most repellent thing he had ever seen, and he could not take his eyes, or his lens, off it for a second. They had once again given him an education. At the end of it, groaning and filthy, one of them lifted the other up, held her round her shoulders as she pissed onto his floor.

'Now you, Rozzie. . . .'

'I can't. . . .'

'Stupid bitch.'

They leant naked against the wall and watched him as he mopped up.

'Did you come, Henry?'

'No. Not this time.'

'Would you like to?'

'No.'

326

They dressed then, and became emotional, came and leant on his shoulders and cried, apologised, said it was only a game, told him they weren't like that really, said he was kind and sweet and they were nasty, horrible sluts.

When they had gone, he exposed all the undeveloped film he had taken, roll by roll.

. . . *six* . . .

A girl alone on a bench in a park on a late summer's evening. At a distance, the roar of traffic; close, the buzz of flies and the soiled heat. A girl: black, or part-black; dark skin, thick mass of black frizzed hair, full mouth, but blue eyes and straight nose; sitting with her legs out, her arms along the bench-back, her spine curved under her, her head tipped back; bare-footed, black toes, pink soles, red nails; jeans frayed at the bottom into ragged tassels, a smock loose about her body and arms, dyed in circles of faint colour; chains of beads, bracelets, long hands with long nails; mouth shut, the bottom lip pushed up firmly; eyes open, looking at the sky which was pink and smoggy and beginning to fill with flecks of birds coming in to roost on the high buildings.

The light was poor, but she was very still. Henry set a comfortable exposure, framed her carefully, not wanting to alert her. He was ten feet from her, kneeling slowly, trying to catch the shape of that body, the way it was thrown back, perhaps in abandon and surrender, perhaps just open. As he pressed the shutter open, she dropped her head to one side to face him, blurring his exposure inevitably. He stood and shrugged and smiled at her, slotted his camera back into its case, turning away.

'Hey, you!'

'Sorry,' he said, looking back at her.

'Fucking tourist.'

'I know,' he said. 'Sorry.'

'Come here, you.'

He went to her, stood close to the bench.

327

'You want to take pictures? Five pounds, you get my tits. The rest is negotiable.'

Her voice was slow, tired, throaty.

He took his wallet from his back pocket and slipped out a five-pound note.

'All right,' she said, looking at the money but not taking it. 'Where're we going?'

'No. I don't want to take any more pictures.'

'Keep your money. What d'you think I am?'

He tucked the money for the time being in his shirt pocket, then sat carefully on the edge of her bench, a clear space between them. She brought her arms down, shifted herself back, leant forward and clasped her hands between her thighs.

'What d'you want?' she said.

'Nothing.'

'Bollocks. Everyone wants something.'

'I just wanted to take your picture, just as you were, before you saw me.'

'I saw you coming a mile off.'

'Ah well.'

She gave a small shudder. 'Got a smoke?'

'No.'

'But lots of money to give away.'

'Not lots.'

'What d'you do?'

'Not much.'

'How come the money then?'

'Well . . . parents, I suppose.'

'Fuck. You suppose? Parents!' She laughed to herself, shook her head at some irony. 'You want to spend money on me?'

'What d'you want?'

'I want to know if you want to spend money on me?'

'All right. Yes.'

'Okay. I eat. Sometimes, I eat. You can buy me food.'

'Fine.'

She looked at him tightly, then past him, behind her, taking a pair of thonged sandals from a bag inside her and slipping them onto her feet.

'Okay,' she said.

They went to a cheap self-service restaurant. She loaded a tray with a sticky bun, an ice-cream sundae, a tinned fruit salad with imitation cream, a milk-shake. He collected a tired sandwich and a small carafe of wine. He also bought twenty cigarettes.

She took a cigarette, produced a lighter and smoked as she ate, which she did messily and fast, concentrating on the food, taking a bite of the bun, a mouthful of ice-cream, a suck of milk-shake. She refused any of the wine.

'Where're you from?' he asked.

'What?'

'Where're you from?'

'Nowhere. Dumb question.'

'Where d'you live?'

'Here. Now.'

'You have a name?'

'Yup.'

'My name's Henry Drewer.'

'Well, that's all right.'

She didn't look at him as she answered, hit his questions back without thought, was not interested in him at all, only in the food. He sat back and watched her, smoked some of a cigarette, drank a little of the wine, which was thin and sour.

'Okay,' he said when she had finished.

'You going now?'

'I'd better go.'

'You want a picture?'

'No. The light's gone. Nevertheless. . . .'

'Nevertheless what?'

'You're very beautiful.'

'Everyone's beautiful. Haven't you heard?'

'Nevertheless.'

He left his change and the cigarettes behind on the table and went home.

It was not a unique encounter. He had before fallen into conversations with girls he had tried to photograph, usually brief, friendly exchanges; occasionally something else had seemed to be being implied or understood and he retreated; as he had done here.

His motives this time were not entirely clear to him. Certainly there was sexual attraction: she was strange and outrageous, and beautiful, not in the shape of her body, which he had not seen, but

329

in her speaking and moving and in the strange amalgam of her features which made her unclassifiable, unpredictable. Such attraction was, in itself, a cause for retreat. There was also a danger in her. He assumed that she was some sort of stray, perhaps even a prostitute of sorts. He had come close, as he had watched her eat, to asking her back to the house, his parents being in Hong Kong for the month; it had seemed a wild thing to do, to oil her with his domestic attentions, to watch her open out. The lunacy of that caught him in time: the imagination of her setting camp, bringing a horde of friends with her, looting and despoiling his safety. But neither the attraction, nor the danger, nor a combination of both of them, quite accounted for how he felt about her once he was home, as the blur of her moving face came out of the white in his developing tray.

It was a strange picture, very dark, almost as if it were very old, from another age, a picture of someone long dead, an obscure life caught for one instant and projected into the future, defying her anonymity. Its very obscurity generated a sad eroticism.

It rained the next day. He found himself waiting for evening and, as soon as the time came, in spite of the rain, he set out to the small park where he had seen her. He had no serious hope of finding her again, nor even a real desire to; it just seemed to be something he had to have done to settle himself, to sign the incident off in his mind.

The rain fell with a vertical persistence, dirty rain emptied from a tired sky, rousing the dust and muck of streets and pavements into movement, sludging gutters and drains. The little park had turned black, its few trees collected the water amongst their leathery foliage which formed urinous flows, burrowing pits in the earth below.

She was sitting on the same bench in the same clothes, drenched, leaning forward, clenched and shivering.

'Where did you and Mummy meet?' Jane had once asked their father.

'She was sitting on a bench in the rain. I sat beside her and asked her to marry me.'

'That's not true, Lewis,' their mother had said quickly, but not without a smile.

Henry had brought one of his father's umbrellas with him and he moved it to cover the globe of her hair and shoulders. After a moment she looked up, wiped her hands over her face.

'Are you the guy who takes photographs?' she said.

'Yes.'

'Okay.'

She stood and the water poured from her, streaking her face, running from the ends of her fingers, the hem of her smock. She put her arm about his waist and they moved away. He didn't understand this, not at all, but could not have devised it more simply and perfectly.

He took her into a coffee bar, led her through a press of steaming bodies to a booth at the back.

'What would you like?' he asked her.

'Whatever.'

He fetched coffees and a plate of chocolate gateau in which she did not take any interest. He had forearmed himself with cigarettes, noted the stiffness of her fingers, the narcotic reaction as she sucked the smoke into her.

'How did you know I'd come back?' he asked.

She closed her eyes, shrugged. The water had run down her face in thick, grimy streaks.

'Anything's possible,' she said, explaining it to herself as much as to him. 'One day, maybe, God will find you and make it all right. Maybe God even exists. Everything's possible. It was possible that you would come back. Nothing else was remotely probable. It was the last chance, probably.'

'Have you somewhere to stay?'

'Possibly yes, probably no.'

'Have you no friends?'

'Possibly, probably.'

'Who are you?'

'At this moment, whatever you want.'

'What can I call you?'

'Whatever you want.'

This was no good. It made him angry, the gutter cynicism of it, the self-degradation that said, clearly, that in her degradation whatever he did would be degraded too.

'You'll have to give me a bit more than that,' he said.

'Take it, whatever you want, whatever you need, whatever.'

'No, you have to give it.'

'Oh, fuck off, will you,' she said wearily.

'All right. In a while,' he said, brightening. 'Drink your coffee.'

He sat her out. It took ten minutes. He watched something rise and fall in her, as if she were trying to get up from somewhere, trying to bring herself to face him one way or another. Her bleak vulnerability had a dynamic which made him shudder with a desire that was only superficially sexual. Just watching her was doing something to him that had not been done before. She had been right: anything was possible, anything.

'Henry?' she said, trying to get it right.

'Yes. Henry.'

She nodded to herself, then, taking a deep breath, lifted her face to him, held it clear from the wretchedness.

'Henry, my name is Bel . . . my name is Arabella . . . Bel . . . whatever . . . I have, as of now, as of yesterday, as of this month, nowhere to stay, no-one to be with, no money. I can't give you any more than this. I don't know any more. I am very, very fucked-up. Will you look after me for a bit? I need to straighten out. That's all. Only, we can't screw. I'm sorry. If you want more then . . . then just give me some money, if you can, if you want to, and I'll make it clear for a bit. If you think that I'll fuck your life up too, then you're probably right, but you're here and I'm here, and this is what you want me to say to you, and this is what I need, this is what I have to say to you. You're white and beautiful and live up there on the surface and I dream about you all the time, and when you go for the dream, then you really get fucked, but that's it, that's where we are, that's it.'

'Bel,' he said sounding the name like a secret at last revealed. 'Come on. I'll take you home.'

Out in the rain she clung to him again.

'Is it far?' she said.

'We'll take a taxi.'

'A taxi? Oh fuck.'

. . . *seven* . . .

When he had closed the front door and led her into the hall from which the house opened up above them, when he turned on the lights to see her, she began to contract, out of her element, frightened. In the taxi, he had told her that his parents were away, that there were a couple of women who came to clean during the day, but that for the time being she was safe, that she only had him to worry about.

'It's all right, Henry,' she had said. 'I won't take much. Just a little time, just a little space. Just hide me away somewhere for a bit.'

She had been easy in the taxi, leaning against him, growing sleepy. She needed a bath, a menagerie of smells coming whenever she shifted herself.

Once he had her safe inside, however, she moved away from him, clasped herself, began to weep. He moved to her, but she shook her head, moved off.

'It's all right, Bel,' he said.

'Can I use your toilet?'

'Come on.'

He took her upstairs to the bathroom, went across to his room and waited for her. It was strange to have her here. He looked about his room and imagined how she would see it, imagined explaining things to her. He began to put things away, records back in their sleeves, magazines in piles, the bedclothes back onto his bed.

He heard the lavatory flush and went at once out onto the landing. She came from the bathroom and leant on the door. Her jeans were undone and she was clasping them to her belly, a twist of pain on her face. He went to her.

'You want a bath? I could probably find you some clothes. They'd be a bit big for you. I have big sisters, but you could wear them while I put your things through the washing machine.'

'I've bled on your floor, Henry,' she said. 'Can you find me a sanitary towel?'

He took her back into the bathroom and turned on the taps, then went to raid Jane's room. When he returned with what she had asked for and with a towel and dressing gown, she was not, as he had hoped, in the bath, but sitting on the floor, huddled against the wall, her face perplexed. He squatted down before her and touched the outer aura of her hair with the flat of his hand. She looked at him, her eyes bloodshot and smoky, her skin giving off a grey perspiration.

'Get into the bath, Bel.'

'I'm sick.'

'Then I'll get you a doctor.'

'Let me be for a while,' she said. 'I don't want you to watch me bleed. I don't want you getting a hard-on when I'm like this.'

He left her then, ashamed of himself. He went back to tidying his room, then left that to go down and put on some tinned soup, rich and nutritious, with some thick bread; but he lost the impetus for that as well, turned off the cooker, left the kitchen and wandered about the house, going into room after room, looking for something, or pretending to look for something. Everything was neat and quiet with a normality that made him angry. He thought about that wounded, bleeding woman upstairs and all this domestic quiet was hypocrisy.

He went and rapped on the bathroom door, asked her if she was all right, if there was anything else she needed. He wanted her to need things, he wanted to go out and plunder for her. She asked him for a pair of knickers. He brought them to the door, but did not take them in.

He sat in his room waiting for her. It was dusk now, a gloom filling the house. He turned the lights out around the house and left his bedroom door open, the light there pouring out onto the landing. He put on a record of slow blues guitar. He lit a cigarette and watched it burn down, taking small puffs of it occasionally.

He heard the bathroom door, but did not move, held himself, posed himself for her to find him there. She stood in the doorway, the dressing gown clutched tight about her.

'Come on,' he said.

She moved in slowly, sat on the edge of his bed. He offered her a cigarette but she shook her head.

'Would you like something to eat?'

'No. Can I sleep now?'

'Sure. I'll put you in my sister's room.'

'Is this where you sleep?'

'Yes.'

'Can I sleep here?'

'If you want to.'

She nodded her head slowly, looked at the bed, looked around the room, looked at him, smiled, then, standing quickly, she shed the dressing gown, pulled back the sheets and slipped into the bed, giving him as she did so a glimpse of her thin, black body, heavy breasts, the white briefs that covered her buttocks. She pulled the covers up, turned and settled on her front. He watched her and knew that she was immediately asleep.

He slept on an air-bed in the room beside her. In the morning, when he woke, she was still asleep. He was supposed to be meeting someone, going to an exhibition, but he missed that. He moved about the house, being domestic, going up every twenty minutes to see if she was stirring, but the hours passed and she did not stir. There was a safety in her sleep. He sat at last and watched over her. He could see only the ball of hair, could not even hear her breathe.

She woke in the early afternoon, very quickly, turned suddenly onto her back and saw him there. She closed her eyes and he could see her hands moving under the covers, saw a small wince as she found some tenderness. She opened her eyes again and looked at him.

'Can I have some water?'

When he brought her the drink, she shifted up onto her elbow and took the water in small sips, then handed him the glass.

'There are some slacks, and a shirt,' he said, 'if you want to get up.'

'Have you been here all the time?'

'Not all the time. You've been asleep, what, about fifteen hours.'

'Where did you sleep?'

'On the floor.'

'Where's my bag?'

'Here.'

'Did you find anything interesting in it?'

'I didn't look. Is there anything interesting in it?'

She dropped back on the bed, stared at the ceiling.

'Where does it hurt you, Henry?'

'Nowhere, really,' he said, not really understanding the question.

'That's probably true, isn't it? Oh well . . . can I use your bathroom again?'

'Of course.'

He handed her the dressing gown, and she sat up in the bed to put it on. She watched as he watched her, then opened the dressing gown for him, held her face away as she did so. This defined for him more clearly than anything so far had done the difference he felt for her and for any other girl he had seen or touched in any way; because he did not turn away; because he looked at those heavy brown breasts which were strangely tapered, black-nippled; because there was a shame in looking; because it was an advantage taken over her, an abuse of her which he felt burning sourly in him; because he continued to look; because he could not look away; because her beauty hurt; because she had shown him where it hurt him; because of his power and her vulnerability, her degradation and his cruelty in that one long moment of revelation.

She did not move until he moved, which he did at last, rising slowly and leaving her there, going downstairs to wait for her.

He had the radio on in the kitchen and she came down to find him, came to the table where he sat and sat opposite him. Jane's clothes were loose about her, and she seemed small, uncomfortable within them. She had brought the cigarettes down and she lit one. He rose, fetched an ashtray and returned to his seat.

'I could use some food,' she said.

'What would you like? Eggs? Bacon?'

'No bacon. Eggs, yeah. Lots of eggs. Scrambled runny. No. Wait. In a bit. I need to talk first.' She smoked silently for a minute. 'You see, I need a doctor, but . . . I've got a dose of something, that's why . . . only, I've got no . . . no cards or anything, no address, no next of fucking kin. All right? You understand?'

She had become aggressive, shamed through to this.

'It's easy,' he said. 'Don't worry.'

'How is it easy? You fucking bastard.'

'Bel, I have an aunt. She's a doctor. She's . . . you'll be safe with her, I promise.' He waited but she did not make a response. 'I'll give her a ring.'

'Tell her . . . tell her my cunt feels like someone's set fire to it.'

'You can tell her that.'

Aunt Naomi had a weakness for her nieces, had come to Jane's help, and to Maggie's too, in different crises, and without troubling their parents. Henry was terrified of her. She had asked him, aged thirteen, if he masturbated, sent him five pounds on his birthday and at Christmas, and argued with his parents whenever she came to the house, which was not often. He had never approached her personally before.

She was brusque when he rang her, assumed at once that he'd got the girl pregnant; when told the problem, asked whether he had given her the infection or whether she had given it to him; asked what drugs she was in the habit of taking; but agreed to come round that evening.

'You stay with me when she comes,' Bel said.

'She won't let me. She scares the pants off me, to tell you the truth, but she's all right with women.'

'Is she lesbian?'

'I don't think so. Would that bother you?'

'No.'

'You ready to eat?'

'Yeah. Maybe.'

Henry cooked for her, ate with her. She ate as if she were being watched, daintily, as if trying to make some social impression. Henry didn't like her like this. He washed up whilst she sat smoking, thinking, nervous of any sound that might be an approach.

Aunt Naomi arrived with a blast of the doorbell that hit her like an electric shock. Henry dried his hands and went to let her in. As he passed, she grabbed his hand and gripped it.

'Come on,' he said.

'You're Bel, are you?' Aunt Naomi said, shedding her mac and pushing it at Henry, looking at her, putting her hands on her shoulders and peering into her eyes. 'Why is it that you young people go so far and know so little. Come on, then. Henry, find a bottle of your father's best malt whisky for me.'

Twenty minutes later Aunt Naomi appeared in the sitting room, sat down, lit a cigarette and wrote a prescription. Henry brought her her whisky, which she took without looking up.

'Have you had sex with her?'

'No.'

'Because, if you have, you'll just pass it back to her. Here. I've written it in your name in case they ask for identification at the chemists'.'

'Is she all right, Aunt Naomi?'

'No, she's not all right. She's undernourished, has been abusing her body with anything that's around. If she dropped dead tomorrow I would not be surprised. The venereal problem is not, however, very serious. Keep yourself completely clear of her genitals for a month, and for God's sake don't get her pregnant, not until she's had a year without drugs, with decent food, exercise.' She drank the whisky.

'Where is she?' he asked.

'I sent her to bed. She's upset. Of course she's upset. You can go up to her in a minute, young man, tell her what a stupid old bitch I am. How long have you known her?'

'Oh . . . a couple of days. I sort of . . . took pity on her, I suppose.'

'I see. What d'you know about her?'

'Nothing.'

'When d'your parents get back?'

'Next week.'

'Are you going to get her out of here by then?'

'I . . . I haven't really thought that far.'

'Henry, you have a very messed-up young woman upstairs. Whatever you do, try not to add to her problems. I could give you some addresses if you want to find someone who can look after her, not that you'd be able to persuade her to take that sort of help. But know this: you run serious risks having her here, risks not to you but to her. I shall hold you personally answerable for what happens to her. You can't pick people off the street like stray animals. Your parents will be very angry if they come back and find her still here; angry with you and more angry with her. So you'd bloody well better know what you're going to do with her before they get back.'

'Yes, Aunt Naomi.'

'I can't believe you're as gormless as you look, Henry. It's the fault of those sisters of yours. They've spoilt you abominably. You've never had to take a serious decision in your entire life. Well, you've got one now, my lad. Right. I'm going home. You've got my number.'

'Thank you, Aunt Naomi.'

'Yes, well, you remember what I've said to you.'

. . . *eight* . . .

She was in Jane's white bed, lying on her back under a mask of tears. He sat beside her and her hand came out and gripped his with a force that hurt him.

'It's all right,' he said.

'I don't want to be here. I don't like it here.'

'Sleep now. I'll get your medicines tomorrow. Then we can decide. . . .'

'We? Who the fuck are "we"?'

'You can decide and I'll try and help if you'll let me help.'

'Fuck off, will you.'

'Go to sleep, Bel.'

'I don't want to go to sleep. I've slept all fucking day.'

'What do you want? We could watch some television, or listen to some music.'

'Have you got any dope?'

'No.'

'There's some in my bag.'

'I don't think. . . .'

'What don't you think? What?'

'The last time I smoked dope,' he said after a moment, 'I had a . . . a bad experience.'

She took back her hand and laughed at him, showing her teeth which were uneven, stained.

'You've having another bad experience now, Henry, or hadn't you realised? Life is a fucking bad experience. You want to hear about some bad experiences?'

'Shut up,' he said. 'Your bag's in my room. I'll bring it through to you.'

When he reached his room, he had tears in his eyes. He smeared his sleeve across his face and began to look for her bag, distracted by the emotions which bulged through him. When he had found it, she

339

had come through, wrapped in the dressing gown. She took the bag from him roughly, turned away to search through it.

'You have been in here, haven't you?'

'No, I fucking haven't been in your bag.'

She burrowed deep, then smiled and withdrew a small oblong of silver paper, unwrapped it, sniffed.

'I'll need the cigarettes,' she said.

When he returned from the kitchen where they had been left, she was sitting on the floor, had spread out the familiar square of rolling papers between her open knees.

'D'you have to do that here?' he said, dropping the cigarettes beside her.

She looked up at him, then stopped, seemed to go dead for a few seconds.

'Henry,' she said distantly. 'Henry, I do need this. I need to come down a little and this . . . this will . . . just take me down, just a little. I know I'm not supposed to, but . . . and I need some company, all right? What I don't need is to be on my own. Now, if that's a problem for you, then I'm sorry. Don't be a prick, now. Please. Put some music on.'

He put on a record of baroque music, on which Maggie was playing somewhere in the second violins. He needed the safety of the nostalgia, needed to remind himself who he was. He sat on the chair by his desk, well away from her, trying to push some distance into his observation of her, trying to push on the time which seemed to have slowed about him.

She had rolled up the sleeves of the dressing gown, had tucked it under her so that it formed a white bundle out of which her dark limbs and head protruded. Her fingers and lips moved slowly in her assembling as if she was having to exercise a fierce control over them.

'This music is like needles,' she said. 'Very hard music, Henry.'

'D'you want me to find something else?'

'No, no. It's part of the scene. It all makes sense if you want it to make sense. I made you hurt. This is your music. That's all right.'

She refolded the silver foil and put it back into her bag, brushed the crumbs of tobacco away, leant back against the bed, shuffled the dressing gown a little looser about her. She put the joint to her lips and applied the flame, inhaled so fiercely that the loose packing of the joint crackled with fire. She coughed a little and spread out her legs.

She offered it to him, but he shook his head.

A while later, he stood up.

'Where're you going?'

'I'm just going to the bathroom.'

'In a while. Just see me through this, will you?'

He sat down again. The record ended. She had grown limp under the drug, looked as if she had been dropped down from a height onto his floor, her movements slow and weighted, her fingers thick, her head loose. Now and then, with considerable effort, she straightened her spine, brought her body forward, dropped back her head, gasped at something within her; then slowly sank again.

The joint at last was done, had extinguished itself. She sucked at it anyway, then looked at it and dropped its remains onto the ashtray.

'All right?' he asked.

She nodded and he went to the bathroom, a cold room after the swirl of the drug in which, passively but willingly, he had participated. His penis was swollen and wet; it revolted him.

When he returned she was lying on his bed, the dressing-gown belted tight about her, staring at the ceiling.

'You want to sleep here again?'

'I can't sleep in that other room,' she said with the aggressive petulance that had begun to sting him. 'It's like a fucking hospital in there.'

'Okay. That's where I'll be if you need me.'

'I need you here.'

'Yes, well . . . well, I need a little space, Bel. Okay?'

She said nothing and he left her, went downstairs to tidy up, to make sure the doors were locked, the milk bottles out, the radio turned off. She had been in the house a day now and the normality of his life was obliterated. It had been a novelty, an excitement, at first. Now the hours were building up and he was becoming lost.

He returned to his room to collect his towel and dressing gown, knocking before entering. She did not respond to his knock, so he went in quietly. She was in bed, lying on her side, smoking a cigarette; the air in the room was thick and stale, the scent of her, the dark reek she gave off, was clearly present, a sexual signal that made his head ache. He found that he had stopped, was looking at her, had again lost his determination. She stubbed out the cigarette, burrowed into the bedclothes and he left her.

In Jane's bed, he could still smell her. He tried to masturbate, but could not begin to bring the pleasure through the disgust. He slept, and had dreams of falling into a great white space that streamed past him, that stung him with a million tiny particles of some terrible disintegration.

He woke in the darkness and something was moving, the darkness was moving. Something touched him. She was opening the sheets, lifting herself, sliding herself down beside him, her legs cold in the dank warmth in which he lay, the hard palms of her hand on his soft side, the dry flesh of her breasts against his breast, the bush of her hair against his face, her mouth on his neck.

'Did you make it?' she asked.

He knew what she meant at once, was appalled at her knowledge of him.

'No,' he said. 'Please, Bel. . . .'

'You want me to help?'

'No. Please, no.'

'Hush, then. Sleep a little. I'll be your sister, your big black sister. Don't be scared. I don't want to be alone any more. You don't want to be alone. There. I can feel how white you are, Henry. It's like you've been inside all your life, pale and soft and scared. You smell of soap and piss, like a little boy.'

'You owe me nothing,' he said limply.

'I'm beginning to, beginning to owe, beginning to know; you too, Henry. Go to sleep now. Go to sleep.'

He slept as if she had simply pushed him off into it; when he woke, he frankly suspected her of this. The curtains were thin and the morning light filled the room. Jane's room, pale and tidy, left behind, the cherishings of her childhood fading on the surfaces; and he in her big white bed with chaos lying beside him.

He lay on his back with his arms at his sides, she on her front, with one arm slung across him. He examined her arm, the flesh thin, the elbow calloused, the hand splayed over his nipple. He touched her arm, felt carefully into the armpit where he found a spray of tough, wet hair. His fear of her beat in his breast and belly.

She woke and turned to him; perhaps she had been awake before him. He closed his eyes, felt her shifting up, felt the sweep of her breasts on his chest, her breath in his face. She kissed him, ran the tip of her tongue over his lips to moisten them, then put her lips on

342

his, breathed from his breath, began to move her lips, massaging him, slipping her tongue into him on quick explorations. He held her head as if he wanted to control this, to know what was pulling his face away from his brain which seemed to fall deeply into the back of his head. He pushed her tongue back with his own tongue and found himself in her mouth, held between her strong lips, sucked, flooded with strange, active liquid.

Their faces parted and coolness came between them. He saw her eyes swimming in tears, her mouth limp, reaching for the air. She lifted from him, taking the bedclothes with her, opening his hot flesh to the light. She knelt beside him and looked along his body, holding her fingers over him but not touching him, leaving an inch of air between her hand and his skin, drawing him out, defining his space. He watched, not her, but himself, felt himself flicker and twitch under her benedictions.

His penis lay flat and hard against his belly and, as she stooped and blew gently onto it, it discharged a long shudder of semen that filled his navel and spilled down his flanks. They watched this happen, he with a small, dark groan, she with a soft laugh. She reached for a tissue and mopped him up neatly, wiping her fingers, then finally ducking down her head and taking the tip of his penis quickly into her mouth, giving him a warm lubrication, taking all the pain away.

Then they slept again.

. . . *nine* . . .

When they were dressed and eating their way through a loaf of bread, with butter and honey and large cups of milky coffee, she asked:

'How long have we got, Henry?'

'What d'you mean?'

'When do your parents come back?'

'Oh. Next week. Tuesday. But. . . .'

'But what?'

He was going to say that wouldn't make a difference. He was going to ask her if she was really going to stay. Her questions had jolted him out of the present and made him think.

'I don't want you to go,' he said simply, foolishly.

'There's nowhere I'd rather be right now than here,' she said, taking his hand, studying his face, letting the questions go for the moment.

Her clothes were clean and dry and she was happier to be back in them, less of an invalid, more herself.

'Do you have other clothes? Other things somewhere?' he asked.

'I don't know. There is a place where I left some stuff, but . . . but the people I was with have gone now, so . . . anyway, I don't want to go back there.'

'Can I buy you some things?'

'Yes. I'd like to be bought some things. Nothing flashy. Some knickers, a new pair of jeans, something to smell good. All of this is free, Henry, giving and taking. If it's going to cost you anything important, then you tell me.'

He took her out shopping, was glad to walk the streets with her, wanted to see someone he knew, just wanted to be seen with her hanging onto his arm, swinging at the end of his hand, walking ahead through the racks of shops, turning back to show him something. He had never done any of this before: before he had met girls in pre-defined situations, had moved from the social to the intimate, all stations part of the same game. This was different, ordinary and miraculous, venturing out into the busy light of day with a knowledge of and assurance in one another that was so simple as to be breathtaking whenever he stopped, which he frequently did, to take stock. He had never felt so immediately present in the world. The sun shone, the streets were bright and open and he was happy.

They ate out, went to a film in which she clung against him and chain-smoked, came out blinking into the late afternoon sun and caught the bus back.

She went up to try on her new clothes and to use her medications whilst he cooked. She didn't eat meat, so his limited culinary skills managed a flabby omelette and something resembling a salad.

She appeared in her new jeans, with a black jumper, and a bra which made her breasts dynamic. She had put on careful black eyeliner and a purple lipstick.

'I haven't dressed up like this in years,' she said. 'I know I look like a tart, but what the hell. D'you like it? D'you prefer the scruffy version? I have this idea that it was the way I smelt that got you going. Tell me what you want, Henry?'

'You look great.'

'I feel great. I've just had my first good shit in weeks.'

She did not talk as she ate, concentrating on the food as she had done that first time, eating with what seemed to be greed, but which he now knew to be pleasure.

'Tell me who you are,' he said, when she had finished, having framed and reframed this proposition for ten minutes.

She looked up quickly, pushed her plate away and reached for the cigarettes.

'No,' she said. 'One day, maybe. Not here.'

'Just one thing,' he said. 'Just tell me if there's anything that's liable to come after you.'

'What are you afraid of, Henry?'

'I don't know. I'm afraid of something . . . of someone coming that I'll have to fight, and I want to know what sort of fight it's going to be.'

'There's nothing like that. I promise you. There's enough to be afraid of without that. Can I ask you something?'

'Please.'

'When I came into your bed last night, was there anybody else involved?'

'What d'you mean?'

'I mean, was I somewhere that belonged to someone else?'

'No.'

'All those girls. . . . ?'

'What girls?'

'In the pictures, in your room, have you screwed them all?'

'No.'

'But some of them?'

'Some.'

'All those pretty little dreamy girls, so clean, so clear, with big houses like this house.'

'They're just girls.'

'No, Henry. I'm trespassing here, I know it. Be careful of me. I'm a bitch. There're times when I want to take you for everything you've got, when I hate you because you're white and rich and so

345

fucking easy here. Then I get afraid because you're taking me, and you're white and rich, and there's a lot of street waiting for me out there. Then I get sad because I want this, I want you, I want to sell myself down for anything you want to offer. And I don't know which one's the real want, the real fear. They're all real. They're all me. So be careful.'

He thought about this, and then said, 'No-one's ever made me come just by blowing on me before. The ultimate blow-job, Bel.'

They laughed at this, and at the memories of that morning that trailed from it.

'Henry?' she said at last, growing serious, coy almost.

'What?'

'Will you take some pictures of me?'

Her face, hair bursting out to the edge of the frame, mouth closed tight, the lips drawn in, the nose a straight line, a dark shine to her skin, eyes open, hard and bright, meeting the black lens-eye with a resolute whiteness.

Her head just turning on the edge of a laugh, the eyes closed, the teeth catching the light, the hair a blur against a white background.

Sitting on a stool with her face down, hidden below the hair, her hands between her knees, her legs straight, an exclamation mark.

Leaning against a wall, in strict profile, hands behind her back, eyes looking at a distance, a static defiance, nose up and breasts defined against the light.

Caught twisted over with a hand up her jumper after an itch, eyes narrowed, teeth set and a glimpse of belly flesh.

Elbows on a table, shoulders hunched, a burning cigarette, the face turning curiously into the lens.

Just the lower half of her face, profile, chin to nose, with the tongue extruded fully, limply, wet, a drip of liquid pearled on its tip, the surrounding skin silkily immaculate with the tongue disembowelled dramatically.

A yawn, the fingers spread over the cavern of the mouth, eyes closed, teeth clear, an enormous mouth gleaming like the underbelly of a machine.

Lying on her side, an elbow lifting her upper body, the other hand hidden behind her, naked, the breasts weighed down, the saddle of flesh between ribs and hips, the belly and pubis presented flat to the

346

lens, one leg up, the other long and pointed, tension in the body, watching in the face.

She had been with him in the dark-room, had shared the magic of the images' emergence, had been very quiet. When it was done, he hung them up and led her back down the narrow stairs, holding her hand, for she was frightened of heights.

They smoked a joint and went dopey to bed, his bed, together, no discussion.

In the morning, he went and brought the prints down, cleared his walls and was going to pin them up, but she didn't want that.

'When I've gone,' she said.

She caught him leafing through them again and again, staring at the images, his excuse a professional exactitude, but she didn't believe that, watched his watching suspiciously, but not without a quiet, smoking vanity. In truth he was using the pictures to try to come to some definition of her; as if he had taken laboratory slices of her that he could minutely scrutinise, quantify, analyse. Her reality was always too quick for him.

She had not wanted to pose naked but, after half an hour, had suddenly conceded, had undressed quickly and nervously, had made him promise not to shoot until she said so, no peek-a-boo, no wanker's meat-shots; but this was the one to which he returned, watching it from a plateau of erotic amazement. He had seen and touched the reality, had it there at his shoulder, there in his bed last night, tonight; but the picture was viewed consciously, requiring only the passive submission to its power that allowed the rest of it, the active twist and shift of her, the slip of her tongue, the clip of her intelligence, her continual search for him, to come clear. This is what I have here, he said to himself. This.

Naked, in his picture, in his room, in his bed, he could not rid himself of the image of her as an animal; no particular animal; many animals; cat and rat, reptile and bird, furred and scaled, padded and clawed, caught out of her habitat, at risk, dangerous. Perhaps it was because she would tell him so little about herself that he could put her in no human context; perhaps it was just the abundance of his erotic greed for her; perhaps, his inherent racism; perhaps just the strangeness of her, and the strangeness of the totality of his feelings for her, the blunt certainty of them, addicted. He wanted to see everything, wanted to be with her when she urinated and defecated, but she would not permit that; the bathroom was her place of absolute privacy, bolted and silent, even her bathing and making-up concealed from him. Perhaps what was essentially animal about her was the immaculate physical dignity with which she moved, touched, looked, reacted, the assurance of herself that grew and flourished day by day, rising from the dirtiness in which he had found her, coming clear of the mess into something clean and certain, the pristine curl and stretch and set of her. In the pictures he could hold it still and know it; otherwise, what could he do but go to her, blinded, doped by her; by her beauty and her grace and the thick miasma of her sex; but above all by her acceptance of him, ironic, knowing; but more than acceptance, more; by her need of him, her delight in him, reaching out with an eagerness that matched his own but outstripped it with its sureness of purpose, the frankness of its pleasure, its shameless consumption of him. What, he asked himself, the stupidest question in the world, have I done to deserve this?

It was strange and exotic to be unable simply to copulate with her, not even to be able to touch her vagina, to be exonerated, forbidden indeed, from making any attempt at her pleasure. His own pleasure she ministered to almost continuously, or so it seemed: a touch, a press of herself, the probe of finger and tongue, a deft friction that would dissolve him. Sex was something that, in the old days, men did to women, that, in the latter days, men had learnt to do with women; this was sex done to him, a copious, liberated operation of a libido that jumped out of him before he was aware of it, but not before she was aware of it. He never once initiated it, never once presented himself to her. It was exhausting, aching, overwhelming; but the critical delight that he took in it was her delight in being able to do this to him. He did not understand it. The emission of semen was smelly and messy; the blob of biological reality left at the end of erotic pleasure that required responsible neutralisation; the shameful ultimate proof, however deferential and considerate he had been, that it was his pleasure that was at work there. All such verities were here irrelevant. She loved it, loved to watch him, to touch him where he shuddered, loved to attend to him afterwards, to settle herself against his repletions.

'This is better than fucking,' she told him. 'Nothing gets lost here. Everything is out in the light. Everything. I know you better than I've ever known anyone, Henry.'

348

Something occasionally made him feel childish in this, usually afterwards when she had dropped into her heavy sleep and he, restless, hot and aching, could not follow her. He wanted to be inside her, properly, man to woman; but he knew, as she knew, that there were weeks before that might happen and they had only a few more days before his parents returned, and then whatever was happening here would have to change.

. . . *ten* . . .

'What time will they be here?'

'Their plane lands at three-twenty. They'll get a taxi, be back here, what, about six?'

'Okay. I'll get myself clear by about two, give you a chance to get the place straight.'

'What d'you mean, Bel? Where're you going?'

'Henry, come on now. Live with it. I have to go.'

'No, you don't. I want you to meet them. I want them to meet you.'

She sighed and let the tears come, let him touch them on her face.

'Please stay,' he said. 'I want them to meet you. I owe them that.'

'And what do you reckon they'll think of me, Henry?'

'I don't care what they think of you.'

'I care what they think of me.'

'Why? You don't owe them anything.'

'This is their house, their food, their money, their son. Of course I fucking owe them.'

He had not thought she would go, had not imagined she would want to, had steeled himself to facing his parents with her. He did not understand this.

'Do you want to go?' he asked quietly.

'I don't want to be here when they get back.'

'But do you want to go?'

'I have to go.'

'But do you want to go, Bel? Please. I need to know that.'

She did not answer and, in the silence, his heart emptied bitterly.

'Where will you go?'

'I don't know.'

'Does that mean you don't want me to know?'

'It means, I don't know, Henry. I don't fucking know.'

'Then stay. Please stay.'

'I'm too scared, Henry.'

'What of?'

'Don't be so fucking naïve.'

'You're more scared of a merchant banker and his wife than you are of the street? What'll you do? Hang about? Wait for someone else like me to come and take you home? There's lots like me, Bel, lots and lots. Would you like me to ring around and see if I can find you someone?'

He expected her to match his anger, to throw her obscenities back at him; he wanted that, wanted to make a fight of it; if she was going, then it was better they fight. But she was not angry. When he had spent his flimsy rage, he found her staring at him with open, frightened eyes.

The refrigerator motor started up suddenly, and they both turned to it in a moment of alarm that made them feel foolish. Then, slowly, she stood and walked from the room, went upstairs. He spent ten minutes trying to find something to do with himself, then he trudged up after her.

She was sitting on the bed surrounded by used paper tissues like the drafts of a failed poem or the detritus of a messy sexual encounter.

'I'll tell you what scares me,' she said. 'Not them; you. I'm scared of how you'll see me when they come back. I know what I am. You don't. You have no idea. But they'll know, and they'll tell you, and I don't want to go through that. So, please, please, Henry, let me go.'

'Let me come with you, then.'

'No. That would . . . be stupid, just be dodging out of it.'

'Aren't you dodging out of it?'

She took another tissue out and blew her nose.

'Come on, Henry,' she said. 'Let me go. Please.'

'I'm not stopping you, Bel.'

'You don't understand, do you? You see? It's fucking hopeless.'

'Don't go.'

'All right. All right. All right.'

He touched her, she lifted to him and they lay down in their tenderness as the hours slipped from under them.

'Hello? . . . Henry? . . . We're home.'

He saw his mother below, a silk scarf over her shoulders, the white line down the centre of her head from which her black hair fell neatly. He came down the stairs.

'Oh, there you are, darling.' She met him with a small kiss, looked at him, and her smile caught on something. 'Go and help Daddy with the cases, would you?'

Out in the street his father was scribbling a cheque for the taxi-driver.

'Hello, Henry. You haven't got a fiver on you to spare me this, have you?'

'Sorry, Dad.'

He picked up the two largest cases and lugged them up the steps into the hall. His mother was sorting through the stack of mail.

'Shall I take these upstairs?' he asked.

'No. Leave them there. There's all sorts of contraband that we need to unload down here. How have you been? Have you heard from that college?'

'They want to see some of my stuff.'

'Have you done anything about it yet?'

'No.'

'Well, we'll have a look at the letter, see what they need. I do hope we haven't left it too late.'

His father then appeared with the rest of the luggage, a clutch of shoulder bags and carrier bags, magazines tucked under his arm.

'We thought you might have come out to the airport,' he said.

'Sorry, I didn't know you'd want that.'

His parents exchanged looks which made him go cold.

' "Welcome home, Mummy and Daddy",' his father said. ' "Did you have a good trip?" Yes, thank you, Henry. We had a wonderful time.'

The banality of this made him shudder.

'Actually,' he said. 'I've got a friend staying.'

'Well. . . .' his father said, 'that's all right. Isn't it, darling? Anyone we know?'

'A girl, Henry?'

'Yes, a girl. No, no-one you know.'

There was a pause in which the house grew very large about him.

'We had thought,' his father began, 'that we might pop out for a meal tonight. I'm sure you've not thought about getting any food in. Er . . . bring your friend.'

'I think that we'd better meet her, Henry, hadn't we?'

He turned and went upstairs. He had believed that, after the first moment, like diving into a cold pool, it would be easy. It was not.

She was standing in his room watching for him.

'Come on. Let's get it over. Oh, and they're talking about going to a restaurant. All of us.'

'Get me out of that.'

'All right. All right.'

His parents had moved into the drawing room. He could not hear them talking, heard the clink of glass, the movement of bodies. Outside the door, she shook away his hand. They seemed, as he walked in with her, very large, grown suddenly into their own importance and power. He watched their faces as they registered her, watched for horror, alarm, amusement; despised them for their social competence which broke into formal smiles upon her.

'Mummy? Daddy? This is Bel.'

'Hello, Bel,' his father said, coming forward and taking her hand.

'How do you do, Bel. Henry, fetch your guest a drink.'

'No,' she said. 'I don't . . . drink.'

'Good for you,' his father said. 'Do sit down. Please.'

She sat on a sofa and Henry sat quickly beside her. She leant forward, elbows on her knees, face down. She lifted her face to look at them.

'Where are you from, Bel?' his mother asked.

'Oh . . . lots of places, really. Nowhere, really. I. . . .'

'Where did you two meet?' his father asked.

'In town,' Henry said quickly. 'She needed some help. I gave it to her.'

'What sort of help?' his mother asked.

'All sorts of help. She was in trouble.'

'What sort of trouble, Henry?'

'She needed some space, somewhere to be safe for a few days, that's all.'

'Safe from what?'

'Darling,' his father said. 'You're upsetting her. Please, Bel. Don't be upset. You're Henry's friend. You're very welcome here.'

'I'm sorry,' she said suddenly, the intonation of which cut his father into silence.

'You don't mind if Bel smokes, do you?' Henry said.

'Of course not,' his father said. 'There are some duty-frees somewhere.'

'It's all right,' she said, fumbling in her pocket for her cigarettes, fixing herself with the drug blatantly.

It was whilst watching her smoke a cigarette that his parents registered their first unmistakable signs of discomfort. Henry saw it, took her hand; she clenched briefly then released him, thrust her own hand deep between her thighs.

'Have you no place of your own, Bel?' his mother asked.

'She's staying here,' he said.

'Yes, darling, but when she's not staying here?'

'There were some people. . . .' she said, 'that I was with. They . . . left. I . . . the place was . . . not . . . I couldn't stay there.' She spoke as if translating, trying to put it into words that would belong here, failing; what she did say was desperate with meaninglessness.

'Well,' his father said, 'I'm going to have a quick shower and change. If we're going to go out, we'd better get going.'

'We'll stay here,' Henry said.

'Well . . . fine, then. We won't be late back. Celia? Are you coming up?'

'In a moment, Lewis.'

His father smiled at them and walked out, briefly touching his mother's shoulder as he passed her.

'Well,' his mother said clearly. 'I won't ask, but . . . but is there anything I should know? . . . Anything that I'm going to find out sooner or later and which is going to have to be dealt with? . . . Well? . . . Henry?'

'No,' he said. 'Bel's staying here for a bit, that's all.'

'Darling, you must understand. . . .'

'What?'

'There are things . . . things that we oughtn't to know about. If you . . . if you let us into your secrets, then we'll probably . . . probably end up interfering. That's . . . that's how families work, you see. Bel, I'm sure you understand that.'

'I don't understand anything,' she said flatly. 'I never had a family.'

'Well. . . .' There was irritation in this, quickly mastered. 'Be that as it may, you will understand, I'm sure, that we have obligations to our son. May I ask how old you are?'

'What's that got to do with anything?' Henry said.

'Henry, I think your friend is quite able to speak for herself.'

'I'm twenty; although some of me is a lot older than that.'

A smile contorted Henry's face for a moment.

'I haven't a clue what you mean by that, Bel; but I really think that if you two want to fuck each other, you should find somewhere of your own to do it.' She rose from her seat. 'I must go and change. Henry, we won't be late. I think we should talk tonight. If you have that letter from the college, I would very much like to see it. I have a busy day tomorrow and if I am going to have to spend most of it sorting you out, I need to know.'

They sat silent until the doors closed upstairs, then he touched her shoulder and found her rigid.

'You were terrific,' he said to her.

'Let me go, Henry. Please let me go.'

They were back by ten. He was waiting for them in the kitchen, having drunk most of a bottle of wine. It had not made him drunk, or if it had he did not notice. He was wound up like a spring. He wanted to get this over, to go up and smoke a joint, to get into his bed, to lose himself in sex and sleep. They came into the kitchen, to locate him, shed their summer coats and jackets.

'Put some coffee on, would you, Lewis?' his mother said.

'I'm going to have a whisky. Would you like something?'

'Just coffee,' she said.

He set up the percolator. She sat at the table. Henry watched his father, was more afraid of him than of her. She was, as always, predictable; he could fight her. His father might have smiled it all away, but would be more likely not to; would anyway have the final decision.

'Where is she, Henry?' his mother said.

'She's in bed.'

'In your bed?'

'Yes.'

'Do you know anything about her?'

'Oh yes.'

'Apart from what you've learnt in bed, which is very, very little, I

354

can promise you. Henry, it is the easiest thing in the world to lie to someone when you're in their bed. I don't mean words, I mean what you do and what it means. I do know, you see, I do know that you've been with girls. Everything is so wonderful for you young people, isn't it? All this quick promiscuity. I thought you would have learnt something from that, some . . . some sophistication at least.'

'What do you mean? That she's not good enough for me?'

She sighed irritably, as if unable to make him understand something simple.

'What I can't understand, Henry,' his father said, 'is why you let her stay when we came back. I mean, she was wretched. You put her through bloody misery in there. What were you trying to prove? Eh?'

'I wanted you to meet her.'

'Why? Did you seriously think we'd approve of her? You can't've thought that. She certainly knew we wouldn't. What is she? Some homeless, helpless thing, probably spent her life being abused by everyone who came near her. You're a wonderful, honest, open boy, Henry, but . . . but quite frankly you are simply not in a position to do anything for her. If you were five years older, if you had a job, something, anything that meant anything to anyone outside this house, then it would be different; but then you would be different and she would not have got near you. I'm not saying that she's calculating or manipulative, just that your honesty, your youth, make you vulnerable, give her something that she can cling onto, something clean and respectable. I think she knows this very clearly. Your mother's right, you know, Henry: what happens in bed is really irrelevant to real life.'

'D'you mean you don't want her staying here?'

They exchanged those horrible glances again, the tokens of adult complicity and hypocrisy.

'Henry,' his father said. 'I'm afraid, old son, that you're going to get hurt by this, by whatever happens. I'm sorry. My advice to you is . . . is to take your own decisions before she, or we, take them for you.'

He had begun to cry then, reduced to the pathetic childishness in which they sought to define him.

'Have you got that letter from the college?' his mother asked.

'Not tonight, Celia. Let him get this sorted out first. Go on, Henry. You go to bed now.'

The light was on in his room, but she appeared to be asleep. That she was still there was a comfort to him, a blind comfort. He turned off the light and pulled off his clothes, stood for a moment naked in the darkness, alone and frightened. She stirred and called his name, and he quickly slid in beside her warmth, wrapped himself in it, submitted to her kisses which flooded him with strength again, filled his mind with desperate decisions.

'You've been crying,' she said.

'It's all right.'

'Henry. Let me go. You must let me go. I don't want to run away, but I'll have to if you don't let me go. It'll come to that.'

'You think they're right about you, do you?'

'It's not right, it's not wrong, it's just how it is.'

'Where could you go?'

'Oh . . . I'll find somewhere. I'm stronger now, better. Could you give me some money?'

'Yes.'

'When I've got myself settled, I'll call you. But don't wait for me. When I go, this is over. When we meet again it will be different. Go to college. Find yourself pretty girls to sleep with, to make you happy again. This has been a little miracle; but don't put your whole life on it. It's not worth that. Let it hurt. Be brave and be proud of it. Let's make love now, and sleep, and then it'll be all right, I promise you, all right.'

She taught him then how to touch her, shifting herself to his touch, lifting her knees and pushing herself up, a dark bolt of flesh under his operations, so immediate, intense, giving off a hot reek from the unfolding of her pleasure, her greed for life, taking and giving. When she came, when he had made her come, he felt a pride and pleasure that made him laugh with delight. If this, this is a lie, he told the image of his mother, then being alive is not worth the effort.

He woke at dawn as she climbed across him and went to the bathroom. When she returned, without looking at him, she got dressed, sorted out her things. There was a picture he had taken of himself amongst the others; she removed it from the wall.

'I'll take this,' she said. 'Is the money in your wallet?'

He didn't reply, watched her. Finally she turned to him and he sat up.

'No. Stay where you are. We've done all that now, Henry.'

'I love you, Bel.'

'Well, fuck off then,' she said, turning and going.

Only in the silence of her absence did he begin to consider the brutality of her departure; as it had happened it had seemed entirely the right way to do it, entirely her, strong, ironic, free. In the wash of it, the pain of her going was stunned by her brilliance; for a while.

. . . *eleven* . . .

He stayed in bed until the afternoon, knew they wouldn't come up to him. He listened and heard them go out, then got himself up, went down to the kitchen and cooked himself a mighty plate of bacon and sausages covered in ketchup, food from his childhood, food that Bel would not eat.

When they returned he was watching television.

'Hello, Henry,' his mother said. ' Where's Bel?'

'Oh, she buggered off. Don't worry.'

'Ah. Well. . . .'

'Is there anything we can do for her?' his father asked.

'Sell everything you have and give the money to the poor,' he said, lit by the inspiration of this, almost laughing, then afraid of what he had provoked.

They stood looking at him as he watched the television, some children's programme telling you how to make a bird-box. Then presumably after a piercing exchange of glances, they left the room.

They did not mention her, which was what he wanted, and he was grateful to them. He did not go out, did not go anywhere. When friends rang, or turned up, he shrugged them off. He stayed in his room mostly, lying on his bed, sleeping a lot, listening to records. He did not know what he was doing really, just consuming endless chunks of time, his tedium self-perpetuating. On good days he thought about her strongly enough to bring himself to pleasure; but it was always worse after he had done so. He knew that he was waiting for her to call him, hopelessly, interminably; there was not much else he could do.

They left him alone, got on with their lives, but the atmosphere was thickening day by day. Occasionally his mother could stand no more of it and turned upon him; which provoked only a deeper retreat, the dullness turning actively miserable within him.

He had to produce a portfolio of his work for the college. The best work he had ever done was hers, but he would not show them that. He wished now that he had not destroyed the pictures of the twins. He submitted to the process of college application, went for his interview, trying not to sulk, but hating the whole atmosphere of the place, the intellectualism, the 'What do you read, Henry? . . . Which photographers do you most admire? . . . What do you consider the main social functions of a photographer?' If this is what college would mean, then he really didn't want to know about it. In the event they rejected him, said they liked some of his work, but that he needed to explore and develop his ideas more consciously, be more critical of what he saw and of the images he made. They advised him to re-apply in a year. He was glad to have got to the other side of this, to be free of his last concrete obligation.

'Well,' said his father. 'What are you going to do with your life? I mean, I could find you a job, I'm sure I could. Something bottom-line, of course, with opportunities to work your way up and all that. But . . . but you'll have to want it, Henry, on one level or another, even if, to begin with, it's just something to do, to get you out of the house and with a bit of independence. I suppose you do want that. Don't you?'

'I don't . . . I suppose so.'

'You're not much use to us here, you know, nor to yourself.'

'That bloody girl,' said his mother at last. 'That's what it is, isn't it? Hasn't she even called to tell you where she's living?'

'If she's living,' he muttered, but they ignored that.

'What I can't understand,' his father continued, 'is your total lack of any sort of ambition. I suppose it's probably our fault; but when I was your age, Henry, I wanted to consume the world. The modern morality, if morality is what it is – and I know that's what it claims to be, very loudly – seems to me to be based entirely upon negatives: money is wrong, families are poisonous, the police are corrupt sadists, all governments are, by definition, crooked; everything's worthless except smoking marijuana, listening to interminable trivial music, and having sex. No-one seems interested in making the world work any more.'

'I suppose what you'd really like,' his mother said, 'is to be drifting about with that girl, living the sort of life she leads. Is that it? Is that the freedom you want, Henry?'

'Perhaps,' he said, 'that's what I do want.'

'Drug addiction, venereal disease, living off others in sordid, squalid rooms. I don't believe even you are that naïve, Henry.'

'Perhaps,' he said, 'I'd like the courage to be that naïve.'

He knew that he would give in in the end, that his father would find him a job, that he would do it, that the years would be clocked up, the waters close over him. That was what life was all about.

Jane came home for Christmas. She was teaching in a comprehensive school in Leeds, came home to make peace with her parents perhaps after years when they had not spoken. Henry found her quieter, older, tireder, happy to be absorbed into the reconciling domesticity of home.

She drifted into his room the day after her arrival. He was sitting on his bed reading an old sex comic.

'You've tidied up in here, Henry,' she said, looking around.

'I've been chucking a lot of stuff out,' he said.

'Clearing out the head. I know. It's a bit stuffy in here. Have you been smoking grass up here?'

'Not recently.'

'Got any?'

'No.'

She was looking at the pictures.

'This is Bel, then.'

'Yes. They told you?'

'Oh yes. And I heard from Aunt Naomi. She was very much on your side, you know. They didn't tell me she was black. That's a point in their favour, don't you think?'

'I don't know.'

'She's very beautiful. Poor Henry . . . what've they said about these pictures?'

'Nothing. We don't mention it.'

'Not even the nude?'

'They don't come in here very often, don't look when they do.'

'That's a stunning photo, Henry. Can I have a copy of it?'

'No.'

'Give it to me for Christmas. Put it in a glossy frame. I'll unwrap it and show it around. Won't we have fun?'

'Leave it alone, Jane.'

She came to him and sat by him, took his hands.

'Oh, my poor little brother. I know what it's like, you know, to have someone who makes you feel so good that it hurts, then to lose them. I do know. D'you think . . . d'you think she'll contact you?'

'No.'

'What was it like with her?'

He felt something knotting inside him, a whole complexity of feeling coming into play, twisting and jamming in him.

'It's all right,' she said. 'If you can't talk about it.'

'I've never felt I was any use,' he said. 'Only with her. I'm not any use, to anyone. I take pictures, but they're not that good, not really. I'm just . . . just nothing, Jane. But when she was here . . .'

'Get yourself away, Henry. Take that fucking job that he's trying to set up for you. That's what's screwing you up. You're still part of the fixtures and fittings here, and it's time you weren't. Whatever that woman did to you, she woke you up. Don't go back to sleep again now. Okay? Now . . . now we've got to work out, you and I, how we're going to get through fucking Xmas without murdering either of our parents or either of our sisters. I would suggest that we get a big supply of dope in and stay happily stoned for the duration. How about it?'

'That's the second one of those I've had today,' his mother said, coming back into the drawing room where they were watching television.

'One of what, darling?'

'I pick up the telephone, start to give the number and it goes dead.'

'Oh?' his father said. 'I had one of those yesterday. Perhaps the line's on the blink.'

Something jumped into Henry. He kept as still as he could for five minutes, until the telephone had been forgotten and the film had re-absorbed their attention; then he stood and wandered to the door.

Out in the hall, he watched the telephone and willed it to ring. Since Christmas he had been ready. His talk with Jane, his progressive sense of nausea at the whole family pantomime, had decided him.

360

He had a bag packed. He had cash. He was ready. He had agreed to go for the interview that his father had arranged, kept them at bay with that, would go to the job if necessary; but it was only waiting, getting through the days, his courage to leave leaking steadily away; but now, at last, the miracle: she was out there, and she was trying to ring through to him.

The telephone rang three times over the next twenty-four hours; twice for his mother and once another silent call that his father took. Then, on New Year's Day, they went out to lunch and it rang for him.

'Henry Drewer here,' he said clearly.

'Henry?'

'Where are you?'

'Graving Street. Off Westbourne Grove. Number twenty. Basement flat. Henry?'

'Can I come?'

'Look . . . I didn't want to. . . .'

'Bel? Can I come and see you?'

'Yes.'

'Now?'

'Yes.'

'I'm on my way.'

. . . *twelve* . . .

He came off a filthy street where filthy sleet ran slashing through, where filthy eyes watched him from paranoia and elysium, and trod his way down filthy steps into a cluttered area full of old refuse. The windows were painted white, as was the glass on the door. The whiteness, covered by a layer of external grime, gave an air of the madhouse, a blindness, somewhere locked in upon itself. He was frightened here, recalled the line of retreat that still lay wide open behind him: he could be back home before they even knew he had gone. He tapped lightly on the door.

She opened it almost immediately. It led into a hallway that was in dense shadow. He could see only her eyes, a brief registering of him, without comment. He went in and she closed and locked the door behind him, opened a door and went into a room. He followed her.

His first impression of the room was of a formless greyness, then she turned on the light, a low, bare bulb that hung from a wire in the centre, and he could see the room for what it was. It was a white room: white-walled and white-windowed, bare of all furniture or decoration. In the middle of the floor was a double mattress with a heap of blankets, her bag, some food wrappings, a couple of books.

'Have you any change for the fucking meter?' she said.

He burrowed in his pocket and held out a palm full of change. She took the coins she needed and went to the edge of the room. The coins clattered, a match struck and with a hiss and a pop the fire was ignited. She sat down before it and chafed her hands. He crossed the room and sat down beside her, to look at her. She knew he was doing this, let him look. She was cold and tired and dirty, but he knew her, recognised the set of her mouth. It was not as bad as he had thought it might be. He began tentatively to be happy.

'Do they know you're here?' she asked.

'No.'

'Can you stay a bit?'

'Yes . . . do you need anything, Bel?'

'Yeah, the usual, the usual, but . . . I had a job, washing . . . washing fucking toilets. I put some money together for the winter. I blew most of it on dope. I could've found another job. I didn't want to call you out, Henry, really I didn't.'

She moved to him and nestled against him, tucked herself into his arms and he let her cry, proud of his being there.

'I'm sorry,' she said.

'It's all right.'

'No, it's not. I got stoned, down here, all alone. I wanted . . . I wanted to go and get fucked. I'm a fucking wreck again, Henry. I wanted to die. I've never wanted to die before. I knew you'd come if I called. I didn't want to call you. Whatever I've got, you're going to get it too this time, but this time it's in here, in my head. I used to be all right on my own, but I'm not any more. Just for a bit . . . stay here . . . give me an hour then you can go home again.'

'I've left home.'

'Bullshit.'

'I mean it.'

'What about that college?'

'They didn't want me, so that's out of the way. Bel, I'm free. Really, I am. Really.'

'You think this is freedom?'

'It's my freedom.'

'You stupid wanker.'

'Oh yes.'

They were quiet for a while, a damaged element in the fire making a slow popping sound which became hypnotic. He felt very still, with the turning of the world heavier and heavier about him.

'D'you want to eat?' he asked.

'In a while.'

'D'you want to make love?' he asked.

'Yes.'

They shuffled themselves across to the mattress and began to undress. It became functional, a sequence of actions rather than a rush of emotions or desires. They looked and touched with a quiet certainty of what they were about. They lay down together, stretched out, covered themselves with blankets, made warmth together. When he moved over her, she clung to him, wrapped her arms and legs about him tightly. He held her head, lifted on knees and elbows, entered her with a sweet ease, stroked himself slowly; about which the steadiness of her clutching, her containment of him, her commitment to him, grew into a sufficiency. He had imagined this many times; but the actuality surprised him. The flaw in his imagining had been the assertion of his own pleasure, the release of her pleasure; this was not the point of it at all. The point was their simple intimacy, being here, doing this, the kindness and care of it, the loose smile that seemed to fill him, the strength of her limbs about him, the flatness of her body against his, the small push and slip of their lower limbs that was all that was necessary, the interchange of tense breathing. He had never been given sex with this completeness before. When he came it was simply an ending, a release of himself, a slide into stillness.

Afterwards, with the same simplicity, they separated, dressed and began a life together in the white room.

. . . *thirteen* . . .

They wintered in the white room, keeping warm, keeping quiet, hiding away and making love.

Often she wept: small, sad leakages of tears, her mind distant, her body poised; or an overflow of sudden shame, sudden remembrance, turing and pressing herself into pillows, locking herself in the bathroom; or a torrent of black misery, curling and violent, beating herself against things, sinking into exhaustion. He was never afraid, watched and waited for her, accepted this, took perhaps a secret excitement in it, in the privilege of these intimacies, knowing that they were, in some way, however closed she seemed, offered to him, knowing that she would turn at last for the comfort that welled inside him, that he learned to give, actively and passively, both, a dance of his needs and her needs.

For her he was a continual miracle. Her ugliness burst from her again and again and she could never push him away; however hard she dug, whatever filth came from her, he was always there with a curious, innocent acceptance, a pleasure even, a devouring interest in her that gave her strange strength, strange freedom, strange belonging, most of all to herself. She wondered what she would have to do to lose him, shuddered at the possibilities, terrified of losing him, terrified of the future that stole upon them steadily. Older than he, she knew that hiding away and making love did not make a world, and that a world would have to be made, some sort of world that would have claims that would have to be met, things that would pull them and shape them beyond their own perfect, hermetic intimacy.

When spring came, they took to the roads. There were financial needs upon them, but firstly it was adventure, escape, releasing themselves into the world. There was a farm in the West Country that she had heard of, a place where some people she knew had once been. They did not know if it existed, nor what sort of place it would be if ever they found it; but they set off for it joyful, the new air blowing into their bodies, shivering over their sensitive surfaces.

Bussing at dawn out to the western suburbs they stood at the mouth of a lay-by, arterial traffic roaring past them, blasting them with exhaust, showering them with dust, their thumbs out into the stream, fishing the traffic for a friend. A lorry driver offered them a ride to Bristol and they bundled into his cab. He spoke little. Bel leant against Henry and relaxed herself into the rumble of the engine, stirring at the gear changes, dozing eventually, whilst Henry looked wide-eyed at the evolving landscape.

They were in Bristol by noon. It took them a while to work their way out of the unfamiliar city, into the open country, south. They caught a lift off a loud woman in an estate car with a mangy dog in the back. They had the name of the farm, and the name of a village which it was near. The woman, dropping them at the edge of a small country town, directed them down a road which, in ten miles, would take them to the village.

The afternoon was hot and, in the small valleys through which the road ran, the light spring heat was compacted about them. When the road rose over a hill-brow, a sharp wind caught them. They hitched when cars came, but the road was narrow and the cars infrequent. They moved more and more slowly, spending time lolling on banks, feeling life slow deliciously about them, wandering apart down the middle of the road, the drift of their freedom directionless. They felt themselves expand after their months of seclusion. They regarded one another and laughed. The sun began inevitably to go down.

Around them woods clustered, enticing with darkness and concealments. They crossed a gate, went down a steep field and spent an hour's solitude in a thick copse, in the chill shadow of dark trees, a little scared, a little lost, the reality of their situation fixing them. They had intended, perhaps, to make love here; but the woodland seemed to expose them to something that they had not counted upon, a starkness below which they were small. They moved there with an instinctive caution, talked in whispers, heard and sensed things continuously, eventually breaking back into the open, striving up the steep field and arriving back on the road, breathless and a little desperate, the shadows now filling the road, a fall of cloud rising behind them.

The rain caught them from behind, the light of the sunset in their eyes, a sudden blast of strong wind, then the downpour. At first they turned into it laughing, flung open their arms, tipped back their faces and danced. Within five minutes they were drenched and shivering and burrowing down against it as it pounded their shoulders and heads, as their flesh grew greasy and the weight of their packs cut into them.

When they saw, off the road, an old barn, dark, open and empty, they bolted for it and stood in its shelter, comfortless and defenceless against the falling night. They looked about them but the gloom of the barn with its reek of petrol and filthy floor offered them no solace. Piles of mouldy sacks and straw against the back wall seemed to move with infestations under their watching.

Bel was better equipped for this situation than Henry, who felt tricked, felt that their luck had turned, that he had led her to this extremity. She held his hand and told him it would be all right, all right. They found a clear space against one of the walls and shuffled up to make some private warmth against the swirl of the wind, the dankness that rose from the walls and floors. They had to be satisfied with jamming their bodies together and generating a small, shuddering friction, slipping into jagged bouts of sleep from which they woke at various times in cramps which invariably led to them both being woken. In the slipstream of dreams they imagined fevers rising into them, dogs bounding in upon them, waking to find the other gone.

At dawn, they rose stiff and unrested with a grey mist cutting them off from the world. They ate the last of their food, Bel smoked the last cigarette. When they were ready to set out again, he called to her and she came and hugged him. Outside a grey world waited for them, larger than he had imagined, with hidden extremities against which the strength of her arms about him, and the small rise of himself towards her, were all that he had to defend himself. A spasm of fear took him, and she pressed herself upon it to hold it down, to gather it in to herself.

Soon they were out in the mist and the barn was lost behind them, and the road was lost ahead of them. They trudged on.

... *fourteen* ...

It was afternoon before, at last, they came within reach of their destination. They crossed a stile and made their way along a footpath between a high hedge and a roughly tilled field, stony and beginning its spring show of weeds. A wariness had caught them both. They were silent, walked single file, Bel leading, walking slowly, registering the landmarks. Henry followed dumbly. The path took a sharp turn and led them into a belt of woodland. The ground sloped under them, drew them down. Henry wanted to stop and sit for a bit, to settle himself, to lean himself against her for a few moments. He was cold with a coldness that seemed to come off his flesh.

'There it is,' she said, halted three yards ahead of him.

He moved up to her and saw the farm lying in the cradle of the valley. It was an old stone building in a litter of outhouses. Smoke rose lethargically from chimneys and various outlying fires. There were goats and chickens, and children running amongst disembowelled machines; various adults moved or lounged or were stooped over various employments. It gave the impression of a camp, somewhere taken over by renegades, pulled to pieces by a sprawl of disordered lives. He registered this as they walked, for Bel would not stop, did not wait for him, pushed on down the track before he could detain her. This was what she had expected. She recognised it from the mess of her past; whatever apprehensions crowded her, this was where they had been heading, and she was driven by a determination to engage with this place quickly, jumping at the darkness within her, trusting him to follow her.

They attracted curiosity but little sustained attention as they passed a group of children who were squatted filthy about a large puddle, playing with wood-chips. The first adults they came upon were two women sitting beside a large tub of water, washing potatoes, great boulders of them, rubbing the soil off with blue hands, working slowly, caressing the potatoes as if each one would reveal something.

Bel squatted down beside them and looked back for Henry, who squatted down beside her.

'Hi,' she said.

'Hi,' one of the women said. She wore a red headscarf which bound an abundance of brown hair. Her cheeks were bright red and her eyes sleepy.

'We've been on the road,' Bel said. 'From London.'

'You come to join in?'

'Is that all right?'

'Sure. Here.' She handed Bel a potato.

'You'd better go see Priest,' the other woman said, older, thinner, watching them with tight lips.

'Priest?'

'He takes the decisions,' the dark woman said. 'You have to see him.'

Bel had begun to wash the potato. 'Where can I find him?' she said.

'In the house.'

'All right. I'm Bel. This is Henry.'

'Hi,' Henry said.

'I'm Tess,' the first woman said with a giggle of embarrassment.

Bel handed her the potato back and stood.

'Thanks,' she said, then looked at Henry, who struggled up and followed her.

Through a thicket of glances and greetings that were sometimes the slight raising of eyes, sometimes a wave and a shout, they made a complex path through the outfall of the farm and its buildings towards the house. The air in the valley was still and sharp with the reek of smoke and manure. Entering the house was a plunge into thick murk: woodsmoke, dankness, dust and flesh. Bel moved carefully towards the sound of voices and came to a large, steamy kitchen.

'Where can I find Priest?' she called.

A woman came from her work and smiled at them.

'Hello,' she said. 'Our first arrivals? I'm Jan.'

She was thin and wore a dark kaftan, had hair that hung down her back. She gave them both quick embraces, presses of her loose body. They told her their names.

'Magic,' she said. 'I'll take you up.'

They followed her through various strange chambers crowded

368

with furniture and heaps of books and clothes. They felt, in their jeans and jackets, with their tight packs, bizarrely overdressed. They ascended a broad wooden staircase through grimy light that fell from above and behind them. At the top of the staircase were large double doors through which Jan, who walked with a light, tiptoe spring, entered.

'Priest?' she said. 'Our first arrivals. This is Bel. This is Henry.'

Priest was a large man in middle age. He sat on a low bed that spread over most of the room. Tall windows threw a curtain of light behind him, but they could see his size, the rolls of naked flesh that covered his body. He sat cross-legged, wearing only a loose pair of silky pantaloons, out of the bottom of which great naked feet protruded with yellow, claw-like toenails. He was bald-crowned but fully bearded. Great clumps of hair sprayed out from his head, from which enormous ringed ears jutted. He viewed them with small, sharp eyes.

'Why have you come?' he asked, almost formally, deep-voiced.

'We need some space,' Bel said.

'Who do you belong to?'

'Only to each other.'

'Show me what you have brought.'

Bel opened her pack and looked to Henry to follow. They sat down, Jan with them, and emptied out everything before Priest. He peered closely down at their things, examined them closely, opening toothpaste tubes, feeling in the lining of garments, flicking through the pages of books.

'Is this all?' he asked.

'Yes.'

'May I have this book?'

'Yes.'

'Do you know where you are?' he said, lifting his face and looking at them, each in turn. 'This is a place of journeys. We are all travellers. Sometimes we travel together, sometimes alone. We live here to help one another on our journeys. Sometimes they are dark journeys. You understand, Bel, but does he?'

'He travels with me,' she said.

Priest nodded judiciously. 'You have brought nothing else with you?'

'No.'

'Are there others who might follow you?'

'No.'

'I need to see everything. You understand? I need to be able to trust you and to feel your trust in me.'

Bel nodded and began to undress, handing everything to him as she did so; not only her clothes, but her earrings, her bracelets. Henry blindly followed. When she was naked, when Priest had felt and sniffed at her clothes, he beckoned her. She knelt beside him and he examined her minutely: her arms, her hair, lifted her breasts, carefully touched her genitals. She stared firmly into his eyes. Henry was terrified, outraged, abandoned, sitting there huddled over his own nakedness. He look at Jan who sat and smiled at him, peering at him.

'Only this,' Priest said, smoothing Bel's forearms.

'Not for more than a year,' she said.

'That is a journey only into the pit,' he said.

'I know.'

'Good. I'm still not sure about your friend.'

Bel reached out her hand and Henry took it, hoping that she might get him out of this, but she pulled and he was dragged over to Priest who began upon him. He knelt up as she had done, leant himself back, trembled as the delicate, precise fingers worked over him.

'There's a lot of soft flesh here, Henry. You have no smell. That makes me suspicious.'

Henry swallowed, closed his eyes, swollen with shame as the delicate fingers weighed his testicles, as mad-head stooped and sniffed at him.

'Only fear,' Priest said. 'A thin fear of being. Henry?'

'What?'

'What are you afraid of?'

'You.'

Priest laughed. 'Put yourself away, Henry. Bel will explain it to you. Bel? You keep an eye on him. I have enough terrors from the drowning, without terrors from those still standing on the edge of the pool. Jan? You've room in the attic, haven't you?'

'Oh yes,' she said enthusiastically.

'Henry?' he said.

'What?'

'You come and talk to me if it gets too heavy for you.'

'Right,' he said. It was already too heavy. He felt hopeless as he followed Jan and Bel, grabbing together his things. He wanted to be alone with Bel, ached for it. His whole life had been lived from a strength of privacy; even at the worst moments he had been able to slide into that. The real nature of this place was becoming manifest.

They were to camp in an attic, bare boards, sky-lit, clean apart from heaps of belongings in various places on the floor. They were not to have a room to themselves; it was stupid of him to have imagined they would have done.

There was one other occupant in residence when Jan took them through; a woman, a girl really, younger than I am, he thought. She lay on a mattress, sleeping, or semi-sleeping, pregnant. Jan stooped down beside her and whispered to her, touched her. Henry watched the girl's hands reach up and engage with Jan as if their conversation was principally in the caresses. He did not like to watch this, turned to Bel, who was looking round the room shrewdly. She touched Henry's elbow and pointed: on the low beams pale membranes were tacked, row after row of them, like strange narcotic plants hung up to dry, but which were not plants, which were exhausted condoms. Bel was watching him, clutched his elbow as he passed through a moment of panic.

'Bel? Come and meet Jo-Jo.'

Bel went and knelt by the girl whilst Jan came and smiled at him, tiptoed past him, brushing the condoms with her hand. They clattered drily.

Their moment alone came when Jo-Jo had risen and waddled off somewhere with Jan, when they were clearing a space on the floor and laying out their sleeping-bags.

'Bel?'

She didn't look at him. He suspected her of muffling a giggle.

'Is this what you want?' he asked.

She stopped, stooped over her things.

'You followed me here,' she said. 'I promise you, I won't let go of you, but you must promise to keep with me. This is the logical thing, Henry. Don't let me down now.'

'Bel, I'm so scared that I can't breathe properly here.'

She turned then and clung herself about him.

'That's all right. Really. It's all right. Being afraid of this is like taking the bandage off a wound. Just go with it.'

371

Jan took them down to eat. They were given bowls of vegetable pottage, full of beans and onion, flabby bits of mushroom and twiggy bits of herb. Henry found it repellent and Bel ate most of his. He had to satisfy himself with a dense cube of black bread and a mug of acid cider. They ate at a table in a large dining room, with Priest presiding and the places around them filled and vacated with a procession of the inhabitants, knotty men with forests of beard, full-fleshed women who heaved their bodies about in kaftan sacks, a scampering squabbling anarchy of children. During the eating, the children chattered and shouted, but the adults remained stolidly silent, concentrating upon the food, masticating with eyes half-closed, reaching across for what they needed. The sounds of their digestion filled the room, Priest watching, apprising, considering. Henry caught his eye on several occasions, blushing, but, after a while, coming to concede the benevolence of this scrutiny, the concern, feeling himself somehow responding, or wanting to respond, or beginning to want to respond to it, something loosening within him; not his bowels, certainly.

From there they proceeded to their attic. Night was falling and the routine of the farm was strictly dawn to dusk. Whether it was the cider, or whether there had been something in the food, Henry felt a narcotic flushing in his blood, the details of the room receding into indistinction, or looming too large to be apprehended. His only point of reference was the quick, quiet body of his lover, which he would not let out of reach.

Candles were lit. Jan was there, sitting with them, and various others. Jo-Jo lay asleep. The condoms flapped and flickered above them. Outside, owls hooted, and within someone was singing somewhere, someone chanting, more than one but not the same chant, a babble of chanting that rose and fell in complex cycles that he imagined as the swirling of water, intricate and unified. Henry leant against Bel who was talking to someone, and the vibration of her voice filled his head. Her fingers were locked in his. He closed his eyes and fell into somewhere soft inside his head.

He felt someone take his loose hand and, when he opened his eyes, Jan was sitting before them, naked, cross-legged, her hair pouring over her shoulders, holding his hand and Bel's hand, lifting them ceremoniously to her breasts. A candle flickered between them, before her, flickering into the splay of her thighs, throwing her shadow onto the ceiling behind. Her open vulva glistened and moved. This was monumental nakedness; it filled him with a flush of erotic energy, blind and universal, as if it had come upon him from outside, as if he were connected to it, had taken root in strange soil and it was flooding up the cell-chains of his body. Hands held his hands tightly or he would have shed his clothes there and then and followed the propulsion of that energy.

Later, Bel had drawn him to the wall where their sleeping-bags lay, was pulling his clothes from him in awkward tangles, undressing him like a child. He was cold and lonely and he whined for her, reached out, suspected her of abandoning him in the darkness, cried out with shame when at last she settled her body against his. He clung to her, urged himself at her to find her, to loosen himself within her whilst she wriggled and pushed him back until he was securely sheathed; then she deftly straddled him and he was safe again, calm, clear, touching the cusps and swells of her body as she rode him with slow lifts of herself.

When the quick rigour had clutched and released them and she lay herself down beside him and covered them against the night chill, he whispered, 'I want you to have my baby here.' This made her cry, shuffling up against him, slipping into her old wretchedness which he comforted, perplexed and flooded with tenderness for her.

They were woken at dawn and went down with the others for the ritual that began the day. They spilled sleepy and bleared from the many chambers of the farm and trooped in heavy silence out into the fields, loose garments flapping, faces grey in the dawn. Henry, happy now, woken in the nakedness of his lover, sticky-fleshed and bathed in the sweat of her, plodded beside her through the dawn, open to anything that might be required of him.

He expected some oblation to the sun-power, not that they were going to see much sun today. He would join in, was glad of the chance to, did not believe in the sun-power but was open to revelation should it be offered to him. Anything was possible.

They moved into a big, uneven field full of stones. They scattered about it in clumps, then proceeded, communally, to manure it. Jan was there, squatted double with her kaftan pulled up about her waist, smiling her smile at him, then tensing and smiling to herself. The acid reek of shit blew across the field. Henry turned to see Bel squatted, bare-arsed, her head buried in her hands. He glanced around the field to see that he was the only person upright, apart from those who had done and were returning. He fumbled at his trousers, closed his eyes and squatted quickly, felt his bowels knot defiantly, felt the wind blowing sharply at his puckered anus.

He looked across at Bel, called to her. She looked up, grim-faced. He shuffled across the ground towards her, stumbling and knocking his knee on a stone.

'I can't manage this,' he said.

She took his hands, gripped them, then relaxed, her face breaking into a beatific smile, her hands reaching up to his face, kissing him, the black smell of her bowels blowing into his nose; at which, with gasp or surprise, he felt the push of his muscles and a long, fluent turd dropped from him.

'Bel?'

'What?'

'Have you got anything to. . . .'

'No. Have you?'

They began to laugh, lolling together with their dirty arses stuck out into the wind in a field full of glistening new shit.

. . . *fifteen* . . .

The seasons of the farm fell fluently upon them, caught them up in their process. If you wish the land to love you, then you must love the land, you must work on it with your hands, measure it with your footsteps, bend your back over it, ploughing and sewing and weeding, anointing it with your sweat, emptying the soil of your bowels upon it, rubbing it into your skin until the stain of the earth is upon your flesh. You belong to the earth and its delights must be your delights, its toils your toils. Thus, in the turning of the seasons, you will come to know yourself, to possess yourself in the full liberty of your nature.

Henry and Bel neither believed nor disbelieved such exhortations; they were simply what life on the farm was about. They were there and they set themselves to work. There were some who did not work, who sat on the edge of fields playing pipes, or who never emerged from the darkness of the house; but they needed the work, needed to belong, needed to be out in the fields, hardening their hands on spades and hoes and scythes, knotting their muscles and feeling the sharp air open their lungs; engaging in the multitudinous struggle of the community to bring forth a subsistence from the wilful, stony soil; moving on the slow wheels of profound, repetitive manual labour.

In the first weeks, they dragged themselves in, ate and fell into exhausted sleep, beyond talking or lovemaking. The work dulled them beyond thought, beyond engagement with any of the others, their brightest moments at dawn, squatting in the field and grinning at one another in the earthy satisfaction of defecation. They kept within sight of one another whilst they worked, ate together, took consecutive turns at the passing flagons of cider, noted the others but did not engage with them, sustained their solitude and fed upon its strength.

There was a strange respect for privacy there, strange in lives that were lived so proximately, where nothing normally kept private was hidden. All external operations of life were held in common, but below that everyone seemed to pursue their private journeys, as Priest had said. The nature of another's private journey was never open. It was, below the confusions of the surface, a place of retreat and contemplation.

What was their journey? To begin with they were just holding on, lifted and dropped by the days in an unreflective blur of immediacy. Even on Sundays, when the work was suspended and everyone lolled about in a communal stupor, they could do no more, were tireder by evening than they were during the week. Bel was worried, watching Henry sleep in the sun, that he was becoming lost here. She pondered the ease of his life compared to hers, his lack of suspicions and aggression, the shallows of his intellectual training; she worried that he would become simply stupid here.

One sunny Sunday, she roused him and took him into the woods where they made love. She found herself tense and desperate below his slow, easy possession of her. She felt that he had lost the sense of her, that this was, in spite of their apparent privacy, another communal physical action, that it might have been anyone, she might have been anyone, he might have been anyone; and being anyone meant being no-one.

When they were done and dressed, and he was rolling a little tobacco in a paper, she said, 'I think I'm going to work in the house for a bit, get in on the centre of things.'

'Fine,' he said.

She had not wanted him to be difficult about this, but his casual acceptance of it irritated her.

'Are you happy here?' she asked.

'Oh yes.' He smiled at her. 'I feel really alive here. Don't you?'

'No,' she said. 'Not yet.'

'What's wrong?'

She had caught him at last, but found the lurch of his concern inhibiting.

'I don't know what I'm doing here yet,' she said, looking down.

They were quiet then, and she looked through the trees to the farm buildings below them. She wanted to go down there and shout at someone, to make something happen there.

'Bel?'

'What?'

He said nothing more until she turned to him and saw that his eyes were full of tears.

'Don't leave me here, will you?'

She held him and they exchanged emotional intimacies that reached her far more profoundly than had their lovemaking.

She attached herself to Jan in the kitchen. The work here was lighter and far less purposeful or organised than the work in the fields. Although there were one or two men who lingered uselessly about inside, it was essentially a province of women. She preferred the rough equality of the fields, but she needed the space to think and look and find herself something to be here, other than a body.

There was baking and cleaning of vegetables, forays out to cull herbs and fungi, and a lot of sitting about talking, exchanging old lives which were offered here in fantasies of brutality and exploitation, escalating mythologies; as if the world they had fled from was, by definition, dark, paranoid, dreadful. For Bel, who told them very little about her past, they were running away from themselves, hiding here from small inadequacies that had shaken them from university courses, from angry parents and blind relationships. She knew that she would never be able to belong to this, that shame and pain and fear could not be avoided so easily.

Jan was one of the brightest of them. She had been here a year, had arrived with a man who had since left. 'He just wasn't big enough for what we have here,' she said. She described her old life as 'sheer constipation'. Her parents, she said, probably hadn't turned the television off long enough to notice that she had gone. 'I'm here for the screwing,' she said. 'One day everyone'll learn the secret, turn to the person next to them on the bus, in the office, in the street, and realise that it doesn't matter who they are. They're just alive and screwing is the only way to prove it.' She believed this, truly, lived in a dream where sex was simple pleasure in a wonderful democracy of bodies.

'Have you never been in a situation where you didn't want what was happening to you?' Bel asked her.

'No. Never. It's never like that. You just have to open yourself, just have to accept everything as real and now and free.'

'And what if your partner doesn't accept all that?'

'They learn. You teach them. You liberate them.'

Bel shuddered to herself.

Henry found that he preferred to be out of sight of his lover during the day, found that he could lose himself in the work more readily, became sociable with the other men, caught up in the concerns of the coarse agriculture, the seasoning of mysticism, the planting to star signs in spiral patterns, the tasting of the earth to see if it was ready, the reverential addresses to growing things. It was all a game, but he played it laughing, uninhibited by Bel's absence, free of her dark distance.

They would meet at supper and, after their separation, their touching grew lively again, their lovemaking pleasant and dreamy; for him at least. He was not unaware of her difficulties, knew that something was being held back in her. He was too tired to struggle with her, believed that the spirit of the place would soak through to her eventually. He trusted her absolutely, lived his freedom always on the basis she gave him, felt that his involvement here was firstly a loyalty to her. He did not think of the future.

He thought occasionally of his parents, of the life that had been his before this; but it had no claim upon him. It was as if it had always been thus, as if he was completely liberated. At times it frightened him: he was free, yes, but whether that meant he was more in control of his life, he did not know; and if he was not in control of his life, what was?

One night Bel woke him and he came unwillingly from his sleep to see a cluster of women about Jo-Jo, heard her cries and knew that she was giving birth. The women, all naked, were clustered about Jo-Jo, soothing her and chanting to her, mopping her brow.

'You'd better go,' Bel whispered.

He went quickly; this was a mystery of women to which he did not belong.

It was a bright night and he wandered out into the yard, into the cool, wondering where he might go and curl himself up to sleep. He heard his name called, and Jan emerged from the shadows, drifting through the warm dark, her hair lifting like a mist.

'Why aren't you up there with your sisters?' he asked.

'It scares me,' she said. 'I don't want to see that.'

'Will it take long?'

'All night, I expect.'

'Oh well, I'm going to sleep in the barn.'

'Can I come with you?'

'Surely.'

It was a long birth. Bel felt more purposeful here than she had felt at any time since her arrival, felt that these limp women were at last being confronted with some sting of reality. One of them had been a nurse, so they weren't entirely without commonsense. At dawn, Jo-Jo, in a motion that seemed more exhausted than anything, at last propelled a large, purple boy into the waiting hands. There were many tears, many hurts and fears brought into the open there; after which they all crawled off to sleep.

Bel woke, sometime late in the morning, to find herself alone in the attic, disconnected with the day. She wandered down to find that the birth had occasioned a day of celebration, of various rituals. A feast was being prepared, a goat killed, the only time they ate meat, apparently. She did not want anything to do with this, so she returned to the attic.

She found Henry there, alone, sitting on their sleeping-bags hunched over. She was glad to see him, sat beside him and put her arms about him, to find him strangely locked against her.

'Did you find somewhere to sleep?' she asked.

'With Jan,' he said bluntly.

She thought of many casual things to say, by which time it was too late to say them; thought no, it doesn't matter, I can cope with this, knowing that it did matter, that she couldn't cope with it.

'Why the fuck did I have to know?' she said.

He looked at her as if this was the worst thing she could have said.

. . . *sixteen* . . .

When Jan came up there were tears and a reconciliation of sorts. They slept together, the three of them, clothed and careful, although Bel awoke in the night to find herself entangled with the restless, sleeping Jan. She freed herself and lay like a chaperone between the sleeping sinners; and indeed she was afraid to leave them even to relieve herself, afraid that when she returned they would have found one another again, half-surfacing from their sleep into some half-willed conjunction.

She knew that Henry had committed no more than one thoughtless carnal act; but that in itself might have unlocked something, might have liberated him from her in ways that he himself did not understand. She knew that at the moment he was perplexed and ashamed, but that it would be easy for such feelings to dull, for the formless tolerations of this place to dissolve him. She imagined him disappearing before her eyes, becoming like all the others, less than the others, a cipher of them. She knew that his beauty was also his weakness. As dawn began to leak into the attic, in the few minutes before she would shake them awake to go down and do their duty in the fields, she knew that she would have to get Henry out of here, and that she would have to fight to do it, that simply to take him and run would not be enough.

Jan had been a treat, a quick, bright pleasure that had come upon him before he had even thought about it. What he could not understand, in the slough of recrimination that followed, was the contempt it generated in him. Jan, in the morning light, had seemed disgusting, ugly, and when she had smiled at him, touched him, he had wanted to hit her. He had run to Bel for help, but she too had become ugly. He had wanted, he supposed, tears and comfort from her, but she had been hard against him. He despised himself for expecting her toleration of his betrayal; and he despised himself for the anger her hardness roused in him. It was as if he had found a side of her that he had never known about; or rather, a side of himself that he had never known about. He became, for the first time since he had left home, actively unhappy.

The attic began to oppress him. It stank of women, of the rankness of their bodies, the heavy reek of their sexual complexities. Jo-Jo returned and their sleeps were broken by the crying of the baby; he could not move in or out of the room, it seemed without the sight of her squeezing her fat breasts into the child's face, grew nauseous at the pallid reek of infant excrement. Jo-Jo herself, coming round after the long sleep of her pregnancy, seemed monumentally dumb, hardly even registering him.

He and Bel did not make love any more. It was not, at least on his part, a conscious decision; and, if she had withdrawn herself from his contamination, it was no deprivation for him. To resume their intimacy would have involved a profound scene of penitence and forgiveness that he did not know how to approach, was not ready for. Whenever Jan and he were alone, she smiled at him with a teasing guilt that he knew had an invitation embedded within it. It made him angry, but he knew that below the anger lay the possibility that, one day, he would give in, would bury himself in it, with Jan or with someone else, with Bel herself even. He felt a fog beginning to close around him.

The summer began to end and he stood working in the fields in rain squalls, the earth turning into a heavy, sucking mess below him, reeking like liquid shit; which he supposed it essentially was, like him, like all humanity, composed of shit of passed ages, held together briefly in a little knot of awareness and discomfort before sliding back into its constituent essence.

She watched Henry's unhappiness and bled for him silently; but it was not in her nature to watch and wait. One autumn morning, she took a pair of scissors to a mirror and cropped off her hair, cutting it close to her scalp, leaving a convict stubble on the dome of her head, from which her ears jutted. She then persuaded Jan to help her carry pitchers of hot water across to the bath-house, filled a tub and washed herself minutely in a haze of steam. Jan watched her curiously, perhaps even erotically.

'It's time you grew up, Jan,' she said as she rose from the water and dried herself. 'It's time you stopped being the farm whore.'

Jan was silent, gazing into the glassy scum on the bath.

'You want the water?' Bel asked.

Jan shook her head, and Bel reached down to pull out the plug, stood away as the water rushed from beneath the tub and coursed across the cement floor to the sluice. Jan was in its path and let it run over her bare feet. Bel stopped and watched her.

'Will you help me, Bel?' she said quietly.

'What d'you need?'

'Will you . . . sleep with me? I hate being alone. I'm afraid of the dark. Sometimes . . . sometimes, it's not the screwing at all. Sometimes I don't even like that any more, not much. It . . . it always goes to the same place, more or less, but . . . but afterwards it's warm. I don't know how to be alone.'

Bel put her arms around her.

'All right. I'll sleep with you for a bit, Jan, but no sex, no little masturbation to help you sleep. That you have to do on your own. Right?'

She nodded.

'And there may be times when Henry needs me more than you do.'

She nodded, looked up, smiled, and gave Bel a schoolgirl kiss on the cheek.

He hated it. He hated Bel's bullet head. He hated them sleeping there, assumed it was an act of revenge against him, the sisters forming a solidarity against him. His first thought was to move out, to sleep down with Bill and Dave and Andy and their women; but after an evening spent down there, watching them slip from laughter and wild-eyed cavortings into chants and songs, palms pressed flat against palms to feel one another's vibrations, and thence folding down into their couplings, and their threesomes and foursomes, multiplications and clusterings, he felt excluded; not that he couldn't have joined in had he wanted to, slipped his nakedness amongst theirs and found his place amongst the slithering limbs and gripping lips; but, watching the promiscuous cycles of it, the purpose of which seemed to be a game of outrage, taking someone by surprise, he felt weary and lonely; and, if he was aroused, it was dumb masturbatory arousal, which shortly he took with him back up to the attic where Bel and Jan were sleeping and Jo-Jo was lying, humming tunelessly with the baby asleep on her belly.

In the morning, Bel came to him, sat beside him and held his hand.

'If you need me. . . .' she said sadly.

'I'm all right,' he said, rolling away from the burden of her affection.

He went to see Priest, didn't say much, sat and let Priest look at him. He felt awkward under their strange mentor's penetration. He shifted about, expecting advice, insight, consolation, something.

'This is all there is, Henry,' he said.

'I know.'

'Isn't it enough for you?'

'No.'

'What more do you want?'

'I don't know.'

But as he sat there, an idea came to him.

'Priest? Is there any paint anywhere?'

There was a whole store of it, boxes of cans, thinners, undercoats and overcoats, a treasury of colours, gloss and matt, brushes of all imaginable sizes. He regarded it with a greedy delight.

He transferred most of this store up to his end of the attic. There was a space of blank wall there which he brushed and washed minutely. The kitchen chimney-breast rose up here, making the work warm. He worked minutely on the old surface, coming to an intimate knowledge of its geography of cracks and patches. When the women returned at nightfall, he realised that he had spent the whole day here. Bel had brought him some food. He slept without thinking about anything except his wall.

The next day, he began to paint. Firstly white; the whole surface covered with a thick layer of emulsion, worked into the irregularities, a fierce unity of nothing. He sat back and stared at it. He did not know what he was going to do with it, but it excited him, generated a blind potential within him. It seemed at last a space in which he could do something. The light began to fade outside, but his wall seemed to glow. He dreamt, or imagined, spreading himself out over this wall, blending into it, becoming invisible before it, filling it with himself spread out in a thin tissue of colour and pattern.

She was alarmed by Henry's obsession with the wall, but she did not interfere. If he was going mad, he was at least doing it quietly, and on his own. She thought that perhaps he was going mad, at times was afraid to look at him; but when she did look, when she came close, he would turn to her and smile his softest smile at her, even reach for her and rub his hand over her stubbly scalp. She was afraid, but she trusted him. She made sure that he had food, but asked nothing, was ready to defend his work, whatever it was.

Meanwhile, she was taking on the women of the farm. What she had begun with Jan was growing in strength and purpose. Jan had been an extremity, but all the others lived, more or less, in the same promiscuous indolence that, Bel felt with a rising, rousing outrage, was ultimately a negation of themselves, a loss of meaning, or integrity. It was somehow different for the men; it involved them less; they had the work on the farm, the old habits of masculine camaraderie, skills of intellect and craft that these women had not the impetus to acquire. They all lived in myths of freedom and of absolute separation from the corrupt world beyond, but the instinctive patterns of that old world were not so easily shed. Because they had no basis of faith or ideology, the old ways would return with the certainty of fingerprints. Ultimately, the women were there to provide food and to be fucked; their general sexual availability, which was asserted as freedom, Bel began to see and to say, was subjection, and ultimately brutalisation.

She began to throw herself into arguments with the women, with Jan a surprisingly loyal convert.

'Ask Jan,' she would say.

'I've come clear,' Jan would say. 'I own myself again. I don't need anyone to tell me that I'm beautiful any more. I am beautiful.'

Some of the women then began to come up to the attic, for a night only sometimes, often to wait out their periods, sometimes to stay. There was much talking, much laughter, confessions and tears late into the night. As the winter came and the land darkened, so did the men, lurking and clustering, going to Priest and accusing Bel of breaking up the community. Priest was inscrutable, detached, ambiguous, whilst Bel was triumphant, watched her women become stronger, going back to their men when they wanted to with pride and with serious psychological demands; and the men came to know that what they did would now be known and judged by that attic court. In the long winter nights, a new dynamic seemed to have entered the community, a new seriousness.

Henry was treated rather like a household pet in the attic. He seemed to accept them, to disappear into himself, neutered amongst them in spite of his general nakedness. He did not go out now, except for necessities. Through Bel, they came to trust his enclosure enough to open themselves within their sorority, even when he came to sit with them, silent and attentive. Perhaps what he saw and heard was going onto his wall.

Long tendrils thickened and thinned, curled and branched and then wound into immaculate spirals. He began with one colour, then blended it with another, then let the second colour take over before blending it with a third, and so on: red into purple into blue into turquoise, livid green, bright yellow, a glow of orange into a blood line, flowing, spreading, intensifying, coiling at last into nothing. The wall was covered, slowly, minutely, in these designs which he evolved to no pattern, following only a logic of line and colour, sustaining somehow a private balance between them. There was no repetition, no overall structure, just the simple delight of filling the whiteness inch by inch with a dazzling filigree, an assertion of intricacy and multiplicity, and of the unity of purpose behind it.

He did not know why he was doing it, still less what it meant. He could place no objective value upon it. There was a futility to it, no more perhaps than a mindless, mind-numbing doodling. He worked, nevertheless, in blind, semi-arousal. He dreamt in spirals and colours, went briefly from the attic to wash or urinate feeling naked and incomplete, feeling mad away from it. He did not believe their praises of it, hated their attempts to understand it. He sometimes fantasised about Bel, imagined painting her dark skin white then covering her with spirals and whorls. Perhaps only dumb Jo-Jo really understood it, sitting cross-legged beside him as he worked, playing with her child or herself, stunned by motherhood, a mute lump of unregenerated physicality.

. . . *seventeen* . . .

As the work on his wall approached its conclusion, as there was only now a contracting white space in the middle for which he was considering something different, considering perhaps leaving it blank, as he was beginning to look at the other walls of the attic and wondering how he could shift things round to begin work on them, for the first time that he could recall, Jo-Jo spoke to him.

'Henry?'

The voice was heavy, almost masculine. He turned and she was very close to him, so close that he stepped away, took a deep breath. He assumed that this was, at last, some sort of sexual approach; chain reactions of desire and anger began within him. He did not speak, backed to put some space between them.

She stayed still, and he recognised the pain in her face, a pleading hurt that began to move him, to calm him.

'Henry? . . . I think my baby's dead.'

She turned and he followed her to the bundle of blankets on which the naked infant lay. There was a bluish tinge to its skin, and a weight, a stillness, the belly bloated tight, the wisps of hair on its scalp matted. She touched it, pressed her hand upon it, rolled it over. Its limbs flopped hopelessly.

He reached over and touched her, but although his hand lay upon her shoulder, he did not seem to reach her at all. The dead child was everything, was final; before it they were suddenly hopeless and pathetic.

'I'll fetch Bel,' he said, rising slowly, watching to see if she needed him, if she wanted him to stay. She did not move. He went.

Bel gathered the women together, sent messages out and drew them up into the attic where they settled themselves about the stooped Jo-Jo and her loss. Below them the whole community turned towards this still, dead space. Somehow they had all let this happen, felt it personally, a collapse of their belief in themselves, a realisation of their lack of belief in themselves. Life, they had thought, was what all this is about; to life at least we are committed. It was not so. They wept, but not the consoling, communal tears of release; hard, private tears that they knew to be selfish. Within each of them, a flaw of guilt opened.

Word came up from Priest that Jo-Jo and her child should be brought to him. Bel felt she ought to go with her, but did not want to, did not want to go down there to the exposure of eyes. Jan went, the brave and resourceful Jan. Only when they had gone did Bel notice that Henry was not at his wall, had not returned, and she knew at once that she wanted him, only him at this moment.

It was a cold day, icy, and they sat and shivered in the attic, spiteful draughts slipping between them. Bel felt a sexual desperation move through them, a need for blind comfort that was bigger, more brutally assertive than the warm unity she had fostered. This was the first serious test of that unity, and it dissolved, had not the depth to sustain them.

She looked up and he was there. She had not heard him arrive. He stood above her, looking down at her, looking around the others who glanced up at him pitifully. He looked at his wall which, in the gloom, seemed only a mess of scribbling.

'Bel? Please, get rid of them,' he said.

'I can't get rid of them.'

He waited for a few moments, then shrugged, moved across to the wall and began to light the lamps before it. They all turned to watch him, bewildered by his purpose, by the drive of his movement which began to frighten them. He stripped off his clothes and they huddled tighter into theirs at the sight of his cold nakedness. He stooped over his paint pots, began mixing and stirring, then rose with a fat dripping brush and began to cover his designs with white paint, a thick, obliterating layer of it, working over patches where the colour showed through.

One by one, with small, timid glances at Bel, the women began to leave. Bel felt herself at the centre of an expanding emptiness, unable to move out of it, enclosed by it, tightened within it. When, however, the last of them had gone, she rose and went to her lover, shed her clothes, found herself a paintbrush and set to at the opposite edge of the wall. The delicacy and beauty of his work reached her in this proximity as it had never reached her before, and she wept as she covered it, shuddering against the cold, numbing, forcing herself, making her whiteness spread towards his whiteness.

Tomorrow, she knew, they would leave.

First thing, they gathered together their few belongings in their rucksacks and went to see Priest. He asked no questions, gave them money, and a piece of paper on which he had written an address. 'This is somewhere for you to start from,' he said. 'I wish you joy.' Within twenty-four hours, they were back in London.

. . . *eighteen* . . .

Priest's address proved to be a squat, a big old house, not, Henry thought with a cold nervousness, unlike his parents' house. The rooms had large open fireplaces in which heaps of rubbish burned. There was water, but no electricity. They were admitted without question, found themselves a piece of floor where they settled carefully and quietly. People watched them from the cold glooms, some drifting over to see what they had, to ask for money or for dope, making offers to show them things, sell them things, restless eyes and nervous limbs. They felt themselves apprised by sharp, predatory senses. In the night they were woken from their sleep by hands burrowing at their belongings. They felt themselves adrift in a sea of nightmares and tucked themselves tightly in the shelter of one another, wary, being careful not to become involved with each other too privately here.

The farm, by comparison, had been organised and purposeful. Shitting in an open field was greatly preferable to a confrontation with the clotted lavatories, the lockable doors of which seemed to have invited a whole range of private suffering and evacuation. Every part of the house seemed, at some time, to have been subjected to desecration, the working out of some misery upon its opulence, the bringing down of everything into a world of trash. People came here, unloaded themselves, then left, or stayed in accumulating nests of garbage. People came here to stay, gibbering in palsies of addiction or psychosis. Although there were couples, groups, families even, the quiet desperation of the place made everyone seem alone; certainly, to leave your friend, to move into the dark corridors of stairways, was to become lost, solitary, wandering through a maze of others, belonging nowhere.

'It'll be better in the spring,' they were told, but they were appalled. This was the end. To have belonged here would have been to surrender, to lose faith in the world outside in a way that even the paranoias of the farm had not achieved. There, the outside was at least imaginable; here, it was non-existent. Coming from the house onto the street, seeing ordinary people going about their ordinary lives, even after one night there, was like looking at a dream world, a distorted hallucination of lost reality. They were out on the street, but could not have gone back there.

They trudged the streets of bedsitters, rapped on doors and offered all the money they had for a room, any room.

'Look,' Bel said. 'We're clean. No drugs, nothing. We're up from the country. We just need a week, just a week to find ourselves some work, get ourselves going here. We'll die on the street. Please.'

The doors closed monotonously, the eyes glazing, the shoulders shrugging, the warmth of the houses retracted, spurning them. Had they been alone, they might have despaired, might have followed the logic of despair into darkness and surrender.

She asked him at last, 'Do you want to go home, Henry?'

'No,' he said, feeling a flush of angry tears come to his eyes.

They persevered, dogged, silent, determined, throwing themselves against the face of the city until it opened for them. At last it did. A door was opened by a bleary-eyed man with a pigtail and, almost before Bel had finished her speech, he had let them in.

'Keep your bread,' he said. 'I'm not the man. There's a room up at the top. He cleared the last freak out of there, had to break the lock. You can crash there. He's away at the moment. When the man comes for the rent, just tell him the man said you could stay.'

The room stank, but had a bare bed and a basin, and a small gas ring. They camped here, crushed together with the screech and whine of the city below them. Through a thin wall they could hear an argument proceeding late into the night; they could not hear the words, but could hear the tedious cycles of recriminations and defiance, could hear the lurch of bodies, perhaps blows, perhaps murder, perhaps only blind copulation.

With an address, they went to the labour exchange and registered, engaged at last with the mechanism of the world. They found work almost at once. Bel changed bed linen and washed bathrooms in a seedy hotel where prostitutes worked and where frightened men, on the further edge of middle age, had come to live ten years ago, as a stop-gap, and were still there. Henry stacked shelves and swept up in a small supermarket. By the time the landlord returned and barged into their room, they had enough money to pacify him. He was impressed by Henry's clean voice, sniffed about, charged them a month in advance, but resigned himself to them, even coming back to restore the lock. They had made a beginning, had acquired somewhere to hold and contain themselves for a while. They worked, had a place, were becoming real.

He enjoyed his work, would perhaps have enjoyed any work that was not actively pernicious. After the hidden imperatives of the farm, the complex significance of everything there, he was glad to be able to arrive on time and leave on time, to have set tasks to complete, to be of simple use; waiting for the delivery vans, loading up the trollies, learning the systems of stock control. He found it easy to be reliable, conscientious, straightforward. The till-girls flirted with him and played pranks upon him. Perhaps they thought he was stupid, but he didn't mind that. He liked to watch them, to see the pattern of moods that moved their features, the sulks and bleariness of their love lives, the gawp of their secrets, their yawns of boredom, the way they could slide things past their tills, ring up the prices, with speed and grace even, but with their minds away in dreams.

Bel, on the other hand, became restless within a month. The hotel was dirty and the lives within it mean and blind. She was paid badly for work she did shoddily, returning to their room, which grew tighter and more sordid everytime she opened the door. Henry was the only brightness in her life and, soon enough, she was jealous, not of his till-girls, but of his contentment, the smiles he brought home and exercised upon her.

On her way home there was a bookshop, a rainbow-painted shop full of radical pamphlets, astrological manuals, erotica, underground comics. She had no money to spend, but she began to spend hours there, browsing, listening in on conversations which began to pull at her. She stayed here until she knew Henry would be home, unable to be in the room without him. She began to be recognised, greeted when she came in.

The shop was run by a woman, tall and blonde and beautiful, who drifted about and, as far as Bel could see, allowed the place to take care of itself. If someone wanted to buy something, she seemed almost surprised. Most of the stock left the shop unpaid for. Bel eventually found the courage, when she and the woman were alone in the shop, to open a conversation.

'You know that guy just left with ten pounds' worth of your books in his pocket?'

The woman shrugged.

'I don't want the pigs in here, do I?'

'You shouldn't be ripped off by people like him. I mean, what was he? Some office boy looking for something to wank off to. He could afford it.'

The woman was resigned, accepted everything. Her name was Leaf. The shop was owned, Bel learned, by a man called Toad. Toad was into the music business, promotions, films. The shop was something for Leaf. Leaf was his woman.

When the conversation moved on to the books, Bel found that Leaf was not the simple dope-head that she appeared, that she had read most of the books, loved them, wanted to spread their messages around the world. She had been to university, studied theology, knew Bel's star sign without being told it, had a vision of the world as a powerhouse of repressed spiritual energy that was, she said, about to be unleashed. She suggested that they close the shop, go upstairs to the flat and get stoned. Bel was tempted but said she had to go home, but that she would be in again tomorrow.

She didn't tell Henry about the shop. She had begun to want to involve herself there, and she didn't want to share that want with him lest she was disappointed. She went and chatted to Leaf every day after work, told her about the hotel, about Henry, about the farm. She met Toad, who surprised her by being large and dirty, a scruffy pig of a man whom Bel could not imagine making enough money to support Leaf and her bookshop, until she had spoken to him for half an hour and begun to notice the shrewdness below the dirt, had begun to see how he had, casually and carefully, been sizing her up. She deduced, correctly as it transpired, that his main source of income came from dealing dope, although he did have contacts in the film and music world, or the ragged, underground end of it. He admired Leaf, in a strange way, appreciated her learning and her beauty. They were even, they admitted rather coyly, married.

One afternoon, they asked Bel to look after the shop for a bit, but she said that she had to get home. Toad had asked her about the shop and she had been quick with ideas and, the next day, on cue, Leaf asked her if she'd like to come and work here. Toad and Leaf were planning a trip to Morocco. They couldn't pay her much, Leaf said, but the figure she mentioned was half as much again as she was making at the hotel; and they offered her the flat above the shop, rent-free.

Best of all was the bathroom, their own bathroom, with a big tub where they could steam and soak and soap one another, splash and play like children. Henry remembered bathtime with his sisters, the warmth and security of it, the openness. He remembered how, as he had grown up, the world had grown a skin of secrecy that he had felt stifling him, retracting him. With Bel's black nakedness slithering against his, he felt that skin peeled back. He remembered her privacy when she had been with him first, remembered the journey they had taken to this fluency of life together, the erotic curiosity spreading through their days; from the bathroom to the bedroom where the light from the night street fluttered across their bodies; across the large space of the big living room where they listened to strange music and smoked Toad's grass splayed in slow, flooded lethargies; into the small kitchen where they elbowed each other in greedy eating, feeding one another, eating off the same plates in a confusion of tongues and fingers; racing through their days to close the door, lock themselves in, loosen the concerns of work, loping about, Bel doing her accounts and Henry cooking, cleaning up; going out to the pub, perhaps, beginning to know people, people who visited the shop, sometimes one of Henry's till-girls and her boyfriend, a movie, then back into the warmth and close focus, tired and clear, confirmed before the world and now with each other.

The summer came and it felt as if they had been together for years, all the shallows and tangles of the past pushed behind them with strong, bright strokes in the warm depths of their pleasure.

. . . *nineteen* . . .

'Were you going to pay for that?'

'For what?'

'For the book you just put in your jacket.'

'Oh . . . they let me borrow books from here.'

'Do you have any identification?'

'What?'

'I need to know who you are.'

'I . . . I'm a friend of Leaf's.'

'Yes, well Leaf's away. Until she gets back, I say what goes here. So, give me the book or pay for it.'

'Or what?'

'Or nothing. Just do it.'

'Look . . . I need the book. I have no bread. Give me a break, eh?'

'No. You give me a break. I make my living here. I don't know who you are, and I can't afford you.'

At last he shuffled and withdrew the book from his jacket, looked at it, considered it. He faced her then, set his mouth, but she had her hand on the book and her grip was tighter than his. He relinquished it, sneered.

'Fascist cow.'

'Parasite.'

She took the book back to the till and watched him. He was large, blond and shabby. He blinked, looked at her furtively, expecting perhaps a change of heart; but meeting her hard appraisal of him, he sank into his humiliation and sloped off towards the door.

'See you,' she called brightly after him.

He paused, turned, but went.

She admitted to herself that she enjoyed these confrontations, enjoyed asserting herself. She wondered what she would do if they flatly defied her, became aggressive. She almost looked forward to that.

She was good at this, ran the shop tidily and tightly. She knew little about the overheads, but in the business of buying and selling, she was making a decent profit. She did not clear Leaf's mystic books from the shelves, but filled the empty spaces with mainstream books that sold more reliably, whilst not neglecting the poets and subversives who came to her with tattered boxes of their small-press pamphlets. The shop was never very busy, so she had time to read, and began to know her way around the stock of the shop, to become caught up with the power of books, the liberating ideas that flowed from the hard privacies of writers into the dullness of the world. She had never had her life so purposeful and settled.

Best of all she liked the women's writing that was beginning to assert its distinction: women writing to women, redefining the world with bright anger. She did not let women steal from her, but she was aware of being gentler with those she apprehended; even, if she knew the face, allowing them to borrow books. It was women who began to form the majority of her regular customers. She began to know them, talk to them, to share the unravelling of their messy lives. She dreamed of doing here, in the real world, what she had done on the farm, began inviting some of them to a social evening in the flat, which became a regular Wednesday evening group, sending Henry off to the cinema or the pub.

They talked about themselves, opened their hurts and shames, struggling to define their constrained sexuality against the long decades of their upbringing, the claustrophobia of what they were meant to be, weeping as they turned against the pain of the wires that bound them, that cut and deformed them. Bel, from the strength of her own past, her own survival, was proud of them, took pleasure in their pain which she felt was the pain of awakening, the beginning of liberation.

When Henry appeared, the group went quiet and slipped off into the night. The meetings made Bel high with an aggression that she could not, without a sense of betrayal, have shared with her lover. Masculinity, within the group, seemed synonymous with aggression and humiliation. To offer herself to Henry's tenderness whilst her sisters were being brutalised, beaten, sodomised and sold, seemed betrayal. He crept off to bed alone whilst she read, chain-smoking, manuals of legal self-help. In the morning, she would rouse to his silent hurt and know again that it was different for her, that he had never, would never, ask anything of her that she was not proud to give him; but there was a growing conflict within her. At times, as they made love, she began to want his cruelty, perversely, for him to reveal himself and justify her new understanding; and to explain also why her sisters, with the dull predictability of addicts, went back to the men who abused them.

'Henry?' she asked him one night, lying under the soft preambles of his touching. 'When we fuck, do you ever imagine hurting me?'

'Sometimes,' he said after a pause.

'How?'

'I don't know . . . sometimes I want to be hurt too. Sometimes, when it goes soft, you know, when you can't stop yourself, then I want it to hurt, to make it, I don't know, sharper. As it happens, for a moment, there seems like there's something else that we might have done, some higher place that we might have reached, something that slips away from me when I come.'

'Would you like to try something?'

'What?'

'I don't know. Whatever you'd like.'

'No,' he said. 'I don't want to lose you.'

'What d'you mean?'

'I dread . . . most of all I dread feeling that I'm doing it alone. Bel?'

'What?'

'I'm not going to lose you, am I?'

'No,' she said, 'no,' reaching down for the softness of his penis, bringing it up into its hard, strong curve.

For a while after their move to the bookshop, he kept his job in the supermarket. When she had been miserable in her work, his work had seemed purposeful; now, however, she had purpose, had leap-frogged him into her new world, and he grew restless. Bel was excited, the world beginning to spin beneath her feet, and he envied her, became afraid that she would outgrow him, that she would need more than tenderness and intimacy, more than the refuge he gave her.

He saved money, browsed in the second-hand shops, purchased at last a battered old camera, a small professional camera that had a perfect big, black eye of a lens, that felt heavy in his hand. He spent hours cleaning and restoring it, carefully dismantling it to repair the shutter release, oiling it, nurturing it, knowing it as he had known his wall, that strange obsessional enclosure keeping him rapt for dissolved spans of time.

He tried his camera on bland street scenes, on parkscapes, but the making of images did not interest him any more. The click of the camera in his hand interested him, and the immaculate moment of chemical impregnation within; these he loved for the control he had over them, the precision. He developed his shots, again for the pleasure of the process, for the active smell of the fluids and the drifting of the images out of the whiteness; but the images themselves, once he had achieved them, were dead for him.

He gave up his job, helped in the shop, ran the domestic life of the flat, cooking and cleaning and removing as many of the complications from Bel's life as he could. When one of Bel's evening sessions led to the breakage of Toad's complex stereo system, he spent a week carefully dismantling it with the help of an electronics manual, fingering the delicate transistors, the soldering of the amplifier and tuner, beginning to reassemble it, testing minutely every connection he made, finally, triumphantly, bringing it to life again, then losing interest in it.

He lived in a silence, a solitude, occupied by his precisions, moving from obsession to obsession, learning. He browsed in the junk shops and bought dead machines home and fixed them, found that he could sell them again, that he could make a contribution. His imagination was in his fingertips moving over the intricacies of cogs and wires, holding himself steady, every move exact, perfect, certain, never happier than when he made a connection with absolute steadiness, absolute knowledge of what he did.

Against this, Bel became his humanity, his external world, the moments when he rose from the tiny solipsism of his work and met her body, growing spacious against her, listening to the tumble of her world that she unloaded upon him, a great soap opera of lives, the occupants of which he knew only by sight, the reality of which he accepted entirely from her, following her excitements and angers with a loyal empathy, trusting her to make sense of it all for him with the certainty of their lovemaking, the pulse between them that never paled.

As the months passed, as letters came from Leaf saying that she and Toad were going on to Kathmandu, that they would be back next year, telling Bel to keep things going, sending her money, as this temporary life grew to permanence, Henry began to feel more certain of Bel, began to know that they had come through to the next stage of their life intact.

In the New Year, when things were becoming complicated in and around the shop, when its success was beginning to attract a wider attention and Bel was becoming something of a figure, interviewed by a newspaper, asked if she could write something for a magazine, she took a decision. She had an accountant now who advised her, and there were aspects of their relationship with Henry that needed, within her position amongst the women with whom she argued and defined herself, clarification.

On a dull Tuesday, therefore, they were married; not that it made any difference to the way they lived their lives, but Henry felt it as a blessing, a confirmation of himself. He could not have been happier.

. . . *twenty* . . .

When Leonie returned from Greece with Lizzie and told the man who had lived with her to leave, told him that she was in love with Lizzie, that Lizzie was going to move in and take his place, he beat her up. 'My last male fuck,' she told Bel, who was dabbing the dried blood off her cuts. He had also, Leonie discovered, sabotaged the house comprehensively in her absence, dismantling the water supply and as much of the electrical wiring as he could, rending it in many places lethal. Leonie had inherited the house from her grandmother, but in the state in which he had left it, it was useless.

'You'll have to stay here until you can get it fixed,' Bel said.

Lizzie, who was far more frightened than Leonie, hugged Bel and wept.

Henry was out and, when he returned, he slipped quietly up to the flat before Bel had had a chance to forewarn him. He discovered their guests in the bath, one of them shrieking at his appearance, the other rising and pushing her nakedness at him, telling him to fuck off out of it.

'I'm sorry, love,' Bel said. 'They'll only be here for a few days.'

He didn't believe that and could tell that she didn't either.

'Could you please go and tell them that I need to take a piss.'

He made them all supper, but Leonie and Lizzie didn't eat more than a mouthful each. Leonie glowered at him, and Lizzie flinched each time he moved. They had camped in an untidy heap in the middle of the living room. He moved warily around the edge of their mess, going to bed early and alone, deprived of his evening stooped over a dismembered tape recorder. His absence made them jovial, and he could hear their laughter, smell the coils of their dope, wanted Bel back.

She came in to him late, stoned and sexy, but their guests were making love with celebrational assertion and he felt, churlishly, that Bel was more involved with them than with anything he had to offer.

'You're not easy about this, are you?' she said.

'I'll get used to it,' he said. 'What are they doing?'

'Making love, Henry.'

'I know, but . . . how?'

'Mind your own business.'

'I wish they'd mind theirs. I'll set up a speaker for them tomorrow. They can broadcast it down the street.'

She giggled. 'You can't play the prude with me, Henry Drewer, not with your cock as hard as that.'

He laughed then, and she sat tucked up upon him, squeezing out his churlishness, goading him on with grunts and squeaks. When they were done, slithering down into sleep, Henry felt a coldness, something external. Leonie and Lizzie had been silent for some while. He sat up and there they were, standing like outraged parents in the dark doorway. He elbowed the dozy Bel.

'Too much,' he said, burying his head. 'Too fucking much.'

'You've said it!' Leonie sneered.

Bel pulled herself out of bed and went through to the living room with them, closing the door behind her.

'We thought he was hurting you,' Lizzie said dismally.

'Oh, come on,' Bel said, tired and floundering to find some bearing in this. 'He's my lover. That's all. It's nothing to do with anything else.'

Leonie said, 'D'you know the way he looked at us, Bel, when he came into the bathroom. He thought it was Christmas. I'll bet hearing us turned him on. We'll go in the morning. There'll be somewhere we can crash.'

'No. I'll go.' Henry had come through in the darkness and was standing a yard from them. 'Give me the keys to your house. I'll fix it up for you. Then you can go back there and I can have my wife back.'

A whole house. He was in the largest toyshop he had ever imagined. He spent a week just camping there, making the water flow but nothing more until he had understood it. Leonie's ex-lover he came to call The Bastard, came to have a private, brutal respect for the man; firstly, for his understandable aggression against Leonie and her mad bigotry; and secondly, as he worked, for the puzzles The Bastard had set him, the traps.

He turned the electricity off at the mains and then patiently traced every wire that came out from the wall, opened sockets to find them carfully rewired to send bolts of charge into any patch of flesh that brushed them. Under the bath, he found a wire attached to the cold water tap that, theoretically, would have boiled anyone careless enough to bathe: that was good, to catch the pair of them and boil them like chickens. Kitchen appliances had been booby-trapped. Under the lids of saucepans, primed mousetraps waited. Furniture had been sawn through. A dead cat festered in the down of a pillow. Piles of clean towels had been systematically pissed into. A rime of powdered glass lay in the kettle and in the whisky bottle. The contents of the gin bottle hissed as he poured them down the drain. The house was a horror-shop of hyperbolic malevolence that frequently made Henry laugh at its manic dynamism. He could understand it, greeted each new discovery with a triumphant whoop. He dreaded The Bastard returning, afraid that he might find him ordinary.

When Bel came to see him and he explained all the devices he had discovered and neutralised, she was appalled and angry. It took a lot of coaxing to bring her down to him, to bring his desire down from the eroticism of his work to an awareness of her.

'You're enjoying yourself here, aren't you?' she said.

'I am, yes. I need you here, though. I'm getting too locked up in it.'

'I know you are.'

'Leave them the flat and come and stay.'

'No. They . . . I need to be there. I need to be with the shop and with the people who come there. It's not just nine to five, you know that. You'll be done here soon, won't you?'

'I suppose so. Bel?'

'What?'

'I could do this well, make money out of it. If we could buy a house, somewhere wrecked and cheap, I could do it up, sell it, buy another.'

It seemed logical, an expansion into permanence. They lay and talked money, bank loans, mortgages, what he would need for equipment, tools and materials.

She was beginning to understand money now, to see, behind the mere earning and spending, the arts of accountancy. Before, money had been the brutal medium of life, clutched in handfuls to stave off wretchedness, hunger, exploitation; always essentially dirty, involving dishonesty to others or to oneself in its acquisition; now, she began to understand the strength of it, the purpose of amassing it, building it into a musculature against the world, the dignity it gave, the freedom. The world was greedy and callous and unjust, but disengagment with the world led to poverty, and poverty was slavery. It was possible to earn and use money honestly and, if she wanted seriously to be subversive, as she did, then money was more effective than explosive; and there was money to be made and, in a small but steady way, she was making it.

She visited Henry on odd afternoons and evenings, when she could get away, never predictably, needing him suddenly, thinking about him and breaking from the interminable ramifications of her work to find the simplicity of a good fuck with her lover; then pulling her clothes back on and rushing back, guilty lest things should have come loose in her absence.

'How's my house?' Leonie would ask sourly, knowing where she'd been without asking.

'Your house is nearly ready.'

'Bel, you reek of him.'

'Good. Good.'

'I thought you were free, Bel.'

'I am free. Freely married to my lover.'

'That's a contradiction.'

'Tell me, Leonie: if you love Lizzie why do you make her cry so much?'

It was no contradiction. It was the certainty of her life. She had no idea what she would be doing in three months, let alone a year, let

399

alone for the rest of her life, but she knew that she would be doing it with Henry Drewer. She now signed herself 'Bel Drewer', and felt, as she had not with her official surname, which had been an administrative fiction anyway, that this was her real name, a name she had chosen, had achieved, to which she belonged. Occasionally she thought of the other Drewers, Henry's family, who existed somewhere and to whom, she considered, she would in some way belong.

. . . *twenty-one* . . .

He finished the house. Leonie and Lizzie returned there, although Lizzie didn't stay long, ran off back to her parents. With shrewd financial bullying, and with a drastic depletion of all she had saved, Bel managed to put her lover into a damp shell of a terraced house in one of the southern suburbs, managed to set him going. She sometimes spent days there, watching him work, feeding off his brightness, joining him with a sander or paint brush, making love in all the different rooms of the house, wondering if, perhaps, they might make a home here, their own home.

'Not here,' he said. 'We'll find somewhere better. This is an experiment. I want to make it work. Prices around here are beginning to move. We'll make twice what we paid for it.'

Then one day she stayed too long, became caught in dreams of the future, returning to find the bookshop full of sour men in raincoats with bad skin and short, greasy hair.

'Mrs Arabella Drewer? We have a warrant to search these premises.'

They did not find her dope, which she had hidden in a tin of curry powder; but they found a great deal of what they called pornography, most of which was available in a hundred other shops; radical erotica, underground magazines, guidebooks of sexual fulfilment. She stood in the midst of their fingering, their prurient disapproval of her stock, and flooded with angry tears. People came into her shop with a lightness, a curiosity, drifted amongst the shelves, browsing and dipping into the books in a liberty that she loved to watch, whoever they were, whatever they sought; amongst her books they were absolved. These bastards barged and soiled and snatched and dropped books, glancing at her with a contempt for her sex, for her colour, for everything she believed in; not even with anger, not really with outrage, but with a sarcastic sneering, a crude reduction of her to the world of their fat, dumb tongues, the sweat of their crotches, the institutionalised deadness of their minds.

'I must ask you to accompany me to the police station, Mrs Drewer.'

'I . . . I need to use the bathroom.'

'Five minutes. Sergeant Black. Keep an eye on her, would you?'

He didn't come into the bathroom, allowed her to shut the door but not lock it. They had been in here, had spilled her talcum powder, stuck their fingers into her ointments. One of them had left his oily urine unflushed in her lavatory. She vomited.

By the time they got her to the police station, she had straightened up, pulled through the fear. She refused to be medically examined, refused to answer any questions, demanded that she be allowed to telephone her solicitor.

The worst time was sitting in a chair in the middle of a bare room, with two young detectives, one lolling against the door, one moving about the room. She wouldn't talk. For ten minutes they watched her, exchanged glances, grins. Then they began.

'How much d'you charge for a fuck, then? . . . I'll bet you're an expert. Joe's been with a wog, haven't you, Joe? . . . Tell you what. Suck me off and we'll forget all those dirty books . . . well? . . .'

She would have killed them if she had had any way of doing it. She thought, with the blood beating in her brain, of accepting the offer, of getting his prick between her teeth and tearing it off. She could've done it, too. But it wasn't a real offer. They were trying simply to humiliate her. She thought of Henry and she wept. It was all going to be taken away from her. She had tried not to let them see her weep, but in the end found the strength to weep openly, to let them snigger and laugh at her because that was their shame, and if they didn't feel it, then they were dead and she was alive.

They kept her there three hours and then, with as bad a grace as they could manage, released her. They had not charged her, although they intimated that there would be charges. Limping palely into the reception area she saw Henry with Claire, her solicitor.

Claire began making a scene, startling the lethargic desk sergeant, threatening, laying down rights. Bel leant against Henry and wept.

'Take me home,' she said.

She insisted on clearing up, more than clearing up. She took every book down, wiped it with a duster, sponged down the shelves, washed the floor, put the books back. Henry helped. They worked all night silently and systematically. Then they went upstairs and began on the flat. They didn't get much further than the bathroom before her exhaustion overcame her and Henry carried her to bed.

In the late afternoon, she woke to find him cleaning the kitchen.

'Leave it,' she said. 'It's all right now.'

'I didn't open the shop,' he said.

'That's okay. Henry? I've been offered a job.'

'What job?'

'With The Lovell Press. They've got a feminist list coming out in the spring. It's Claire's idea. Her husband works there.'

'Good. Great. What about the shop?'

'Fuck the shop. Find us a house, Henry.'

'All right.'

When, that night, she went to put in her diaphragm, in the light of the bathroom, a disgust overcame her, the rememberance of her sickness, of the policeman outside the door. She dropped it into the bin.

'I didn't put it in,' she said, suddenly, when he was inside her.

He stopped.

'No,' she said. 'It doesn't matter.'

'You want to make a baby, Bel?'

'Why not?'

He lay inert upon her as if she had stunned him. She was about to ask him what was wrong when, without another movement, he ejaculated.

'Oh . . . oh shit . . . I'm sorry.'

She giggled and cuddled him, patted his head and blew into his ear.

. . . *twenty-two* . . .

When he returned from a city dinner to find his wife in a coma induced by a bottle of sleeping-tablets, Lewis Drewer felt only a numbness of inevitability, an irritation that she should so disturb his life. He rang for the ambulance. He decided against ringing Susan or Maggie until he had some idea of how serious it was going to be. He sat on the edge of her bed, watching her breathing catch and strive. He did not believe that she would die; perhaps he wanted her to die and he had ceased to believe in a world that worked to his wants; perhaps he simply would not accept that it would end; perhaps, beneath the insulating pall of his indifference, some terrible reaction waited.

He touched her skin, which was spongy and wet, drew back the sheets to see her nakedness, the slackness of booze and pills into which she had lapsed, filling the emptiness in the middle of her; where I should have been, he thought, the pain beginning to reach him, as it always did, as it always had done, the leaking shame of his life.

When the doorbell rang, he did not at first connect with it, wondered who it might be, began to determine to ignore it; then, in a fluster of confusion, he was running downstairs, fumbling at the latch, letting them in, the purposeful uniforms who took the briefest of directions from him, who took over. He stood looking out at the wet night, at the blue blip of the ambulance light, at the curious passers-by who gathered and peered into the open door as if it were a wound from which his life flooded. He wanted them to see, strangely, wanted them to know. He felt he deserved this, bowed his head before their silent reproach.

They wheeled her away into the bright chambers of the hospital and left him to wait with other stooped figures in the reception area. He glanced at them briefly, trying to find some empathy for them or from them; but was incongruous in his light overcoat, his sharp creases, glassy shoes. He imagined them gloating that for all his money he was brought, like them, to this, to the squalor of attendance off-stage in the shadows of pain and loss.

He did not think about her, did not seem able to: either there would be her survival, her convalescence, a world of waiting and caring, of picking over the past and trying to make of the pieces something that would be sustainable a little further into the future; or there would be her death, the obligations of grief, the whole horrible process of funeral and family, beyond which all he could see was a featureless fall of days. He had not loved her, in any active sense, for years; but he could not imagine his life without her. He shuddered and shuffled and lit a cigarette and knew, at least, that he wanted her to live, perhaps for entirely selfish reasons, but it was a start, at least that.

There had been too many funerals, lights going out around him; each one, as this one would, exposing the survivors in the squalor of their continuance . . . Uncle Harry buried in the small grey church where he had not been since before the Great War, with Hanni shuddering inconsolable and the strange boy, their son, staring about him as if waiting for a train; the family gathered then, his parents, Naomi, Helena with her perfect husband and the perfect twins, Susan and Charles in their shabby intelligence, Maggie and Maurice, cultured, sophisticated, all the right responses, the house full of Drewers, fuller than it had ever been that he could remember; and it had been, for an evening, as if that was where they belonged, their home; and blind old Brady in her room hoarding them all up about her, knowing all their names and the dates of their births and what they were all about now out in the world, full of disapproval and loyalty; and waking in the middle of the night to Celia's crying, 'We would have been so happy here, so happy', and in the sadness of that, a sense of beginning, a sense of renewal, a determination to bring it together and hold it together, making love there for the last time that meant anything, but knowing the moment it was done that it was an illusion, that she was right, that the house belonged to Hanni who had no need of this clutch of selfish strangers who had come to the death of a man they had neglected for the long, hard years of his dying, who had rights of birth there but not of belonging, as she belonged, and Brady, and Max; dispersing next day, shame-faced with promises to return, to keep in touch, to help if she needed help, 'Nothing, I thank you, nothing, nothing', her terrible reproach upon him . . . and then Naomi suddenly calling him to her hospital bed, unrecognisable, wasted in a few months to a shrivelled mummy, the cancers knotting her with pain, the drugs she would not take, determined to be alive to the last moment, angry and bitter with all her strength, knowing something, wanting to tell him something but unable to bring it out of her mind bleached with pain; her funeral a perfunctory crematorium ceremony with the family out of place amongst the strange set of her friends, lovers and patients and colleagues who wept a burning personal loss of her, shaming the family, apart from Jane, apart from Jane; and her parents, his parents, waiting out the years for their children to come to them, to bring their lives back home, lost in an England they had never understood, relying on ties of loyalty and love that had somehow failed to come through, for which they blamed themselves, uncomprehending, standing at the ceremony for the death of their youngest, brightest child and not knowing where they were, who they were, very old, very old . . . going to see them in the months after Naomi's death, feeling strange with them, their frailty now so intimate, so minute; Lionel and Anna Drewer, forged in a terrible war that had become historical, irrelevant, serving fifteen years an empire now compromised, abandoned, wreaking its legacies of pride and racism in dark cities; and us with nothing to say to them any more, the children one by one subjects that might not be mentioned, Naomi dead, Helena marking time in her hollow marriage with her selfish, spoiled daughters, and Celia, how was Celia? We'd love to see her again . . . my father, aged ninety, running out of life at last; my mother coming in from the garden to find that he'd slipped away, dissolved in the thin dozing that occupied so much of his time; his funeral bitter with absences, Naomi, Helena in California under therapy, Charles having one of his turns and Susan having to be with him, Maggie there, immaculate, detached, 'Maurice and I are separating. Did you know?'; and Jane; and Jane; and Mummy, watching the long coffin going down into the earth, quietly, certain with the strength she had always had that she would not be long in her loneliness, that death was a doorway out of the house into the night, that it would be so easy for her, contented to be the one left, at peace with herself, looking at them as they came to her with condolence and concern, smiling her brightest smile, free of them all now, free of everything but herself, every obligation filled at last, 'I don't believe that Lionel and I will meet again in a better world, in any world. There is no other world, but, it doesn't matter', answering his weekly calls, refusing to move, waiting, each day a quiet grace, a logical routine, small pleasures of remembrance, irritated perhaps only by Helena's return, by the fussing of Helena's conscience, made to respond again, 'Mummy, I should have been here, I should have been here.' 'Why? What could you have done? Everything was done that ought to have been done. It's all so very wearisome', going quite suddenly when Helena was there as if to make her a present of it; the older generation now gone, Mummy's funeral pitiless, pointless, indicating our solitudes, our failures, nothing to speak of any more; and Jane stayed away, couldn't bear another one, knew Granny wouldn't know or wouldn't've cared . . . and then Jane . . . and then Jane, driving tired, late into the night, going to see someone in trouble, spinning on the ice, hearing it in my dreams, the single crack, the sudden click, the world moving on in all its hideous banality from where she had been; too late then for the hurt between us to be resolved, too many melodramas, too many times the weighty father with his sour disapproval, his hard mockery of the bitter tears as she had fought to bring herself clear of the proliferating mess of her life; and had he really preferred the hard manipulations of Maggie? Susan's rancid intellectualism? Oh yes, of course he had, for they played his games, gave back in kind, kept the cancerous mess of their lives neatly hidden behind smart answers, strategic lies, irony, hypocrisy; Jane always wanting to fight, wanting to know, wanting to have it all out in the open, and they had despised her; she had wanted their understanding and they had despised her; as she had followed herself into trouble and pain, she had wanted their loyalty, their love, and they despised her, and her dying had slashed them open like a razor, the worst of them all, each death a reproach, but hers a damnation; and now this death, Celia's death, the closest, the most intimate, the most wearisome, no-one to share the burden of it, the most unnatural, Naomi and Jane dying at the random will of the world, Celia dying by her own will, defeated by his active neglect, his contempt for her in the bleak emptiness of his contempt for himself, where they had begun, where they had always been going once the pull of sexuality had dulled, once the weight of middle age had slowed and tired them from the fight where they had once made something of one another, once, no more, not for a long time, too late, too many betrayals, marks scored against one another, only mean spites, only this, only this, waiting for her to be dead in a cold hospital, for her to consummate the final spite against him, throwing herself into the pit and leaving him for the rest of his life looking down into the depth of it, the stench of it rising, rotting him in his own self-disgust; and he wept then, for himself and for her and for the wretchedness they had made of themselves, the nothing they had given to anyone, finally, finally, finally; and with a twist of hard pain he knew that in all his thoughts he had not found Henry.

Henry.

. . . *twenty-three* . . .

She did not die. Perhaps, they said to him, she had not meant to, not finally, although she had come very close to it; perhaps, they said, it was a plea for help. He could not imagine this of her. He sat with her in the hospital, watching her drift in and out of consciousness, of awareness of him, looking at him there waiting for her. He tried to construct some implicit plea amongst the drawn lines of her face, but he could not. They had nothing to say to one another.

She came home and Maggie came to stay with her two boys, a move that, in the circumstances of her divorce, seemed to become quickly permanent. The house had children again, the babbling and bickering of family life that made it lively again, but which saddened him, excluded now, Grandpa, out to work, marking off the final years of his employment, the stuffy old senior partner on whom young men with wide lapels and flopping hair sharpened their financial teeth avoiding and outwitting. He became cantankerous and small-minded, felt himself becoming so; it seemed his only assertion, his only possibility, holding on, marking time, growing irrelevant.

'One day,' she said to him, 'he'll come back, and he won't come begging, and he won't be defeated, and then you'll have to face it squarely.'

'Who are you talking about?'

'You know bloody well who I'm talking about, Lewis.'

'He's dead, Celia.'

'No.'

'I . . . I had a letter, a couple of years ago now. I . . . I didn't want you to know.'

'You're a liar, Lewis. If you'd had such a letter, you'd have rubbed my nose in it the moment you took it out of the envelope.'

'I won't discuss this.'

'I'm not discussing it. I'm stating the truth, although, since the subject is between us again, I will say this: your denial of him is pure dishonesty, Lewis. You pretend that you have suffered some dreadful betrayal; but you never even tried to love him. Your inability to love has maimed us all; he least of all because he had the strength to walk away and not come back. I hope that he will return. I even pray for it. Yes, I have begun that again.'

'I wish you well with it. Goodnight.'

He stooped over her and placed his cold kiss on her forehead. An urge to strike him rose in her steeply but did not quite translate into action. After he had gone, she felt better; he had made her angry again and the charge of that drained from her hotly. She lay back in her bed and felt tired, cleanly tired. Tonight she would sleep without a pill. Tomorrow she would go for him again.

He sat at his desk and took out the folder of photographs Henry had taken of his black street-whore. He spread the pictures across the desk under the strong light of the lamp, within the surrounding darkness of the room, the ticking of the clock, the rumble of the city beyond. He did this often, was terrified that the door would open and Celia would appear, would catch him at this secret pleasure, would know the truth about him; although what that truth was he could not clearly have said; she would know at once, though, would break it over him. Sometimes when the house creaked in the darkness he thought she was coming, thought he was going to be caught, his heart pounding, the sweat starting on his face. Perhaps he wanted her to catch him, perhaps that was what this was all about. Meanwhile he peered at the images of this woman and was overcome by her beauty, by the defiant liberty with which she offered herself to the lens, the trust and the love which she opened; and if he thought of his son at this time, he did so with a hot sexual jealousy.

Your inability to love has maimed us all.

He accepted this condemnation as a simple truth, and wondered how he could have failed, what he had not done, what pattern of circumstances in his past had crippled him in this way. Sometimes he blamed his parents for their desertion; sometimes he blamed school; sometimes Celia; but it always came back to him. He did not know what love was. He knew the ferocity of sexual desire and its completion, but that was not it. He knew the emotional comforts of marriage, of parenthood, the understanding and solicitude; but that was not it. He had seen, in his parents if nowhere else, the triumph of love over the extremities of life. Amongst the dead and dying in a concentration camp, he had recognised the absolute reverse of love. But in the silence of himself he had never known it. It was a final, annihilating numbness within him; and what was most appalling about his son's betrayal was that he, perhaps, with the innocence of the true fool, had found love, perhaps here with this half-caste, perhaps now at this moment somewhere out there in the night, a tender erotic awareness that spread from their bodies confirming and liberating them in ways that he imagined with actual physical pain: the pain of envy and failure and loss, the inability to lift himself, to turn into a light that he felt would shrivel him. He wept.

. . . twenty-four . . .

One morning, Max Brand woke and realised that he was mad. It was a resolution of so much that had been troubling him for so long. He cursed himself for having missed a solution so simple to problems that had seemed so complex. It absolved him. He felt as if he had been travelling in a car that did not work properly along roads whose destination was never apparent on a journey whose purpose he had never understood; now, suddenly, he had stopped the car, turned off the engine, opened the door and stepped out, finding himself in a pure, clear landscape that he did not recognise, in which he did not belong, but which had, at last, no claims upon him. He made this image distinctly, clearly and, as he made it, he recognised it as part of a recurring dream that he had had for years. At last he had caught it, put it into words and was free of it, free of everything, free of himself.

He sprang from his bed, crossed the carpet in three purposeful strides and pulled open the curtains, unlatched the shutters, let the light in like a trumpet blast. Fiddling with the old brass window catch, he flung open the sash, and stood naked in the swirl of misty morning air that rushed in, that laid the fetid dust of the night and dried the sweat on his skin. Before him lay the troubled acres of his birthright, the tussocky lawn and straggling woodlands. For a moment he was detained by this sight, remembered all the things that ought to be done, all the duties that lay there unfulfilled; but with a shake and a shudder in the cold air, he rose above all that, asserted the freedom of his lunacy, thrust himself forward and sent an arc of urine out into the morning, heard it splatter on the gravel below him.

Turning from the window, avoiding the mirror until he had wrenched a blanket from his bed and thrown it over the glass, he pulled on his clothes in a muddle, had to stop, strip again, slowing himself, putting on each garment with sustained deliberation. Then he was ready, and he began to feel afraid, set his teeth. He went to the door and unbolted and unlocked it. What he was going to find the other side of it was completely new, completely strange: he reminded himself of this, put his mind to it.

Opening the door slowly, receiving the images of the still house, the landing, the wide staircase, the stale light that fell over everything, he had to concentrate to feel it, to feel the strange vibration of newness that lay below the surface, to know what he saw as part of his dream, the truth below the veil of the quotidian, the lurching unpredictabilty. Everything was suddenly alive, conscious, active; as he was. The bannister rail as he touched it seemed to slither, the stairs as he trod them seemed to shrug, the portrait of his grandfather, old Henry Brand, was deeply affronted by him, wanted to know who the devil he was and what the devil he was doing in this house. They were pertinent questions which set him running, bounding down the stairs like a surprised house-breaker, leaping clear of the walls which bulged out at him, the stairs which jerked up to trip him, coming down on all fours on the flagging of the hall and glancing around him.

He had forgotten the mirror there and he suddenly saw his double staring out at him, wide-eyed, open-mouthed, a thin excrescence of pale stubble on his face. He slammed his hands flat on the mirror surface expecting it to shatter, instead feeling its cold moistness like a disease. He dodged quickly away, went into the small lavatory and scrubbed his hands at the basin, remembering that mirror and closing his eyes.

Returning circumspectly to the hall, moving backwards, sideways, he reached the front door and fumbled at its lock and latch, pushing it open and moving out of the malevolence of the house into the freedom of the open air.

He had not moved five yards from the house when he began to be afraid. The air, when it had blown in through his bedroom window, had been cleansing: here, where it was everywhere, it was abrasive, aggressive. He found it difficult to breathe. He shivered and quivered and squatted down on the weedy gravel. He did not belong out of the house. He ought to have known that. He did not want to go back, but could not stand it out here, not for any length of time. He would die out here, of exposure; he would dissolve, evaporate; he quite liked the idea of that, the idea of being dead, anyway; but it would take too long this way, would hurt too much. He was not good with pain; and anyway, someone would come and stop him.

He then knew that he was being watched, and that straightened him up. He did not know who, or where, or how many, but he was being watched. He walked evenly back into the house and closed the door behind him. He was still being watched so he had to be very, very careful. He turned left into the library, again closing the door behind him. He stepped into the middle of the room and looked about him at the uniform leather spines of the books.

He had never dared touch any of these books; their age and obscurity had always frightened him. There was so much of the house that he had never touched. It was his house, or his and his mother's, but she didn't count, being a woman, being foreign. He was the man, the squire; he had the power of his wealth and birth and station, and they were watching him, expecting him to rise to the challenge, to guide this great ancestral enterprise into the harsh waters of this wretched century.

He understood the watching now, in the clarity of his madness, knew who they were and what they wanted of him; and he knew his failure, his absolute, final, terminal failure. He had failed to make contact with any of it, with any of them. His madness was only an acceptance of what he had always been, spinning pointlessly into the void, incapable of any decision, of making any use of anything. He remembered the blind old man he had called 'Daddy', but he was not that man's son: it was inconceivable. He thought of his mother, lurking about somewhere, arthritic and muttering, saving apple cores to make chutney, endlessly counting sheets and towels, fussing over the way vegetables were peeled whilst the old house leaked and crumbled, going into frightful rages of foul German, breaking into inconsolable, inexplicable tears over him: if he belonged to her biologically, it was a bizarre natural accident. He belonged to no-one. He remembered the horrible isolation of school. He remembered the lost years at university making sense of less and less and less of it, until he had come home defeated and bewildered. He remembered his one attempt at copulation, the hotel room, the willing girl who terrified him and disgusted him, who found him amusing, then pathetic, then frightening. He had not known what he had been doing, not then, not ever. As a boy they had made decisions for him, had tried to fit him into a tight glove, but he did not have the right number of fingers for it, or it flapped about him stupidly, or his hand was so gross that it ripped the seams. In the library he knew, at last, that those books contained the chronicles of his life, that every twitch and blunder he had ever made, the entire composition of his life was here logged and noted. In his madness he knew it and he knew what the implication of it all was, closing like a noose about his neck.

Brady, dozing in her room, living in a watery, pastel world where there were no solid distinctions between sleep and waking, heard it as a door slammed deep in the body of the house that brought her to the surface clearly for a moment, where she took deep breaths of the lavender air of her room and lapsed back into the flow of dream and remembrance and imagination. She dreamed of the war, of the colonies, of the young Drewers at dances, at the births of their children, a multiplying world which she stored in her silence, their lives somehow charging her, the living and the dead having no distinction in her. She had become religious in her old age, took weekly visits from a Catholic priest who gave her the host, who gave her absolution, who spoke to her of the journey into the presence of the Redeemer, which she understood and took as a simple fact: one day her bodily needs and discomforts would dissolve and the dreaming would flow unstaunched, and the figure who floated about in the mist that enclouded her would be as real as she was. She was old now, lamented at times the loss of her powers, but had no more regrets, no more desires, no more illusions that the world might, be, might ever have been, other than it was.

She felt someone come into her room.

'Is that you, Jimmy?' she said, for he was the only one who came in to her without knocking, the boy who looked after her, whom she had never seen, but whose mother and grandmother she had tended through their service at the house.

It was not Jimmy, for there was no reply.

'Father MacPherson?'

No, not he either.

'It is I, Brady.'

'M'm?'

'May I sit down?'

She sat. Brady reached out her hand, but it was not taken.

'Brady, my son has taken his own life.'

There was nothing to be said. Brady slipped into a sort of sleeping, felt him there, young Max, moving amongst the ghosts in her head, spinning and spinning there, slowly becoming still, slowly realising where he was, allowing the others to come about him, to absorb him, to understand his seriousness and his unhappiness. Father MacPherson would be very cross, but she would tell him that there was no need to be cross, that he was at peace now, that he was in the hands of the Redeemer now just like all the others.

'What will become of us now, Brady?'

'M'm?'

'It is over here now. I hoped that he would . . . he would be all right, but that was foolishness. Now it is all over. Perhaps I am relieved. Is that a terrible wickedness?'

'You must send for Master Lewis, m'm.'

'Must I?'

'Oh yes. That's what you must do now.'

'I think I only want to be dead now, Brady.'

'Hold my hand, m'm, if you please.'

She felt the long knotty fingers mesh with hers, felt the lips touch her skin, the scalding, silent tears. She lifted herself and placed her free hand on the stooped head, felt them move into a moment from which time dropped like a sloughed skin, a moment of pain and peace that glowed with eternity.

. . . *twenty-five* . . .

On a sudden impulse one day, he rang Aunt Naomi's flat, but she no longer lived there. He tried the hospital where she worked, but the receptionist checked and said that no-one of that name worked there.

He told Bel about this.

She was quiet for a moment then said, 'I'm glad you tried.' Later she asked, 'Are you going to try your parents?'

'When the baby's born, maybe.'

Bel giving birth was monumental. She screamed and raged and fought and laughed. Henry gave her his hand to hold and she crushed it, tried at one point to put it into her mouth and bite it. The midwife and the doctor seemed unconcerned, professional, practical, and Henry hated them, determined that if they should ever do this again, he would learn up about it and dispense with them.

A boy. Benjamin. Dark-skinned and black-haired with blue eyes. Beautiful, miraculous.

The house quiet, attentive to his stirrings, Henry slipping up to fetch him to her breasts, watching him suck and bubble, seeing her nakedness in a new manifestation that brought on a wicked randiness, deferred, lying in wait for her.

She asked him if he had thought any more about his parents, but he hadn't. With the arrival of Ben, life had become busy and intricate, the days crowded with demands on his various energies. It would not have been true to say that he did not have the time; but he did not have the space, he felt, to go through all that. One day, he promised himself, and her, he would give them a ring, just to see what was going on.

Tom came fourteen months after Ben, and Martin two years after Tom. Henry and Bel prospered and were fecund. He restored houses and she worked with writers. They made money and they made love, and in their different ways strove to make the world better. They were busy and contained, sociable and happy, and then one day a woman appeared in their life.

'Hello,' she said.

Henry had thought he was alone. It was a new project, a commission, a large detached house that they were going to convert into flats. He had been pacing the rooms, gathering ideas when suddenly, from nowhere, this woman had appeared. She was tall, gaunt, stubble-headed and might have been a squatter.

'Henry Drewer,' she said, identifying him.

'What can I do for you?' A job, presumably; or someone who wanted to get to Bel. He moved away a little, disliking this sort of opportuning.

'You don't remember me, do you?' she said.

He turned back, regarded her from a different angle, with a deeper suspicion.

'No. I'm afraid I don't.' Bookshop? Farm? Perhaps before that. He did recognise something. 'Put me out of my misery,' he said.

'Miranda Graves.'

'Good God.' He remembered. 'Miranda. How are you?'

'Much as you see me, Henry.'

'And Rosalind?'

'Oh, I don't know. I stopped being part of all that a long time ago. I think she was going to be married. You're married now.'

'Oh yes.'

'Three children.'

'Yes. You?'

'No. I . . . I fucked up, very badly. I left and didn't go back. They wouldn't have had me back. I was . . . a junkie for three years. I don't deserve to be alive, probably. I met your wife a few years back. She'll remember me. I knew she was your wife then, but . . . I suppose I want to get back now. I suppose that's what I want at last.'

'I . . . I haven't been back.'

'No?'

'Not at all. I tried to ring Aunt Naomi a while back.'

'She died. Cancer. Grandpa and Granny Drewer, they're dead too. They may all be dead by now, though. You haven't been back at all, then?'

'No.'

'Ah well. I thought . . . I thought you might, I don't know, help me back, but . . . but there we go. See you round, maybe.'

'Wait.'

He was supposed to call her back. He could see the smile of calculation at the edges of her face, the manipulation that he remembered.

'You need help?'

She moved into the room, a large room with bare boards and tattered wallpaper, looked about her, keeping to the edges, avoiding his eyes, performing for him. She sat, at last, up against the wall between the two big windows, in the shadow of the grey day that lay outside. She spread her knees and began to roll a cigarette between them, began to talk.

'One of us had to go wrong,' she said. 'One of us had to have it all, the other nothing. My fucking twin sister. We always went so far together, then she stopped at the edge and pushed me over, watched, waited, found out what it was like from me, never got herself dirty. When I began to sink, that bitch was nowhere to be seen. I've not seen her for over five years now. And . . . since when, nothing . . . I've shot up, tripped out, been fucked and fucked and fucked . . . nothing. I just don't feel anything any more, like there's no more room for anything in me. I'm just numbed. I think the only thing that would give me any pleasure would be watching Rosalind suffer, preferably from something I'd done to her.' She lit her cigarette, looked up at him clearly. 'Well? That turn you on, Henry?'

He squatted down before her.

'You stupid bitch,' he said.

She laughed, then burst into tears, threw herself forward and sobbed into his dusty shoulder.

Bel remembered her, hated having her in the house, hated the claim she had made upon Henry, hated the way she was able to ignore the boys as if they weren't there, hated the way she used everything, took whatever she wanted. When she was in the bath, Bel knocked on the door.

'It's open . . . oh . . . hi, Bel.'

'Who were you expecting?' Bel asked.

Miranda laughed. 'Father Christmas, probably.'

'Listen, Miranda. Whilst you're here, no dope, no men, and what you want you ask for, every time.'

'Sure. Fine. I won't get in the way.'

'You're already in the way.'

She pondered this, soaped her scrawny body carefully, as if to draw Bel's sympathy to its wastage and abuse.

'Does Henry still take photographs?' she asked.

'No.'

'He took some of Roz and me once.'

'I know. He told me.'

'Has he still got them, d'you know?'

'No. He destroyed them, didn't even develop the film.'

'That's a pity.'

Thereafter, she took to crying at unpredictable moments, stopping conversations, asserting herself with sudden flows of emotion. Bel went hard, could not understand why this woman, of so many women she had fought for, aroused only her contempt. She did not go out, did not seem to do anything apart from watch television with glazed boredom; but finally, finally, she reached Bel with her pitifulness, every gesture still a calculation, but below the calculation, nothing; even her desires were automatic, expressive of no real need in her.

Henry at last, with Bel's help, wrote to his father:

Whether anything about me means anything to you any more, I don't know. I am married now, to Bel. We have three sons. I am working restoring houses. We have Miranda staying with us at the moment. She has been through a lot of trouble and would like to contact Aunt Helena. She told me about Aunt Naomi, and about Granny and Grandpa, and I am very sorry. I would like to see you and Mummy again, if you would like to see me. I hope you are both well. I hope you can forgive any pain that I have caused you. I am well, and happy, and think of you a great deal.

Love, Henry.

There was no reply for a month; then it was his mother who replied.

Your father has given me your letter, for which we have been waiting for ten years. I do not want to be reproachful, but I must say that I think we deserved something from you in all that time. I am very glad to hear that you are well and happy. Will you come to see us? I think we would prefer it if you came alone in the first instance. We have had much pain and many sadnesses in the family which I will tell you about if you come. I cannot share them with you in a letter, not knowing how you really feel about any of us any more. We would be very happy to see you again. Let us say, next Saturday, the 20th – we will be in and alone. I have written Aunt Helena's address on the back of this, and if Miranda would care to contact her, I'm sure she would be able to do something for her.

Love, Mummy.

. . . *twenty-six* . . .

At fifteen minutes past two the doorbell rang and Lewis, without looking at Celia, who did not look at him, rose from his chair and went through to the hall, to the door. What am I expecting? he thought. Something in a long black cloak with a scythe, probably.

'Hello, Daddy.'

'Henry.' He was dressed neatly, with a tie loosely tied in a floppy collar, a long, loose jacket. He was clean-shaven and his hair was tidy. His face looked bright, more substantial in a way, but instantly recognisable. He did not smile, waited. 'Come in, come in.'

He came in and waited for his father to close the door.

'Go through. Your mother's in the drawing room.'

He did not move at once, seemed to be expecting something, some embrace perhaps. Lewis, careful to avoid contact, moved around him and led the way. He followed.

'It's Henry, darling,' he said, feeling fatuous.

'Hello, Mummy.'

'Hello, Henry.'

Again he hovered, again expectant.

'Sit yourself down, then,' Lewis said, going to sit beside Celia, pulling up his trouser creases.

Henry looked about him, then selected a chair, cautiously, opposite them.

'You're looking very well,' Celia said.

'Yes. I am well.'

418

He did look well, frighteningly fit and assured, strange, dangerous.

'And . . . your wife?'

'She's well, and the children. How are. . . . ?' He stopped, waited.

'Jane died, you know. In a car crash. What is it, Lewis, five years ago now?'

'Five years, yes.'

'I didn't know. I'm very sorry.'

'You heard about Naomi, and your grandparents. Susan and Charles are still in Cambridge, although Charles is mostly in hospital now. Maggie and Maurice have parted. She lives here now, with the boys. They're away at school. She's playing with her orchestra on the Continent. Helena . . . Uncle Freddie died. Rosalind married an American. Max Brand . . . you remember Max? He . . .'

Lewis watched her throughout this recitation, saw how she was enjoying it, driving each of their tragedies into him like nails, blaming him. Lewis had thought that she had wanted him back to be reconciled; he had not known there was all this spite there, welled up in her, fired out of her now. Henry had bowed his face before her onslaught. He was weeping. They sat and watched him weep, not daring to look at one another.

'Your mother's not been well,' Lewis said.

'I'm sorry,' he said, taking a handkerchief and wiping his face, lifting his head but unable to look at them.

'For what are you sorry, Henry?' she said.

'For everything. I can't . . . this is a mistake. I shouldn't've come. I'm sorry. I'll go.'

'No,' she said. 'You've come. These things must be faced. Lewis, you'll support me on this, won't you.'

'Yes,' he said flatly, without agreement, but at least with solidarity.

Henry leant back, tipped up his head and took deep breaths; then faced them again. Lewis could see again the strangeness, the newness, the maturity. He took her hand, afraid of what she had provoked.

'What do you want of me?' their son asked of them. 'I can't make anything better here. I fell in love and I went away, and I made that work. I couldn't have done that here. You don't want what I've got now: a wife you despise, three sons with brown skins. I'm sorry

419

about Jane, and Aunt Naomi, and Granny and Grandpa. If I'd been here, it might've been easier for you. I know that. You want me to be ashamed of not being here? Yes, I'm ashamed. I took decisions. I lived with them. I still live with them. I'm not ashamed of that. I'm proud of what I am and what I've done. I'm proud of Bel, proud of my children. I was never proud of anything here, not of you, not of myself, not of anything I did or might have done here. I think, if I'd stayed, I'd have been another one of your problems.'

Lewis left a space to be sure that he'd finished, then said, 'You're very hard upon us, Henry.' He felt his wife's hand knotted tightly in his own.

'I don't mean to be hard.'

'You're a father yourself now. You'll understand in time.'

'Your cousin Maximilian blew his brains out,' Celia said.

He considered the weight of this; it perplexed him.

'Why?'

'I suppose,' she said, 'because he didn't see any point in being alive.'

'I . . . I didn't really know him. I'm sorry.'

'You restore houses now?' she continued.

'Yes. I . . . I've got a small company. I've a friend whose an architect. Bel deals with the money. She's good at that. She . . . she works in publishing. We're doing all right.'

'The point that your mother is making is that . . . on the death of your Aunt Hanni, and on my death, both of which are perhaps within the foreseeable future, you will inherit the house, the Brand estates, or what's left of them.'

'I don't think I'd be interested in that,' he said carefully.

'That's a pity, Henry,' Lewis continued. 'Your house-restoring skills would be very useful. There are other concerns, too, family concerns. I think, perhaps, this is what this is all about today.'

'What will you do?' Celia said. 'You will inherit an estate worth probably a million pounds. Will you give it away?'

'I don't know.'

'She'll tell you to give it away, I suppose. She'll tell you it belongs to the people, to the working class.'

'Surely,' he said, 'it would be more appropriate for Susan or Maggie to have it. You're right, that sort of money would be point-less for me. Yes, I'd probably make some sort of gesture with it. I don't know. And yes, I'd talk to my wife about it. But please, Mummy, if you make judgements on her, I'll go.'

'It's not money, Henry,' Lewis said. 'It's a responsibility.'

'I believe that all right,' he said.

'I love that house,' Celia said. 'I always hoped it would be ours, that we could bring our children up there. Now Hanni wants us to go and live up there. Your father retires next year. We'd like you to come up with us, to put the house right. It would be. . . .'

'A reconciliation,' Lewis said. 'Ours as much as yours. We have . . . not done well with our lives, perhaps. We want to try to put things right, and it seems to us that . . . that going north, trying to put some of that back together again, might make some sort of recompense for the things that have gone wrong. It's to do with the past, I suppose, where we came from, where we belong. I don't think we've ever been a family in that sense, and I think we ought to have been. Perhaps it's an old man's sentimentality. I don't for a moment expect that you'll agree, but I felt . . . we both felt that you should be told, that you should at least have the opportunity to say no. Your letter came, in fact, at the perfect moment, just when we were beginning to take decisions.'

'That's why we didn't want your wife here,' Celia said.

'If she'd have come, I'd have brought her anyway,' he said sourly.

'Does she hate us?' Celia said.

'Why should she hate you? She's, I suppose, a bit afraid of you.'

'Why on earth should she be afraid of us?'

'Because, I suppose, of what you might make me do.'

'Have you anything to say about my proposal?' Lewis asked.

'No. Nothing to say. I don't understand it yet.'

'It's hardly complicated,' his mother said.

Henry looked at her with the ghost of a smile. Lewis could see him remembering her talking to him like that.

'No, Mummy, it's not complicated. But I still don't understand it, understand what it will mean for me, and for Bel, and for the children.'

Another small impasse occurred here.

'Three sons, then,' Lewis said.

'Yes. Ben is nearly five, Tom three, Martin not quite a year. We were together for a couple of years, then we decided to marry, then it was right to have children. We were trying for a while, then all of a sudden they began to come in a rush. We may have more. We'd like a daughter.'

'Who looks after them?' his mother asked.

'We both do; me, I suppose, during the day, although there's a crèche if we need it.'

'We'd like to see them,' his father said.

'Really?'

'Of course we would.'

'Mummy?'

'Oh yes.'

'Well, you know where we live. You have the number. You'd be very welcome. I . . . I don't think I could bring them here, really. They're a bit wild, Tom particularly. I don't think they'd cope with the cakes and orange squash bit.'

'You haven't dismissed our proposal out of hand, though?' Lewis said.

'What can I say to you, Daddy? I like the idea of rebuilding that house; but it's not my decision. I want what Bel wants, and there's nothing, nothing, that you could do or say, no amount of moral blackmail that you can pile on me, that'll change that. It's to do with love, you see. Somehow I lost that here. I'm not blaming you, but I don't think I loved you when I left. I don't see how I could've done. And that was ten years ago. Maybe we can learn to love each other again, but . . . but you have to be able to love Bel too and that's going to be more difficult for you than anything you've asked of me; but that's the price.'

'You use that word "love" very glibly,' his father said.

'Do I? I'm sorry. It's what I believe in now. I can't see much point to anything else. I mean, I thought that's what families were all about.'

When he had gone, a white vibrant space remained.

'Lewis?'

'What?'

'Fetch me those photographs.'

'What photographs?'

'Oh, Lewis, Lewis, stop . . . stop *lying*.'

He did not move. He felt cold under her knowledge of him. He had imagined her discovery of his secret; had even planned to tell her, perhaps this evening, to bring them out. That she had known about them all along made him feel pitiful.

'Where are they? I'll fetch them.'

'No.' He rose, needing anyway to be separate from her, not sitting beside her where Henry had left him, propped against her. Henry's departure had altered the balance; he always sat facing her when they were alone.

He brought the manila envelope from his desk without even thinking about what it contained. It was no longer magical, no longer a fantasy. He returned briskly and dropped it in her lap, moved across and poured them drinks, listened to the slicing sounds as she moved through the stack.

'Is she beautiful?' she asked.

'Yes, she is. Tell me, Celia; was he right? Do you despise her?'

'I want to. I feel that I ought to. She frightens me more than anything else. When I think of how he used to be, when I remember all the things I worried about him, I never remotely imagined this. She . . . she is beautiful, yes, but that makes it worse. I have imagined her as some monster, some vampire who devoured him. Seeing these again . . . I think I was right, Lewis.'

'We're going to have to meet her.'

'Is it worth it?'

'I think we are committed to play this out to its conclusion.'

As he handed her her gin, she looked up and he saw her eyes filled with tears.

'Lewis. Thank you for keeping these. Thank you for being with me through this. There is still hope, you know, I mean, even if this doesn't work.'

He reached down and touched the tears so that they spilled down her face.

. . . *twenty-seven* . . .

Bel picked up the telephone on her desk without thinking, her mind on the wording of a press release that had suddenly gone hollow and pretentious on her.

'Bel Drewer,' she said.

There was a pause which irritated her.

'Hello?'

'Bel? It's . . . Henry's father here. Look. I'm sorry to sneak up on you like this. I wondered if you had a free lunch hour next week. I'd like to meet you on neutral ground.'

Her mind blanked, jumped, derailed, then lurched out into space.

'Right. Yes. Er . . . Tuesday?'

'I shall look forward to it. Do you know Blewings'?'

'Yes.'

'Shall we say twelve-thirty?'

'One o'clock.'

'Splendid. Till Tuesday, then.'

The line went quickly dead. She listened to it buzz for a few seconds, then replaced her receiver carefully, dropped back in her chair and felt that she'd been the victim of some sort of hit and run.

He arrived at Blewings' at twelve-thirty, not wanting to give her the advantage of first arrival, of sitting there waiting for him. He expected something outrageous; denim and badges, a t-shirt under which her breasts flopped. Blewings' was respectable to the point of stuffiness, and he had chosen it to give her no chance to obscure any gesture she might try to make. He smoked a cigarette and drank dry sherry, leafing through the *Financial Times*, flicking his eyes carefully up at the least movement into or out of the quiet bar. He had not told Celia of this engagement. He was profoundly excited.

She was suddenly there, had seen him and was moving clearly towards him. He had to drop the paper in a muddle to be standing before she reached him. She was a model of elegance, in a black suit, calf-length skirt, blue blouse, the darkness of her dress making her skin seem creamy, warm; not the harsh charcoal of the photographs. She took his offered hand and shook it briefly, a jangle of bracelets at her wrist. She sat on the edge of her seat, refused a cigarette, would drink only mineral water.

'Thank you for coming,' he said.

She nodded in acknowledgement. He called for menus.

'I don't eat meat, I'm afraid. Is that a problem here?'

'They do excellent salad, and wonderful omelettes. Will that be all right?'

'Fine. Thank you.'

He had expected her to come quickly to a point of confrontation; now she was here, he did not know where to begin. She daunted him. He asked about her job and she spoke freely and intelligently. Henry had been right to say that she understood business. He was impressed, kept trying to move back from her properly to admire her, but she seemed to keep close to him, to allow him no vantage-point upon her, no pauses in the conversation within which he could simply observe her.

They moved to their table.

'A little white wine, Bel?' he asked.

'I'm sorry to be boring, but I don't drink alcohol.'

'Is Henry vegetarian now?' – the first time he had been mentioned.

'He eats anything,' she said with a smile. 'I don't think he really notices if it's meat or not.'

'May I ask . . . did you tell him you were lunching with me?'

'Yes. Shouldn't I have done?'

'Tell me about his business.'

'He buys derelict houses and restores them. Recently, he's been taking commissions from people, which is financially better, but that's not really the point. He enjoys his work and is good at it.'

'It's remarkable,' Lewis said. 'I could not have remotely imagined him doing something like that.'

She watched him, and he saw the accusation in her eyes that had bounced off this comment of his.

The food arrived and he had a chance to watch her as she ate, which she did rapidly and neatly, concentrating on the food, clearing her plate before he had managed half his sole, which he abandoned, too nervous to enjoy it, drinking too much wine.

'You want Henry to come and restore the family home,' she said. 'Do I have it right?'

'Yes. It would be a very large project, I think.'

'How long would it take, d'you think?'

'He would be out of London for the best part of a year.'

She considered this.

'We had assumed that you would oppose such an idea,' Lewis said.

'I would certainly not want to be separated from my husband for a year, Mr Drewer.'

'Could you come too? Your work. . . .'

'It's not impossible. We have three sons who don't see enough of either of us, and who are beginning to need more space than London gives them.'

'It is a wonderful house for children, Bel. I spent my childhood there. It needs children, needs family life.'

'Whether it needs our family life is another question, however. I don't want you, in six months' time or whenever, to realise you have made a dreadful mistake. We're strangers to you, Mr Drewer, even Henry. We have habits of intimacy and a need for privacy, a need to possess the space we inhabit, however temporarily.'

'It is a very big house.'

'It would need to be.'

'Will you consider it?'

'Certainly. As a straightforward business proposition, it has many attractions; but we're playing games here, Mr Drewer. This is the second time we have met; and during the ten years since our last meeting, we have lived with strange images of one another, become parts of one another's private mythology, I think. All this. . . .' indicating the restaurant, her clothes, their situation, '. . . this is wonderful. We can be perfectly civilised, exchanging good manners, that ultimate English vice. I wonder what you think of me, Mr Drewer?'

'And I wonder what you think of me?' he said quickly, for she had suddenly become dangerous.

'Let me put it like this,' she said. 'I think we have the potential to bring chaos into one another's lives; and if you understand that danger, if you accept it, then perhaps, perhaps, we have something to work on.'

'I will confess,' Lewis said, feeling the warmth of this opening him up, 'that for years I despised you, felt that you had abused and perverted my son. What else could I think? I was afraid of you too. I . . . I have those photographs Henry took of you. But seeing him again . . . what can I say, Bel? I'm proud of him now, and that is your achievement.'

She nodded seriously under this, thought how she might reply.

'I cannot,' she said at last, 'be as frank with you as you have been with me. I don't know you. I have no image of you distinct from what Henry has told me. Perhaps we will come to know one another better. I hope so. Will you do me a favour?'

'If I can.'

'Will you destroy those photographs, please?'

'If you wish.'

'I do. I think . . . I think I should go and see your wife.'

'Yes.'

'I will go now.'

'Very well.'

'It will not be inconvenient?'

'No. I . . . I don't think so.'

'Good, then.' She relaxed. 'And thank you for lunch. I lost a bet with myself, you know.'

'What bet?'

'I bet myself that you would say, "Please call me Lewis".'

'I wouldn't have dared.'

They exchanged smiles of mutual acknowledgement.

The call of the doorbell in mid-afternoon brought Celia Drewer to a state of fear. In the silent chambers of her house, the outside world was sealed out. She lived in a dull calm, filled increasingly with a pleasant melancholy. Life was better now: she could remember sections of the past with pleasure and could believe again in the possibility of the future. The clanging of the bell brought a whole range of unidentified terrors into play. She constricted herself in her chair, but did not move.

The bell rang again. She rose quickly, turned off the wireless and returned to the chair, lowering herself down in it and holding her breath. Again the bell came and she began to whimper with frustration and fear. The fourth time it came she was waiting for it, had pulled herself together and stepped out into the hall to send whoever it was smartly on their way.

'Mrs Drewer? May I come in?'

The social machinery bore her through and, with thoughts of slamming her out, of crushing her with her anger, she led her mutely into the drawing room, indicated a seat for her, took her own seat and lit herself a cigarette.

'Bel, isn't it?' she said distantly.

'Yes.'

'I'm so sorry. Would you like a cigarette, Bel?'

'No, thank you. I have just had lunch with your husband.'

'Oh?'

'He didn't mention it?'

She battened her anger upon Lewis then, which made the immediate situation easier. She regarded this woman for the first time, noted her sober presentation, curiosity and suspicion moving her forward and back in small twitches.

'What can I do for you, Bel?' she said.

'Well . . . I've been talking to your husband about the work he wants Henry to do on your house. . . .'

'Not in fact *our* house.'

'Your family's house, then.'

'Your family too, I suppose, or don't you see it like that?'

'I'm not sure.'

'I see,' Celia said, looking down as if no longer entirely involved.

'Can I ask . . . do you really want Henry to do this work for you?'

'He is capable of it, I understand?'

'Yes, I think he probably is capable of it; but that's not the point, is it? I mean, you could easily hire a local contractor who might very well make a more professional job of it.'

'We'd rather it was Henry.'

'I just need to be sure that you do really want Henry, or rather, that you want us, for I assume that the invitation is for myself and our children to come north too. As I said to your husband, I need to have the implications of this thought through.'

'It would be your decision, would it?'

'Henry will not agree unless he has my support.'

'And what are your terms?'

'My terms? Mrs Drewer, I have no terms. I only want to know what you want, what you really want out of all this.'

This question was outrageous. She thought of the photographs, of the pornography of those images, the erotic complicity they implied,

428

the brute shamelessness of this corrupt woman, for all her glossy sophistication.

'I want my son back,' she said.

'Your son now has a wife and three children. What you want doesn't exist any more.'

'That is untrue. You took him; I want him back. I want you to give him back.'

'I took him; he took me; I went; he followed me; he left here; I did not take him away . . . I don't think we will get very far if we are going to argue on these terms. I think we must concern ourselves with the situation as it is now. Don't you, Mrs Drewer?'

'If you are the price I have to pay to have him back, then I accept. He belongs to our family. You belong to our family. Your children also.' She began to like this, the hard punitive logic.

'You want me to come and live in the same house as you somewhere in the north?'

'Yes.'

'I don't believe you. I don't believe that is what you really want. I think you imagine that after a few months I will crawl away and leave him behind, taking your little wog grandchildren with me. Is that what you imagine, Mrs Drewer?'

She would not answer this, stared at her antagonist, knew, recognised her with a sudden spurting insight, knew what Henry had found in this woman. After all the prevarications and compromises, all the hypocrisies of all the Drewers, she at last faced someone who spoke to her in her terms. It was a consolation, a resolution. She felt a smile coming, then saw how this woman drew back from it insulted.

'I don't think we have much more to say to one another, Mrs Drewer. I'm sorry to have disturbed your afternoon.' She began to move forward, to rise.

'Wait a moment. Please. You are wrong, quite wrong.'

She waited. Celia allowed the tension to sag a little.

'May I get you some tea, Bel?'

'No. Thank you.'

'Coffee?'

'A glass of water, if I may.'

She rose and went into the kitchen, found herself light and happy. She ran the tap to let the water come cold, filled a tumbler with its brightness. It was possible, so possible.

When she handed her the glass, Bel looked up cautiously into Celia's smile. After a moment, Celia returned to her seat and lit herself another cigarette.

'I *am* glad that you came to see me, Bel. I wish we had got to know one another before. You should've found us earlier, you really should've done. I really don't foresee any difficulties. You have done so much for Henry. I am really very happy for him. I will admit that I had formed quite the wrong impression of you, but in the circumstances I don't think that was entirely unnatural. I think we will understand one another.'

'I think,' Bel said after a pause, 'that, if your understanding is based upon your contempt for me, then it will not be a very productive understanding, Mrs Drewer.'

'My dear girl . . . there is no . . . contempt. There was . . . anger at what you took from me. There was . . . perhaps contempt for what I imagined you to be. Oh, these men! These bloody Drewers and their bloody houses! And you have got three new ones waiting to eat you up, Bel. Perhaps you should keep Henry away from it all, but I don't think you will. I don't think he wants to be kept away. We'll all go north, back to do our bloody duty by the bloody family. We must come to an understanding, Bel. You must call me Celia and we must stand together, you and I, against the whole battalion of sons and husbands, not that the daughters are much better. I need to be fighting again. There was a time when I gave up fighting and nearly died of it. Be my ally, Bel. Could you?'

Celia watched her puzzlement, her caution, watched her beginning to try to smile, thought for a moment it was a smile of pity, the humouring of a madwoman. She tensed and waited.

Then she laughed and said, 'Yes. I will be your ally. Thank you.'

'Splendid. We are agreed then?'

'I hope so.'

'I am going to have a gin. Will you join me?'

'No. Thank you. I . . . actually, I'm pregnant again.'

'Good Lord! Another one? You *must* enjoy it.'

'I do. Yes.'

'I always thought pregnancy was a penance, the miserable punishment for being born a woman. We must talk about this.'

'Yes.'

. . . *twenty-eight*

Across the north blew the night rain, a slanted driving downfall, across moor and fell, through woods and the slatey streets of closed towns, slashing the surface of lakes and rivers, covering the roads in a slithering, leaping skin of water; the manifestation of the black, iron wind.

The big house became stone in the rainfall: in the sun it glowed and softened, blended into its surrounding leafage; but the rain brought out the underlying stone. There were no lights in any windows: where there might have been lights the shutters were fast, latched and covered with heavy curtains. No-one was expecting anything tonight. The rain was like a heavy band of static through which no signals could be received.

It was late, long gone midnight. All had retreated to their rooms to make their private journeys through the dark. The communal chambers and arteries of the big house were empty and dark, prey to the rattling of the wind at the shutters, the slithering cross-currents of draughts, the creak and shift of old timbers, the clamp of the dankness, the various small steppings of the various old clocks.

In the patchwork of her dreams, Hanni Brand lapsed freely into her native tongue, had bloody arguments with all of them whilst they stuttered and hobbled through unfriendly grammar. She was the stranger here, stranger and stranger as the months passed and the Drewers gathered, massed to recover their birthright from her failing tenancy. She had come again to hate them all with a fine fighting hatred that she had known as a girl, as a young woman when first she had arrived here, had fallen in love with a monster, had betrayed herself into wifehood and motherhood. All that had dried in her hands and crumbled away. They had come to take the last of it away from her and, whilst there was nothing that she cared for any more, nothing that she would not have brushed from her thoughtlessly, she would fight them, a great struggle of futile purity to keep her soul from them. She plotted and connived, writhed with an ecstasy of liberty that made her arthritic bones clatter within her against the long, poised aching of the day ahead of her, the day behind her, the endless staircase of days that she hobbled up. In her dreams she heard the wind and the rain and she opened her heart to them.

Across the landing, her arch-enemies, Lewis and Celia Drewer, slept in separate beds, corresponding light sleeps, a little softness, a little looseness coming into the angularity of their bodies in which the morning would re-attire them. Their dreams corresponded in ways they would have found surprising and pleasing, had they had the liberty to speak of such things to one another, which they did not have, would never have now. They dreamt simultaneously of punishments, the cleansing bite of retribution where everything was resolved; and they were happy in their dreams.

For Lewis, such dreams were explicitly sexual, the re-ignition of that part of himself which, day by day, had become completely dormant, not mentioned, not even considered; that was all over for him and he was thankful. In his dreams, however, it returned in the beautiful safety of involition, surprising him, a gift of delight. Strong women summoned him and scalded his trembling flesh, making him smart and swell and glow: his mother . . . his aunt . . . his wife . . . his sisters . . . Bel . . . he was a little boy again and they beat him until he wept, then they forgave him, comforted him, brought him their peace. It was a wonderful secret, opening in his dreams like a blossom, allowing him to face the day in a quiet, clean sobriety, his mind sharp, his manners, amongst the proliferating tensions of the house, immaculate and assured, solicitous to Celia, consoling to Hanni, the good father, grandfather, all that he was supposed to be; believing, with a faith that was almost religious, in the truth of his dreams, in the reality of that punishment and in the certainty of its absolution.

Celia did not dream of others, did not dream of places even. Vague shapeless terrors bred of her own corruptions and the corruptions of others surrounded and penetrated her, clogged her face and strapped her limbs, snaked between her legs and wormed up into her. She had to lie absolutely still; had she moved they would have devoured her. The lying still required intense effort, a gripping and setting of herself to keep them all at bay; and in her achievement of this, in her readiness and certainly before whatever came at her, lay an iron triumph. She might have identified her terrors with any one of them, for they were all against her, ultimately, in their own secret ways. In her dreams they were abstracted into essences of retribution and she withstood them all, rose in the morning clean and bright, vindicated, accepting Lewis's neat kisses, occasionally even admitting him into her bed for a few minutes' sentimental embrace; then up for a cold bath and a girding of her milky flesh in sheaths of strong material; then out into the day, to her station in the drawing room, with the children, the grandchildren, in the kitchen, a figurehead amongst the women whether they wanted it or not, the standard to which they all aligned themselves or against which they set themselves; proud in her predictability, untouchable at last; and really quite content.

Meanwhile they slept, Lewis and Celia Drewer, pretending to the room and the house and the wind and the rain that they had been here forever, that they belonged here, that they were this place, that their gathered family gave them at last their significance. They were no longer perhaps real people except in the profound, shadowy ecstasies of their dreams but that, they would readily admit, was enough, was more than they deserved.

A floor above them, but an age away, at the other end of reality, slept Ben and Tom and Martin, the ragamuffin half-castes, full of squeals and fights, guzzling and laughing, dragged in filthy, washed cleaner than anyone; too young yet to belong to anyone beyond their mummy and daddy, Henry and Bel; unaware of the weight of family, the landscape of psychological elevations and rifts, their inheritance; yet belonging in this house with an unequivocation that was quite beyond their elders, as they belonged in the world, a comfortable place of small needs and small frustrations, resoluble quickly in the completion of delights that filled them completely, asleep now in the peace of their infancy; the quiet chomp of Ben's mouth over his thumb, the indistinguishable muttering that rose from the depth of Tom, the warm reek of Martin's solidly filled nappy, the wind and the rain like everything else that did not concern them, not even noticed.

A light fell from the door of the adjoining room where Bel and Henry slept, keeping guard over them in an old brass bed that creaked and jangled; surprised to be parents, surprised to be so promiscuously fecund, no idea where it was all going to lead, letting it come out of them with the bewilderment of delight, half-ashamed amongst the urbanity of the others, secretly certain of each other, of

433

the world, day by day, and late into the clutches of the darkness. . . .

. . . Bel's great whale-belly glistening with oil, the navel pushed up like a button, within which tomorrow's Drewer turned and lumped; and she woke, gasping under the weight of it, drew up her knees, tucked down her elbows, forming her body into a cradle for her new child, her rich breasts falling to either side of her, a runnel between them damp with the perspiration of her effort, the effort simply of being, the ache of her thighs, the dryness of her throat, the internal pressures of this burden upon her spine and bladder, the concatenation of a unified physical purpose beneath which she had no independence, no energy; within which she was safe; and in these, the final days of her pregnancy, she felt that it all led to this, all the hurts and delights of her life gathered in her to the purpose, to the great biological cataclysm that was about to pull her open again, to separate another world from her; and she was afraid; and she was excited; having lapsed in these last days into cow-like passivity, coming now to the point where she would have to fight and scream and struggle, to throw herself into it, this great making, again, a new heart, a new centre for her writhing affections, afraid of her weakness, afraid of what might come upon her from her womb, afraid, in this house at this time, of the raw demands of family affection which the rituals and structures of the house seemed, she comprehended, designed to blunt and blur, to leave unsaid, resolving into silence and dust, into tumours of unfulfilment; and at this moment she knew she was more than they were, more alive, that she would swallow them before they would ever swallow her; and coming awake with a wrench that she knew, yes, perhaps, the beginning, turning to Henry to wake him, her heart beating, waiting, suspended there, mustering the catch of breath in her throat for the cry, she knew that she belonged here, yes, more than they belonged, that they would die, would go, would leave her here with her children, her husband, with a world to be made, a new world, beyond the imagination of their privilege, a new belonging branded with this birth, here in the centre of a storm, here in these still chambers, the breaking of the waters, the flood of herself upon which would float her child at whose coming she wept with the weakness of joy. . . .

. . . and turned to Henry beside her, but would not wake him yet, not yet, watching him sleep, lying on his belly, his hands tucked comfortably beneath him, the natural looseness of his features very

434

much as they were when he was awake; knowing him, the comfort of his lean body, knowing how it fitted her body, how they absorbed one another, became thus the parts of something else, something strange, vague, fanciful; until the children came and it was real, beyond them, apart from them, what they had done together that was more than they were, the miracle, beginning again, renewed, here, now, in a little while, not yet, not just yet. . . .

. . . whilst Henry dreamed of a room, a white room where he was working, mending, painting, preparing it for someone, filled with the need to perfect it for them, to make it just right so that he could slip away from it and leave them to their joy there; and as he worked, lithe, naked girls came to wash themselves in this room, their flesh silvery, their breasts heavy, their buttocks lean and muscular, bodies strong and purposeful, belonging elsewhere, coming here to be private, to cleanse and know themselves, to be right for the tumbles of the world beyond the white room where they would be dressed in argument and assertion, vulnerable and hurtful; but here, in the anonymity of their flesh, at rest; and he watched them as he worked, turning to see them, receiving their smiles; for they accepted him clearly, and if he rose to their beauty that was all right, it was simple and honest and meant nothing, for they had no desires here, no fears, nothing but their beauty, their innocence irrespective of who or what they might be beyond the room; and he knew none of them and would never know them, although they all knew who he was and that made him proud, and he turned to his work and worked for them, covering the wall in a whiteness that was somehow infinitely complex, requiring the utmost of his skill and commitment to perfect it, for it had to be perfect, it had to be; and then one was beside him, touching him and something leapt inside him for he had only been waiting for this. . . .

'It's starting,' she said.

He was awake at once, and within the bed was a furnace of body-heat and the monumental tension of his lover; and beyond the rain and wind lashed the house.

'I'll ring the hospital.'

'No time . . . don't go . . . hold on . . . hold on to me. . . .'

Brady knew what was happening but could have done nothing even if she had imagined there was anything to be done: there was nothing to be done, not any more. Existing faintly, somewhere between the living and the dead, she was sensitive to birth, she could imagine it vividly, as vividly as anything in her sealed world where the events of the quotidian were the inexplicable, the estates of her memory populous and active. She knew birth, knew the silence that surrounded it, within which the rending of flesh from flesh roared oblivious. It was the only thing that mattered, the first mystery: where we were and where we went, our continuous becoming; these she understood, but where we came from was ineffably miraculous, the moving power of God. She offered a prayer of welcome for the new-born.

She liked Henry and she liked Bel; of all the Drewers, she liked them the best. They all came to see her, to do their duty before her as if she were some sort of household saint before whom they had to make their token genuflections. She didn't mind that, didn't mind anything now, too old to mind, had outlived them all. She remembered when Lewis had been born, she remembered when Hanni had first come, she remembered when Lewis had brought his wife, newly pregnant; all that, working itself out in the house above her; she had outlived all that; but Henry was a fine young man, with a newness that made her warm. Everything seemed, more and more, to have been feeding off the past, turning forever inward until it would all disappear; he alone of all his family seemed free of that. He was like his Uncle Harry, his Great Uncle Harry, but untouched by war. How wonderful, at last, to have a generation not shrivelled by war, not burdened with the pain and shame and responsibility of that.

And his fine wife would come and sit with her, come to rest her big belly in her room, asking her about the family, about the past, wanting to know, her curiosity precise and thorough, shaking Brady's memory, making her bring it all out of the shadows, making it all alive again, taking it on.

'Why did Max kill himself, Brady?'

'Because he was afraid of himself, m'm. So many of them are that, you know. You must be careful.'

'Why did Harry marry Hanni?'

'Because she was strange and strong, and he was blind and useless, and because she fought him and because he loved her.'

'Is it true Henry's grandfather went mad in the First World War?'

'Yes. He had always thought that being a man was enough. They all thought that in those days, you know. But it wasn't enough.'

'Why have you spent your life here, Brady?'

'Because it's where I belong, m'm.'

'You might have married, had your own life.'

'There needed to be someone to keep an eye on things. I couldn't have done that if I'd had my own husband, my own children. I don't regret it, m'm. Don't you go feeling sorry for me, now. I'm better off than any of them in the end.'

'Brady, sometimes I think they're all monsters.'

'Not Master Henry, m'm, surely.'

'No, not Henry; but he's not really one of them.'

'Oh yes. I can hear it clearly. And you, you know, m'm, you're one of them too, now you're here. You remind me of Master Henry's grandmother.'

'Brady, I have a black skin.'

'Well, I don't know anything about that, but I don't see why you shouldn't have.'

Was it simply because Henry reminded her of Harry that his wife should remind her of Anna? A wishful connection to tidy it all up at the end? Perhaps. But perhaps if she could match up Bel with the shadow of Anna Drewer, she would come to possess that shadow. Brady believed in such things, had come through unscathed to a complacent old age, snug in her blindness from distraction and dis-appointment, remembering, when Bel had left her, her own young womanhood, taking out her unabsolved sins like stolen treasures, remembering with a shiver through her old, numb nerves the cold and the warm, the opening and closing of the flesh, remembering with a sudden steep limp of her heart that all the men with whom she had joined in the dark flash of sin were now dead, gone before her into a world where, whatever else, none of that would matter, the flesh at least at rest there; and perhaps this alone frightened her about death, kept her alive a little longer, squeezing out the last drops of physical memory before she slipped away to join the ranks of the dead.

And as Bel was giving birth, Brady felt the congregation of the dead about her, slipping through the thicket of her flesh to nestle against the warmth of her heart, the thrill of their lives touching hers, drinking at the source of her fidelity: Max Brand and Harry Brand, Naomi Drewer and Lionel Drewer, and young Jane, and Anna to whom she gave her life, loving whom she loved with the force of her blindness, in the clarity of the light that was within that blindness;

and old Mrs Brand and the old world that lay behind her nodding with satisfaction. It was done. It continues. What belongs here must be resolved here in all its distortions. The many debts it owes to the world must be paid.

And the wind and the rain came driving in from the west, blending the house into the darkness, seeking out the flaws, asserting the futility of it all, pressing the final blind obliteration against the blindness of arrogance and the cruelty of self; and only those who could turn with love to another would ever find the strength to be safe from the storm in the blindness of a beauty that would not be betrayed.

A Selected List of Fiction Available from Mandarin

While every effort is made to keep prices low, it is sometimes necessary to increase prices at short notice. Mandarin Paperbacks reserves the right to show new retail prices on covers which may differ from those previously advertised in the text or elsewhere.

The prices shown below were correct at the time of going to press.

All these books are available at your bookshop or newsagent, or can be ordered direct from the address below. Just tick the titles you want and fill in the form below.

Cash Sales Department, PO Box 5, Rushden, Northants NN10 6YX.
Fax: 0933 410321 : Phone 0933 410511.

Please send cheque, payable to 'Reed Book Services Ltd.', or postal order for purchase price quoted and allow the following for postage and packing:

£1.00 for the first book, 50p for the second; **FREE POSTAGE AND PACKING FOR THREE BOOKS OR MORE PER ORDER.**

NAME (Block letters) ....

ADDRESS ....

....

☐ I enclose my remittance for ....

☐ I wish to pay by Access/Visa Card Number ☐☐☐☐☐☐☐☐☐☐☐☐☐☐☐☐

Expiry Date ☐☐☐☐

Signature ....

Please quote our reference: MAND